The Cavendon Women

Barbara Taylor Bradford was born and raised in England. She started her writing career on the *Yorkshire Evening Post* and later worked as a journalist in London. Her first novel, *A Woman of Substance*, published in 1979, became an enduring bestseller and was followed by many more, including the bestselling Harte series. Barbara's books have sold more than eighty-eight million copies worldwide in more than ninety countries and forty languages, and ten mini-series and television movies have been made of her books. In October of 2007, Barbara was awarded an OBE by the Queen for her services to literature. She lives in New York City with her husband, television producer Robert Bradford.

The Cavendon Women is her thirtieth novel and also available as an audiobook and ebook.

For more information on Barbara Taylor Bradford please visit www.barbarataylorbradford.co.uk or visit her at Facebook.com/BarbaraTaylorBradford or on Twitter @BTBNovelist where she would love to hear from you.

Books by Barbara Taylor Bradford

SERIES
THE EMMA HARTE SAGA
A Woman of Substance
Hold the Dream
To Be the Best
Emma's Secret
Unexpected Blessings
Just Rewards
Breaking the Rules

THE RAVENSCAR TRILOGY
The Ravenscar Dynasty
Heirs of Ravenscar
Being Elizabeth

THE CAVENDON SERIES
Cavendon Hall
The Cavendon Women

OTHERS
Voice of the Heart
Act of Will
The Women in His Life
Remember
Angel
Everything to Gain
Dangerous to Know
Love in Another Town
Her Own Rules
A Secret Affair
Power of a Woman
A Sudden Change of Heart
Where You Belong
The Triumph of Katie Byrne
Three Weeks in Paris
Playing the Game
Letter from a Stranger
Secrets from the Past

EBOOK-ONLY NOVELLAS
Hidden
Treacherous

The
Cavendon
Women

Barbara Taylor
Bradford

HARPER

HarperCollins*Publishers*
1 London Bridge Street
London SE1 9GF

www.harpercollins.co.uk

Published by HarperCollins*Publishers* 2015
This edition published by Harper 2015
1

A catalogue record for this book
is available from the British Library

ISBN: 978-0-00-750326-1

Set in Sabon LT Std by Palimpsest Book Production Limited,
Falkirk, Stirlingshire

Printed and bound in Great Britain by
Clays Ltd, St Ives plc

MIX
Paper from
responsible sources
FSC
www.fsc.org **FSC C007454**

For Bob, with all my love always

CONTENTS

CHARACTERS

<u>ABOVE THE STAIRS</u>
<u>THE INGHAMS IN 1926</u>
Charles Ingham, 6th Earl of Mowbray, aged 57. Owner
   and custodian of Cavendon Hall. Referred to as Lord
   Mowbray.
Felicity Ingham, his ex-wife, the former Countess of
   Mowbray, aged 56. An heiress in her own right through
   her late father, an industrialist. Now remarried to
   Lawrence Pierce, a noted surgeon.

<u>THE CHILDREN OF THE EARL AND FORMER</u>
<u>COUNTESS</u>
Miles Ingham, heir to the earldom, aged 27. He is known
   as the Honourable Miles Ingham, lives at Cavendon
   and is learning to run the estate. Married to Clarissa
   Meldrew.
Lady Diedre Ingham, eldest daughter, aged 33, living in
   London. She works at the War Office. Single.
Lady Daphne Ingham Stanton, second daughter, aged 30.
   She is married to Hugo Ingham Stanton. They live in
   the South Wing of Cavendon with their five children.

Lady DeLacy Ingham, third daughter, aged 25, living in London. Divorced from Simon Powers, and has reverted to her maiden name.

Lady Dulcie Ingham, fourth daughter, aged 18. She lives at Cavendon.

The four girls are still referred to affectionately as the four Dees by the staff.

The children of Lady Daphne and Mr Hugo Stanton are Alicia, aged 12; Charles, aged 8½; the twins, Thomas and Andrew, aged 5, and Annabel, aged 2.

OTHER INGHAMS

Lady Lavinia Ingham Lawson, sister of the Earl, aged 53. She lives at Skelldale House, on the estate, when in Yorkshire. She is mostly in London. She is now widowed. She was married to John Edward Lawson, known as Jack.

Lady Vanessa Ingham, the spinster sister of the Earl, aged 47, who has her own private suite of rooms at Cavendon, which she uses when in Yorkshire. She spends most of her time in London.

Lady Gwendolyn Ingham Baildon, the widowed aunt of the Earl, aged 86, who resides at Little Skell Manor on the estate. She was married to the late Paul Baildon.

The Honourable Hugo Ingham Stanton, first cousin of the Earl, aged 45. He is the nephew of Lady Gwendolyn, the sister of his late mother, Lady Evelyne Ingham Stanton. He is married to Lady Daphne.

BETWEEN STAIRS
THE SECOND FAMILY: THE SWANNS

The Swann family has been in service to the Ingham family for over one hundred and seventy years. Consequently, their lives have been intertwined in many different ways. Generations of Swanns have lived in Little Skell village, adjoining Cavendon Park, and still do. The present-day Swanns are as devoted and loyal to the Inghams as their forebears were, and would defend any member of the family with their lives. The Inghams trust them implicitly, and vice versa.

THE SWANNS IN 1926

Walter Swann, valet to the Earl, aged 48. Head of the Swann family.

Alice Swann, his wife, aged 45. A clever seamstress who takes care of the clothes and makes outfits for Lady Daphne and her daughters.

Harry, son, aged 28. A former apprentice landscape gardener at Cavendon Hall; he is now learning estate management and works with Miles Ingham.

Cecily, daughter, aged 25. She lives and works in London, where she has become a famous fashion designer, with three shops.

OTHER SWANNS

Percy, younger brother of Walter, aged 45. Head gamekeeper at Cavendon.

Edna, wife of Percy, aged 46. Does occasional work at Cavendon.

Joe, their son, aged 25. Works with his father as a gamekeeper.

Bill, first cousin of Walter, aged 40. Head landscape gardener at Cavendon. He is widowed.

Ted, first cousin of Walter, aged 51. Head of interior maintenance and carpentry at Cavendon. Widowed.

Paul, son of Ted, aged 27, working with his father as an interior designer and carpenter at Cavendon.

Eric, brother of Ted, first cousin of Walter, aged 46. Butler at the London house of Lord Mowbray. Single.

Laura, sister of Ted, first cousin of Walter, aged 39.

Housekeeper at the London house of Lord Mowbray. Single.

Charlotte, aunt of Walter and Percy, aged 58. Retired from service at Cavendon. Charlotte is the matriarch of the Swann family. She is treated with great respect by everyone, and with a certain deference by the Inghams. Charlotte was the secretary and personal assistant to David Ingham, the 5th Earl, until his death.

Dorothy Pinkerton, née Swann, aged 43, cousin of Charlotte and the Swanns. She lives in London and is married to Howard Pinkerton, a Scotland Yard detective. She works with Cecily at Cecily Swann Couture.

CHARACTERS BELOW STAIRS

Mr Henry Hanson, Butler
Mrs Agnes Thwaites, Housekeeper
Miss Susie Jackson, Cook (niece of Nell, who has retired)
Mr Gordon Lane, Head footman
Mr Ian Melrose, Second footman
Miss Jessie Phelps, Head housemaid
Miss Pam Willis, Second housemaid
Miss Connie Layton, Third housemaid
Mr Tim Hartley, Chauffeur

OTHER EMPLOYEES

Miss Margaret Cotton, the nanny for Lady Daphne's children, usually addressed as Nanny or Nan.

Miss Nancy Pettigrew, the governess, usually addressed as Miss Pettigrew. The governess is not at Cavendon in the summer. The children are not in school.

THE OUTDOOR WORKERS

A stately home such as Cavendon Hall, with thousands of acres of land, and a huge grouse moor, employs local people. This is its purpose for being, as well as providing a private home for a great family. It offers employment to the local villagers, and also land for local tenant farmers. The villages surrounding Cavendon were built by various earls of Mowbray to provide housing for their workers; churches and schools were also built, as well as post offices and small shops at later dates. The villages around Cavendon are Little Skell, Mowbray and High Clough.

There are a number of outside workers: a head gamekeeper and five additional gamekeepers; beaters and flankers who work when the grouse season starts and the Guns arrive at Cavendon to shoot. Other outdoor workers include woodsmen, who take care of the surrounding woods for shooting in the lowlands at certain times of the year. The gardens are cared for by a head landscape gardener, and five other gardeners working under him.

The grouse season starts in August, on the Glorious Twelfth, as it is called. It finishes in December. The partridge season begins in September. Duck and wild fowl are shot at this time. Pheasant shooting starts on 1 November and goes on until December. The men who come to shoot are usually aristocrats, and always referred to as the Guns, i.e., the men using the gun.

PART ONE

A Family Reunion
July 1926

'The little world of childhood with its familiar surroundings is a model of the greater world. The more intensively the family has stamped its character upon the child, the more it will tend to feel and see its earlier miniature world again in the bigger world of adult life.'
Carl Jung, *The Theory of Psychoanalysis* (1913)

ONE

Cecily Swann knew it well, this path. She had walked it all of her life, and it was an old familiar. Lifting her head, she looked up at the grand house towering above her on top of the hill. Cavendon Hall. One of the great stately homes of England, it was the finest of all in Yorkshire.

The house was her destination this morning, as it had been so often when she was growing up. Her parents and her brother Harry lived in Little Skell village, at the edge of Cavendon Park, just as their ancestors had done. For over one hundred and seventy years, in fact.

It was a lovely Friday morning in the middle of July, and there was no hint of rain today. The sunshine streamed down, bathing the house in that crystalline northern light which gave the exterior its soft, peculiar sheen at different times of day.

Cecily glanced about as she walked on. She had half expected to see Genevra loitering here. But there was no sign of the gypsy girl. The Romany wagons were visible on the hill at the far end of the fields; Genevra's family still lived on the 6th Earl's land – that was a given. He had always permitted it; she supposed they would stay there forever.

But so much else had changed. Cavendon Hall looked the same, but it wasn't what it used to be. It was a different place; in fact, many things were different now. The Great War had changed everything. And everyone. As her father, Walter, was forever saying, the good old days were over, and nothing would ever be the same again. And his words were only too true.

Thankfully, her father and her brother had come back safely from the Great War, but Guy Ingham, the heir to the Mowbray earldom, had not. He had died for his country fighting in France, and was buried there alongside his comrades in arms.

They had all mourned him, every person in the three villages around Cavendon, as well as his family. Not because he was the heir, but because he had been one of the nicest of young men. Now it was Miles who would one day inherit the earldom and everything that this entailed.

Miles Ingham.

Her heart tightened at the thought of him. He had been her constant companion throughout her childhood, her best friend and later her sweetheart. She had loved him with all of her being; she still did. And he had told her many times that he felt the same, and that one day they would be married. But that had not happened.

Miles had been forced to marry another girl. A suitable girl. Clarissa Meldrew, the daughter of Lord Meldrew. The right kind of girl, who would give Miles an aristocratic heir. That was the way it was with the gentry: future heirs dominated their lives and their destinies.

Cecily came to a stop as a sudden thought struck her. After a moment, she veered to her left and headed in the direction of the rose garden. She needed a few moments to think, and anyway she was too early for her meeting.

A few seconds later, she was pulling open the heavy oak door and going down the steps. It was a fragrant

4

spot, this old walled garden, filled with the scent of late-blooming roses. She breathed in the heady smell as she sat down on a wrought-iron garden seat. This spot had always been a haven of peace and beauty.

Holding herself completely still, she closed her eyes, wondering why she had agreed to do this – to help Miles manage the events planned by the Earl for the family reunion. It was probably the most stupid thing she had ever done in her life.

Only if you are stupid, she told herself. Obviously Aunt Charlotte thinks you are capable of handling a difficult situation, or she wouldn't have asked you to help out.

Her aunt's voice echoed in her mind as she went back to the discussion they'd had a week ago. She remembered her aunt's words very well. 'Lady Daphne is the only one capable of managing the weekend with Miles, but she has so much on her hands, what with running Cavendon and five children underfoot. I personally would appreciate it if you would help him, Ceci.'

She thought now of the way she had tried to wriggle out of it, not liking the idea at all. She had muttered something about one of his other sisters being better at that job. But her aunt had batted her objections away with a dismissive wave of her hand. 'There might be difficulties, Ceci, and we need someone strong like you. Someone who can be tough, if needs be.'

Well, she could be tough, she knew that. But mostly she would have to be tough with herself. And with Miles Ingham.

She had not had a conversation with him for the last six years. They'd spoken, the odd times they had run into each other, here at Cavendon, or waved, but that was all. Six years ago she had vowed never to let him near her again, and her aunt had nodded her approval when she had confided in Charlotte.

'I'll walk alone and devote myself to my career as a

fashion designer,' Cecily had said, and Charlotte had looked pleased, and relieved. Unexpectedly, Charlotte had asked her to help Miles out now, and it puzzled Cecily. Actually she had no choice.

Cecily sighed, and sat up straighter. She owed Charlotte Swann everything. It was her aunt who had backed her fashion business, presented her with her first shop in the Burlington Arcade, made her career possible. And it was Charlotte's money which had originally funded the venture. They became business partners, and they still were, and worked extremely well together.

She trusts me to handle myself correctly, Cecily decided. She knows I won't succumb to his charms, become involved with him on a personal level. She understands that the pain he caused me runs far too deep. Besides, she's fully aware I'm devoted to my business, that it's my life.

Standing up, Cecily walked out of the rose garden, and went on up the hill towards the house. She felt better. She could handle Miles Ingham. She wasn't afraid of him. She wasn't afraid of anyone, for that matter.

In the past six years she had learned to be truly independent, to stand on her own two feet, and to make her own decisions. Furthermore, she was a big success. Women loved her clothes; they bought them by the cartload. And not only in London, but in America as well. Already, she had made two trips to New York, and her name was well known on both sides of the Atlantic.

Miles had his problems. And so did Cavendon.

Her future was full of brightness and challenge, and – with a little luck – even more success. Miles Ingham was part of the past. Her eyes were focused on the future.

She would help him out this weekend, and then she would go back to London and get on with her work, and leave Miles to his own devices. There was no place in her life for him. She would never forget that day, six years ago, when he had told her he was getting married to another woman. He had broken her heart, and she would never forgive him.

TWO

Miles Ingham bent down, picked up the small pieces of cork, and placed them on the mantelshelf, next to the carriage clock. Only Miss Charlotte knew how to properly wedge them behind the two horse paintings by George Stubbs, so that they would not slip. She had been doing it for years, and no one else had managed to master the technique.

Turning, he walked over to his father's desk and sat down, staring at the list he had made earlier. All were points he wanted to take up with Cecily, regarding the next few days.

Cecily Swann.

He longed to see her, to talk to her, to just be near her. And yet, at the same time, he dreaded it. For years she had been merely civil to him whenever they ran into each other here at Cavendon.

Her demeanour had been so remote, so cold, he had been unable to breach those icy walls she had erected around herself. She had frozen him out, and he fully understood why. He had hurt her immeasurably, and the hurt had never healed. It was an open wound.

This now presented a problem, since they did have

to be cordial with each other for several days in order to carry off this unusual family reunion. He had realized, the other day, that he must come up with a modus operandi, and it had to be one she found acceptable.

Sighing to himself, he jumped up, suddenly overcome by nerves. He paced up and down the library, attempting to get a grip on his flaring emotions. She would be arriving at any moment, and he had no words ready, nothing formulated in his mind, no greeting prepared for her. He was also at a loss about the days ahead, and how they would manage them.

There had been a moment last week when he'd begun to wish his father hadn't decided to invite the family home for a weekend visit.

On the other hand, there hadn't been any parties or get-togethers at Cavendon for the longest time. Nothing to celebrate, what with the family's money problems, the loss in the Great War of men who had worked their land, the scandal surrounding his mother, which they all tried to ignore. And then there was DeLacy's worrying depression about her divorce, not to mention Hugo's huge financial losses on the New York Stock Exchange.

And what a mess his own life was. Miles was acutely aware that he had no life, actually. He had grown to detest Clarissa, who, he had swiftly understood, was dense beyond words, a spendthrift whose only conversation was about clothes, cosmetics and jewels. All of which bored him. And she was a gossip. She loved to talk about her friends, and she wasn't always nice about them. He despised her for her mean comments about other women.

He had also come to dislike her father, Lord Meldrew. He overindulged his only child, giving Clarissa anything her heart desired. That in itself had created a rift between them; he loathed spoiled women, and she was particularly greedy.

Miles had long accepted that he was saddled with a dud of a wife; and, worst of all, one who had been unable to conceive.

He was still without that much-longed-for heir. Not only had she proved to be barren but, much to his dismay, she had soon developed an aversion to Cavendon Hall, and would not come to Yorkshire.

'Not a country girl at heart,' she had informed him, fairly early on in their marriage. What marriage? he now wondered, and strode over to the window, gazing out across the terrace, looking towards the park.

A moment later he stiffened. Cecily was coming up the terrace steps and every thought in his head fled. He felt as if he had a tight band around his chest, and for a moment he could hardly breathe. Then he swallowed, took firm hold of his emotions, and went to open the terrace doors.

He was stunned by her loveliness as she came towards him: the richness of her luxuriant hair with its russet lights, her ivory skin, her smoky-grey lavender eyes, which told the world she was a Swann born and bred. They all had those eyes.

Cecily was wearing a white dress, trimmed and belted in navy blue, and yet it was loose, casual, the silk skirt floating around her long legs.

Finding his voice, he said, 'Hello, Cecily.' His heart was pounding in his chest and he was genuinely surprised that his voice wasn't shaking. To his relief, he sounded quite normal. 'Thank you for coming.'

She simply nodded, and took hold of his outstretched hand. Shaking it, she dropped it instantly, and stepped back. Giving him a cool glance, she murmured, 'I hope this weather lasts for the next few days.' Her voice was soft, calm.

'Yes, so do I,' he agreed, and was then unexpectedly tongue-tied. Putting one hand under her elbow, he ushered

10

her across the terrace, into the library, and closed the door behind them.

Cecily immediately gravitated to the fireplace, as almost everyone usually did. This room was always cold, even in the summer months.

'I want to apologize,' Miles announced, as he quickly followed her across the room.

'What for?' she asked a little sharply.

'Being remiss . . . never congratulating you over the last six years. For your fantastic success as a fashion designer, I mean. You've done so well, wonderfully well, and I want you to know how thrilled I am about that. And I'm very proud of you.' Miles cleared his throat, added, 'I did attempt to write to you, but every time I started a letter, I threw it away. I couldn't quite get the words right. And, anyway, I thought a letter from me might annoy you.'

'Yes, it might have done, under the circumstances.'

Cecily sat down in a chair near the fire. As she settled herself, straightening the skirt of her dress, she couldn't help thinking that Miles didn't look well. He had lost weight, and there was a curious gauntness about him, as well as an aura of sadness. This was particularly apparent in his blue eyes, and she felt for him, knew he'd had a hard time.

Following her lead, he went over to the sofa and seated himself opposite her. In a low voice, he said, 'I have a list of things I'd like to go over with you, about Saturday and Sunday, but first I need to discuss something else.'

Cecily's eyes were focused on him, and she nodded. 'Please, tell me what's on your mind.'

'It's about our attitude towards one another. We've been civil when we've run into each other over the years. But that's all. And I do understand why. However, it's going to be a bit awkward for the next few days, if we're unfriendly, especially in front of the family. Don't you agree?'

11

'Yes. It's occurred to me that my antagonism towards you could present a problem, and I suppose I must mend my ways.'

'And so must I, Cecily.' A faint smile flickered on his mouth, and he added, 'It struck me yesterday that we might be able to slip back into the past; maybe we could behave like we did then. We had fun, we were happy.'

When she remained silent, he said, 'Well, we did have fun, and we were happy.'

'That's true, but I hope you don't think that I'm going to go up to the attics with you and revisit our "love nest", as you used to call it.'

She had said this so solemnly, and her face was so serious, Miles burst out laughing, surprising himself; it was the first time he had laughed in months. 'Of course not,' he spluttered. After a moment, he contained his hilarity. 'I'm speaking about our demeanour,' he explained.

Cecily had managed to remain poker-faced, although there had been a moment when she had almost laughed with him. But she wasn't going to give him an inch. Not ever.

Eventually, she answered, 'I think if we try to erase the last few years, and remember our youthful friendship, it will work. I will try hard, because we must make this a perfect celebration for Lord Mowbray.'

'Thank you, Ceci, I knew you'd see the sense of striking a bargain.'

'More like a compromise, I think, Miles,' she answered stiffly.

Ignoring her iciness, he shifted slightly on the sofa, and went on, 'There is just one thing I want to explain, something you should know.'

His voice had changed, was now extremely serious, and she glanced at him swiftly. Knowing him as intimately as she did, she was positive he was about to say something of genuine importance.

'Tell me then.' Her gaze was level, steady, as she looked across at him.

'I'm going to London next week. I haven't been for ages, and I shall ask Clarissa for a divorce.'

Cecily had not anticipated anything like this, and she was shocked. Before she could stop herself, she blurted out, 'But what will the Earl say?'

'Papa knows the marriage hasn't worked. We are not compatible in any way. Clarissa hates the country; furthermore, she has never conceived. She hasn't given me an heir, and this troubles my father as much as it has upset me. And it won't happen now, because we have been separated for some time.'

When she made no response, he said, 'But then you know that. Because you're a Swann, and the Swanns know everything about the Inghams.'

'Not always everything,' she remarked. 'But yes, it's true, I did know that your marriage was not happy, Miles. Great-Aunt Charlotte told me. I'm sorry it didn't work out.'

'So am I,' he mumbled. 'In view of the sacrifices I made.'

'I know,' was all she said, thinking about the sacrifices she had been forced to make as well. But this was best left unsaid.

Miles continued, 'I shall make Clarissa a generous offer – alimony, the house in Kensington my father gave us for a wedding present. But I'm not at all sure she'll agree to a divorce.'

A frown brought Cecily's brows together, and she asked in a puzzled voice, 'But why not? She's young enough, and pretty; she could get married again. And consider what she would bring to a new marriage. Alimony, and a lovely house.'

'The alimony would cease if she remarried, but she would keep the house. However there's a problem, you see.'

'What is it?'

'She wants to have a title, to be a countess, and so she'll try to cling on. When Papa had his heart attack last year, there were moments when I thought she was positively gleeful, anxiously waiting for him to pop off and clear the way for me. And for her, of course.'

'But how awful that is, Miles! Horrid.' Cecily sounded aghast.

'You're telling me! It was preposterous, especially since we were separated by then. But I shall win, I'm quite certain. Papa has spoken to his solicitor, and the way through this is for me to take the blame, provide evidence of adultery, so that she can sue me for divorce. If she won't agree to that, I might well have to divorce her. According to Mr Paulson, Papa's solicitor, I do have grounds. Not of adultery, but of abandonment. You see, she packed all of her things and left me here at Cavendon. In other words, she left the marital home.'

Cecily leaned back in the chair, thinking of the last six years. For Miles they had been wasted. But for her they had been productive, because she had started her fashion business, and it was thriving, making money.

'Penny for your thoughts,' Miles said quietly, watching her carefully.

'I was thinking of all the years you lost,' she murmured, as honest as usual.

'I know. On the other hand, I did learn a lot about agriculture, livestock, the land, the grouse moor, running the estate. And I keep on learning.' He leaned forward and looked at her intently. 'When I'm finally free, divorced from Clarissa, would there be any chance for me?'

'What do you mean exactly?' she asked, her mouth suddenly dry, a feeling of alarm running through her.

'You know very well what I mean. But I'll spell it out, clarify it. Is there a chance for me with you, Ceci?'

14

Cecily was not surprised by this question, because she knew he still loved her, just as she loved him. Nothing would ever change their feelings. There would never be anyone else for her, and she knew he felt the same way. But he was different in one thing. He was the heir to an earldom, and his father would most decidedly want an aristocrat for a new daughter-in-law. Not an ordinary girl like her. DeLacy had pointed that out to her six years ago, when she had blurted out that Miles was getting engaged to an aristocrat. 'He could never marry an ordinary girl like you,' DeLacy had said, and she had never forgotten those words.

'You're not answering me,' Miles said, his blue eyes suddenly filled with love for her. That awful sadness was now expunged.

The way he was gazing at her, his face full of yearning, touched her deeply. His expression was signalling so much to her, and it reflected what she had felt for years. She said slowly, 'When I was twelve, you proposed to me and I accepted. But we were too young. When I was eighteen you proposed again and I accepted. However, you married another woman. What are you saying to me now, Miles? Third time lucky?' An eyebrow lifted quizzically.

He nodded, and a smile broke through his gravity. 'Yes, third time lucky indeed! So you will marry me when I am divorced?' He sounded excited, and his voice was lighter, suddenly younger.

'I don't know,' she replied. 'Actually, I don't think so. I've changed in many ways, and so have you.' She paused, took a deep breath. 'But the situation hasn't. I'm still an ordinary girl. I can't make that kind of commitment to you now, Miles, nor should you to me.'

'You still love me, Cecily Swann. Just as much as I love you. I've never stopped loving you, and you know that.' He sat back, a reflective look crossing his face, and then he said in a low, tender voice, 'We belong to each other, and we have since we were children.'

She was silent, her face wiped clean of all expression. But inside her heart clenched. She wanted to say yes to him, to tell him she did belong to him, but she did not dare. She could not expose herself to him. Because it was his father, the Earl of Mowbray, who would ultimately have the final word in the end, not Miles.

Almost as if he had read her mind, Miles announced, 'First things first, Ceci. I must get my freedom, and then we will talk again and sort everything out. Will you agree to that?'

Cecily could only nod.

Miles said, 'Now, let's get down to the business of the next few days, the events. This is what I thought we should do about Saturday evening.'

He began to outline the initial plans, but inwardly he smiled. He was going to have Cecily for himself, whatever she believed. The Ingham men and the Swann women were irresistible to each other, and he and she were no exception. It was meant to be.

THREE

It was a wonder, this garden, with its low privet hedges in front of the raised banks of glorious flowers. So beautiful, in fact, it took her breath away.

A smile of pleasure crossed Charlotte Swann's face, and she felt a rush of pride. Her great-nephew, Harry, had created this imaginative effect in the pale green sitting room of the South Wing.

It reminded her of the indoor garden she herself had designed for this same room, some years before. Thirteen years, to be exact, and she had built it for the main summer event that year, the annual supper dance, to which the aristocracy of the county was invited.

The evening had been memorable in every way, and Lady Daphne had stunned everyone with her incomparable beauty, wearing a gown of shimmering blue-green beads the colour of the sea. Everyone had talked about it for weeks, and Charlotte had never forgotten how she'd looked.

Her mind still on Harry, Charlotte suddenly thought what a pity it was he'd had a change of heart. He was such a gifted gardener, with a great eye for form and colour, and his gardens outside were works of art, in her opinion.

Unfortunately, he had lost interest in being a landscape

gardener. Instead he wanted to be an estate manager, relishing the idea of working with Miles and learning from Alex Cope, who had replaced Jim Waters as estate manager at Cavendon two years ago.

Harry's rebellion had taken place at the beginning of the year, and it had shaken his father, Walter, who had felt betrayed when he realized his son was contemplating leaving Cavendon.

His mother, Alice, hadn't been quite so surprised. She had known from the moment Harry had returned from the Great War that he had been changed considerably, affected by the brutality and wholesale killing he had witnessed at the front.

All the returning soldiers had been changed by their experiences, even her husband. While Walter was more contemplative, her son had acquired an independent attitude, become quite ambitious for himself; he felt he was owed something by society.

It was Cecily who had asked Charlotte to intervene, and she had. It had taken only a few words with Lord Mowbray, and then Alex Cope, for her to help Harry up the Cavendon ladder.

'Is it all right, then?'

Charlotte jumped, startled at the sound of Harry's voice. She swung her head. He was leaning casually against the door frame, a quizzical look on his face.

'More than all right,' she answered. 'It's beautiful. Harry, you've outdone yourself.'

'I think I inherited what bit of talent I have from you, Aunt Charlotte.'

'Oh, you're a much better gardener than I am, a true professional, and it was good of you to take the time and trouble to create it. Thank you, Harry.'

'It was my pleasure, and my way of saying thank you to you for helping to sort things out with Dad,' he answered, and strolled into the room. 'I'd like to ask you something . . .' He stopped, became hesitant, as if changing his mind. He let his sentence trail off, stood silently next to her chair, obviously at a loss.

She looked up at him, thinking what a handsome young man he was. At twenty-eight he was tall, like his father, and had inherited the striking Swann looks, his features chiselled, the thick hair the same russet brown as hers. He even had her greyish eyes with that odd tint of lavender peculiar to the Swanns.

'Is there something wrong, Harry?' she asked. 'You seem worried.'

'Not worried, just curious, I suppose. I've been wondering why you asked Ceci to help Miles? With the upcoming events tomorrow, and on Sunday. Couldn't he have teamed up with one of his sisters?'

She shook her head. 'Daphne is too busy, Dulcie too young, DeLacy too depressed. As for Diedre, she's far too intellectual for such mundane matters like arranging events for a family get-together. Ceci was my only choice, because I think he needs back-up.'

'Poor Miles. I feel sorry for him, working with my sister. He'll get frostbite.'

Charlotte laughed, shaking her head. Harry's tone had a pithy edge, but then he always had an appropriate retort on the tip of his tongue.

'I did have another reason though,' Charlotte now volunteered.

'I thought as much,' Harry answered. 'He's so worn out and damaged. Miles needs some kindness. And Ceci will be kind to him, even though I know that deep down she's still angry.'

Charlotte eyed Harry, thinking how astute he was at times. But then he knew his sister well, and he and Miles had been friends since boyhood, had grown up here.

'It did strike me I might be playing a dangerous game, getting them together,' she said. 'But then I realized they are both adults. Grown up enough to handle themselves, and their problems.'

'I agree.' He moved away, went to look at the flower beds, took a dead head off a bloom, put it in his pocket. Without looking at his aunt, he murmured, 'You're expecting some sort of trouble, aren't you?'

'To be honest, I'm not sure. A lot of mutterings and dire warnings perhaps, nothing we can't cope with. On the other hand, I thought it better to be prepared. And there's nobody like Cecily, when it comes to taking control of a difficult situation. Also, she can be neutral, very calming and rational. I've always told her she would've made a good diplomat – she's a really good negotiator, you know.'

'Who's a good negotiator?' Lady Dulcie asked from the doorway, and walked into the room, looking beautiful in a primrose-yellow summer dress. At eighteen she was very much the same person she had been as a child: outspoken, with a quick, facile tongue. She was no longer afraid of Diedre, but cautious around her eldest sister, and automatically wary. Self-confident, sure of herself socially, she had a superior intelligence.

To Dulcie, Charlotte was like a mother; she had brought her up, alongside Nanny Clarice, and with Daphne's help. These three women had been the biggest influences in her life.

Gliding across the room, her face filled with smiles, Dulcie went straight into Charlotte's outstretched arms. The two women hugged, and then stepped apart.

Charlotte said, 'It's lovely to see you, I'm so glad you're back. I've missed you. London was nice though, wasn't it?'

'It was, Miss Charlotte, and I really enjoyed staying with Aunt Vanessa. She helped me so much with my art

20

history studies, but I'm very happy to be home.' Glancing at Harry, whose eyes had never left her, she blushed slightly as she said, 'Hello, Harry, it's nice to see you.'

He inclined his head, his face also full of happiness. 'Welcome back, Lady Dulcie,' was all he managed to get out. Inevitably, he became tongue-tied when the Earl's youngest daughter was present. She was so beautiful, he became lightheaded whenever he was in her company. He adored her, secretly yearning to know her better.

Charlotte took charge. 'Look at the beautiful garden Harry's created, Lady Dulcie. For the dinner tomorrow evening. It's superb, isn't it?'

'I've never seen anything like it,' Dulcie answered. Turning to Harry, she added, 'Congratulations, you're a true artist.' Then she laughed. 'I remember now, I did see one like it years ago, when I was about five. I barged in here, all covered in chocolate, just before the big dance was about to start.'

Charlotte smiled, remembering this incident herself. She hadn't been present, but she had certainly heard all about it the next day.

'Apparently none of the ladies was able to come near you, since you were covered in that chocolate. At least, so I was told. They were afraid of the chocolate getting on their gowns.'

Dulcie grinned, then asked, 'Where's Daphne? Do you know, Miss Charlotte? I haven't been able to find her.'

'I'm sure she'll be back in the conservatory by now. She told me she was going there to check on all her seating plans.'

'Then I shall go there. Once you've told me who the good negotiator is.'

'Why Cecily, of course,' Charlotte answered.

FOUR

'Welcome back, darling,' Daphne said, as Dulcie rushed across the conservatory, and flung her arms around her favourite sister. 'I've missed you,' she added, and then held Dulcie away, staring at her intently. 'More beautiful than ever,' she pronounced.

'No, no, no, you're the renowned beauty of this family,' Dulcie exclaimed, and went on swiftly, 'I couldn't get here quickly enough, I've so much to tell you. And mostly about Felicity.'

Daphne nodded, and guided Dulcie over to the wicker loveseat, where they sat down. Ever since their mother had left Cavendon, Dulcie only ever referred to her as Felicity, never Mama. Sometimes she even referred to her as 'that woman who abandoned me', and had a string of ridiculous and rather nasty nicknames for her.

Daphne understood why. Felicity had been too pre-occupied with her sister's fatal illness, and her own personal problems, to pay too much attention to Dulcie when she was little, and the child had never forgiven her. Now that she was a young woman, that animosity still lingered.

Settling herself on the loveseat, Daphne said, 'So, tell me everything, I'm all ears.'

'I've been informed that Felicity is going to throw out Lawrence Pierce, that knife-wielding maniacal quack – and, by the way, that's not the only thing he wields. From what I understand, he's quite the womanizer, wielding his manhood everywhere.'

Dulcie sat back next to her sister and waited for a reaction, her eyes fixed on Daphne's face.

Daphne burst out laughing, as always genuinely amused by Dulcie's extraordinary use of language. Their father constantly said she had a unique way with words and should have been a writer, and Daphne thought the same thing.

'Who told you this?'

'Margaret Atholl's mother,' Dulcie answered. 'Lady Dunham. She also said there's a rumour that the marriage is unhappy, and Felicity is planning to return to Cavendon. She won't come back, will she, Daphers? I couldn't bear to have that greedy, man-hungry creature here. Papa wouldn't fall for her again, would he?'

Shaking her head, the laughter bubbling inside her, Daphne answered, 'She won't even attempt it. And certainly Father is not interested in her one iota. This is just idle gossip you've heard. However, perhaps she is going to throw the surgeon out. I, too, have heard stories about his behaviour.'

'A flagrant and very experienced adulterer, who thinks he's the Don Juan of all Don Juans, impossible to resist. And very conceited about his . . . hidden charms, shall we say?'

Daphne couldn't help laughing again, and then she finally managed to say, 'All surgeons think they're God, according to Diedre. Because they save lives, I suppose.'

'Or ruin them,' Dulcie shot back. There was a moment of silence, and then Dulcie moved closer, confided, 'I think Aunt Vanessa might marry her artist friend. He's awfully nice, by the way, and he's from the very proper Barnard family, and well connected. He was very kind to me, helping me with my art history course.'

Daphne was taken by surprise and gave Dulcie a penetrating look. 'Are you sure there's an engagement in the wind?'

'I'm not absolutely certain, but it looks like it to me. He practically lives at her house, and they're never apart. They sort of . . . drool over each other.'

'Papa doesn't know. He would have told me. But then Aunt Vanessa doesn't have to report to him, since she's in her forties and can do whatever she wants.'

'Gosh, I wouldn't want to wait so long to get married! Is that too old to have babies, do you think, Daphers?'

'Perhaps,' Daphne answered.

Dulcie, who was facing the door, jumped up when she saw her father standing there. He looked furious, and she wondered if he was angry with her. Because she hadn't gone to see him first.

Daphne also caught sight of him at the entrance to the conservatory, and instantly knew something had happened. The angry stance told her that. What had upset him? He was usually easy-going, genial. She cringed inside, prayed it wasn't anything to do with the events planned for the next two days.

'Hello, Papa,' Dulcie said as soon as their father came to a stop next to them. 'I just arrived,' she explained swiftly. 'I was about to come and say hello to you, Papa.'

A smile flitted across Charles Ingham's face, and disappeared at once. He brought his youngest daughter into his arms, kissed her cheek. 'Welcome home, darling. Glad to have you back, and also that you're early.' He paused, released her and asked, 'Have any of your sisters arrived yet?'

'Not that I know of, I think I'm the first. I wanted to get here in time for afternoon tea.'

He nodded, and then turned his attention to Daphne, who had risen from the loveseat. 'I need to speak to you about something. Privately. And it is rather urgent.' He glanced at Dulcie. 'Would you excuse us, Dulcie, please?'

'Yes, of course, Papa. I must go up to my room. I left Layton unpacking my suitcases.'

Once they were alone, Daphne gave her father a questioning look. 'Papa, whatever's wrong? I can see you're angry.' She felt taut, anxious, though she tried to conceal this.

'I'm angry, upset – and totally baffled. I went down to the lower vaults to get something from one of the safes, and I discovered there are pieces of jewellery missing.'

Daphne couldn't hide her shock. 'But how can that be? Only you have the key!'

'That's true, and it was in its designated place. I took it, opened the main vault, went to a safe, took out a case, and found a pair of earrings missing. Diamond earrings. I looked in several other cases, and they were empty. I was in shock, Daphne. I couldn't believe my eyes.'

'Please, Papa, let's go down there at once. And we had better check all the jewel cases. Don't you agree?'

'I do indeed. I was so upset I just rushed up here without doing that.'

'Do you think somebody knew where the key was? Took it, went down there – let's say during the night – and made off with those pieces?'

'How can I say? Who would know where the main key is kept?'

'Have you mentioned this to Hanson?'

The Earl shook his head. 'I came straight up here, looking for you. Let's go, Daphne, and bring a piece of paper and a pencil with you. We'd better make a list of everything that's missing. How unfortunate I discovered this now, with all the things we have going on these next few days.'

Although there was a silver vault on the kitchen floor, which contained the pieces used all the time, there were other, older vaults, on the floor below in the lower cellars. These vaults had been built by Humphrey Ingham, the 1st Earl of Mowbray. He had planned them with the architects, when the house was being built in the 1700s. They were cavernous, and not only housed a huge collection of jewellery, but also all the most important and valuable pieces of silver made by the great master silversmiths of the eighteenth century.

As they hurried down the lower staircase, Daphne asked, 'When was the last time you were in the jewellery vaults, Papa?'

'Not recently, that's a certainty. We haven't been having parties, so no one thought of taking jewels out to wear. I'm puzzled, I truly am, but we must solve this mystery and reclaim the pieces. My father, my grandfather and my great-grandfather always called these vaults our safety net. The pieces were bought for investment purposes, as well as to be worn and shown off. A lot were bought by the 1st Earl when he was a trader in the West Indies and in India. He purchased diamonds from the famous Golconda mines, and those pieces are unique.'

When they arrived at the iron door, Charles unlocked it and stepped inside the huge vault, turning on the light. 'It's a good thing my father put electricity in down here, otherwise where would we be today?'

'Putting it in ourselves,' Daphne muttered, and followed her father over to one of the larger safes; it sat against a wall at the far end of the vault.

Charles opened the safe and lifted out a worn, red leather case. 'There were diamond earrings in this. From Cartier. As you can see, it's empty. This other one held a single strand of diamonds, also from Cartier.'

Daphne nodded, and reached into the safe herself. Her fingers curled around a blue leather box, stamped with gold edging, and as she took it out she said, 'This is the brooch I wore at my wedding, Papa.'

'I'm afraid not, darling, that one is empty, too.'

'I can't believe it!' she cried, and lifted the lid. 'It *is* empty, and it was one of my favourite pieces. I wore it on my wedding dress, and then later Mama wore it at the dinner we had in January 1914, after Alicia was born—' Daphne cut herself off, swung to face her father, and cried, 'I know who took the jewels.'

Charles stared at her, frowning. 'Are you about to point a finger at your mother?'

'I most certainly am, Papa! She was the last person seen wearing the diamond bow brooch.' Placing the empty jewel case on the table that stood in the middle of the room, Daphne looked in the safe again and pulled out two more cases. 'In here should be a small diamond and ruby tiara, and in this one a matching diamond and ruby bracelet.'

When she opened them, she nodded. 'Papa, she took these pieces, I know she did. They were her favourites, and so were the Marmaduke pearls. They're in the other safe, aren't they?'

'Yes, they are. We'd best investigate, ascertain what's missing from there.'

The pearls, dating back to the eighteenth century, were highly valuable, and had been treasured by the Inghams over many years. They were large, had been carefully matched, and were of opera length, long and elegant. The single string was so precious it was hard to evaluate. Daphne had come to believe the pearls, if auctioned, would go for a lot of money.

The box was heavy, and she knew at once the pearls were safe, that they were inside. When she lifted the lid, she nodded, smiled in relief. 'At least she didn't grab these, Papa.'

'I was sure they were here. Pearls have to be taken out from time to time to, sort of . . . well, be allowed to breathe. And I've taken the box upstairs quite frequently for that reason,' Charles explained.

'I just know Mama took the other jewels. She knew where the key was, nobody else did, except for me and

Miles. And we didn't steal them. She did it. Your former wife and my mother, and I am going to get every single piece back from her. She's met her match in me. I won't rest until the Ingham jewels are back in their rightful place.'

'How are you going to do that, Daphne? And how are you going to prove she has the jewels? Your mother will never admit she took something she shouldn't have from Cavendon.'

Daphne was silent for a moment or two, and then she confided, 'I have an ally. Someone who will help me. I know that for an absolute certainty, Papa.'

He frowned, and a sudden look of concern settled in his blue eyes. 'And who is that? Who is going to help you?'

'I'm afraid I can't tell you, Papa. It's not that I don't trust you, because obviously I do. Nonetheless, I simply can't tell you. At least not now. When I've done it, and given the jewels back to you, I will explain everything.'

Charles let out a deep sigh. 'When are you planning to confront Felicity?'

'In the next few weeks, when you are away. And I shall force her to hand them over. Obviously we cannot take any steps right now. Nevertheless, I have no worries. She can't possibly sell them, not ever.'

'That's right. We would know immediately if they went on the market.'

'So, let's lock these safes, and the vaults, and forget about the missing jewels for the next few days. And I will make the list next week and check every box in all the safes, I promise.'

'It is a little worrisome,' Charles murmured, and closed the safe door.

'I know it is, Papa, but we must not let this problem affect the . . . family reunion. It wouldn't be fair, would it?'

'No, it wouldn't. As usual, you are making perfect sense, Daphne. Whatever would I do without you?'

FIVE

There was no doubt in Daphne's mind that the moment her father had seen the empty cases, he had known at once who had taken the jewels. But he had waited for her to make that very obvious connection.

Daphne sat back in the chair in the conservatory, thinking about her mother, a woman who had changed so drastically she seemed like a stranger. Daphne blamed Lawrence Pierce. It was his fault. He had been a bad influence on Felicity, and no doubt he still was.

She sighed to herself. There was nothing much any of them could do about their mother. She was married to Pierce and, seemingly, he ruled the roost, as Miles so aptly put it. Her mother had created a scandal when she had run off to be with the surgeon in London. But somehow her father and the family had managed to weather it all, and their standing was still intact. Anyway, almost every family they knew were having some problem or other, whether marital or financial.

It seemed almost inconceivable to her that their mother had just pocketed the jewellery, as if it were her own, and gone off to London to join her lover, without giving it another thought. Not about the jewellery she was taking, which was not hers to take. Or the children she was leaving behind. That had happened twelve years ago.

Little Dulcie had been only six, and baby Alicia, her mother's only grandchild, was not even one year old.

But Felicity's children had managed. They had not only had each other, they had had their extraordinary father, a very loving man, who was the personification of decency.

And she herself had also had her darling Hugo, and their first child. And all the Swanns. Whatever would they have done without the Swanns? Most especially Charlotte.

Normally, Daphne would have run straight to Charlotte today, to tell her about the missing jewels and ask for her help. But she could not do that. Charlotte had her hands full, and she didn't need this worry to cope with.

Closing her eyes, Daphne wondered what she could do. She had told her father she had a plan, but she didn't really. Her only thought was to go to London to confront Felicity.

But her mother would deny having the jewels, wouldn't she? Obviously that would be Felicity's only course. And how could Daphne prove otherwise, without ransacking her mother's house? That wasn't a possibility, under any circumstance. She did have an ally, as she had told her father. That at least was the truth. But just how much could that ally do?

What she really needed was a reason to invite herself to tea with her mother. But it would have to be a genuinely good reason, because they had all shunned her, off and on, over the years.

'There you are, my darling,' Hugo said, interrupting her whirling thoughts as he came striding into the conservatory, at forty-five as handsome as ever. Daphne swung around in her chair, beamed at him.

Bending forward, her husband kissed her on the cheek, and sat down. 'I've been looking all over for you,' he said.

'Good news from New York to impart at last! I just heard from Paul Drummond, and he's finally managed to sell those old factory lofts I bought in downtown Manhattan, near the meatpacking district. And for an excellent price. The money can be put to good use here at Cavendon.'

'Oh, that's wonderful news, Hugo!' Daphne exclaimed, her eyes filling with love for him. He was doing his best to help keep Cavendon afloat, which was drowning in taxes and other problems. She and Hugo stood right behind her father, helping to prop everything up. She was very happy that the strained look had left his face this afternoon.

She now said, 'Papa will be grateful, and so am I. You do so much, we can never thank you enough.' She paused for a moment, and then added softly, 'It will certainly give Papa a lift. He discovered something quite awful today.'

'What on earth happened?' Hugo asked, leaning closer. There was a certain kind of disquiet about her, which was not like her at all. She was usually ebullient and positive, whatever problems she faced.

'Papa went down to the big vault, to get something or other out, and he discovered there were quite a few pieces of jewellery missing. Obviously, he knew at once that my mother had taken them—'

'Who else?' Hugo interrupted in a terse voice. 'Only a Countess of Mowbray knows the hiding place for the key. If I remember correctly, those are the ancient rules followed by the Inghams for generations.'

'Yes. And the butler always knows where the key is too. But I can assure you, Hanson hasn't stolen diamond earrings to give to his lady love.'

'Does he have one?' Hugo asked, and couldn't help laughing, despite the gravity of the matter.

Daphne laughed with him, and then went on, 'I told Papa not to worry about the missing pieces; that whilst he was away I would get them back.'

'And how do you plan to do that?' Hugo asked, a brow lifting. 'Are you going to take Felicity on, and demand their return?' He shook his head, before saying, in a low tone, 'You know, you would be accusing her of stealing, since they are actually the property of the Earl of Mowbray, her former husband. I don't think your mother will take very kindly to that sort of accusation, my darling.'

'You're absolutely right, Hugo, she won't, I'm well aware of that. But I must confront her. I've no alternative. And I do have an ally.'

'Ally or not, I shall come with you to London. I'll certainly not allow you to go alone under the circumstances. Not to Felicity's house. Lawrence Pierce may well be there and I don't want you to end up doing battle with him.' His glance was long and speculative. 'And who is your ally, may I ask?'

'I will tell you, Hugo, but it is in confidence. I didn't say who it is to Papa.'

'I shall not tell a single soul, I promise.'

'It's Wilson.'

A knowing look crossed Hugo's face, and he nodded. 'Of course it's Wilson. Olive has a very soft spot for you. She always has, and I don't believe your mother is her favourite at the present time. On the other hand, your mother pays her extremely well, so why would she jeopardize her job?'

'Because soon she'll be working for me, as my lady's maid. In a few months. She finds the situation untenable at Charles Street, and confided in me that she was going to give Mama her notice. And she has. She told Mama she wanted to retire. Felicity made a fuss, didn't want to let her go, but Olive was adamant, very determined. The point is, when she confided in me, I asked her to come to Cavendon as soon as she was available.'

'I see,' Hugo murmured, and sat back in his chair, wondering what Wilson's wages would be.

As if reading his mind, Daphne swiftly said, 'You mustn't worry about the cost, Hugo. I shall pay Wilson myself. I have my trust, and I plan to use some of that to pay her salary.'

'When does Wilson plan to retire, so to speak? And then come here?' he asked, thinking that Felicity would not like this turn of events.

'Not until September. So there's plenty of time to deal with my mother regarding the jewels.'

'Whatever your mother says, I know that Wilson will tell you the truth. That is why you're calling her your ally, isn't it?'

'Yes, Hugo. Wilson helps my mother to dress every day. She's in charge of her clothes, and, presumably, her jewels.' She stared at him, and added quickly, 'I know that look on your face, Hugo. You think Wilson should've told me before . . . about the jewels. But you see, Olive Wilson doesn't know that they're not Mama's, not her own personal possessions.'

'She has no idea they're family heirlooms?' he asked, sounding sceptical.

'How could she? My grandfather was a wealthy industrialist, and I'm quite sure Wilson thinks my mother's jewels were given to her by him. Or by my father. There's no way she would know that the jewels Mama wears must remain in the care of the current Earl, that they aren't actually hers to keep, only on loan.'

'You make sense, darling,' Hugo murmured, and stood up. 'I'd better go back to the annexe for a short while, I'll see you at teatime.'

'Oh no, no, Hugo, you must come to the little gathering Papa is having in the library, at three thirty. Just the girls, Miles and you. I know your presence is important to him. You haven't forgotten, have you?'

'It did slip my mind, but I shall be there,' he answered, going over to kiss her cheek.

She moved her head slightly, and, as he bent forward, her face was bathed in the sunlight streaming in through the window. He was instantly struck by her loveliness this afternoon. At thirty, Daphne was at the height of her beauty. Thirteen years, he thought. It didn't seem possible that they had been married almost that long.

As his lips brushed her cheek, and he squeezed her shoulder affectionately, he thought of their children. Genevra's prediction had come true . . . the gypsy girl had foretold that Daphne would bear five children. And she had. They were Inghams through and through, beautiful girls and handsome boys. He loved them dearly and spoiled them atrociously. But why not? Along with Daphne, they were his life.

Walking back to the annexe, Hugo's thoughts were still with Daphne. What a truly wonderful woman she had become over the years; she had helped her father run Cavendon, and done it well. He smiled inwardly, when he pictured his wife being 'the general in charge', as she called herself. Some general, indeed. She was still beautiful, glamorous really, with her abundant golden hair a soft halo around her lovely face. No chic 1920s crop for her; and those glorious eyes were as blue as ever, her skin clear and perfect. I've been lucky, so very lucky, he reminded himself. We both have good health and we're still in love. Miraculous.

SIX

Diedre stood in the middle of her bedroom, slowly turning, her eyes resting on some of her favourite things. The large antique silver mirror standing on her dressing table, given to her when she was a little girl by her mother, the collection of lace pillows on her bed, made for her by Mrs Alice, and the tortoiseshell and silver brushes, comb and mirror set, a gift from her father for her sixteenth birthday.

All were beloved things, just as this room, which had always been hers, was one of the most special places in the world to her. She had missed it, and as she walked forward to sit down at her small Georgian desk, she felt unexpected tears welling in her eyes.

No one had kept her away from Cavendon; she had just not come, and that was of her own volition. She had not been home because she had been in a state of grief for a long time, and she had not wanted anyone to witness it.

Her grief for the person she had loved the most in her entire life was extremely personal, and therefore absolutely private. And since she was not able to talk about it, at least not coherently, there was no one who could give her comfort. Except, perhaps, her father, who was the most compassionate and sympathetic of men.

Brushing away her tears, Diedre sat down at the mahogany desk and immediately felt truly at ease. Her sister DeLacy loved fancy, frilly bedrooms, whilst she had usually had her eye on the best desks at Cavendon, had often rummaged around in the attics, looking for hidden treasures, mostly amongst the fine antiques.

This was a desk she had chosen years ago, and it became her favourite, with its many drawers, little cubbyholes and polished green leather top.

Unexpectedly, a wave of lovely memories washed over her, and she was surrounded by the past for a few moments. The first diary she had kept, when she was a little girl, had been written here, and her first love letter. She had done her homework at this desk, always diligent about such things; gift cards to her family had been written in this spot, along with Christmas and birthday cards.

Funny how she had liked desks so much when she was younger. She still did. She had three in her flat in Kensington. That was another safe haven. Thankfully, she could afford it, because of the trust from Grandfather Malcolm Wallace. Only she and Daphne had been given these trusts, because Grandfather Wallace, their mother's father, had died before the other daughters were born.

Leaning back in the chair, Diedre let her eyes wander around the room once more. It was light and spacious, and had a lovely oriel window with a window seat. The pale lavender-grey walls and matching silk draperies created a restful feeling; she felt so comfortable here, and secure.

Now she wished she hadn't been so silly, that she had come to Cavendon more often in the past few years. After all, she had grown up here. She loved every inch of the house and the parkland, not to mention the gardens. The history of this estate was the history of the Inghams, and therefore part of her.

Her father was a little hurt that she had not been home more often in the last few years. She had suddenly become conscious of this earlier today, when she had first arrived and gone to see him in the library. He had said this lightly, but she had caught a hint of sadness in his voice, and then it had passed. He was clever at hiding his feelings, of course. He would have made a good actor, she often thought.

She had pointed out that she had seen him frequently at the Grosvenor Square house; he had laughed, informed her it wasn't the same thing.

He had obviously been very happy when she'd arrived this afternoon, most amiable and kind. Well, she was his eldest daughter, his first-born girl. As she was leaving he had reminded her there was to be a small gathering, here in the library later, before tea, and that she must be there.

And she would be. And at tea as well. Diedre hoped she could walk Great-Aunt Gwendolyn home, so that she could talk to her, confide her problem. A small sigh escaped her and she bit her lip, the worrying problem suddenly seeming insurmountable as she thought of it again. Her close friend, Alfie Fennell, had recently told her that someone was out to cause trouble for her at the War Office. He didn't know who this was, or the reason why.

And neither did she. Diedre loved the work she had been doing during the Great War, and had stayed on after the war had ended, remained in the same division. She had gone to work there in 1914, when she'd been twenty-one. Now she was thirty-three, and it was her life. Without it she would be lost.

Alfie's news had shaken her up, shocked her, and she had found it hard to believe. She didn't want to be pushed out; she was frightened by the mere idea of this. It would ruin her life – what was left of it, now her one true love was dead and gone.

When she had finally railed at Alfie and demanded he tell her everything he knew, he did so. And it wasn't much, as it turned out.

His cousin, Johanna Ellsworth, had been the first person to hear the rumour, and she had told Alfie at once, suggested he alert Diedre, inform her of a possible problem. Johanna was well connected and mixed in political circles.

'But it is only a rumour,' Alfie had said last week. 'Rumours don't mean much, now do they?'

Diedre thought they did mean something, and said so, adding that many people thought there was no smoke without fire.

Now she focused on the word rumour. Who had started it? And why had they? Was it someone with a grudge against her? A competitor? Did she have an enemy inside the War Office? Was it from inside? Or outside? Was someone trying to scare her? If so, why? Part of her job was asking questions, and now she was asking them of herself, racking her brains. Alfie had hinted she was supposed to have made a bad error in judgement.

There was one thing she did know. All of those who ranked above her, the top brass, were truly satisfied with her work. If a rumour had first been started at the War Office, it was obviously coming from a person in the lower ranks.

Diedre felt certain that her great-aunt would be able to help her, because of her connections in the British government. She knew everyone of any importance, and was considered a genuine friend by many, and if anyone could get to the bottom of this, it was Lady Gwendolyn. And a lot of people were indebted to her.

This aside, her aunt and she were very much alike, and were unusually close. Great-Aunt Gwendolyn was willing to listen to her any time, and to give her considered opinion, as well as good advice. Diedre couldn't wait to confide in her. It would be a great relief just to unburden herself.

SEVEN

Henry Hanson sat in his office in the downstairs quarters of Cavendon Hall. Leaning back in his comfortable desk chair, the butler reread the menu for the dinner to be held on Saturday evening. It had been created, as usual, by Lady Daphne, and it was perfect as far as he was concerned. But then she couldn't do much wrong in his eyes; she had long been his favourite.

Lady Daphne had chosen vichyssoise to start, and after the cold soup there would be Dover sole with parsley caper sauce. The main course was rack of baby lamb, fresh green peas from their own vegetable garden, and rösti. These were shredded potatoes, fried in hot oil until they became a crisp potato cake, a Swiss dish introduced into the household by Mr Hugo, which everyone enjoyed.

He glanced at the wine list, written by His Lordship earlier today. He smiled to himself. As usual, Lord Mowbray had chosen his own particular favourites, but the Pouilly-Fuissé was a good choice for the fish, and the Pomerol would be perfect with the main course.

The Earl had made a note on the card, suggesting Hanson select the champagne himself. This would be served with the dessert, and he immediately thought of

Dom Pérignon, but he would go to the wine cellar later. Perhaps something else might catch his eye.

Rising, Hanson walked over to the window and looked out at the blue sky. It was a lovely day, very sunny, and he hoped the weather would last for the next few days. But, come to think of it, rain wouldn't dampen anything, he decided. Happiness didn't get diluted by rain.

Hanson was excited that the Earl had decided to have this family reunion, the first in six years, and delighted he had picked the middle of July.

It smacked of old times, when all was well in the world and they gave the big summer dances, always a hit with everyone in the county. But the county wasn't invited tomorrow, just the family.

The last time there had been a reunion was the marriage of Miles to Clarissa Meldrew, a lovely affair, but everything had later gone askew for those two. He felt extremely sorry for Miles, who did not deserve the treatment meted out to him by Miss Meldrew.

Aristocrat my foot, he thought, with a flash of snobbery mingled with anger. Nouveau riche, he muttered to himself, and the title very new, given for some kind of business endeavour. Hardly a match for the heir to the earldom of Mowbray, centuries old, created in the mid 1770s. Miles's pedigree is bred in the bone, and he's to the manner born, Hanson thought, and she's a nobody. Certainly she's shown that to the world. And with bells on. Sometimes he wondered what that young woman would do next to upset Miles.

Henry Hanson, who was now sixty-four, had worked at Cavendon Hall for thirty-eight years. The stately home and the Ingham family were the be-all and end-all of his life, and he was devoted to both.

He had arrived here in 1888, when he was twenty-six, hired by the famous butler, Geoffrey Swann, who had seen great potential in him. He had started as a junior footman, and risen through the ranks, well trained by his mentor.

When Geoffrey Swann had died rather suddenly, ten years later in 1898, the 5th Earl, David Ingham, had asked him to take over as butler. He had done so with great alacrity, and never looked back. The 5th Earl had trusted him implicitly, and so did his son, Charles Ingham, the 6th Earl. He had proved their faith in him many times.

So much so, the Earl had recently confided in him, explained the real reason for this reunion with his children and the rest of the family. Hanson was sworn to secrecy, and he would tell no one, as the Earl well knew.

Hanson was aware that Lady Daphne and Mr Hugo also knew what this reunion was all about, and no doubt the Swanns did too. They usually were aware of everything, and that was the way it had been forever . . . since the time of James Swann, liegeman to Humphrey Ingham, who became 1st Earl of Mowbray and built Cavendon Hall.

The Swanns were true blue, in Hanson's opinion, and he had a lot of time for them. And whatever would the Inghams have done without them? God only knew. He, personally, was grateful for their existence.

Turning away from the window, Hanson decided he would go to the wine cellar, look at the different champagnes. Dom Pérignon was undoubtedly the best, though. He would also look in on Cook, reassure her about Saturday's dinner. She was a wonderful cook, had inherited the culinary talents of her aunt, Nell Jackson. Tomorrow there would be nineteen people for dinner, and she understood she had to be deft, prompt, swift and on her toes the entire time. She was a capable young woman, but she had told him last week she was concerned about the big dinner. He knew she would be fine, do well, but now he must go and give her a boost.

Hanson went out of his office, thinking about Nell,

41

Susie's aunt. He had been sorry to see her retire, but after standing on a stone kitchen floor for hours on end, day in, day out, cooking for the Inghams for the best part of her life, she had started to have problems with her legs. They were always swollen and red and painful, and she had backache, which troubled her greatly.

In the end, retirement had been the only solution, but she still lived in Little Skell village and had stayed in touch with them.

There was a lot of the Jackson flair around Cavendon because of Susie. Nell's niece was like her in every way, not only in her cooking; although she was taller than her aunt, more heavily built, and a comedian at times, making all of them laugh.

'Mr Hanson! Hello!' she exclaimed as he strode into the kitchen a moment later. 'You've arrived just in time for a cup of tea. And how about a few sweet biscuits?'

'Thank you, Cook, I wouldn't say no,' he murmured, and sat down. 'I just wanted to pop in to tell you to stop worrying about tomorrow evening. You'll manage very well. I have no doubts about you, Susie. And you know the footmen and the maids are well trained, they'll help you no end.'

She laughed, poured tea into two cups. 'That's what Auntie Nell said this morning. I went down to the village to have a word with her, and she was very reassuring.' Susie smiled at him and added, 'Can you believe it? She said I was a far better cook than she'd ever been. That I was really a chef and that, if I went to London, I would easily get a job at the Ritz.'

'I think she's right,' Hanson answered, genuinely sincere. Nell had been a good cook, with long experience, but Susie was more inventive and imaginative with food, which put her in a different category altogether.

They sipped their tea and munched on their biscuits in silence for a few seconds, before Susie threw Hanson a

42

questioning look. 'We're not looking for any maids, are we, Mr Hanson?'

He stared at her, frowning. 'Why do you ask?'

'Because my friend, Meg Chalmers, has just lost her job. She's been a maid at Fullerton Manor for quite a few years. Now the family is closing the manor, throwing dustsheets on the furniture and locking the house up. For an indefinite period. They're going to stay at their London residence. They've let all of the staff up here go, and everyone's down in the dumps and desperately looking for work.'

Hanson felt as if he had just been hit in the stomach with a sledgehammer. He had heard that the Fullertons were in a bad way, but had not realized how bad. Yet another aristocratic family feeling the pinch, going under, he thought, and then said quietly, 'No, we're not hiring at the moment, Cook,' and left it at that.

Whatever anybody else thought, he knew that Cavendon was still safe. Lady Daphne had assured him of that. Nonetheless, he did worry a lot, even though he knew she would never lie to him. Lately there had been a lot of penny-pinching and cuts, and Lady Daphne had discovered a new phrase. 'We're on a budget, Hanson.' When he heard those words he cringed.

But Lady Daphne and Mr Hugo were clever, and now that they were involved in the running of Cavendon there was a great deal of efficiency. Not that His Lordship was inefficient, but his heart attack, which had felled him last year, had slowed him down.

Mr Hugo had insisted on taking matters into his own hands, and so had Miles. They all worked well together, made a good team.

Last year, Miles had turned to him for guidance, and he had been happy to explain certain matters to do with the house. In fact, he had given him what turned out to be a short course on the house, and the many valuable possessions in it. All were exceedingly precious, from the paintings and the silver to the magnificent antiques.

The paintings in the Long Gallery included some extraordinary masterpieces, such as those by Constable, Gainsborough and Lely. These three great portraitists had painted the Ingham ancestors, and there were also Canalettos, Van Dykes, and Rembrandts. 'Another safety net the earlier Inghams provided us with,' Lady Daphne had said to Miles one afternoon last week. He had looked at her askance. 'Would we ever sell any?' he had asked, sounding slightly aghast. Hanson remembered now how she had answered in a low voice, 'If we have to, we will.'

He himself had jumped in and exclaimed: 'It will never come to that, surely not, Lady Daphne.' And he had flashed her a warning signal with his eyes.

Understanding him immediately, she had smiled at her brother and murmured, 'However, things are improving, and Hugo has sold some of our Wall Street investments, so we have money in the bank.' She had then turned to Hanson, and said, 'Let's continue our little tour of the house, go up to the attics, and Miles can view the rare antiques stored there.'

'About the Sunday luncheon,' Susie said, rousing Hanson from his reverie.

He nodded, and replied at once. 'Buffet style, as we decided, Cook. We always served the food that way when we had the summer cotillions. Lovely evenings they were. Well, not to digress. Lady Daphne's menu is a good guideline for you, but you can add other dishes if you wish. Perhaps cold poached salmon, asparagus and smoked salmon, dishes like that.'

They went on talking for a few moments, and then finally Hanson left the kitchen, made his way to the wine cellar to select the champagne for tomorrow's dinner. Definitely Dom Pérignon.

EIGHT

The light knocking made Diedre sit up straighter at the desk. She called, 'Come in,' and looked at the door expectantly.

It was Dulcie who appeared in the entrance to her bedroom, and for a second Diedre was astonished by her appearance. The girl bore a strong resemblance to how Daphne had looked when she was eighteen – was actually her spitting image. All blonde and golden and blue-eyed . . . well, they all had blue eyes, of course. But here was the most gorgeous girl she had ever seen, except for her sister Daphne at the same age.

Smiling hugely, Diedre got up and walked across the room to put her arms around Dulcie; she gave her a big bear hug, held her close for a moment, then stepped away.

Dulcie was astonished by this gesture from her sister, who had scared the life out of her when she was a child.

Diedre smiled at her once again, added, 'I haven't seen you for almost two years; you've become a true beauty, Dulcie. You look so much like Daphne when she was your age, it's quite startling.'

Even more taken aback, Dulcie could only nod. After a split second, she found her voice. Peering at her eldest sister, she said, 'What happened to you, Diedre? You were always the mean sister, saying very nasty things to me. Unkind things. Have you been taking nice pills?'

Diedre stared at her, and then began to laugh. 'You seem to have taken a leaf out of Great-Aunt Gwendolyn's book—'

'No, yours!' Dulcie shot back swiftly, cutting her off. 'Definitely yours . . . there's nothing quite like learning at the knee of the master, is there?'

'Too true,' Diedre replied, laughter still echoing in her voice. Years ago she would have taken umbrage at Dulcie's attitude and comments. But not now. The death of her lover had changed her, given her a different approach to life. She was much kinder and nicer. Intense grief had taught her a lot about people, and about herself. Death had softened her; loss had taught her compassion.

Now Diedre said, 'I must have been really mean to you when you were little. I was, wasn't I?'

'I'll say!' Dulcie answered sharply, walking into the bedroom and sitting down in a chair near the oriel window. 'I couldn't do right for doing wrong, as far as you were concerned. You were nasty, said some really rotten things. You called me a little madam, for one thing.'

Diedre shook her head, shocked to hear this. 'How terrible, so awful of me actually. I must have been going through some strange stage myself.'

'I doubt it, because you were always like that. Truly mean. At least to me. But, in a way, you toughened me up, and that's served me well,' Dulcie replied in her normal blunt manner. 'However, there was no reason for you to be so cruel. I was only five. Just a little girl,' she finished in a sharp tone.

'I'm so very sorry, Dulcie,' Diedre said, her voice filled with sincerity as she sat down at her desk and looked across at her sister. 'I can't bear the thought I treated you badly. That I was mean, unkind. Will you accept my apology? Can we be friends?'

'I suppose so. It all depends on how you treat me now, you know. I won't stand for any of that old nonsense.'

Diedre wanted to laugh at her outspokenness, but she swallowed hard and said, 'I promise I won't verbally abuse you. Or upset you in any way.'

'All right.' Dulcie now gave her a pointed look. 'Why are you being so nice to me?'

'Because I like you. No, I love you. You're my sister, after all, and we should all stick together, be close. Closer than we've been in the past.'

Dulcie was still wondering what this was about. She exclaimed, 'That's an odd thing for you to say. You used to behave as if I was a poisonous snake.'

A look of chagrin flowed across Diedre's face, and she felt a tightening in her chest. How could she have behaved in such a dreadful way towards her baby sister? It was suddenly incomprehensible to her. And then it hit her. She had been unhappy at that time, at odds with the family, and she had taken it out on a child. Shame filled her, rendered her silent. She had been a mean-spirited woman, it seemed, and she was saddened.

After a moment, Dulcie said, 'You're looking morose. What is it? Is there something wrong, Diedre?'

There was such concern in her sister's voice, Diedre felt even worse, and she did not answer. After a short silence she finally said, 'I am feeling very ashamed of myself for treating you the way I did . . . After all, you were only a child, as you've just reminded me.'

'Perhaps you were a little jealous because Papa spoiled and pampered me.'

'You might be right,' Diedre concurred. Thirteen years ago she had faced many problems in the family; jealousy one of them.

'I was his favourite and still am,' Dulcie now announced, giving Diedre a hard stare.

47

With a faint smile, Diedre replied, 'He's clever, our darling father, and he always has been. He makes each of his four daughters feel special – that each one of us is his favourite and the one he loves the most. And, in fact, he loves us all equally.'

'True. More than I can say about Felicity. She was no mother to me. She's an odd one. Everyone says it's because she's under the influence of the knife-wielding Lawrence Pierce . . . that she's so strange these days, I mean. What do you think? And is he really a blond Adonis, with the glamorous looks of a matinee idol jumping around a stage in the West End?'

Diedre burst out laughing. 'My goodness, what colourful language you use, Dulcie. You're certainly a chip off two old blocks: mine and Aunt Gwendolyn's.'

'Am I supposed to take that as a compliment?' Dulcie asked, a blonde brow lifting.

'Our great-aunt would think it was. I have a feeling she's rather proud of her way with words, even if she's a bit tart at times. As I often am myself.'

'So be it. Have you ever met Felicity's little playfellow?'

'Once or twice, in the early days of their relationship, just after the war started. And yes, he is very good looking, loaded with charm, but full of himself. He's a brilliant surgeon, everyone says that. But doctors like him, who save lives and perform miracles of a sort, are egomaniacs. They think they're to be revered on bended knee.'

'I've heard that before, and the quote about being God is always attributed to you, Diedre, if you care about such things.'

'I don't, and you were a neglected child, in my opinion – at least you were neglected by Felicity. Others loved you very much and took care of you in her absence. Still, our mother was behaving in a weird way in those days, and her mind was elsewhere.'

'I can well imagine exactly where it was. On the scalpel-happy doctor. And a certain part of his anatomy.'

Diedre stared at her, pushed back a chuckle, and asked, 'Have you ever thought of being a writer, Dulcie?'

'Occasionally, but I'm studying art history . . . I love paintings, and occasionally I've thought I might open an art gallery when I grow up.'

'I think you're grown up now. And that's a great idea. In the meantime, has DeLacy arrived yet?'

'She has, and I heard her crying a short while ago. I went into her bedroom and comforted her. I think she regrets her divorce, but I told her to buck up and get ready. So she pulled herself together, and said she was glad to be here with all of us . . . "in the middle of the clan Ingham" was the way she put it.'

'Shall I go and see her? She is all right, isn't she?'

'She is, I'm sure of that. She was focusing on what to wear when I left her room, so you don't have to go and see her.'

'And why did you come to see me? Since I was so horrid to you?'

Dulcie walked across to Diedre, stood in front of her. She said, 'I wanted to find out if you still frightened me. I was relieved to discover you don't. And, listen, we can be friends now. After all, we are sisters . . .' She let her sentence drift away, and went to the door, opened it. 'I'm going to go and get ready.'

'I shall too, Dulcie. I'll see you downstairs,' Diedre answered, feeling better than she had in a long time. Her chat with Dulcie had cleared the air.

Also, she was very taken with her youngest sister, the baby of the family. She had been a pretty child, and had grown up to be a true beauty. She had a glamour about her, with her flowing blonde hair, worn shoulder length. Her face was soft; her full mouth, high cheekbones and arched brows gave her a strong look of Daphne at the same age.

She's got it all, Diedre thought, walking over to the wardrobe to take out a frock. She'll go far, our little Dulcie.

49

NINE

Anger had replaced DeLacy's tears, as she discarded dress after dress, throwing them on the bed, a look of disgust on her face. There was nothing in her wardrobe here at Cavendon that she liked; they were old frocks, out-of-date for the most part, and not so flattering any more, she was sure of that.

She stood glaring at them scattered across her bed, when there was a knock on the door. Before she had a chance to speak, Miles walked in.

'I came to see what you were doing. My God, DeLacy, you're not even ready!' he exclaimed, slightly annoyed.

'Only because I've nothing to wear,' she wailed, staring at her brother. 'I brought several things for the evening, but I didn't bother about day frocks . . .' Her voice trailed off helplessly.

Miles came over to the bed and started to examine the dresses. Finally, he picked out a pale grey and white silk afternoon frock with a full skirt, a square neckline and flowing sleeves. 'This looks quite stylish. I'd wear this if I were you.'

'That's a funny expression to use, Miles, since you're

a man. But no doubt you like it because it's an old Cecily Swann frock.'

He nodded, and smiled knowingly. 'Of course it is; her style is inimitable. That's why she's the success she is today.' He noticed DeLacy's mouth tighten, and he knew the reason why. Cecily and DeLacy were no longer friends, and had not been for years.

He glanced at his watch. 'Come on, put this on. It's really beautiful, Lacy, and certainly it doesn't look dated. With some jewellery, it'll look quite different. Smart.'

DeLacy sighed. 'I suppose I have no option. All right, I'll wear it. But I don't have time to ring for Pam and wait for her to come up. You'll have to help me.' As she spoke, DeLacy picked up the dress and hurried into the bathroom. 'Wait for me, Miles, please, don't leave.'

'I'll be here,' he promised. He strolled over to the window and glanced out. In the distance he could see the lake and the two swans floating across the water. It had been his ancestor, Humphrey Ingham, who had decreed there would forever be swans at Cavendon, in recognition of James Swann, who had been his liegeman all those years ago, and the truest friend Humphrey had ever had. And they've been true ever since, Miles thought. For more than one hundred and seventy years . . .

'Here I am!' DeLacy cried, sounding more cheerful and swinging around. 'If you could do the buttons for me, Miles. Then all I have to do is put on a string of pearls and earrings, and I'm ready.'

He did as she asked, saying as he did, 'You look beautiful, and the dress is lovely. By the way, I think you and Cecily should make up, become friends again.'

'I've tried. Many times; even asked her aunt Dorothy to let me buy clothes there. But I've been rejected every time. They just don't give an inch.'

'Maybe Ceci will relent, if I ask her,' Miles murmured, fastening the last button. 'I'll talk to her later today.'

'She's here!' DeLacy exclaimed as she turned around to face him, surprise in her eyes. 'And she's talking to you?' DeLacy was astonished.

'Yes, actually, she is,' Miles answered carefully.

'I can't believe it! I thought she would never speak to you again. Why didn't you tell me she was going to be here?'

Miles sighed. 'I've been far too busy; I wasn't keeping it from you. But please, Lacy, hurry up. We mustn't keep Papa waiting.'

'Just another second, and do let's go downstairs together. I won't be a moment.' As DeLacy spoke she hurried over to her dressing table, took out a string of pearls, put them on, began to look for the earrings that matched.

Miles said, 'I shall talk to Cecily later this afternoon, and perhaps I can persuade her to relent, now that six years have passed. Perhaps she'll agree to a rapprochement. Do you want me to do that?'

'Yes, I do, Miles, as long as there are no recriminations, or anything like that . . . I mean the placing of blame, I've been blamed enough of late.'

'By Simon, you mean?' her brother asked, looking across the bedroom at her.

'Oh yes, and yes, and yes! Long ago, I discovered he loves to whine. And he's doing it now, moaning and groaning that the failure of our marriage is all my fault.'

'Is it?' he asked.

DeLacy swung around to face him, shaking her head. 'Maybe. Or maybe it's his . . . to tell you the truth it's nobody's fault. It just happened . . . it's the way it is. And I know I can't remarry him as he wants me to. I simply can't, Miles.'

'You don't have to protest to me. I know exactly what you mean. When a relationship doesn't work it's hell on earth.'

Although Miles had told DeLacy she looked beautiful, he was nonetheless worried about her. She was much thinner, and had a gauntness about her. Yes, her face was still delicate, beautifully proportioned, but her shorter hair did not really suit her. He was not particularly enamoured of these sleek, cropped hairdos; he found them masculine. He thought he could get Cecily to become Lacy's friend again, and she would influence his sister. As they walked downstairs together, he made up his mind to help DeLacy through this difficult period of her life. Fragile though she was at this moment, he knew she was strong. After all, she was an Ingham.

TEN

The library door was closed, but Hanson opened it without even knocking, and walked in. The Earl was expecting him.

Charles Ingham was sitting at his desk. He looked up and nodded at the sight of the butler. 'I'm assuming all my daughters and sisters have arrived, Hanson?'

'That is so, m'lord,' Hanson answered, walking forward. 'The young ladies are in their rooms, and I have spoken to Lady Gwendolyn. I told her tea will be at four thirty today, and I've given the same information to Lady Vanessa, as you requested. She is also in her suite. Apparently Lady Lavinia was with Lady Gwendolyn when I telephoned, and the message was relayed to her, Your Lordship.'

'Thank you, Hanson. As I told you earlier, I don't want to be disturbed once my children have come down.'

Hanson said, 'I understand, Lord Mowbray.' There was a momentary pause, then Hanson murmured, with a slight twinkle in his eye, 'I could stand guard outside, m'lord, if you so wish.'

Charles burst out laughing. 'I don't think that will be necessary, but thank you for offering.'

The butler inclined his head and excused himself. Charles rose, and walked across to the hearth, where he stood with his back to the fire, thinking about his children. He had no qualms about what he was about to tell them. He was quite certain they would understand; his plans made good sense. His daughters were intelligent; they cared about his wellbeing and trusted his judgement. Miles already knew, as did Daphne. As for the world at large, he had long since realized he didn't care about what strangers thought.

Daphne was the first to arrive with Hugo. When she joined him by the fireside, she said, 'I have told Hugo about the missing jewels, Papa.'

Charles turned as the door burst open.

'Here I am, Papa!' Dulcie cried in her usual flamboyant way, floating towards her father in a cloud of pale blue silk.

Charles embraced her. 'Like Daphne, you look beautiful, Dulcie.' A smile tugged at his mouth. 'You're both wearing blue. And taking a huge chance. Aunt Gwendolyn will tease you mercilessly about wearing frocks to match your eyes.'

'She will,' Dulcie agreed. 'But we don't care, do we, Daphers? We love blue, it suits us – and anyway, she wears blue as well. Because she has the same blue eyes. It's a family distinction.'

Daphne laughed, and went and sat on the sofa, where Hugo joined her.

A moment later, the door burst open again and Diedre, DeLacy and Miles came in together in a mad rush. 'I hope we're not late, Papa.' Diedre hurried forward, with DeLacy right behind her; Miles closed the door and joined his sisters.

Charles greeted them, and was relieved to see that Diedre had chosen pink and DeLacy was in a pale grey frock. No doubt they remembered how their great-aunt frequently made fun of them. Even though she was now in her mid-eighties, she was full of life, and mischief.

Charles let his eyes rest on his children for a moment, and admiringly so, and then he gave them a warm smile.

'It's really wonderful to have you here together . . . I should have done this before, had a family reunion. But, as you know, we've had our hands full, keeping Cavendon on an even keel. And it is safe, by the way, thanks to good management, wise counsel from Hugo, and innovations created by Miles. And also a great deal of prudence on Daphne's part in the running of the house. Anyway, I know we're going to have a truly happy few days together . . .'

Pausing, Charles moved away from the fireplace and sat down in a chair. Leaning back, making himself comfortable, he went on, 'I have several things to tell you. But first, let me explain that I am well, truly recovered from the heart attack I had last year. Doctor Laird has given me a great bill of health. He says I'm fit, and that I can lead a normal life. Which is tremendous news.'

'It is indeed, Papa!' Dulcie began to clap her hands, glanced around, and her siblings joined in, clapping with her, laughing together. They loved their father, who had been the true constant in their lives.

Charles still had a smile on his face when he continued. 'On Sunday afternoon, once lunch is over, I will be leaving Cavendon. I've decided that now is the right time to take a holiday. Just for a few weeks, but it will be a welcome respite—'

'What a wonderful idea!' DeLacy cut in. 'It will do you good, Papa—'

'Where are you going?' Dulcie asked, interrupting her sister. 'Somewhere lovely, I hope.'

'I'm going to Switzerland,' Charles said, his keen eyes roaming over them once more. 'To Zurich, to be exact. Hugo has very kindly offered me his villa, and for as long as I want.'

'What a treat.' Diedre smiled at her father lovingly, and

then a thought suddenly occurred to her. 'You'll be by yourself, and you might feel lonely, Papa. Would you like one of us to accompany you?'

Charles shook his head. 'Thank you, Diedre, for such a kind thought. I would like all of you to know that I won't be alone. You see, I'm getting married. The holiday is actually my honeymoon.'

Three pairs of blue eyes, wide with shock, were staring at him. Diedre, DeLacy and Dulcie were speechless, unable to say anything for a few seconds, taken by surprise as they were.

Daphne stood up and said, 'I think congratulations are in order, don't you?' She eyed her sisters, her own face wreathed in smiles of happiness for her father. 'Congratulations,' they all said in unison.

'You haven't told us who the bride is, Papa.' Diedre stared at her father, a quizzical look on her face. 'Do we know her?'

'Of course you do,' Miles said, walking over to join Daphne in front of the fire. 'Very well, in fact.'

Charles also stood. 'It's Charlotte. I'm going to marry Charlotte Swann. Whom I love and cherish and wish to spend the rest of my life with.'

There was a sudden excited rush towards him.

As usual, Dulcie was the first to spring forward and into his arms, followed by DeLacy and Diedre. Within seconds, three of his daughters were hugging him so hard he was almost knocked over.

'Goodness me!' Charles cried. 'That's a truly genuine endorsement, if ever I've seen one.'

Diedre exclaimed, 'She's been like a mother to us, Papa, and she's certainly held this family together for years. I'm very, very happy for you.'

'So am I,' DeLacy said, meaning this as much as Diedre did.

'I'm so happy for you and for Charlotte, Papa. I don't know what I would have done without her when I was little,' Dulcie announced. 'She gave me so much motherly love.'

'I know, darling,' Charles murmured. 'She's always been loyal, and she gave love to each and every one of us.'

After a few minutes, when everything had calmed down, it was Diedre who looked across at Daphne and then at Miles. She said softly, 'You both already knew, didn't you?'

They nodded, and Miles explained. 'I had to know, because I'm the heir, and I have to understand all of my father's actions. Daphne had to be told, because it is she who had to plan the wedding.'

'I understand,' Diedre said in an even voice, not at all jealous or put out that two of her younger siblings had known before she did. She was fully aware she had been sadly absent from Cavendon, and for quite some time, and so she didn't really know what had been going on over the years.

'When are you getting married, Papa?' Dulcie asked, as she hovered next to him near the fire.

'On Sunday morning,' he answered. 'Tomorrow evening will be . . . our engagement party . . .' He paused, then finished, 'On Sunday morning, Charlotte and I will be married in the church here on the estate. There will be a buffet luncheon for the Inghams and the Swanns, and then we shall depart for London, en route to Zurich.'

DeLacy asked, 'Papa, does Great-Aunt Gwendolyn know? And what about Aunt Lavinia and Aunt Vanessa? Have you confided in them?'

Charles shook his head. 'They don't know, not yet. I'm going to tell them in a short while, when we have afternoon tea. You see, I felt it was only correct to explain everything to my children first. But, in all honesty, I don't need anyone's approval, as you well know. I am a grown man, fifty-seven years old, and I can do as I wish. I told you first because you have a right to know. And I am going to tell them as a matter of courtesy.'

Diedre said quietly, 'Great-Aunt Gwendolyn might say you're stepping out of your class, and—'

'I don't care what she thinks – or anyone else!' Charles interrupted somewhat peremptorily. 'It's my life, and I shall live it as I see fit. I thrive when I'm with Charlotte. I shrivel up when I'm without her. I want to be happy in these last years of my life.'

'The world has changed, Diedre,' Miles interjected. 'Sadly, many aristocratic families are suffering because of the heavy taxes imposed on us by the government. And for many other reasons. I don't believe anyone we know is going to pay much attention to what you do, Papa, with all due respect. They're all bound up in their own ghastly problems, trying to survive the best way they can.'

'Well said,' Hugo agreed. 'No one can live their lives by what the world thinks. Charles must do as he wishes.'

'Can I be a bridesmaid?' Dulcie asked, throwing her father an engaging look.

He smiled, then looked across at Daphne, a brow lifting.

Daphne addressed her sisters when she said, 'Yes, Dulcie, you can, and you, too, DeLacy, and you, Diedre. I shall be matron-of-honour, since I'm a married woman. And I'll ask Alicia to be a bridesmaid too.'

'We don't have bridesmaids' frocks,' Dulcie murmured, making a *moue*.

'I thought the three of you could wear something really summery and pretty,' Daphne answered. 'As for me, I shall be wearing blue.'

Her sisters began to laugh, and Diedre said, 'And so shall we. None of us are short of blue dresses, so at least we'll match each other. Oh, how wonderful . . . a wedding at Cavendon.'

ELEVEN

As Cecily turned the bend on the dirt road she saw Genevra sitting in her usual spot on the dry-stone wall. She waved.

The Romany girl waved back, jumped off the wall, and stood waiting for her.

Cecily noticed at once that Genevra was wearing one of her old frocks, and she couldn't help thinking how well it suited her. She had not seen the gypsy in a long time, and now she realized how she had blossomed, was actually quite beautiful in an exotic way.

'Yer mam give it ter me,' Genevra explained, touching the white collar of the cotton dress. Her head on one side, she studied Cecily for a moment before adding, 'It's me favourite.'

'I'm glad you like it.' Cecily hesitated for a moment before asking, 'How old are you now?'

The girl grinned. 'Twenty-seven. Same as Master Miles.' Genevra glanced up at the great house towering above them on top of the hill. 'Big 'appenings going on up yonder, ain't that so, Cecily?'

'All the girls are here to visit Lord Mowbray.'

'Did yer keep that bit of bone I carved for yer?'

Cecily nodded. 'I did. But why are you asking me about it now?'

'It's lucky. A charm.' She waved a finger at Cecily. 'Don't lose.'

'Of course I won't lose it, Genevra. I treasure it,' Cecily responded, meaning every word. Somewhat superstitious by nature, she believed that the Romany girl did have the gift of sight, as she had always claimed over the years. Some people on the estate laughed at Genevra behind her back, and belittled her, but Cecily understood how clever she actually was, and she was fond of her.

'Did Miss Charlotte keep hers?' the gypsy asked.

'I'm sure she put it away carefully.'

Stepping closer to Cecily, Genevra opened her clenched hand, showed her a newly carved piece of bone. 'Tek it, Miss Cecily. It's a charm. I carved it for Master Miles. Give it ter Miles. Go on, tek it.'

Cecily reached for the bone, stared down at it. There were six small crosses and two hearts carved on it, with tiny strips of scarlet and blue ribbon tied on one end.

'It's like mine.'

'No, it's not.'

'I meant the ribbons.'

'True. Tell Miles it's lucky. Keep Miles safe, liddle Ceci. Keep him near yer.'

'I will,' Cecily answered, knowing full well that she would indeed do that. She had no option. After all, when she was just a young girl, she had taken the Swann oath: To protect the Inghams.

As she walked on up the hill, Cecily paused at one moment and looked across towards the fields. In the distance, she could make out the figure of Genevra, and, on the far horizon, the Romany wagons. There were three now; the family had grown.

61

It was Charlotte Swann who had told her why the 6th Earl allowed them to live on his land. Many years earlier, during the period when the 5th Earl had been the head of the Ingham family, Genevra's great-grandfather, Gervaise, had done him many services. One was discovering and catching the poachers who raided Ingham lands. The reward Gervaise and his brood were given was the right to inhabit the area near the bluebell woods for all time. The 6th Earl was just upholding that promise.

Romany wagons were a common sight in the lanes and woods of the English countryside, and had been for years. Cecily had always thought of them as picturesque. Some of the gypsies moved around, travelling from village to village, while others chose a particular area, and stayed if they were allowed. They kept to themselves, did not cause trouble.

Cecily couldn't help thinking about Genevra's cautionary words to keep Miles safe. She wished now she had asked her what she had seen in the future, although questioning the Romany would not have made her confide. Genevra had always been wary of issuing predictions. Who would want to harm Miles? Clarissa, his estranged wife? Clarissa's powerful father, Lord Meldrew? Someone unknown? Cecily could not pinpoint anyone as she hurried on, heading for the long terrace at Cavendon where Miles was waiting for her. She pushed worrying thoughts to the back of her mind.

Miles stood at the top of the steps, leaning against the balustrade, and she thought at once that he did not look good. He was wearing a navy blue linen suit that was far too big; it swam around him. Poor choice, Cecily thought, as he kissed her quickly on the cheek and then walked her along the terrace. She was going to have to take him in hand, do something about these awful clothes. Linen was not her favourite fabric. It creased in seconds.

'What happened?' she asked, as they sat down at the wrought-iron table in the centre of the terrace.

'It went really well. Diedre, Dulcie and DeLacy were thrilled about Papa and Charlotte, so no problems there.'

'I didn't think there would be. After all, my aunt practically brought them up.' Cecily sat back in the chair, put her hand in her pocket and brought out the piece of bone, then quickly told Miles about her encounter with Genevra.

After examining the bone, turning it around, he asked, 'What do the little engravings mean?'

'I don't know. She never explains. I have a bone, so does Charlotte, and she made one for Daphne years ago. When Hugo was going off to fight in the Great War, Daphne begged her to explain the carvings. Sympathetic to Daphne's worries, Genevra finally gave in. She said Daphne would have five children. And she did.'

'The bits of ribbon I understand completely. They represent the House of Ingham. Scarlet and azure are our colours.'

Cecily simply nodded.

Miles said, 'And you believe in Genevra's claim that she can see into the future, don't you?'

'I always have. I know she's strange, and some people say she's crazy, but I think she's just different. And gifted in a certain way.' Cecily shrugged. 'You're to keep the bone safe. It's a lucky charm, according to our gypsy girl.'

Miles put Genevra's gift into his jacket pocket, and murmured, 'When you run into her again, thank her for me. If I see her I will do that myself.'

'She means well, Miles. And I mean well when I tell you that you must not wear this suit ever again. It wrinkles quickly. It's too big for you. And navy blue is not your colour.'

Miles started to laugh. 'So I do matter to you, Miss Swann?' He raised a brow.

Cecily felt the warmth on her neck, and she realized she was blushing. Swiftly, she said, 'Clothes are my life, and I tell everyone if a garment doesn't work for them.'

'Oh, so I'm one of many, eh?'

'I wouldn't say that. I do care how you look.'

'Why?'

'Because you're my friend.'

'Thank you, Ceci, for being my friend. And you know I feel the same way about you.'

'I do. And I think we can manage to make this weekend work, if we're cordial with each other, as we agreed to be earlier today.'

He smiled at her and stood up. 'I think we'd better go inside; it's teatime, and Papa is expecting you to join us.'

TWELVE

'You're getting married!' Lavinia exclaimed, her incredulity apparent as she stared at her brother.

'I am, yes,' Charles answered, sitting back in his chair.

'To whom?' Lavinia asked, 'And when?'

'I'm marrying Charlotte, of course, and then—'

'Thank heavens for that!' Great-Aunt Gwendolyn instantly cut in, detecting a critical nuance in Lavinia's voice, wishing to avert any unpleasantness. 'And it's about time, too. I, for one, am thrilled to welcome Charlotte to this family.'

'So am I, Charles,' his youngest sister, Vanessa, announced, smiling at him. Looking pointedly at her great-aunt, she then added, 'But, actually, Charlotte's been a part of this family since we were all children, growing up together.'

'There might well be gossip, you know,' Lavinia interjected, focusing on her brother. 'You're marrying out of your class, for one thing, and you're fifty-seven, Charles. Why get married at all? Why not just continue in the same situation? I think your actions might seem inappropriate to many people, especially your friends. You know how you loathe scandal touching the family.'

The yellow drawing room went unusually quiet.

There wasn't a sound. Not one person said a word. No one moved, not even slightly. The stillness was overwhelming.

Miles glanced across at his father and saw at once how stunned Charles looked. He was about to get up, but Dulcie beat him to it. His sister sprang to her feet, flew across the room and stood behind her father's chair, one hand on his shoulder.

She said in a cutting voice, 'With all due respect, Aunt Lavinia, I don't believe Papa was seeking your approval. What he chooses to do is none of your business . . . nobody's business, in fact. He was actually being courteous. He wished to tell us he was getting married to Charlotte, and discuss the weekend events—'

'And I'm in charge of those!' Miles exclaimed, also jumping up, taking over from Dulcie, seizing his chance to change the direction of the conversation. He said in a strong, determined voice, 'Cecily has been helping me plan things. So let me proceed. Tonight it will be the usual quiet family dinner, just Inghams present. But tomorrow evening will be a different thing altogether, an engagement party – a gala, in a sense, as engagement dinners usually are. Harry, Cecily, Mrs Alice and Walter will be joining Papa and Charlotte, and also—'

Cutting across Miles in the rudest manner, Lavinia addressed her brother. 'I assume you haven't invited any of your friends, Charles. And perhaps that's for the best.'

'Actually, Charlotte and I have kept it to a minimum. We wanted a small family wedding, with just a few close friends. But we will be giving a party when we return from our honeymoon,' he finished, his blue eyes icy. Turning away from his sister, Charles said in a softer tone to Miles, 'Please continue, Miles. Sorry you were interrupted.'

'Thank you, Papa. On Sunday morning, Charlotte and Papa will be married in the church on the estate. After the service, Cecily and I will host a luncheon. This will be in a buffet style, as we favoured for the cotillions in the past. In the afternoon, the bride and groom will leave for their honeymoon. Of course, all of the Swanns are invited, as well as the Inghams.'

Dulcie said, 'The four Dees and Alicia are going to be bridesmaids. Well, three of us. Naturally, Daphne will be the matron-of-honour.'

Daphne, relieved that Miles and Dulcie had stopped Lavinia's idiotic chatter, stood and walked across the room. She said to Charles, 'I think I should tell Hanson we are now ready for tea, Papa.'

'What a good idea,' Charles replied. He was proud of his children for taking over, and so expertly squashing Lavinia, who had been unusually rude. She had over-stepped the mark, and he would put her in her place later.

Reaching the door, Daphne jerked it open, much to the surprise of Hanson, who was standing guard outside. 'Goodness me, Lady Daphne, you really made me jump.'

'I'm so sorry, Hanson. And you can stand down now. His Lordship has broken the news to his sisters and Lady Gwendolyn.'

'How did they take it, Lady Daphne?'

'I must admit, Aunt Lavinia seemed utterly taken aback, but not Aunt Vanessa, who was lovely about it. As for Lady Gwendolyn, she seemed positively elated.'

'Oh yes, she would be, m'lady. She admires Charlotte. Mind you, she's always been on the side of the Swanns, very partial to them.'

Daphne glanced at the butler, frowning. 'That's a strange word to use, Hanson . . . partial.'

'What I meant, m'lady, is that she likes them, but then we all do. Now, if you'll please excuse me, I'll have tea brought up immediately.'

'Thank you, Hanson,' Daphne answered, and watched him rush downstairs to marshal his troops. She herself went back to the yellow drawing room, and purposely avoided looking at Lavinia, who had been so snobbish and oddly belligerent.

Daphne was glad to hear the cheerful buzz of conversation as the family chatted with each other. She took her seat on the sofa next to Hugo. He was her rock – and everyone's rock these days. He was wonderful at keeping everyone's spirits up, and he did a lot to help her father hold Cavendon steady. Her father had recovered from his heart attack, but there were times when she thought he wasn't quite as strong as he looked.

Taking hold of her hand, squeezing it, Hugo said, sotto voce, 'That was a rather ugly performance from Lavinia. I was appalled at her attitude, and she spoke so rudely to Charles, who has always been so good to her. I'm happy Charlotte wasn't present.'

'So am I, darling. But Cecily's here, and although her face has remained inscrutable, I'm sure she was a bit hurt. And nobody can blame her for that. Don't forget, my father put her and Miles in place because he didn't want to cope with any problems or trouble. He believes Miles and Cecily can handle anything, keep everything on an even keel.'

'I'm well aware of that, and together they can be extremely tough. Unfortunately your father did get a bit of a shock a few minutes ago. Lavinia was mean-spirited, and really out of step with the times.'

'She was ghastly. Still, she's not been very nice to anyone since Uncle Jack died. Grieving for him, I suppose.'

'I doubt that. I don't think there was much love lost there. Jack adored her, and all he got in return was unhappiness. Buckets of it, according to Miles.'

'Miles?'

'Yes, Miles. They were rather close. He was Jack's favourite – surely you can't have forgotten that, Daphne?

He treated Miles like the son he never had. That's why Jack set up a trust for him in his will. It was small, though.'

'How stupid I am, Hugo. Of course, I remember now. Papa told me Lavinia wasn't too happy about that trust, but it was rock-solid legally. Lavinia couldn't do a thing.'

Daphne turned, glanced at the door as it opened. There was a sudden flurry of activity as Hanson swept into the yellow drawing room, leading his team.

Right behind him was Gordon Lane, now the senior footman, accompanied by Ian Melrose, the second footman, and Jessie Phelps, the head housemaid. The three of them were pushing tea trolleys laden with finger sandwiches, scones, strawberry jam and clotted cream, and all the usual fancy buns and cakes.

'A sight for sore eyes,' Hugo murmured. 'I've been so busy today I've worked up quite an appetite.'

'I know, so have I. But mostly I just want a good cup of tea,' Daphne said.

Miles, who had been talking to Lady Gwendolyn, now walked over to join Diedre, who was sitting with Cecily. 'I'm sorry about that, Ceci,' he said quietly. 'I hope you didn't get upset.'

'No, I didn't. But what your aunt did do was alert me, and I hope you, too. We'll have to make sure she doesn't do anything to upset Charlotte and your father at the dinner tomorrow – or, even worse, create some sort of scene in the church on Sunday.'

'You're right on target. We'll keep a sharp eye on her.'

Diedre said, 'She's preposterous, not to mention stupid. What in God's name did she think she could achieve by making those awful comments?'

'Let's just dismiss it now, and put it down to dim-wittedness,' Miles said. 'She's always been somewhat stupid, in my opinion.'

'That's right,' Diedre agreed, and rose. 'I'm going to sit

with Great-Aunt Gwendolyn. I want to speak to her about something, if you will excuse me.'

Once they were alone, Miles took hold of Cecily's hand; to his surprise and pleasure, she didn't pull it away. She simply looked at him, her eyes questioning.

'There's something I need to ask you,' he said, and paused, looking uncertain about continuing.

Cecily remained silent, hoping he wasn't going to talk about something personal . . . about them and their relationship.

After a moment, Miles plunged in. 'Look, DeLacy really wants the two of you to become friends again. She's genuinely missed you over the years, Ceci. And she's ready to apologize.'

Cecily didn't answer at first, and then finally she said: 'We can be friends again, of course. It's silly to hold grudges, and of course I'll accept her apology. But there is just one thing, Miles . . . I do work. Very hard and long hours. Just so long as she understands this, and that I won't always be available.'

'I'm sure she will. I'll make sure she does.' He squeezed her hand, and then let go of it. She had a sudden look of discomfort on her face, and he realized that it wasn't going to be easy, winning Ceci back into his arms.

A moment later, Dulcie came and flopped down in the chair next to the sofa. She grimaced. 'If Aunt Lavinia dares to make another rotten comment, I promise you I'm going to grab the first cream bun I see and shove it in her mouth. If that doesn't shut her up, I don't know what will.'

Cecily began to laugh and so did Miles. Glancing at Cecily he said, 'Don't think Dulcie's joking, because she isn't.'

'Of course I'm not joking,' Dulcie assured them, frowning, wondering why anyone would think that. She always did what she said she was going to do. She was an Ingham, after all. And Ingham women, especially, always stood up to be counted.

THIRTEEN

The house was still. So quiet that Cecily was alarmed. She stood in the small entrance foyer, her head cocked, listening for sounds of life.

Nothing stirred. This worried her. Her aunt had not looked well earlier; rather tired, worn out, actually. She hoped Charlotte had not collapsed, taken to her bed.

Cecily had come over to her house to help her try on the last of the clothes she had brought from London. That was an exhausting exercise, fitting frocks and outfits, and she hoped Charlotte was up to it.

Cecily walked towards the sitting room when she heard noises on the floor above and stopped. 'Are you up there, Aunt Charlotte?' she called, and immediately began to climb the stairs.

Charlotte appeared on the landing, looking down at her great-niece.

'Cecily! I didn't expect you until later.'

They hugged when Cecily stepped out onto the landing, and then they went into Charlotte's bedroom together.

Cecily noticed the photograph in the silver frame at once. It was of David Ingham, the 5th Earl, for whom

Charlotte had worked from the age of seventeen until his death. She had been his personal assistant.

Over the years their relationship had grown much more personal, although they had been so discreet that nobody knew for certain if they had been lovers or not. Except for the Swanns, who were aware of everything that went on at Cavendon.

The frame on the bed was next to a number of leather-bound notebooks and a pile of legal documents. And instantly Charlotte noticed a peculiar look on Cecily's face, and followed the direction of her gaze. She asked, 'Why are you so interested in David's photograph?'

'I was wondering why you have it in your bedroom? After all, your fiancé might find it strange, having his father's image staring back at him all the time.'

Charlotte burst out laughing. After a moment, when her hilarity had subsided, she said, 'It's usually locked up in a drawer. But I've been making a special list for you, and the code number for my main safe is on the back of his picture. That's why it's here.'

As she was speaking, Charlotte took the photograph out of the frame, and showed Cecily the number neatly written on the back. 'This is the combination for the big safe, where I keep my jewellery and those documents.'

Reaching for the list on the bedside table, she gave it to Cecily. 'I just added the number here. And, by the way, those are some of the record books. They are kept with many others in the second safe. I've been rearranging them, putting them in order.'

Cecily nodded, glanced at the list. 'And what are these other numbers?'

'I'll explain the list later. I want to tell you something else. When I die, you will take my place and keep the record books. Until you die. Before that happens, you must designate the person who will replace you to keep the records.'

Suddenly troubled, Cecily asked, 'What's wrong, Aunt Charlotte? Are you ill?'

'No, I'm not, don't be so silly.'

'Then why are you talking about wills and dying, when you're about to get married?'

'You of all people should know how practical I am. I want my affairs in order before I marry Charles. Also, we are going abroad, we'll be travelling, and I am fifty-eight years old. So, just in case—'

'Just in case what?' Cecily interrupted sharply.

'Don't get het up, Ceci dear. I'm perfectly well, and fit, and sound of mind. However, I do have quite a few possessions, such as this house, jewellery David bought me over the years, certain investments he made for me. I just want everything to be quite clear to you. I'm not going to die for a very long time, I promise you.'

'I'll hold you to that.'

'I won't let you down. Nobody knows what's going to happen from one day to the next. We are not in control of life. Life controls us. We have to handle what befalls us the best way we can. And hope and pray that it comes out right in the end. Remember this, Ceci.'

'I do take what you say seriously. I do listen to you,' Cecily reassured her.

Picking up one of the notebooks, Charlotte opened it at a certain page, handed it to Cecily. 'Please read this particular entry.'

Staring at the page, Cecily read the words which had been penned in a beautiful copperplate handwriting.

> *In mine own hand. July 1876.*
> *I loveth my ladie. Beyond all.*
> *The swann fits the ingham glove tight.*
> *I have lain with her. She is mine.*
> *She gives me all. I got her with child.*

Oh our joy. The child dead in her belly.
Destroyed us. She left me.
She came back to me.
My nights are hers again.
Til the day I die. M. Swann.

Still holding the book, Cecily gazed at her aunt. 'That's so sad . . . they lost a child.' Her voice was thick with emotion. 'Do you know who the person was? The man who wrote it? The Swann?' She was intrigued, curious as well as touched.

'I think so, but only because of the date. I believe it was Mark Swann who wrote it, the father of Percy and Walter. He was head of the family at that time. Obviously I have no idea who the Ingham woman was. For obvious reasons, he didn't write her name in the notebook. Protecting her. At least that's my opinion.'

'Why did you show me this entry?'

'For the same reason I told Charles about it a few years ago. I wanted him to understand that there is something mysterious, yet inevitable, about the Ingham men and the Swann women being together. I wanted you to understand that, too.'

Cecily's dark brows drew together in a frown. 'I'm not sure I'm following you. What do you mean?'

'I have been involved with two Ingham men. One died. The other I am about to marry. And what about you and Miles?' Charlotte paused for a second, and gave Cecily a penetrating look. 'You and Miles have been extremely close since you were children. And I know you love each other.'

'Yes, it's true,' Cecily admitted, having denied it for years.

'And there hasn't been another man in your life, has there?'

'No. I'm far too busy working. I don't have time.'

74

Charlotte bit back a smile. 'You're in love with Miles,' she said again. 'Other men don't interest you, hold no attraction for you.'

When Cecily was silent, Charlotte asked, 'Am I not right?'

'You are,' Cecily answered in a low voice.

'And he's in love with you. I believe that's one of the reasons his marriage failed. Clarissa played a role, of course. She wasn't a good wife. And she never conceived. Anyway, this is the point . . . he'll come after you, Ceci. Be prepared. That's the way the Ingham men are. With us. They just won't let go.'

Cecily sighed. 'He told me this morning that he is going to ask for a divorce. He said he hoped we could be together once he was free, because he loved me.'

'And how did you answer?'

'I told him I didn't know how I would feel. I really meant that, Aunt Charlotte. I don't believe I can go back to him. Ever. He hurt me so much. I can't forgive him. Or ever forget his treachery.'

'Oh darling, it wasn't treachery,' Charlotte said softly, her heart aching for Cecily, knowing how she had suffered. 'He had to do his duty as the heir. Whatever his feelings were for you, he had to put them aside. He had no alternative.'

'You're defending him!' Cecily pursed her lips and gave her aunt a hard and knowing stare.

'No, I'm explaining to you what Miles Ingham faced. It was his duty,' she emphasized again. 'He had to marry her, produce an heir.'

'And, once he's free, he'll have to do his duty again! Marry an aristocrat, beget an aristocratic heir. The Earl will see to that,' Cecily shot back vehemently.

'No, no, that won't happen,' Charlotte replied. 'I promise you. Very recently, I reminded Charles about that entry you've just read, which fully illustrates how long these liaisons have gone on. Over a hundred years. I told him he had to agree that Miles must seek a divorce. That is an imperative. I also explained that he could not interfere in the relationship which Miles would likely have with you later. And the world has changed radically, which Charles accepts.'

Genuinely surprised by this statement, Cecily just sat there, gaping at Charlotte, rendered speechless for a few moments.

And then it hit her. 'You did this, didn't you? You put us together this weekend. It was you who told the Earl that Miles and I worked well with each other, that we should handle everything. The events. Any problems or trouble that might arise. It was you, Aunt Charlotte. You manipulated all of us.'

Charlotte shook her head. 'No, I didn't. What I did was arrange a situation in which you and Miles would be helpful to us if anything went amiss. And at the same time I knew it would give you both a chance to connect again.'

'You're splitting hairs.'

'Maybe I am. But I've watched Miles in his awful misery for six years. Very painful to witness. And I've seen how you work and work and work. To counteract your own sorrow and loneliness. You're both broken. I hoped I could help to mend the two of you somehow.'

When Cecily remained silent, Charlotte went on quietly, 'Well, I suppose I am guilty as charged. Still, there's no getting away from the fact that Miles must produce an heir for Cavendon. And the only woman he wants in his bed is you. And that's that.'

'You've put me in a terrible position!' Cecily protested.

'No, I haven't, and actually you are holding all the cards, if you think about it. I really do believe you have the winning hand. However, let's move on. I need to continue to explain about my will. You are my main heir. Harry is my only other heir. I've looked after him, so there's nothing to worry about. I've left my house to the two of you. However, I have also left all of my shares in Cecily Swann Couture to you. It is your business, and you should own it fully.'

'Thank you, thank you very much, Aunt Charlotte. But what about Aunt Dorothy? She has some shares.'

'Not many. I'm going to buy her out, and she'll be happy to sell. You don't need any partners. Always remember that. Anyway, they're a nuisance in the long run.'

'You've never been a nuisance,' Cecily pointed out softly, having regained her composure.

'Thank you for saying that. I've tried to stay in the background.'

There was a moment of silence, and then Cecily said, 'You have some dresses to try on, you know.'

'Let's lock up the record books and the documents, and then I will concentrate on my trousseau, I promise.'

FOURTEEN

Diedre enjoyed her early morning walk to Little Skell Manor, which took her through the park at Cavendon, past the lake where the two snow-white swans floated together in contentment.

She paused for a moment, watching the swans, remembering that they mated for life. If only she had been able to do that . . . She pushed sorrowful thoughts to one side, and moved along the path at a steady pace. Put the past behind you, she reminded herself.

At one moment, she lifted her head, glanced up at the sky. It was a clear blue on this sunny Saturday morning, and she hoped the good weather would last. She wanted it to be a perfect day tomorrow for her father's marriage with Charlotte.

How glad she was he had taken this step at long last. There was not a single doubt in her mind that Charlotte would be a wonderful wife . . . she had actually been exactly that for many years, without the benefit of a legal document.

Diedre had felt the warmth and love of her father, Miles and her sisters last night at the family dinner. It had been like old times, and she had realized how much she had missed everyone.

Funny, she thought now, how we become so entangled in our everyday doings, consumed by our worries and problems. Selfish really, not giving a thought to others.

She aimed to make amends, to stay in touch with her sisters, most especially DeLacy. It struck her last night how fragile DeLacy was – nervous, on edge. At one moment after dinner she had asked Miles if their sister was all right. Miles had said DeLacy was unhappy about the divorce, yet could not live with Simon. Their married life had been full of terrible quarrels and violent upsets that had inevitably torn them apart in the end.

Diedre focused on Miles, who had also been unlucky in love. If he'd ever loved Clarissa, that is. Duty had been at the root. What rotten luck that Clarissa had not produced an heir. On the other hand, perhaps it was for the best. Miles had confided to her that he was going to seek a divorce. Far better in this situation that there were no children involved.

Daphne's been the luckiest, Diedre thought, her mind suddenly settling on her sister's adorable and beautiful children. As for Dulcie, she has her life ahead of her. I'm going to take her under my wing; I'm determined to make up for the way I treated her when she was a child, she muttered to herself. Deep inside she was still ashamed of the way she had behaved.

As she walked up the garden path to Great-Aunt Gwendolyn's house, Diedre managed to empty her mind of these thoughts, and tried to concentrate on what she had to say.

One thing she did know, she could not waste her great-aunt's time. She wouldn't sit still for small talk, always needed to get to the heart of the matter. And immediately.

Gwendolyn Ingham Baildon was blessed with great intelligence and practicality. Diedre thought she had the most wisdom of anyone in the family.

Lifting the brass hand-knocker on the front door, she banged it once. Almost instantly the door was opened to reveal Mrs Pine, Lady Gwendolyn's long-time housekeeper, standing there.

Smiling, greeting her warmly, Mrs Pine led her through the front hall and into the parlour. This attractive room, filled with mellow antiques, comfortable sofas and chairs, had two large mullioned windows which overlooked the gardens. The gardens were beautiful; they had been lovingly cultivated by Harry Swann until he had become Miles's right-hand man, learning estate management with him.

Her great-aunt was sitting on a sofa, waiting for her. 'There you are, my dear,' Lady Gwendolyn exclaimed. 'Punctual as always. I do like that characteristic in people. Those who arrive late are thoughtless. They're stealing one's time, don't you know.'

Diedre nodded. 'That's correct. And thank you for agreeing to see me this morning.' She bent over and kissed her aunt's cheek.

'I'm happy to have a little private visit with you, Diedre. Do sit down, my dear, don't hover.'

Taking a chair next to the sofa, Diedre said, 'I've been informed by a very good friend, a trusted friend, that I have an enemy at the War Office. I was stunned when I heard this. My work has been excellent, and I've had promotions over the years. My friend said this enemy could prove dangerous to me.'

Lady Gwendolyn sat up straighter on the sofa and gave Diedre a penetrating look, her eyes narrowing slightly. 'I don't like the use of the word "dangerous", Diedre. Dangerous in what way?'

'I'm not sure. I think that whoever is against me wants me to be dismissed – pushed out, in other words.'

'What exactly is it that you do at the War Office? No one seems to know, and you've been very wary about discussing it over the years. Which leads me to make the assumption you are in Intelligence. Is that so?'

Diedre leaned forward slightly and said in a low voice, 'I am not allowed to discuss my work, Great-Aunt. But let me just say that I have never known you to be wrong about anything, and most especially in your assumptions.'

A twitch of a smile crossed Lady Gwendolyn's face, and she nodded. 'Now, do you have any indication who this enemy might be? Were you given a name? Or do you suspect anyone of wanting to harm you?'

'The answer is a definite no to all of your questions. I was rather dumbfounded, actually, when I was told I had an enemy, someone who was out to make trouble for me. I've wracked my brains, and I haven't been able to pinpoint anyone.'

'Who was the person who informed you, may I ask?'

'A very old friend, Alfie Fennell,' Diedre answered. 'And he was so sincere I believed him.'

'Is he any relation to Sir Hubert Fennell?' Lady Gwendolyn asked.

'Yes. That's his uncle.'

'How did young Fennell get to know about this so-called enemy of yours?' Lady Gwendolyn now asked.

'Through Johanna Ellsworth. They are cousins. Neither have anything to do with the War Office. Alfie is a barrister, and Johanna does not work. She has a private income.'

'It seems that your friend Johanna knew about this first and passed it on.'

'She told Alfie she had heard a strange rumour about me, and she wanted him to alert me, even though she said it was only a rumour.'

'I think you have to find out who told her.'

'I did do some probing, and I know the right questions to ask. I gathered that it was just . . . out there.'

Lady Gwendolyn was silent for a moment before remarking, 'You say you can't think of anyone who might want to cause you trouble. But maybe it's not someone . . . highly visible. Have you ever offended anyone, without realizing it? Have you rejected a would-be suitor who you didn't know was a suitor? Is someone in competition with you?'

'None of those things. At least, not that I know of. I just plough into my work every day and keep my head down.'

'Have you told any of your colleagues at the War Office about this rumour?'

'No, I haven't. I thought it better not to say a word to anyone except you. Obviously, I know people there, and we're friendly as colleagues, but I don't have any bosom chums. Actually, I'm baffled at the mere idea of an enemy.'

'How can I help you, Diedre?'

'I'm not sure. Being able to talk to you about this helps a lot, because now I don't feel so alone, coping with this problem.' Diedre let out a small sigh, shook her head. 'I thought you might know someone at the War Office, or in the government. But now, as I'm saying that, I know you can't just start asking your friends who my enemy might be, now can you?' Diedre began to laugh at her own absurdity, and so did Lady Gwendolyn.

After a few moments, Diedre added, 'I suppose all I can do is just wait and see who tries to make trouble for me.'

'That is true, my dear, in one sense. But I'm afraid I can't just leave it at that. Let me think about this. I am going up to town next week. I have several engagements to fulfil, and who knows what I might find out as I circulate in Mayfair and Westminster with my friends.'

'Thank you, Great-Aunt Gwendolyn, I do appreciate your help. I love my work . . .' Diedre broke off as her voice started to quaver unexpectedly. She was on the verge of tears. Swallowing, promptly taking hold of herself, she continued, 'The War Office is a huge part of my life, as you know. I've been there twelve years, and I love what I do. Without it I would be lost.'

'I truly understand,' Lady Gwendolyn murmured sympathetically, having always been aware that Diedre found great fulfilment in her work, and was dedicated to her professional life.

FIFTEEN

It was a weird and dubious story at best, and if anyone else had told her this strange little tale, Lady Gwendolyn would have doubted its veracity.

Since it was Diedre who had related it, though, she believed it was the truth. Her great-niece was honest and dependable, not given to flights of fancy.

Leaning back against the iron garden seat, gazing out at the flower garden, she relaxed, let her mind wander.

She knew nothing about Diedre's work, other than that she was well thought of by the powers that be. Only today had Diedre strongly implied she was in Intelligence, which Lady Gwendolyn herself had long suspected but never mentioned to anyone. She was always cautious when it came to such things.

As the daughter of one of the foremost earls in the land, with a title in her own right, her niece mixed in the best of circles, was genuinely popular, and was on the invitation lists of everyone that mattered in London society.

There had never been any gossip about Diedre . . . no Chinese whispers. Lady Gwendolyn sat up with a start, frowning to herself, suddenly recalling Maxine Lowe, one of Diedre's closest friends. She had been found dead in suspicious circumstances at her house in Mayfair, four years ago now.

At the time, Lady Gwendolyn had been annoyed when Diedre had been interviewed by Scotland Yard. But her worries immediately vanished when her great-niece told her that all of Maxine's friends had been questioned by the police.

Diedre had then gone on to explain that the big boys at the Yard thought they might be looking at a murder; some agreed with this theory, others focused on the idea of suicide.

Then a different verdict altogether was announced by the coroner at the inquest. Maxine had indeed died from poisoning, and the substance ingested was arsenic. But the manner of death was declared to be undetermined. Leaving the verdict inconclusive in this way meant that the case was open to speculation; there had been a lot of talk about Maxine's sudden death in the circles she had moved in – mainly high society and the artistic world. In the end, nothing ever came of the police investigation. Her death remained a mystery to this day.

Now Lady Gwendolyn focused on Diedre's present problem, and her razor-sharp mind told her one thing . . . the rumour about Diedre being pushed out by the War Office had nothing to do with her personal life. She believed it had been started by a colleague with a grudge against Diedre.

Nothing else made sense, actually. Obviously there was someone who wanted Diedre out of the way. Jealousy, envy and ambition. A fatal combination. Malice, she said to herself. It's driven by malice aforethought.

If you wanted to punish a person, the only way to do it without causing them bodily harm was to attack whomever or whatever they loved the most. Hit their vulnerable spot hard.

This might be another human being, such as a spouse, a child, a parent, siblings. Or a lover, perhaps. A person who could be physically damaged, maybe even killed. She dismissed the idea of a lover. Diedre had become very much a career woman. But she was beautiful, with her chic hairdo and lovely face, not to mention her stylish clothes.

Alternatively, a career that was relentlessly attacked could ultimately be totally destroyed forever, never to be rekindled.

These were the only two choices, as far as she was concerned. Hurt someone Diedre loved. Or destroy her career totally.

Discovering the identity of Diedre's enemy was an imperative. Until they knew who it was, they would be whistling in the dark. Whom could Lady Gwendolyn turn to for help? Which of her friends had real power? Whom did she trust? And who would actually be willing to poke around for her?

The answer came to her immediately. Only someone in politics and someone with access to the top brass at the War Office.

Staring into the distance, she thought of those friends who were connected to politics. She knew Lucy Baldwin quite well, had been at her wedding to Stanley in 1892. But she could hardly go to the Prime Minister's wife with this.

Winston. Of course! Not only was he a good friend, he had just the right temperament to get involved. He would relish it, in fact. But how could she ask him at this particular time? Once again, Winston Churchill was in the middle of the fray, dealing with the coal strike for Baldwin. Perhaps—

'Excuse me, Lady Gwendolyn,' Mrs Pine said, intruding on Lady Gwendolyn's thoughts, coming down the steps into the garden. 'Lady Lavinia is here. She apologizes for being early for lunch.'

Pushing herself to her feet, Lady Gwendolyn said, 'That's perfectly all right, Mrs Pine. I was just about to come inside anyway.'

Lavinia was waiting for her in the parlour; as she turned around to greet her aunt, Gwendolyn was struck by the tiredness etched on her niece's face. 'Are you feeling all right, Lavinia?' Lady Gwendolyn asked. 'You look a little under the weather, my dear.'

'I'm tired. I didn't sleep well last night.' A faint smile lingered on Lavinia's face as she followed her aunt across the room.

Sitting down in a chair opposite her, Lavinia went on, 'I'm afraid the unexpected news that I was going to attend a wedding on Sunday – my brother's wedding at that – rather startled me. It also upset me.'

Lady Gwendolyn simply nodded, made no comment. She had fully intended to chastise her niece over lunch today, for being rude to Charles yesterday. But now she changed her mind.

As she studied Lavinia's face, she realized there was something else radically wrong with her. In fact, she thought her niece might be ill. She looked pale, wan, and her blonde beauty had faded somewhat. I'd better not chide her at this moment, she decided. 'We were all surprised, except for Miles and Daphne, who knew about it all along. But I'm happy for Charles, and delighted he is marrying Charlotte.'

Staring at her aunt, raising a blonde brow, Lavinia exclaimed, 'I know you are! And I must admit, I was taken aback yesterday when you voiced that opinion about this unfortunate union. He's marrying out of his class. He'll be ostracized.'

'Don't be ridiculous!' a voice exclaimed from the doorway.

Lavinia's sister glided into the parlour.

Drawing to a halt next to her aunt, Vanessa said, 'I'm not late, am I, Aunt Gwendolyn? Hello to you, Lavinia. I'm afraid you're going to have to join the multitudes who are cheering on the sidelines. Otherwise you'll be the one who is ostracized . . . you'll be sent to Coventry.' Bending over her aunt, she kissed her cheek, then seated herself on a nearby sofa.

Vanessa couldn't help thinking how elegant and distinguished Lady Gwendolyn looked. Long ago her abundant blonde hair had turned to silver. Now it was pure white, and beautifully styled as usual. Her blue eyes sparkled brightly this morning and there was no hint that she was eighty-six. She looked much younger and was agile of mind and body.

Lady Gwendolyn smiled at Vanessa and glanced across at Lavinia. Two sisters entirely different in personality and character. She knew which one she had always preferred: Vanessa, liberal-minded, ready to accept people on face value, and in step with the times they were living in. The 1920s, not the 1800s.

Lavinia, throwing her sister an icy look, asked, 'And what about you, Vanessa? When are we about to hear that you are finally getting married?'

Vanessa began to laugh. 'Oh, I don't know, I'm not sure I'm ready to do that yet,' she answered casually, still laughing.

'Is there a nice young man in your life, darling?' Lady Gwendolyn asked. 'And if indeed there is, who is he? I would love to know.'

'His name is Richard Bowers, and he's very nice. And the next time you come to London we'll have dinner, or lunch – whichever you prefer, Aunt Gwendolyn.'

'I'll be up in town next week. We must meet. That would be lovely. Is he by any chance related to the Barnards?'

'His mother Valerie is a Barnard,' Vanessa answered. 'I think you know her, Aunt.'

'I do indeed. We're acquaintances, but not close friends. She is a very nice woman.'

It was during lunch that Vanessa mentioned that Daphne had shown her the guest list for the wedding earlier. 'I was happy to see Hugo's cousin, Mark Stanton, is coming, and so is Paul Drummond. Also a number of—'

'Who is Paul Drummond?' Lavinia cut in, staring across the table at Vanessa. 'I've never heard of him. He must be a new friend.'

'No, actually he's not. Paul Drummond is an American. He has worked with Hugo for many years,' Vanessa explained. 'Paul runs the New York end of Hugo's business and, since he happens to be in London at the moment, Charles wanted him to come.'

'An American! That explains it perfectly. I can assure you none of Charles's close friends will be there. How could he invite them when he's not marrying an aristocrat?'

Vanessa, appalled by Lavinia's comment, said slowly in a firm tone, 'Stop harping on about the aristocracy. It's falling apart. It has been since the end of the war. Because of high taxes imposed by the government. No men to till the fields, run the factories or go down the mines. All dead on the blood-sodden fields of France – including our nephew, Guy. Half of Charles's friends are busy trying to stay afloat, keep their stately homes running, and many are not succeeding. Do you really believe they're concerned about Charles's new wife? Not one iota. They're trying to save their skins. So shut up about Charles marrying out of his class. I for one think you're totally out of line.'

Lavinia sat back in her chair, gaping at Vanessa, astonishment washing over her face. For once in her life she was speechless, shaken by her sister's verbal attack.

Seizing the moment, Vanessa continued, 'Everyone said it was the war to end all wars. But what the Great War actually did was end the British Empire. Nothing is the same any more. England's stony broke. The landed gentry are being diminished. The working man is looking for a fair deal. There was a General Strike, in case you didn't notice, and the coal strike. The country's spinning on its heels, and talk of a Depression is constant. And you're going on about class. Just grow up, Lavinia. Join the world we're living in today.'

Lavinia still remained speechless, even more shocked by her sister's attitude and her angry words.

Lady Gwendolyn studied Vanessa, and then nodded. 'Well put, my dear. I'm afraid I do have to agree with you.' Focusing on Lavinia, she continued, 'No one likes change, certainly not I, but times have indeed changed, Lavinia. And we must all change with them, keep in step. And that includes you.'

Lavinia had become paler than ever, and she replied in a low, slightly nervous voice, 'Why are you both so annoyed with me? It's the truth.'

There was a small silence. No one spoke. And then a moment later, Mrs Pine came into the dining room with the parlour maid, and they served the dessert.

Vanessa, wishing to change the subject, smiled at the housekeeper, and said, 'I do love crème caramel, Mrs Pine. It's my favourite.'

The housekeeper merely smiled and nodded.

Once they were alone again, Lady Gwendolyn sat up straighter in her chair, and peered at Vanessa and then at Lavinia. Both of them knew a pronouncement was coming and they sat perfectly still, not uttering a word or touching their food.

After a long moment, Lady Gwendolyn said in a steely voice, which was also as smooth as silk, 'Because I am matriarch of this family, its oldest and most senior member, I can break the rules and make the rules.' She paused, took a sip of water, and shifted slightly in her chair.

Her voice had a little less steel and more silk to it when she explained, 'I am making a new rule. Since I am most approving of my nephew's choice, this will be the last time a pejorative word will be uttered about Charlotte. Ever. By anyone. On Sunday she will become the Countess of Mowbray. She will be treated with the respect she deserves, and which she has actually earned through a life of devotion to this family. Charlotte has been a boon to us all. And frankly your brother would be dead by now if it were not for her.'

Still the sisters said nothing.

Lady Gwendolyn was fully aware that she had got her point across to them. Vanessa was at ease, whilst Lavinia looked shaken. Picking up her spoon, Lady Gwendolyn tasted the crème caramel, then she said quietly, scrutinizing Lavinia, 'Are you all right, my dear? I hope my words haven't upset you too much.'

'No, not at all, Aunt Gwendolyn,' Lavinia answered, her voice still low, but steady. 'And I'm sorry if I offended you, Aunt. It won't happen again. Surely you must know that I love my brother, and I do want what's best for Charles.' Lavinia stopped, took a deep breath, and finished. 'I am fully aware that Charlotte is devoted to him, and we do owe her a lot.'

Lady Gwendolyn offered Lavinia a warm smile. 'I am very glad to hear those sentiments.'

Wow! Vanessa thought, pushing down the laughter bubbling inside. Wow oh wow! I never thought I'd hear anything like this from Lavinia's mouth. She's always been jealous of Charlotte, ever since we were children growing up together. She was constantly in a sulk because Charles treated Charlotte like his best friend. And she hated it when they called each other Charlie.

91

SIXTEEN

They had arranged to meet at the gazebo, situated halfway between Little Skell Manor and Charlotte's house at the edge of the village. After lunch, once Vanessa and Lavinia had departed, Lady Gwendolyn set off to keep her appointment.

She walked slowly along the path, as usual wanting to savour the beauty of Cavendon. For her it was the one true place on this planet, the place she was happiest and most content.

Gwendolyn Ingham Baildon had been born at Cavendon, had grown up there. When she was twenty she had married Paul Baildon in the small church on the estate. She and Paul had had a wonderful ten years together, and then he had died, quite suddenly, after a botched operation for appendicitis.

It should not have happened. He had been far too young to die, and she had been devastated by the loss, as had everyone else. At thirty she had become a widow, and she had been a widow for fifty-six years. Paul had been buried in the cemetery alongside her ancestors, such a long time ago now.

They had never been lucky enough to have children, but the memories were there, to be recalled at will and mulled over . . . they were almost living things, so vivid in her mind and in her heart.

As she strolled along, Gwendolyn glanced around. The park at Cavendon was always beautiful, whatever the time of year, but today it was spectacular. It was a perfect July afternoon, the bright sun shining in the light blue sky, everything so green and verdant. The great oaks were ancient sentinels along the path, their thick branches forming canopies of dark leaves high above, offering cool shade in this warm weather.

Within minutes she saw the gazebo ahead. Charlotte was standing on the steps waiting for her. Charlotte Swann. A remarkable woman. She had known her since the day she had been born, fifty-eight years ago, and there was a certain closeness and friendship between them; they were comfortable with each other, but then Charlotte never overstepped the line, was never out of place, and Gwendolyn was open-minded and without an ounce of snobbishness in her character.

Charlotte, her face full of smiles, said, 'Good afternoon, m'lady.'

'Hello, Charlotte, my dear.' Lady Gwendolyn took the hand being offered, and mounted the few steps.

After ushering her over to a white wicker chair, Charlotte said, 'I'm glad you suggested meeting here. Cecily and Miles are still going over details for the weekend, and Mrs Alice is finishing my packing. I'm afraid it's a bit busy at the house.'

'I rather thought there would be quite a lot of activity around you, and this seemed the most suitable spot to meet for a quiet chat. We'll be undisturbed.'

Charlotte sat down at the table. 'What did you wish to speak to me about, Lady Gwendolyn?'

'I'm sure Charles has already told you how delighted I was to hear his news at tea yesterday. However, I did want

93

to tell you that myself, and to congratulate you. I'm very happy you are marrying Charles, Charlotte. I have something for you.'

Lady Gwendolyn opened her handbag and took out a package wrapped in blue silk and tied with white ribbon. She placed it in front of Charlotte.

A moment later, Charlotte found herself holding a brooch in her hands. It was made of gold, designed in the image of a swan. The gold was carved to look like feathers on a plump body, and around the swan's long neck there was a narrow band of diamonds. The swan's eyes were made of small sapphires, its beak formed of slivers of mother-of-pearl and ebony.

'It's beautiful, Lady Gwendolyn!' Charlotte exclaimed. 'Thank you so much. I can see it's old.'

'Very old, in fact,' Lady Gwendolyn replied. 'The worn box is obviously ancient. There's no jeweller's mark or name on the pin, or on the box, but it is so beautifully crafted it must have come from a fine shop.'

Charlotte nodded, touched by this gesture on Lady Gwendolyn's part. Her eyes filled. After a moment, clearing her throat, she said, 'I shall treasure it always.' She glanced down at the brooch. 'May I ask who gave it to you?'

'My mother,' Lady Gwendolyn answered without hesitation. 'The brooch has been passed down for years. I decided you should have it. You're about to become an Ingham, and you are a Swann. A fitting token from an old woman who thinks the world of you.'

Charlotte experienced another little rush of emotion. After a moment, she said, 'You've always been so kind to me, Lady Gwendolyn, and you've never passed judgement on me.'

Staring at her, frowning, Lady Gwendolyn asked, 'Because of your love for my brother? Is that what you're referring to?'

'Yes.'

'Why would I judge you? You made David happy, gave him a new lease on life. And he loved you, Charlotte.'

'He helped to make me who I am. He taught me so much, and he gave me a wonderful life.' Charlotte laughed. 'In secret, of course.'

'I knew about the two of you,' Lady Gwendolyn murmured. 'I never said one word to anyone.'

'Thank you for that.'

'Stop thanking me, Charlotte. It is I who should be thanking you for all you've done for us. And I just want to add this . . . welcome to the Ingham family officially.'

Walking back to Little Skell Manor, Lady Gwendolyn chastised herself for not telling Charlotte the truth about the brooch. She had suddenly lost her nerve, if the truth be known. But she must know more of the story, she murmured to herself. And I will tell her when she comes back from her honeymoon.

If I haven't died by then. This thought made her chuckle. I've no intention of dying just yet. I've too much damage to do, and I have to help Diedre find her enemy and make her problem go away.

SEVENTEEN

Daphne sat at her desk in the conservatory, a room which had become her own over the years. No one else ever used it. She was making a last-minute check of the guest list for the engagement dinner that evening, and contemplating the placement of everyone at the two dinner tables.

Nodding her head, deciding that it could not be improved on, she sat back in the chair, sighing to herself, finally relaxing. It had been an extremely busy day, and she was relieved she had asked her father to cancel afternoon tea. The staff were overburdened as it was, and Hanson was all for it. Fortunately, her father had understood.

At the sound of footsteps on the terracotta-tiled floor, she turned around in her chair; her face lit up when she saw Peggy Swift coming towards her, carrying a tea tray. She was Peggy Lane now, having married Gordon Lane after the war, and was the mother of a little girl who was called Daphne, named for her.

'I thought you might be in need of a nice cup of tea, Lady Daphne,' Peggy said, placing the tray on the table next to the sofa. 'You haven't stopped for a minute today, so Hanson tells me.'

'It has been busy, Peggy, and by the way, I must thank

you for stepping into the breach this afternoon, coming in to help out. We really needed you. How is Mrs Thwaites?'

'She's all right, m'lady. Resting in her room. Hanson told me it's not the first time she's fainted lately. It's happened before. She's very dedicated to her job. Hanson says it's probably just tiredness, nothing serious. But he's told her she must go to the doctor on Monday.'

Standing up, Daphne walked over to the sofa. 'I'm glad Hanson insisted on that. She's not getting any younger, I'm afraid.'

'Neither is Hanson, m'lady.'

Daphne glanced at her quickly. 'Have you noticed something I haven't, Peggy?' she asked, worry creeping into her voice.

'No, no, just making a casual comment, Your Ladyship. By the way, I've tried twice now to get hold of Olive Wilson, but there's still no reply at Lady Felicity's house – I mean Mrs Pierce's house.'

'Thank you, Peggy. Please try the number again later.' Then Daphne's blonde brows drew together in a frown, and she added, 'Actually, I'm not sure there's anyone at the house. My mother usually goes to Monte Carlo in the summer.'

'I'll try again, anyway,' Peggy murmured. 'Shall I pour you a cup of tea, Lady Daphne?'

'Thank you, Peggy.'

'Surely they'd have one staff member there, don't you think, m'lady?'

'I do indeed. The housekeeper.'

Peggy said, 'That's right, Your Ladyship, a house like that would never be left without a caretaker.'

Daphne watched her hurrying out, thinking what a lovely woman she had become. Her marriage to Gordon, now the senior footman, had been successful, and they were obviously happy together.

He had risen in the ranks of Cavendon after the war, and was a superb head footman, as well as a good right-hand man to Hanson. She relied on Gordon for many things, and he was willing to pitch in, clever in a variety of ways.

I'm glad we gave them the biggest cottage in the village, when it became vacant, Daphne now thought as she took a sip of the tea. And that we broke the rules and allowed Gordon to sleep in his own home. The arrangement has worked out well. Changing times have their assets, it seems.

Daphne's thoughts slid back to her mother, and the missing jewels. She would get them back no matter what. She knew her father was worried about the stolen pieces. But she had pointed out that there was no way her mother could sell them. Every jeweller in London would know if they went on the market. The Ingham Collection was famous and well documented.

There was a little cough and a shuffling of feet. When Daphne glanced up, she saw her daughter Alicia hovering in the doorway, looking discontented.

'Darling, why the long face? And do come in, don't stand there.' Daphne gave her a welcoming smile, struck by her glowing face despite the sulky expression. She could see the woman in the child, and she realized yet again that her daughter would grow up to be stunning, a true beauty.

The twelve-year-old girl, tall for her age, blonde and blue-eyed, came running in and stopped in front of her mother. She asked in a somewhat plaintive voice, 'Am I going to be a bridesmaid or not, Mama?'

'Of course you are, darling, I told you that last night, and we've already picked out a blue frock for you.' Daphne threw her a puzzled look. 'Why are you so upset?'

'Charlie said it wasn't true . . . about me being a

bridesmaid. He said only the aunts were, and that you weren't a bridesmaid either.'

'I'm not, actually, I am the matron-of-honour, you see, because I am a married woman and no longer a maiden.' Daphne shook her head. 'He's a scallywag, that brother of yours, he just loves to tease you.'

Daphne stood up, took Alicia in her arms, held her close. 'You'll be the most beautiful of us all. I know that.'

Alicia, who adored her mother, clung to her for a moment longer, and then stepped away, glanced up at her. 'No, you'll be the most beautiful, Mama. Everyone says you're the great beauty of the Ingham family.'

'Oh, they're just prejudiced, my sweet,' Daphne laughed.

Alicia's troubled expression had dissolved. Eagerly, she asked, 'Shall I tell Nanny she can iron the frock?'

'Why don't you do that, Alicia? I'll see you shortly . . . for the moment I must continue my work.'

With a smile, Alicia skipped across the room, happiness obviously restored. Staring after her, Daphne felt a sudden glow inside. This child had turned out to be perfect. No, almost perfect, she corrected herself. I want her to be human, with a few naughty traits. There weren't many, she had to admit that. She was a good girl, but sensitive at this age, and her brother did enjoy teasing her – too much at times.

Returning to her desk by the window, Daphne picked up the guest list, then put it down again. Almost at once, her mind strayed to her mother. The last time she had spoken to Olive Wilson, her mother's maid had told her that Felicity was unhappy in the marriage.

When Daphne had asked her what had gone awry, Olive had fallen silent, glumly shaking her head, and had changed the subject.

'We're not intruding on your privacy, are we?' Miles asked from the doorway, where he had suddenly appeared with Cecily.

'You are,' Daphne answered. 'But come in anyway.' She smiled at them and went on, 'Cecily, you do look lovely. What a smart dress. But then you know that. You designed it. I'm wearing one of yours this evening, that lovely turquoise and green chiffon you made for me in May.'

'It really suits you, Lady Daphne, and the colours are wonderful for you.'

'Thank you, Cecily, that's what my husband says.'

'Can I look at the guest list?' Miles asked, businesslike as he usually was.

'Of course.' Daphne held it out to him and spoke to Cecily again. 'Tell me, how do you manage to stay cool and calm with so much going on around you? Cavendon has been in an uproar all day.'

Cecily, who had seated herself in a chair, smiled at Daphne. 'I ignore it. Concentrate on whatever project I'm working on. I won't allow anything to distract me.'

'That's probably one of the secrets of your great success in business,' Daphne remarked, meaning this.

'You can be sure of it,' Miles interjected. 'Focus, determination and desire to do it right. That's always been Ceci's rule, even when she was little.'

There was such admiration in his voice, Cecily was taken by surprise at this unexpected praise, and looked across at him. How weary he was, and depleted. Her heart went out to him. She had begun to understand how much he had suffered in the last few years. Harry had told her a lot last night, and she knew her brother spoke the truth.

Miles walked over to Daphne and sat down in a chair next to her, studying the list. 'Who's this Richard Bowers chap? His name rings a bell.'

A wry smile touched Daphne's mouth. 'He's Aunt Vanessa's current boyfriend. It's serious. She told Papa they will be announcing their engagement soon. Apparently she had been intending to tell Papa about him this weekend, and so she asked if she could invite him to the wedding, to meet Papa before he went on his honeymoon. Our father agreed. What else could he do?'

'So there's going to be another wedding?' Miles said.

'Seemingly so, but listen, the two of you, what I've just told you is confidential. Vanessa doesn't want to announce the engagement yet. He's from the Barnard family, or rather his mother is, and Great-Aunt Gwendolyn knows her.'

'I think I know him,' Miles said. 'He's with the Foreign Office, a diplomat.'

'No, that's his brother, Clive. Dulcie told me that Richard is in the arts. I'm not sure what he does.'

Miles nodded, then murmured, 'Ah, I see Mark Stanton is coming, and also Paul Drummond. I'm glad there are a few extra chaps. We can dance.'

'Dance? What do you mean?' Daphne asked, her voice rising in alarm.

'I've booked a quartet to play after dinner.'

'Miles, you didn't! That's so expensive,' Daphne protested.

'It's all right, Daphers, I'm footing the bill. It's . . . well, sort of my wedding present to Papa and Charlotte, and Cecily has offered to pay for the fireworks display.'

Daphne gaped at her brother. 'You can't be serious,' she spluttered. Sudden anxiety echoed in her voice. 'Papa and Charlotte wanted a small, very quiet wedding, no fuss. I'm sure this news will upset them.'

'No, it won't, you'll see,' Miles reassured her, sounding confident. 'I have been inspired by Aunt Lavinia's mean-spirited attitude. Cecily and I decided we needed to give the engagement dinner a little bit of a boost.'

'It will give Aunt Lavinia a bit of a shock,' Daphne exclaimed, and then laughed when she saw the look on her brother's face. 'She will certainly think that a fireworks display is vulgar.'

'But it's nicer than having a cream bun pushed in your mouth, don't you think?' Dulcie said as she walked into the conservatory.

Miles said, 'She will be apoplectic when the fireworks start.' As he looked from his sisters to Cecily, there was a wicked glint in his blue eyes.

Later that afternoon, when Daphne told Hugo about the quartet and the fireworks, he burst out laughing. She was so taken aback by his hilarity, she could only stare at him nonplussed.

Once he had stopped, she asked, 'Why are you laughing? Papa and Charlotte won't like it: dancing and fireworks and all the fuss. They wanted a quiet wedding.'

'Yes, I know. Don't worry, darling, I do believe your father is aware of Miles's plans.'

Daphne frowned. 'You think Miles has told Papa?'

Hugo nodded. 'The other day Charles made an odd remark to me, about being a bit rusty for the dance floor. He then went on to say something about the villagers coming to the park on Saturday night. Before I could question him, we were interrupted by a very important call from New York. And then I forgot all about it. You know how I am when business intrudes.'

Daphne shook her head. 'I wonder why Papa didn't mention it to me? He usually consults with me on everything.'

'He probably thinks you're too busy. You do have a lot to deal with, Daphne.' There was a small pause before Hugo added, 'Miles would never do anything rash. He would always seek advice from your father.' Hugo laughed. 'Hadn't you noticed he always plays by the rules? His disastrous marriage to Clarissa is a good example of that.'

When she was silent, Hugo said, 'Miles looks more cheerful, no doubt because Cecily is with him, and frankly, I think he's enjoying having a bit of fun with the wedding.'

'Yes, you're right,' Daphne agreed, realizing that Hugo was making sense. She knew Miles was a little bit in awe of their father, and of course he wouldn't want to upset him in any way. 'I suppose I worry too much,' Daphne finally murmured, and smiled at her husband. 'And, like Miles, I plan to have a good time tonight.'

'And so do I. Will you promise me the first dance?'

'I will. Every dance for the rest of my life.'

EIGHTEEN

In all the years he had worked at Cavendon Hall, Hanson had never heard such a raucous noise coming from the servants' hall. Much laughter, voices raised. A din to end all dins.

He moved swiftly on silent feet, hurrying down the corridor, and paused just before he reached the door. It was ajar, and he could hear everything clearly.

Never in his life had he actually eavesdropped, but he was doing so at this moment. He needed to know what this was about. The laughter had ceased. A woman's voice echoed.

'And Vanessa was right angry, that she was, and she told Lavinia off, told her to stop talking about class. Lavinia's against this marriage, I can tell you that. As for Lady Gwendolyn, she's all for it. I don't understand why. I mean, Charlotte Swann's a nobody and—'

Outrage bubbled inside Hanson. He moved at speed, threw open the door and strode inside. Those sitting there were rendered speechless by his sudden and unexpected arrival. There was total silence. Everyone gaped at him, taken by surprise. They were also fearful.

His rage was apparent as his eyes swept over the

assembled group. It was composed of Ian Melrose, the second footman, Tim Hartley, the Earl's chauffeur, the head housemaid, Jessie Phelps, and the two other house-maids, Pam Willis and Connie Layton.

They were all seated at the long oak table, having their tea. And, at the far side of the table, sat Adelaide Pine, Lady Gwendolyn's housekeeper, who had been hired by Mrs Thwaites, before she was taken sick, to help out that evening.

'I see you've made yourself at home, Mrs Pine. Holding court here. And speaking out of turn, it seems to me,' Hanson snapped in an icy voice, focusing on her.

She flinched under his dark and angry gaze, but remained silent, knowing it was better to keep quiet.

Hanson's eyes swept around the room again, and he continued, 'Never, in the thirty-eight years I've worked here, have I heard such a hullabaloo coming from the servants' hall.'

He stared at Mrs Pine. 'And your behaviour is outrageous, madam. Nobody, but nobody, gossips about the family I serve. Under their noses, in their own home, no less. In their great house, one of the greatest stately homes in the whole of England. I will not stand for it! Do you hear me, Mrs Pine? And it goes for you lot, too. If any of you ever utters one word of gossip about this family we serve, you will be dismissed instantly, and there will be no refer-ences given. Now, all of you, finish your tea and make haste, prepare for your evening duties. It's going to be a busy night.'

Cowering in their chairs, some of them cursing Mrs Pine under their breath, the staff was silent, did not dare move a muscle. As for Mrs Pine, she was unusually pale.

Hanson gave Mrs Pine a withering look, and said in that same icy voice, 'Come with me, Mrs Pine. I will speak with you in my office.'

Without another word, he swung around and left the room. After a moment's hesitation, Mrs Pine got up and went out, followed Hanson down the corridor, quaking.

When he reached his study, Hanson opened the door wide and said, 'Inside, please.' He stepped aside, so that she could enter first.

Hanson closed the door behind him and leaned against it for a moment, staring at the woman who had so affronted him.

She stared back, a nervous tic making her mouth twitch. She knew she was in serious trouble.

He said, 'I will not tolerate gossip in this house. You overstepped the mark, and you will collect your things and leave immediately. You cannot work here this evening.' He went across to his desk and stood behind it, glowering.

Mrs Pine nodded and began to walk to the door. She said, 'You're not going to say anything to Lady Gwendolyn, are you, Hanson?'

'No, not at the moment. But once the marriage of the Earl has taken place, I shall indeed speak to Her Ladyship. She must know what happened here today, Mrs Pine. It's my duty to inform her. You live and work in her home. What she does is her decision.'

'But I didn't mean any harm—' she began.

Hanson cut her off sharply. 'Gossip can be very harmful. It has been known to destroy people. And those who gossip are extremely dangerous, in my opinion. All they do is cause trouble for others. But not here, they won't – not anywhere here at Cavendon. This place is sacrosanct and under my watchful eye.' He paused. 'If I were you I would resign.'

Without another word, Adelaide Pine shot through the door, and banged it hard behind her.

Staring at the door, Hanson shook his head, and then

moved with speed, returning to the servants' hall to take charge.

It was quiet when he went in. He noticed that the chauffeur had disappeared, and so had the second footman. The three housemaids were clearing the dishes.

Addressing the head housemaid, Hanson said, 'Jessie, come over here, and let us sit down together for a moment. I need to speak to you.'

'Yes, Mr Hanson,' she responded, her voice quiet. She joined the butler at the oak table.

He said, 'How could you let that happen, Jessie?'

'What do you mean?' she asked, frowning, not understanding at first.

'Why didn't you stop that woman spouting off the way she did? Gossiping about the marriage of the Earl and Miss Charlotte. Not a good idea, Jessie. She didn't speak nicely about them, now did she?'

'She'd said much more before you came rushing in. And I did try to stop her, Mr Hanson. She just wouldn't shut up.' Jessie hesitated, and then added softly, 'I thought she was a bit malicious, Mr Hanson, to be honest.'

'Yes, she was, from what I heard. But how could you laugh? I heard the laughter as I came down the corridor.'

'Oh we weren't laughing at anything she said. A few minutes earlier, Tim had been telling us about his brother's wedding a few weeks ago, and how so many things went wrong. He was a real comedian, like in a variety show. He made us laugh, not Mrs Pine, Mr Hanson.'

Hanson simply nodded his understanding.

Jessie said, 'It was after that she started to talk about the wedding again, the Earl's wedding, I mean. She repeated what she'd heard at lunch, and we just listened, we were taken aback.'

Hanson stood up. 'As the head housemaid, Jessie, I expect you to be in charge of the other maids. Speak out

107

if something untoward happens. And put your foot down. We must have decorum at all times.'

'Yes, sir, I will.'

'I'm going upstairs to the South Wing to check on the tables Lane and Peggy are setting.' At the door he turned around. 'Where's Melrose?'

'He went to change his clothes for the evening shift, Mr Hanson.'

'I think you and the other maids must do that as well, Jessie. Time is running out.'

Hanson's anger dissipated the moment he hurried into the pale green sitting room in the South Wing. Lady Daphne was standing there with a huge smile on her face, and Gordon Lane and Peggy were with her, also looking pleased. Thoughts of Mrs Pine no longer existed in his head, that ugliness pushed away at once.

'Hanson, just come and look at the room, now that Gordon and Peggy have brought out the small chairs and several love-seats. Isn't it a perfect place for everyone to gather tonight? Thanks to Harry's garden as well.' As she spoke she gestured to the privet hedges and the banks of flowers that gave the room a sense of summer and the outdoors. 'It's magical, isn't it?'

'You're right, m'lady,' Hanson replied. 'Harry's outdone himself . . . it's just beautiful.'

'Come with me to the pink dining room, Hanson. Lead the way, Gordon and Peggy,' Lady Daphne instructed, hurrying out.

The others trooped through into the pink dining room, where Gordon and Peggy had already set the two circular dining tables. Under the chandelier, crystal and silver glittered in the bright light, and the silver bowls of colourful flowers were the perfect finishing touches on the tables.

After walking around both tables, inspecting them,

Hanson nodded his approval. 'Well done, the two of you,' he said, glancing at Gordon and Peggy, smiling at them. 'Perfection, not a thing out of place.'

At this moment the unexpected arrival of Dulcie made everyone turn around, and Daphne said, 'You look excited. What's happened, darling?'

'Good news! Vanessa asked me to come and tell you that Richard Bowers is definitely coming. He'll be here in time for dinner. He's already on the train from London. And I just ran into Mark Stanton; Hugo was showing him to his room. Apparently he caught an earlier train than planned.'

'I'm glad to hear that. And also that Richard Bowers is confirmed. No need to rearrange the table, Hanson.'

'Yes, m'lady.'

Daphne looked at Hanson and then at the Lanes. She said, 'Thank you. I'm able to relax and leave it all to you.' Taking hold of Dulcie's arm, she went on, 'I need to have a word with you. Let's go to the conservatory.'

'Excuse me, Lady Daphne, but shall I put Mr Bowers in the Chinese bedroom?' Hanson asked.

'What a good idea. I'm sure he'll be comfortable there.'

Daphne and Dulcie left the pink dining room and, as they walked out of the South Wing, Daphne said, 'What's he like? Richard Bowers, I mean? You said you've met him several times. Are they very taken with each other?'

'Yes. He's lovely, and has a lot of quiet charm,' Dulcie answered. 'And he's good looking, but not flashy good looking. More normal – a bit like Papa, in a way.'

Daphne smiled. 'I hope he's as nice as Papa. I think he must be, because Vanessa is a good judge of character. Is it serious between them?'

'I think so.' Dulcie was thoughtful, then added, 'I'm sure it is now . . . bringing him to meet Papa is significant.'

NINETEEN

She had expected it to happen and it did. They closed ranks on her; shut her out of the inner circle.

She wasn't shunned – they didn't exactly send her to Coventry, as it was called. In fact, they were civil, and greeted her when she went into the pale green sitting room on Saturday evening.

But it had vanished, that familial warmth, that sense of inclusion, the shared inner knowledge that they were a clan, special, different, a unique tribe. They were the Inghams, and there was nobody like them in the whole world.

It was the ice in the blue eyes that said it all.

Lavinia was well aware she had blundered badly, had made a grave error speaking to Charles the way she had. Her brother was the 6th Earl of Mowbray, the head of the family, one of the premier earls of England, and she had criticized him, questioned his judgement. Worst of all, she had verbally demeaned the woman he adored and was about to marry. A good woman, one who had devoted her life to this family. Her heart tightened, and there was an ache in the pit of her stomach as she walked across the room; she was fully aware there would be no reversal, no acceptance in the inner circle ever again.

Not for her. She had been stupid, and regretted it, but there was nothing she could do. She was in no man's land. And there she would stay.

Lavinia stood admiring the extraordinary garden which had been created near the windows, calming herself, when she became aware that someone stood immediately behind her. Glancing over her shoulder, she saw that it was Mark Stanton. He was Hugo's cousin, but he looked more like his brother.

'Good evening, Lady Lavinia,' he said, smiling, coming forward, adding, 'What an enormous amount of talent went into the creation of this . . . work of art. Because that's what it is. Somebody with a fantastic eye for colour and flowers certainly had a big hand in the making of it.'

Relieved that it was Mark and not an Ingham, Lavinia smiled at him, her natural charm surfacing. 'It was Harry Swann. He has always had a marvellous flair for gardening, but now he's learning about estate management, you know. He's got good ideas, and I think he can really help to modernize the running of the estate.'

'So Hugo mentioned to me recently . . .' Mark broke off. There was a sudden flurry of excitement near the doorway, and both he and Lavinia looked across the room.

Vanessa stood there, tall, graceful and elegant, holding the arm of a good-looking man. The entire room was smiling at them as Vanessa led Richard Bowers forward, to be introduced to her family.

Miles, Cecily and Dulcie hung back, allowing the others to meet him first. Dulcie said, 'I feel such a fool. I thought Richard was an artist, or owned an art gallery, or something like that, mostly because he knew so much about art. But I got it all wrong. Art is merely his hobby.' Dropping her voice, Dulcie added, 'You'll never guess what he does.'

'So tell us, don't keep us in suspense,' Miles said.

'He's a policeman . . . Just imagine, we've got a posh copper in our midst – and, who knows, maybe it's forever.'

'Who's a posh copper?' Diedre asked, joining them, staring at Dulcie with interest.

'Richard Bowers, Aunt Vanessa's new gentleman friend. Papa told me earlier that he's with Scotland Yard.'

Diedre gaped at her sister and remained silent. Any mention of Scotland Yard brought memories of Maxine's untimely death rushing back. She held herself still, pushing dire thoughts of that tragic event aside. She was trembling inside.

'I wonder why Vanessa never told me when I was staying with her?' Dulcie muttered to herself, baffled yet again, as she had been earlier in the day.

Miles, who missed nothing, noticed Diedre's curious reaction, saw she was upset for some reason, and immediately took charge. 'Let's not stand here gawking at the poor man. Let's go over and welcome him to Cavendon. At the moment we're being frightfully rude, staring at him so blatantly.'

The four of them made their way across the room just at the same moment Vanessa led Richard over to meet Lady Gwendolyn. Undeterred, Miles ushered Cecily, Dulcie and Diedre forward to join the group.

Daphne and Hugo, who had met Richard Bowers with Charles a short while ago, sat down on the sofa. Daphne, her eyes roaming around, said, 'Still a few people missing . . . DeLacy, late as usual, and Paul Drummond hasn't arrived yet, Hugo. Oh, and Papa and Charlotte.'

'Here's Paul now. Your father told me he would wait until everyone else was here before joining us. But I had better introduce Paul to those members of the family he hasn't met before.' Hugo rose, touching Daphne's shoulder lovingly as he went to greet his colleague and friend from New York.

Daphne nodded, leaned back against the sofa cushions, trying to relax. Her eyes sought out Miles. He saw her

112

looking at him, raised a hand in salute, signalling he was there and in charge.

Suddenly, Daphne spotted Mrs Alice, and immediately jumped up, hurrying over to join her. Alice had saved her life, her honour, and had made sure she stayed safe through an extremely harrowing period. For Daphne there was no one quite like Alice Swann; she loved her deeply, was devoted to her.

After greeting Alice warmly, Daphne spoke to Dorothy Swann, who was married to Howard Pinkerton, a detective with Scotland Yard. The two of them had come up to Yorkshire especially for Charlotte's wedding; Charlotte was Dorothy's cousin, and it was Dorothy who managed Cecily's business.

After being introduced to Richard Bowers, Miles took Cecily's elbow and guided her away from the crowd. He stationed them both near the door in the entrance hall of the South Wing. In a low voice he said, 'Diedre was upset to learn Richard Bowers is with Scotland Yard. No doubt because of Maxine's strange death, and the fact that she was interviewed by the Yard. But then all of Maxine's friends were.'

'I saw her stiffen myself. I wonder if he knows Uncle Howard, Dorothy's husband?' Cecily said, a thoughtful look crossing her face.

'Maybe. Bowers looks to me as if he's top brass. In management. Not a copper on the beat walking the streets. He's hardly the local bobby.'

Cecily laughed, her eyes merry.

Suddenly there was DeLacy, hurrying through the entrance hall, a tentative look on her face. She slowed when she saw them and came to a stop, hesitating.

Cecily, fully understanding her sudden wariness, took a step forward, grasping DeLacy's hands in hers. She said, in a warm tone, 'It's lovely to see you, Lacy. Let's be friends again, shall we? I really do want that.'

Tears filled DeLacy's eyes. She moved forward and into Cecily's arms. They held each other close, and DeLacy said, 'I've missed you so much, Ceci. Really missed you, and I've never had another friend like you.'

'Neither have I,' Cecily answered. Stepping away, looking at DeLacy, she smiled lovingly. As her eyes swept over her, she said gently, 'I think you'd better come to the shop next week. That's an old frock I made for Daphne. Two years ago now. You need something new.'

DeLacy began to laugh, and so did Miles, who said to his sister, 'Ceci will get you into the right clothes, old thing.'

'I know she will.' With a small smile, DeLacy said, 'I didn't want to be the only one here tonight not in one of your frocks. So I asked Daphne to lend me something.'

'She picked the right one for you,' Cecily replied and, slipping her arm around DeLacy, she began to walk her to the pale green sitting room. She thought Lacy looked too thin and her eyes were so filled with sadness.

A sense of relief settled in Miles. They were going to be fast friends again, as they had been in childhood. DeLacy needed Cecily's strength, just as he did. DeLacy had not been herself for some time. He thought she was depressed.

The three of them paused at the entrance to the sitting room, and Miles said softly, 'Aunt Lavinia's aware she's no longer in the inner circle, Lacy.'

Cecily nodded, and DeLacy said in a whisper, 'She ought to have known better. She shouldn't have said those things.'

Leaning closer to Cecily, Miles said against her hair, 'I have to talk to you later. Privately.'

'What about? Tell me now,' she insisted.

'I can't. Oh, there's Papa and Charlotte coming down the hall.' As he spoke he drew Cecily and his sister away from the doorway and guided them inside the room.

A moment later the Earl and Charlotte Swann entered

together, smiling and nodding to everyone as they moved forward, walking towards the indoor garden.

There was total silence as the couple moved through the room. Miles thought he had never seen his father looking healthier or happier, and Charlotte was stunningly beautiful.

'She looks gorgeous,' Miles said in a whisper. 'And the gown is sensational.'

Cecily gave him a knowing smile.

The evening gown, made of crepe de Chine, was a soft mauve colour. It was extremely plain, but cut in the flowing Princess line and elegance personified. It had a round neckline, and the narrow sleeves became bell shaped from the elbow down. The dress was just above ankle length, showing elegant satin court shoes dyed mauve to match the gown. As with all of Cecily's clothes, the cut said it all: couture at its best.

Charlotte wore the famous Marmaduke pearls. These were large South Sea pearls of a lustrous white, each one carefully matched. It was a long single strand that sat perfectly on the dress. Her earrings were of pearls and diamonds.

Cecily was filled with pride and satisfaction when she saw how the rest of the guests looked at Charlotte. With awe, she thought; they're all awed by her. It was as if they had never seen her aunt before. And they hadn't, in a way. Certainly not looking like this, with her glossy, luxuriant hair cropped in the latest fashionable style, her perfect complexion glowing in the lamplight. Cecily knew that the mauve colour of the gown brought out the faint hint of lavender in Charlotte's smoky, grey-blue eyes.

She's going to be the next Countess of Mowbray, Cecily reminded herself. And she looks every inch the countess. Elegant, confident and distinguished. Little did Cecily know that everyone else in the room was thinking exactly the same thing.

TWENTY

Daphne was troubled. Even though everything was going well, she felt on edge, a little nervous.

Glancing around the pink dining room in the South Wing, seeing how lovely it looked, she chided herself silently for being silly. Anticipatory despair, she reminded herself: to be avoided at all cost.

In the candlelight the room appeared to glow, and it had a warm and intimate feeling. The two tables were uniquely beautiful, as were the floral centrepieces.

Delicious food and superb wines had been served with precision and elegance by Hanson and his footmen, and she could see how pleased her father looked. As for Charlotte, she was radiant; her face was serene, and there was a calmness about her that reflected her self-assurance and confidence.

Daphne herself had placed the guests, and now she was wondering if she had made a few mistakes. No, she scolded herself, I haven't. It was obvious everyone was enjoying themselves and getting along with their dinner partners.

It struck Daphne then that perhaps this was one of the problems. Two of the men seemed rather friendly with two of the women. Her sister Diedre, seated at her table, was looking relaxed with the handsome blond Paul Drummond at her side.

Her eyes went to the other table. Mark Stanton seemed about to be devoured by her aunt Lavinia; an older woman, a widow losing her blonde good looks. What could Mark possibly see in her, she wondered? As Daphne continued to gaze at them she saw they were oblivious to everyone else, caught up in each other. Well, well, well, she thought, there's no accounting for taste. Who would have thought Lavinia still had it in her to entice a man like Mark?

Now Daphne's attention swung to Lavinia's sister, Aunt Vanessa, her own favourite. Vanessa was truly gorgeous this evening in a pink chiffon dress, obviously designed by Cecily. It was the glow in her blue eyes that said it all. Vanessa was in love. And of course it's serious, Daphne thought – and who wouldn't be serious about Richard Bowers? Good looking, a perfect gentleman, and obviously as liberal-minded as Vanessa. The moment he had spotted Howard Pinkerton in the pale green sitting room, Richard had gone over to speak with him and to shake his hand. The two of them had chatted for a few minutes, and Howard had obviously felt extremely flattered to be sought out in this way.

Her father had told her that Richard Bowers had a top job at Scotland Yard and was Eton and Cambridge educated. Although he had a law degree and could have been a barrister, he wanted to be at Scotland Yard.

But he's not a cop on the beat, she thought, smiling to herself, just as Miles had pointed out earlier. She glanced at her brother, who was sitting between Vanessa and Diedre, and noticed that he only had eyes for Cecily on the other side of the table.

I want Miles to be happy, Daphne suddenly thought. I really do. Those two belong together, and surely Papa will understand that. After all, he's about to marry Charlotte . . . breaking the old rules himself, setting a precedent in a way. And times had changed.

But there was a genuine stumbling block, Daphne was aware of that. Clarissa. Miles had told her he was going to get a divorce, but Hugo and she believed Clarissa was more than likely going to be difficult. And not as easy to handle as Miles thought. There might not be a divorce for years. If ever.

Howard Pinkerton, who was sitting next to Daphne, said, 'I was surprised to see Mr Bowers here, Lady Daphne. I just wanted to say that we all look up to him at the Yard. He's that kind of man, you know, a true leader. He inspires the men, and he's known for his integrity.'

'That's wonderful to know,' Daphne responded, and suddenly looked at Miles, who had just risen. She also noticed Hanson standing in the doorway, flanked by the two footmen.

'I would like everyone to come outside to the terrace,' Miles announced. 'For a little entertainment.'

None of the guests had expected to see a fireworks display, and they were fascinated as the night sky exploded with Catherine wheels and sunbursts and rainbow colours. It was magical. All of the villagers had been invited to come to the park, and they were clapping and cheering along the paths below the terrace as the fanciful patterns erupted above them. It was a show that became more spectacular by the minute.

Only Daphne noticed the two couples who slipped away discreetly. Diedre and Paul Drummond disappeared first, followed a few minutes later by Lavinia and Mark Stanton. Slipping her arm through Hugo's, Daphne led him down the terrace. Once they were alone, she whispered, 'Looks as though there are two romances blossoming here.'

Hugo glanced down at her, frowning, 'What do you mean?'

'Paul seems to have taken quite a liking to Diedre, whilst Aunt Lavinia has gobbled up your cousin Mark.'

Laughter filled the air, and then Hugo spluttered, 'You can't be serious, darling. Now come on, tell me it's a joke.'

'It's true. And, by the way, Howard Pinkerton gave Richard Bowers a great review. He said all the men at the Yard looked up to him.'

Hugo nodded. 'He is that kind of chap, you know. I spotted it right away. He's made of fine stuff, the type you know you can rely on in a crisis or a disaster.'

'So I'm definitely going to London on Tuesday,' Miles said, looking into Cecily's eyes. 'I aim to move quickly. I want to see Clarissa and work out the terms of the divorce.'

'I hope she agrees,' Cecily answered, staring back at him. 'You know she's not in a hurry to give you your freedom.'

'I've got to do it, Ceci. I must. The point is, will you have supper with me in London? I'll be staying in town for several days.'

There was a moment's hesitation and then Cecily said, 'Yes, I will, Miles.'

He was so happy he grabbed hold of her and pulled her to him. Against her cheek, he said, 'It'll be like old times.'

Cecily Swann did not answer. She was rendered speechless at this thought . . . old times indeed. Whatever was she going to do? She had no answer for herself. All she knew was that the barrier went up again. She must protect herself against heartbreak and pain. Miles had no control over Clarissa. Or his father. The status quo was unchanged, she was aware of that. On the other hand, she did have control of her own life, her destiny.

TWENTY-ONE

The matriarch of the Ingham family was the first guest to arrive. Charles had sent the car for her, and when Hartley pulled up outside the small church on the estate, Lady Gwendolyn saw the four ushers standing on the steps, each with a white rosebud in the buttonhole of his lapel and a huge smile on his face.

It was Hugo who stepped forward, opened the car door, and helped her out. After greeting her warmly and kissing her on the cheek, he led his aunt up the few steps.

Harry Swann, Mark Stanton and Paul Drummond were the other ushers; behind them was Miles, who was to be his father's best man. Each of them had a special word of welcome for her, especially Harry.

Oh dear, all this blue, Lady Gwendolyn suddenly thought, when she saw the bridesmaids waiting just inside the church. They were looking truly beautiful, each holding their posies of white and pink roses.

The four Dees, and Daphne's twelve-year-old daughter, Alicia, wore elegant dresses, all different in style, but of the same delphinium blue, an Ingham favourite. Dear oh dear, and then she laughed to herself, thinking: Oh well, who cares? This is such a wondrous day.

Lady Gwendolyn was thrilled that an Ingham was marrying a Swann at long last. This thought lingered as she walked down the aisle, arm-in-arm with Hugo.

Although Lady Gwendolyn had no way of knowing it, Charlotte Swann was thinking exactly the same thing about the Inghams and the Swanns at that very moment.

Charlotte stood in her newly decorated dressing room at Cavendon Hall, which she had not used before, waiting patiently as Cecily fastened the twenty-two buttons running down the back of her wedding gown.

Her mind was centred on her marriage to Charles, due to take place very shortly. After so many years of close ties between them, a Swann was marrying an Ingham for the first time. She knew only too well from the record books that there had been a lot of intermingling between the two families for over a century and a half, but never a wedding.

Charles had been asking her to marry him for the last five years, constantly listing all the reasons why they should take this step. They loved each other; he genuinely wanted her to be his wife; he had a pressing need to know she would be safe and protected in every way if she outlived him.

She had always refused, understanding the ancient rules between the aristocracy and the other classes, and also she was aware of the many pitfalls such a union could create. It was only after his heart attack last year that she had finally succumbed to his endless pleading that they wed.

He had succinctly pointed out, in no uncertain terms, that if he fell ill again, and perhaps became mentally impaired, his children would be in charge of him and his life. He had added that if he could not do his own thinking, he wanted her to be the one to do it. And no one else. He

121

then reminded her that they had grown up together, understood each other completely, and looked at life in the same way. 'You must become my wife, we must make it legal,' he had said in a most determined voice, and she had finally agreed they should get married.

That would happen in about half an hour, and then they would start a new life together. They were both in their fifties, and she did not know how long they would have together. That did not matter. They would live each day to the fullest, and she would look after Charles, and endeavour to protect him as best she could.

His constant anxiety about Cavendon Hall, the running of the estate and the financial burdens of it were ever present and debilitating at times. This was one of the reasons she was glad he had agreed to remain abroad for three months, and not three weeks as everyone thought.

Charlotte believed it would do him the world of good to be away from the pressure of business, the awful worries about DeLacy and Miles and their unhappy lives, and the absence of a grandson who would inherit the title from Miles and ensure the continuation of the Ingham line. And now there was the hideous problem of the missing jewels. When Charles had confided in her on Friday, he had added that Daphne was going to deal with Felicity, and immediately she had been heartened and also relieved.

Despite her great beauty, her appearance of fragility and femininity, Daphne was tough, had a backbone of steel. Charlotte was absolutely certain Daphne would win the battle with her mother. There was no doubt in her mind about that—

'All right! The last button fastened!' Cecily exclaimed, interrupting Charlotte's thoughts. 'And now for the cape.'

'Can I go and look at myself?' Charlotte asked, glancing at her great-niece.

'No, no, not yet,' Cecily answered in a firm voice.

At this moment the door of the dressing room opened; Cecily's mother, Alice, walked in, and stopped. She stood staring at Charlotte, surprise flashing across her face. 'Oh my goodness! Don't you look—'

'Don't say a word, Mam,' Cecily instructed, staring hard at Alice. 'I want Aunt Charlotte to be just as surprised as you are.'

Alice nodded, fully understanding what Cecily meant. Charlotte looked extraordinary, so beautiful in the wedding gown, that Cecily wanted her aunt Charlotte to see the transformation for herself.

The gown was made of the palest of grey-blue silk crepe de Chine, and although it was simple in style it was a marvel. It had no side seams, only one seam down the back, which would be hidden by a cape. Essentially, the gown was a long, rounded tube, with a scooped-out neckline and long, narrow sleeves ending at the wrist.

Alice knew that Cecily, wanting to be sure that the dress hung correctly, had sewn tiny lead pellets in the hem. Now she realized that the small weights worked to perfection. Nor were they visible, because the crepe-de-chine gown was lined with silk. She's clever, Alice thought, as always filled with pride in her daughter, often awed by her talent.

Cecily said, 'Mam, come and help me, will you please?' As she spoke she placed a matching pale blue crepe-de-Chine cape on Charlotte's shoulders.

'Of course,' Alice replied, hurrying across the room.

This was not a typical cape, full and flowing. Instead, it was very narrow; Cecily called it 'skinny'. It sat on the shoulders only; did not even edge out onto the neck bones, and it merely grazed the sleeves. The back of the cape hung straight down, and was extremely narrow.

Looking at her mother, Cecily said, 'I've used hooks

and eyes. Obviously the hooks are on the inside of the cape, the eyes on the shoulders of the gown. Here, take a look before we fasten it in place.'

Within a second the cape was attached, and Cecily announced, 'There you are, Aunt Charlotte! You're ready to walk down the aisle. Now you can come and look at yourself. And, don't forget, you will feel the small weights in both the cape and the dress as you move, but they don't show, I promise you.'

'I trust you implicitly,' Charlotte answered, smiling at Cecily, and then she turned and slowly walked over to the cheval mirror at the other end of the dressing room.

Charlotte was startled when she saw her reflection. She could not believe how she looked in the gown and cape. She had tried on both items of clothing in London, and had had several fittings, but the finished effect was extraordinary. The narrow gown and narrower cape made her look slimmer, taller, and pale grey-blue was a flattering colour for her. The pieces were elegant couture at its best, and they told her why Cecily was a genius.

As she stared at herself, wondering who she had suddenly become, Charlotte realized Cecily had been right to insist she use cosmetics. Her complexion was clear and translucent; she did look younger than she was, and had few wrinkles. But the touch of lip rouge on her mouth and mascara on her eyelashes enhanced her face.

As for her hair, the cropped style suited her; it was sleek and modern. Her only pieces of jewellery were a pair of small diamond studs in her ears, and the sapphire engagement ring that Charles had given her before the dinner last night.

'You're not saying anything,' Alice said at last. 'Don't you like the way you look, Charlotte?'

'I do, I do. I'm just astonished,' Charlotte replied with a small laugh.

Cecily laughed with her. 'You look beautiful, Aunt Charlotte, and now it's time for us to leave for the church.'

Walter Swann had an expression on his face that was a mixture of astonishment and delight. His aunt, looking half her age, was a picture of elegance and grace, and he knew she would make every head turn in the church. As for his daughter Cecily, she had taken her marvellous talent to yet another even higher level. The pale blue gown and cape were incomparable, and his pride in these two Swann women knew no bounds.

Alice understood exactly what her husband was thinking with just one glance at his face. 'They've both rendered you speechless, haven't they, Walter?' She said this with a warm but knowing look. 'I do believe it's a grand day for the Swanns.'

'It is indeed,' he agreed, walking over and kissing Cecily on her cheek. 'Congratulations, you've outdone yourself.'

Turning to Charlotte, he continued. 'And you, Aunt Charlotte, are without a doubt the most beautiful Countess of Mowbray I've ever seen. Congratulations to you, too.'

'I'm not a countess yet.'

'You will be shortly, and you're going to knock their socks off.'

The three women laughed, and Cecily announced, 'We must go.'

Walter offered his arm to the bride. 'I'm thrilled I'm the one to give you away.' Glancing across at Cecily, he added, 'Now I understand why you've had a tarpaulin laid from the end of the stable yard up to the church. To protect the hem of the dress and the pale blue shoes.'

Cecily nodded. 'Correct. But it wasn't my idea, actually, Father. Miles thought of it when I told him Aunt Charlotte must walk to the church because I didn't want her to crease her gown sitting in a car.' Now, hurrying across the

125

grand entrance hall where Walter had been waiting, she added, 'And now it's time to take that walk. Come on, all of you, let's go to the church.'

The small church stood on a rise behind the stable block. It had been built when Cavendon Hall was erected and was made of the same stone.

Charlotte was well aware how meaningful it was to the Inghams and the Swanns, who had worshipped God here, held their christenings, marriages and funerals in this sacred place.

Standing at the top of the nave, clinging to Walter's arm, its ancient history seemed to wrap itself around her, and comfortingly so. The past was the present . . . immutable. Those long gone were part of them, had made them who they were, and there was something reassuring to her about their lineages, the way they were bound together . . .

She glanced up at the high ceiling, crossed with dark beams, and then her eyes lighted on the marvellous stained-glass windows, their brilliant jewel colours glittering in the bright July sunlight filtering through. They depicted long-dead Inghams, resplendent in their armour, bearing their shields. Proud and valiant men.

The church had a timelessness to it. She knew it would stand forever, defying the passage of time, would be a place of sanctity and comfort for those who would worship there in the future long after she was gone.

Suddenly she became aware of the cold, and shivered, as she usually did here. Then she took a deep breath and settled herself. The air smelled of mildew and dust. But today the mustiness was overlaid with the intense scent of flowers – every kind of flower, it seemed to her.

Her eyes roamed swiftly around; she noticed the tall urns of blossoms running along each wall on either side of the nave. The altar was a mass of roses in tall vases, and was breathtaking. She was certain this was Harry's work. Still, there was no doubt in her mind that Miles and Cecily had been behind this profuse floral display. They so wanted to make this day special for her and Charles.

For a few seconds, Charlotte got lost in her thoughts. Earlier she had looked in the cheval mirror and seen another woman. And, in fact, she was exactly that. In a few minutes her life would change. She would become a woman who had just taken on enormous responsibilities as the wife of the 6th Earl.

She knew it was her duty to help Charles uphold the honour of the Ingham name, support the entire family, protect this great stately home, its three villages and the villagers who lived there, and to do everything in her power to ensure the Ingham bloodline. She did not shirk these duties, she welcomed them.

The pressure of Walter's hand on hers increased, and she glanced at him. At the same moment she became aware of low-level noises . . . the rustling of clothes, whispers, hurried voices, a few coughs and clearing of throats, the murmur of the bridesmaids behind her. Suddenly, Mrs Parkington began to play the first strains of the wedding march on the organ.

'It's time,' Walter whispered, and began to slowly lead her down the middle aisle.

Charlotte fell into step with him.

She carefully avoided looking from side to side and smiling at those seated in the pews. Instead she stared straight ahead, her eyes focused intently on Charles Ingham.

He was standing at the altar with Miles, waiting for her, a look of anticipation on his face . . . that face she had known and loved all of her life. As familiar to her as her own. As she drew closer, he began to smile, and he was still smiling when Walter put her hand in his, then stepped back and away from the altar.

They stood together in front of the vicar, who began the marriage ceremony. It seemed to Charlotte that the words rushed by, and that she answered by rote, as did Charles. And then, quite unexpectedly, there were gold wedding rings on their fingers and they were pronounced man and wife. And Charles was holding her in his arms and telling her how much he loved her.

Charlotte felt slightly dazed when, a few seconds later, they were walking down the aisle together, arm in arm and clinging to each other.

When they stepped out of the church and into the sunlight, they saw a sea of smiling faces. The grass lawns on each side of the stone path were filled with villagers, who had come to wish them well.

They threw confetti and rose petals and cheered Charles and Charlotte. Someone began to sing, 'Here Comes the Bride'. And there was a lot of clapping and cheering once again. No one doubted how much the villagers cared for the couple who had just been married. The 6th Earl could do no wrong in their eyes; he deserved his new Countess.

Laughing in the rain of rose petals, Charles and Charlotte walked down the path, across the tarpaulin, and onto the terrace. All of a sudden they found themselves entirely alone, standing in the pale green sitting room of the South Wing.

Charles took her in his arms and kissed her, and she kissed him in return, and then they stood apart and simply stared at each other. Both looked slightly stunned.

'The deed is done,' Charles finally said. 'No going back now. You're finally actually mine.' Then he added, the sound of wonder in his voice, 'Thank you for making all my dreams come true, my darling.'

'And thank you, Charles, for doing the same for me. I . . .' She broke off as Miles and Cecily came rushing into the room, smiling but also looking very purposeful.

128

After they congratulated them, Miles announced briskly, 'I'm afraid we must now go to the yellow drawing room, Papa, the photographer is waiting for us there. The wedding pictures have to be taken before lunch. Right now, in fact.'

'Of course,' Charles said, taking hold of Charlotte's hand.

Charlotte was delighted that Cecily appeared to be more relaxed when she was with Miles, and he had grown more cheerful, less tense and anxiety-ridden. And she now believed everything would be fine, would work out the way she had hoped. All would be well with the Inghams.

She was wrong. Things were not going to be fine. Storm clouds were gathering over Cavendon and trouble was brewing.

PART TWO

Deceptions Revealed
September 1926

I expect to pass through this world but once; any good thing, therefore, that I can do, or any kindness that I can show to my fellow creature, let me do it now; let me not defer or neglect it, for I shall not pass this way again.

Proverbial saying

Love comforteth like sunshine after rain.

William Shakespeare

TWENTY-TWO

James Brentwood jumped out of the cab when it came to a halt, slammed the door shut, pressed far too much money into the cabbie's hand, and rushed into Brown's Hotel.

He was late for an appointment, which irked him. He enjoyed his reputation for never being late; nor did he wish to be stopped by passers-by eager to congratulate him. Many had already done so in the last week. He wasn't displeased by shows of affection from the public – in fact, he rather enjoyed hearing their praise; but, very simply, he was in a hurry this afternoon.

James slowed his pace as he strode across the hotel's front lobby, began to walk in a more sedate manner. Smiles and whispers of congratulation from the various staff members floated around him. He nodded and smiled and murmured his thanks, as always gracious, his charm surfacing naturally, as it usually did. He was a man blessed with enormous charisma and good looks.

James Brentwood, called Jamie by his family and close friends, was one of England's most renowned actors, a living legend at the age of thirty-three, acclaimed by critics and the public alike. A week ago it had been announced that he was to receive the most prestigious award from the Critics Circle, an important group in the world of classical theatre. Ever since then, congratulations had been flowing in, and the press coverage was endless.

When he reached the lovely formal drawing room where afternoon tea was being served, James saw that it wasn't too full, and this pleased him. He paused in the entrance for a few seconds, his dark brown eyes glancing around, seeking his agent and manager.

Felix Lambert, seated in a discreet corner reading a piece of paper, knew at once that James had arrived. The room had gone suddenly quiet. Silence reigned. And there was a sense of excitement in the air.

Looking up, Felix watched the actor walking across to him, noticed how men threw curious glances at him, the women more adoring looks. He smiled inwardly. Not bad for the docker's lad from the East End, Felix thought, and instantly had a picture in his mind's eye of meeting the young Jimmy Wood. Jimmy had been fifteen at the time, bursting with tremendous talent and charisma, even at that tender age.

Felix and his wife, Constance, had discovered Jimmy at Madame Adelia Foster's Drama School for Children. Constantly on the lookout for new young talent, they always went to Adelia's annual summer concert.

What guts, nerve and confidence the boy had shown, Felix thought now. Jimmy had walked out onto the empty stage, dressed only in tights, a jerkin, and a single piece of armour – a metal breastplate. He had stood and recited one of the great Shakespearean speeches from *Henry IV*, quite an undertaking for any actor. Jimmy had mesmerized and intoxicated the entire audience, who couldn't stop clapping at the end.

That evening Felix and Constance had told Jimmy they thought he should attend the Royal Academy of Dramatic Art, and explained that they were certain they could get him accepted. Jimmy had obviously liked the idea, but had swiftly pointed out that they had to speak to his three sisters, Ruby, Dolores and Faye, who were in control of his career – and of his life, actually.

A few days later they all met. The three sisters had not needed any persuasion, because they understood that RADA was a big step up the ladder to stardom for their beloved Jimmy, the apple of their eyes. That he would be a star was a foregone conclusion in the Wood family. Felix had come to realize this at once. Jimmy was their hero, their rescuer, the bringer of good fortune to their little clan.

'You have a weird look on your face,' James said when he arrived at the table.

Felix jumped up, laughing as they embraced each other. He said, 'I was watching you navigate the room, looking for all the world like the great star you are, and remembering little Jimmy Wood from the docks that first night I met him all those years ago.'

'I often think of that night, and how lucky I was that you and Constance were there. You changed my life, you know.'

'It would have happened anyway. You were loaded with talent, had everything you needed to walk onto a stage and take total command of it. By the way, I've ordered the full tea for both of us. I missed lunch, and you always eat at this time before going to work.'

'Thanks; I am rather hungry myself.' Settling back in the chair, James said, 'What's all this about a musical, of all things? I couldn't believe my ears when you phoned me this morning.'

'It's a thought I had the other day, when I had lunch with Mortimer Jackson. He's just come back from New York, and he'd been spending time with Jerome Kern. Kern told him he was trying to buy a new novel by the writer Edna Ferber. It's called *Show Boat*, and Kern thinks it would make a sensational musical. He would write the music, and he's managed to get Oscar Hammerstein II to agree to write the book and lyrics. They want to produce it on Broadway some time in 1927, about a year from now. Then they would bring it to the West End. That's when I jumped in, and suggested you for the lead when that happened.'

'Good God, Felix, that's a long way off! What am I going to do in between? You know I soon get itchy feet.'

'I know, and you do only have a few months left in *Hamlet* at the Old Vic. This last year has been wonderful for you, Jamie, but frankly I'm surprised you're not bored with *Hamlet* by now.'

'Some days I am; then when I walk the boards something extraordinary happens . . . I can't help myself. I just become Hamlet again, throw myself into the part.' He grinned at Felix. 'Funny, mate, innit, but I ain't got no choice,' he added, reverting to Cockney.

A waiter arrived with teapots, plates of small finger sandwiches, scones, strawberry jam and clotted cream, and all the paraphernalia of afternoon tea. They fell into silence until the waiter poured the tea and left.

James said, 'You can tell Mortimer Jackson I might well be interested when he has the show up and running on Broadway. Then I'll go over to New York to see it, and give him my answer.'

Felix chortled. 'Very clever, me lad, very clever.'

James merely smiled, and glanced around the room again, as several people came in. It was then that he saw the two women seated in the other corner. At once he recognized Olive Wilson, lady's maid to Felicity Pierce. He had no idea who the other woman was, but she looked familiar. He was frowning when he turned back to Felix and reached for another cucumber sandwich.

Felix said, 'The beautiful blonde caught your eye, did she?'

136

'Not really, although she is very beautiful. I know the other woman. Well, I don't actually know her, but she works for Felicity Pierce. I've bumped into her when I've been at Felicity's house at dinner parties. Her name is Wilson, and she's Felicity's lady's maid.'

Felix, glancing across at Olive Wilson, nodded. He studied James for a moment before saying, 'I hope you don't see much of Lawrence Pierce. He's got the most unsavoury reputation, Jamie. He even offers his friends his widow's gym for an illicit rendezvous, and then asks if he can come and join in. Or at least watch them having a go.'

James was gaping at Felix. 'What's a widow's gym, for heaven's sake?'

'Never heard the expression before?'

'No, I haven't, I'm afraid.'

'A widow's gym is a man's secret flat or set of rooms, where he takes his women. Widows, spinsters, married women, very young women, sometimes very young girls. He takes them through his form of gymnastics, they say. He's known for throwing orgies as well. It might be better not to be seen in his company too often, Jimmy lad.'

'I agree. In fact, I'd heard quite a few strange things about him, and I've steered clear. He's never been my cup of tea. I've never liked him, actually.'

'I can't imagine why Felicity stays with him. She's a wealthy woman in her own right, so I'm told. She's in control.'

'I think she is wealthy, through her late father. He left her a fortune, according to Pierce. I've also been led to believe that once he's bedded a woman she's his for life. Something about his technique between the sheets and ecstasy.'

Felix shook his head. 'Remind me, if ever I need special surgery, to avoid Mr Lawrence Pierce. It seems to me he might be burning the candles at both ends, and that he might have shaking hands in the morning . . . hands not quite perfect for surgery.'

'I'm so glad you telephoned me on Wednesday, Lady Daphne, and thank you for inviting me to tea. I was hoping to hear from you, even thinking of getting in touch with you myself,' Olive Wilson said.

'It must have been telepathy,' Daphne answered warmly, smiling at her. 'Certainly you've been on my mind a lot.'

A worried frown knotted Olive's brows, and she said quickly, 'I know I promised to come to Cavendon by the end of September, but I don't think I can, m'lady.'

'My mother won't accept your resignation now, is that it?'

Olive shook her head. 'Oh no, she did accept it, months ago. But as I told you on the phone, she's not well, Lady Daphne, and I'd like to see her back on her feet before I leave Charles Street.'

'I didn't realize she was that ill. What's wrong?' Daphne was suddenly worried, thinking of the rumours about Lawrence Pierce.

'She caught a bad cold in Monte Carlo and it's turned into bronchitis,' Olive explained. 'But her doctor says she's making good progress after a few days spent in bed here. I'm sorry I can't come just yet, m'lady.' Olive Wilson hesitated, and then asked, 'That is why you phoned me, isn't it?'

'Actually, it's not. I wanted to ask you something rather important, Wilson, and confide in you about a problem.' Leaning forward, Daphne murmured in a low tone, 'I know you must handle my mother's jewellery, and I was wondering if you had come across a ruby and diamond tiara and a ruby and diamond bracelet, as well as Cartier diamond earrings and a diamond bow brooch?'

'Yes, of course, I have, Lady Daphne. Not that she's

been wearing the tiara lately, only the bow brooch and diamond earrings.' Olive stared at her, saw the concern in her blue eyes. 'What's the matter, m'lady? I know there's something wrong . . . terribly wrong.'

'There is indeed. Those pieces of jewellery do not belong to my mother. They are the property of the Ingham Estate, and are only on loan to whomever is the current countess.' Daphne shook her head, and grimaced. 'My mother had no right to take those pieces with her when she left Cavendon.'

'Did she know that?' Olive asked, and then exclaimed, 'How stupid I am, of course, she would know. Every titled woman has knowledge of the family's rules.'

'Quite so, and I have to get them back, and as soon as possible. My mother won't want to let go of them, or any of the other pieces she has. But there is no alternative.'

'Perhaps not, although Lady Felicity has always been a reasonable person. It's only lately she's been difficult, and that's because she's never really well—'

'Does he hurt her?' Daphne interrupted, giving Wilson a pointed look. 'Mr Pierce, I'm talking about.'

'Not physically, if that's what you're getting at, Lady Daphne. But he can be mean, plays games with her, hints that there are other women . . .' Olive broke off, and whispered, 'It's a kind of mental torture, that's what I think.'

'That's horrible. I can't imagine why she doesn't kick him out!' Daphne exclaimed, sudden anger surfacing.

'Oh, he's got a hold over her all right, that I'm sure of. Also, she loves him to death.'

Daphne was silent, looked thoughtful, then she said, 'When she's better, I will come to tea, and I will ask her nicely for the jewellery, point out that she must give it back to the estate as an honourable woman.'

'What if she won't? If she refuses?' Olive wondered out loud.

'I have two alternatives. I can take the matter to my father's solicitor, and have him start legal proceedings—'

'She won't like that!' Olive cut in. 'And she'll deny she has the jewels.'

'Or I can steal them.'

'Lady Daphne! You wouldn't dare!' Olive sounded horrified.

'Yes, I would. And you can help me.'

Olive Wilson turned pale. 'I couldn't do that!' she cried.

'I realize you're reluctant. But you could show me the cupboard, or wherever it is all kept. And possibly get me the key?' Daphne raised a brow.

'She would never give it to me, m'lady, and I don't know where she keeps that key, honestly I don't.' Olive now sounded calmer but she was still pale.

Daphne nodded, and after a moment a little ripple of laughter crossed her mouth. Leaning towards Wilson again, she said, sotto voce, 'Eric Swann knows all sorts of people. Some nice, some not so nice. I shall ask him to find me a thief, and I'll take the fellow over to Charles Street and he can pick the lock of the cupboard. I aim to get our property back.'

Olive had no words. She sat staring at Daphne, looking totally flabbergasted.

Daphne had the good grace to laugh, and exclaimed, 'But I don't think it will come to that, Wilson, so don't look so shocked. Oh my goodness, James Brentwood the actor is sitting over there, and he's staring at you. Why, he's smiling at you. Do you know him?'

'Not exactly, my lady. He's a friend of your mother and Mr Pierce. He's seen me at the house. Oh heavens, I hope he doesn't tell them he's seen us together . . . that would seem very strange to Lady Felicity.'

'You can't use her title any more, Wilson. She's Mrs Pierce now. I keep on telling you that.'

140

'I know, m'lady. But old habits die hard.'

'I think I had better go over and speak to Mr Brentwood. I shall ask him to keep our secret,' Daphne announced, and immediately stood up.

'No, no, my lady, you can't go over and speak to him just like that. It's not proper for a lady like you,' Wilson exclaimed, sounding nervous.

Daphne gave her a wide smile. 'Of course, I can, Wilson. I can do anything I want. After all, I'm a married woman, and that gives me quite a lot of leeway.'

Felix Lambert had just spread clotted cream on his scone when out of the corner of his eye he saw a flash of apricot fabric, and the lovely blonde woman from across the room walking directly towards them.

He exclaimed in a low voice, 'There's the most gorgeous female heading right for you, James, my lad. You'd better stand up, and so should I.'

Taken aback for a moment, James stared at Felix and saw him rising, and knew he was not joking. As he pushed himself to his feet, the beautiful blonde came to a halt in front of them.

'I'm so sorry to intrude,' Daphne said. 'But I do need to have a word with you, Mr Brentwood.' She thrust her hand out. 'I'm Daphne Ingham Stanton, and I believe you know my mother, Mrs Pierce.'

James took hold of her hand and shook it. 'I'm pleased to meet you, Lady Daphne, and I do know your mother. May I introduce Felix Lambert?'

'How do you do?' Daphne said, taking Felix's outstretched hand.

Felix smiled at her, appreciating her beauty. 'I am honoured, Lady Daphne.'

'Please, do join us,' James said, and guided her to a chair. Once they were all seated, he said, 'How can I be of help?'

'Olive Wilson, my mother's lady's maid, realized you had recognized her. She is nervous about being seen with me because my mother and I are estranged. Wilson thinks my mother will be angry with her if she discovers we meet from time to time. You see, Wilson keeps me informed about my mother's wellbeing. So, may I ask for your discretion, Mr Brentwood?'

'Of course, Lady Daphne,' James answered. 'I'm not likely to be seeing Mr and Mrs Pierce. I'm working most of the time. However, I would never mention seeing Miss Wilson with you.'

'I know that, actually,' Daphne said, smiling at him. 'But I did want to reassure Wilson, and approaching you was the only way to convince her.'

James thought she was the loveliest woman he had seen in a very long time. The bloom is on the rose, he thought: a happy woman in her prime.

Lady Daphne now said, 'Congratulations on your Critics Circle award, Mr Brentwood. As it happens, my husband and I are coming to see you in *Hamlet* next week. We are really looking forward to it.'

'Please do come backstage after the play,' James said warmly, then asked, 'What night are you coming next week?'

'On Tuesday, and thank you so much for the invitation.' Daphne stood up, and so did the two men. She shook hands with them again, and returned to her table at the other side of the room.

Both men watched her glide across the floor, and then sat down and stared at each other. James said, 'What a beauty, and a charming woman.'

'And married,' Felix thought to point out.

'All the good ones are,' James said, shaking his head. 'That's the problem.'

*   *   *

'He won't say a word,' Daphne told Olive Wilson when she returned to the table. 'I didn't think he would, but I do believe I was right to ask for his discretion.'

'Thank you, Lady Daphne,' Wilson said. 'And I apologize for putting you to all this trouble . . . going over to speak to Mr Brentwood, I mean.'

'Please do be at ease, Wilson.' Daphne then went on, 'Please explain to me where the cupboard is actually located in Charles Street.'

Olive did so and, after she had finished, she looked at Daphne, to whom she was devoted, and said, 'My lady, I do hope you didn't mean it when you said you might employ a burglar to help you.'

Daphne smiled at her reassuringly. 'Of course not, Wilson! I was just teasing you, the way I did when I was a little girl.'

Olive sat back, filled with relief.

Daphne thought: I must speak to Eric Swann the moment I get home. I feel sure he knows someone who can pick a lock.

TWENTY-THREE

Unexpectedly, Miles experienced a sense of unease as he approached the house. The time he had spent there with Clarissa had not been happy, and he had never really liked the architecture and interiors of the place. It was not his style. But she had hankered after it, and so his father had finally bought it for them as a wedding present, but had always held the deeds himself.

The door was opened by Mrs Kennet, the gloomy-faced housekeeper – Clarissa's other choice, but a woman he had disliked on sight. And still did.

As he stepped into the front hall, he said, 'Good afternoon, Mrs Kennet.'

'Afternoon, sir,' she said in a curt voice, and tried to usher him towards the drawing room. Walking around her swiftly, he said, 'I'm going to the library, and don't bother to accompany me, Mrs Kennet. I know the way. In case you've forgotten, this is my house.'

The woman glared at him before turning on her heels, heading towards the kitchen without uttering a word.

So much for the warm welcome, he thought, striding into the pine-panelled library, a room his sister Daphne had helped him decorate.

It was the one room in the house he had enjoyed, his own small private haven, with its fir-green leather Chesterfield sofa, matching green velvet armchairs and draperies, and the colourful red and gold Oriental rug underfoot.

As was his habit, Miles strolled over to the bookshelves surrounding the bay window, and stood looking at his collection of history books. He had loved history since his schooldays and was well versed in this subject. His eyes caught his favourite leather-bound books on the life of Julius Caesar, and he took one off the shelf. It was a much-loved book, familiar, and he held it for a moment before putting it back.

One thing he was certain of was the decision he had come to last week. He had finally made up his mind to have his books and every personal possession packed by their London butler, Eric Swann, who would take them to his father's house in Grosvenor Square, which Eric ran.

It was a relief to know that Eric would take care of everything. He had worked for the family for thirty years, since he was sixteen, and he was the most dependable man. He had been trained by Hanson at Cavendon, and was, in fact, Hanson's younger version.

Hearing footsteps, Miles walked out into the corridor, and recoiled in shock when he saw Clarissa coming towards him. She looked unkempt, and she had put on weight.

Dismay lodged in his stomach. What man would even look at this blowsy, bedraggled young woman, never mind marry her? Instantly he reminded himself that she had a wealthy father; no doubt quite an inducement for some fellow to turn a blind eye to the way she looked.

Without greeting him by name, Clarissa said, 'I have arranged for Mrs Kennet to serve afternoon tea in the drawing room, so let us proceed there, shall we?'

145

'That's fine, and hello, Clarissa. How are you?' he asked, as always a gentleman.

'Perfectly well, thank you,' she answered, and went on ahead of him.

Walking behind her, Miles couldn't help thinking she had become the size of a London bus, at least the back of it. Sadly, his hope that his estranged wife would have a romantic encounter with an eligible man and want to remarry instantly fled. He also felt sorry for her, because at heart he was a kind man, and once she had been quite pretty.

Seating herself on the chintz-covered sofa, Clarissa arranged her floral silk afternoon dress, and sat back, regarding Miles intently.

Absently, Miles wondered why she had chosen that particular dress. It matched the sofa. He stifled the sudden urge to talk to her about her weight; that was not the reason he was here, so he refrained. He also reminded himself that although she was stupid in so many ways, she had a certain shrewdness. He cautioned himself to be wary of her, on the alert at all times.

'I was surprised you were in London,' Clarissa said, speaking at last. 'I know how devoted you are to Cavendon. Your trip to town must be something of a novelty.'

'I wouldn't say that. And yes, I am caught up in the running of the estate in Yorkshire. Especially at the moment, since Papa is abroad.'

'Oh, yes. Indeed. He got married. I don't suppose it was a very fancy affair, under the circumstances. I mean the circumstances of his new wife, and her background.'

'You don't have to qualify that rather rude remark, Clarissa,' Miles shot back swiftly. 'I know exactly what you mean, and you will not speak ill of my stepmother, who is now the Countess of Mowbray. And, by the way, Papa is in marvellous health. So I won't be inheriting his title for a very long time, I can assure you of that.'

'And I won't agree to a divorce, I can assure you of that!' she exclaimed.

Ever since he had arrived, Miles had been expecting this announcement. He said quietly, 'I don't understand why not. We are living apart. There is no possible chance of a reconciliation, and you don't want that either. Be honest, Clarissa.'

Leaning forward slightly, he added, 'I have spoken to our solicitor and he will work out a very favourable settlement with you, and your solicitor.'

'I don't want a divorce, so don't bother telling me about the settlement,' she responded coldly.

'I can't fathom you out. What have you to gain by being so obdurate? Living in this big house alone, leading a somewhat circumscribed social life, passing the time with your women friends, going to lunches, going shopping. It seems like a pointless existence to me.' Miles stared at her. He looked puzzled.

'I'm happy. So you don't have to concern yourself with me, or try to fathom me out, as you call it,' she snapped.

'I know my father will give you the deeds to this house, Clarissa, and I will pay you suitable alimony until you remarry, which I'm sure you will.'

She gaped at him, then laughed hysterically, exclaiming in somewhat shrill tones, 'What man will even look at me? Haven't you noticed I've put on weight, Miles? Surely you're not blind.'

'I had noticed, but you're a young woman. You can take off the weight, if you commit yourself to a regime.'

She opened her mouth, a sharp retort on the tip of her tongue, then stopped. At that moment Mrs Kennet came in with the parlour maid, who was pushing the tea trolley.

Wisely, Clarissa remained silent until they had poured the tea and passed around plates of sandwiches.

Once they were alone, she said in an icy voice, 'There's

not much more to discuss about the divorce, Miles. I won't agree to one. I don't care about this house, or alimony, since my father is a very, very rich man. He will always take care of me. As he did before I was married to you.'

'I'm aware there aren't many financial inducements to make you change your mind,' he remarked. Miles sat back, lifted his cup, took several swallows of his tea, and put the cup back in the saucer with a clatter. He said, 'I'm not your enemy, and I presume you're not mine. It seems to me that we can have an amicable divorce and then get on with our own lives as single individuals. We're both young enough to start anew.'

She remained silent, staring at the sponge cake oozing thick cream, salivating, clearly longing to devour it. That must be her main occupation these days. Eating. And eating more. And wallowing orgiastically in the rich food Mrs Kennet made. Delicious, comforting food.

Miles cleared his throat several times.

Clarissa finally looked across at him. 'Would you like a piece of the cream cake? Or would you prefer a tart? A cherry tart, actually.'

He shook his head, frowning slightly, noting something odd in her tone of voice.

'Of course you don't want this tart. You've already got your own, and you gobbled her cherry years ago,' she announced. 'In fact, you've never stopped gobbling her cherry. You were doing it before we were married, and continued after. You're still doing it now.'

Astonishment crossed his face. He glared at her, immediately understanding the innuendo.

Before he could answer her, Clarissa rushed on, 'Long before you began to court me, when I was being eyed by a variety of eligible young men, my father warned me about the likes of your lot. He said I must never forget that aristocratic men prefer working-class girls because they are juicy tarts.' Sitting up straighter on the sofa, she gasped, 'And it was always your tart you loved. Not me!'

Miles was on his feet and leaving the drawing room before she could catch her breath and utter another ugly word.

Once he was outside, he rushed down the street, wanting to put distance between himself, that house – and particularly its disturbed occupant. Because there was no doubt in his mind that she was disturbed. He was filled with anger and disgust, and he never wanted to set eyes on Clarissa again.

Eventually, he slowed down, leaned against a brick wall, and managed to calm himself. He had been accused of something that was untrue. This had infuriated him, especially when he thought of the last six years: his lack of contact with Cecily; his loneliness and pain. And he understood what everything was about now. It was called Clarissa's Revenge. How she had changed, and in several ways. She had been rather lovely six years ago: fine features, large luminous eyes and soft brown hair framing a pretty face. She had not been mean. In fact she had been humorous.

As Miles Ingham made his way back to his father's house, Detective Inspector Howard Pinkerton, Dorothy Swann's husband, was crossing Piccadilly, heading in the direction of Berkeley Square. The lovely, leafy park in the centre of the square was a favourite spot of his, an oasis of calm in the middle of Mayfair.

The park was empty except for a courting couple wrapped in each other's arms, sitting on the other side, and he smiled as he lowered himself onto a bench. He hoped they would be as lucky in love as he had been. He had found the love of his life when he met Dorothy. They had both been twenty and had married within three months.

Not long ago they had celebrated their thirtieth wedding anniversary, and were still in love.

A little rush of warmth enveloped him when he thought of his wife. On Sunday they were going out in their brand-new motorcar, making a long overdue trip to Bath to visit his cousin, Patsy. It was a huge improvement on their first motorcar, and they were excited about this particular purchase.

Howard was a big fan of Henry Ford. Although recently he had come to realize that Mr Ford's invention had created the heavy traffic he sometimes had to confront on the roads these days. And no doubt the skies would soon be full of aeroplanes, he decided, thinking about those adventurous young men attempting to fly the Atlantic.

It seemed to Howard that 1926 was a spectacular year, with so many new and diverse things to experience and enjoy, alongside the many changes in society. The Roaring Twenties, they were now calling this era. And so it was – or the Jazz Age, another name that people used. Nightclubs, cafés, and parties. Young women in shorter and shorter skirts, who had become independent and sexually liberated. They smoked, drank, and drove motorcars, and even had careers. He liked the changes and the new names for this era. They were apt, and he considered progress important and to be welcomed. He thought of himself as a modern man.

Taking out his pocket diary, Howard turned the pages until he came to today's date, Friday 3 September. There was only one notation on the page.

At six o'clock he was to meet with Lady Gwendolyn to discuss her great-niece, Lady Diedre. After once again checking the exact number of the flat in Mount Street, Howard put the diary back in his pocket. He could walk there in three minutes.

Howard had set out early from Scotland Yard, in order

to have this half-hour alone in the park. It gave him that bit of quiet time he needed to consider the upcoming meeting with the matriarch of the Ingham family.

He liked Lady Gwendolyn, found her open and outgoing, a most approachable woman who was highly intelligent. It was these reasons which had led him to agree to help her sort out Lady Diedre's problems; he would do a bit of investigating in his own time, he had told her.

He had found out a great deal; some of the things he learned had genuinely surprised him. He was positive they would surprise Lady Gwendolyn as well.

Suddenly, he wondered how much he ought to tell Lady Gwendolyn at this moment in time. He still had several people to speak to, and he also wanted to assess a number of files he had read at the Yard.

These had to do with the death of Lady Diedre's friend, Maxine Lowe. He had been taken aback to discover that those files were inadequate and lacking information. It was a dead-end case, with no leads. Yet the case had never been closed; he had found this odd the other day, and he still thought it so.

Settling himself comfortably on the iron garden seat, Howard closed his eyes, mentally focusing on the Lowe case, puzzled by several aspects of it.

In doing this Howard Pinkerton was in his element . . . analysing. He was considered to be the most brilliant detective at Scotland Yard, and over the years had moved up through the ranks very rapidly.

To work at Scotland Yard had always been his childhood dream. He had made sure he knew its entire history, and had committed everything to memory by the time he was ten years old. He was much encouraged by his clever father, who was proud of his talented child.

If anyone asked Howard a question about Scotland Yard when he was growing up, he would immediately explain that it was the headquarters of the Criminal Investigation Department of London's Metropolitan Police Force. The CID. He would even reveal that it was named after the short street where the building stood, on the site of a twelfth-century palace, of all things. He would tell anyone who would listen that the palace had been the residence of the Scottish kings when they visited London centuries before; that it had become the centre for the police force in 1829, but sixty-one years later, in 1890, new quarters had been built for the CID on the Thames Embankment. New Scotland Yard it was called, but few people ever used that name, Howard would tell them.

Howard's father, Lionel Pinkerton, was clerk to a famous barrister with chambers in Gray's Inn at the Inns of Court. Lionel was a man who made it his business to be on good terms with everybody. He believed that courtesy, charm and general helpfulness were vital, and that being accommodating, whilst offering a wealth of knowledge, paved the way to success. And he was right. When it came time to get his beloved son into Scotland Yard, he did so with ease.

Opening his eyes, Howard sat up on the bench. Something about Maxine's death, which had troubled him, was unexpectedly very plain to see. Leaving the park, he made his way to Mount Street. He glanced at his watch. It was just six o'clock. Straightening his back, striding out, he braced himself to meet Lady Gwendolyn, wondering how she would react to some of the strange information he was about to impart.

TWENTY-FOUR

'I don't understand you, Inspector Pinkerton,' Lady Gwendolyn said, peering at Howard. He was seated opposite her in front of the fire in the drawing room of her Mount Street flat. 'Are you saying there is no rumour?'

'No, I'm not, Lady Gwendolyn,' Howard answered swiftly. 'There is a rumour . . . that Lady Diedre might have problems at the War Office regarding her job. However, it's what I would call more of a whisper.' Clearing his throat, he added, 'I think her friend Mr Fennell might have exaggerated a bit.'

'Why on earth would he do that? It sounds rather strange.'

'Not really, m'lady. I think a whisper about someone can become more, just through repetition. Things get left out, other things are added. I've only enquired at a lower level in the hierarchy. Quite frankly, I prefer not to draw attention to Lady Diedre unnecessarily.'

'I like your way of thinking, Inspector, and your discretion,' Lady Gwendolyn answered, and sat back in her chair. 'Have you any thoughts about who could have started this . . . whisper, shall we call it?'

'No, I don't. I do have an opinion, though. I'm not so sure the rumour is emanating from someone who works with Lady Diedre.'

'Are you suggesting that the rumour was started by a person in her private life?' Lady Gwendolyn raised an eyebrow questioningly, sounding surprised.

'I am, yes. The colleague of Lady Diedre I talked to was dismissive about the little rumour, as he called it. He spoke in glowing terms about your great-niece, confided that the top brass at the War Office think her work is exemplary. I doubt she has any enemies there, Your Ladyship.'

'That's lovely to know,' Lady Gwendolyn replied, and then frowned. 'However, it is rather ghastly to think that a friend of Diedre's may be trying to hurt her.'

Howard said, 'I agree. However, I do think we must consider that possibility. Do you know many of her friends, Lady Gwendolyn?'

'I don't. I only ever met Maxine Lowe, who died in rather strange circumstances. I'm sure you know all about that, Inspector Pinkerton.'

'I do,' he replied. 'Although it wasn't my case.'

After a moment's thought, Lady Gwendolyn said, 'Are we perhaps bashing our heads against a brick wall, Inspector?'

'I don't think so. With a little more poking around I might find out who is attempting to frighten Lady Diedre, because that is what this is all about, I suspect.'

'Then we are in agreement,' Lady Gwendolyn murmured.

'Did you ever meet Laura Upton Palmer, my lady?'

'No, I didn't. Nor have I ever heard of her. Is she a friend of Diedre's?'

'No, not any more, I am afraid. Unfortunately she died about six years ago. It was very tragic, she was so young.'

Shocked, Lady Gwendolyn sat up with a sudden jerk, staring at Howard. 'Another friend of my great-niece died! Oh my goodness. Not in peculiar circumstances, I hope? Then there would be something really amiss, I do believe.' There was a moment's pause, before Lady Gwendolyn asked, 'How did the young lady die?'

'Mrs Palmer died of leukaemia, m'lady.'

'I see. Why did you bring her name up, Inspector?'

'It occurred to me you might have met her, m'lady. Maxine Lowe, Lady Diedre and Laura Upton Palmer were great friends, best friends. In 1914, just before the war, the three of them went on a trip to Europe, which ended in Berlin. They were a popular, well-known threesome, more or less the same age and background. It was Maxine Lowe who invited them, and paid for the trip. As you know she was an heiress, and very generous to her friends. So I've been given to understand.'

Lady Gwendolyn was shaking her head. 'Diedre never mentioned Laura Upton Palmer to me, and she and I are rather close. How odd that she did not confide in me. I might have been able to comfort her. Oh dear, how sad for her. Diedre must have been so upset, losing two close friends like that, and in just a few years.'

'I'm sure she was, and from what I can gather she was especially grief-stricken about Mrs Palmer's death – and probably still is, I think.'

Lady Gwendolyn, nobody's fool, was studying Howard intently, and after a moment she asked, 'Is there an implication behind those words, Inspector Pinkerton?'

Howard shifted slightly in his chair, and did not answer for a few seconds, wondering how to properly proceed.

Lady Gwendolyn's eyes narrowed. 'I am a woman of a certain age, Inspector, and I have seen and heard so very many things in my long life. Nothing you tell me could possibly shock me.'

Staring back at her, he thought: What a wily old bird she is, and then said, 'I realize that, Your Ladyship.' He took a deep breath and jumped in. 'Lady Diedre and Mrs Palmer eventually were more than just friends, they became . . . romantically involved.'

155

'Are you saying that Lady Diedre and Mrs Palmer were lesbians, and lovers?'

'I am.'

For a moment, Lady Gwendolyn did not respond. Finally she said in a very steady voice, 'Perhaps that's why my great-niece never mentioned Laura, or introduced me to her. However, wasn't Laura a married woman?'

'She was married to Ralph Palmer.' Understanding that Lady Gwendolyn was taking everything in her stride, and very calmly, Howard decided to continue. 'Mrs Palmer left her husband for Lady Diedre. In turn, Lady Diedre broke off her relationship with Austin Morgan. I'm sure you remember that the family believed she was about to get engaged to him.'

Lady Gwendolyn sat very still, indeed remembering everything about that possible engagement. She knew Austin Morgan's father, who had been one of her oldest friends. And his only son had been killed in the Great War, and Rodney Morgan had never really recovered from his sorrow. He grieved for Austin until the day he died.

Now, looking across at Howard, an expression of puzzlement in her blue eyes, she asked, 'I suppose we must accept that my great-niece and Laura would be considered bisexual? Isn't that so?'

'It is, Lady Gwendolyn.'

'I would say we had two rejected, angry men seeking to hurt Diedre. However, Austin Morgan was killed in the Great War. Could Ralph Palmer be out for revenge?'

'He too died in the war, Lady Gwendolyn.'

'So that theory doesn't work. I would like to get to the bottom of this situation. Obviously Diedre doesn't have any idea who might be endeavouring to harm her with Chinese whispers, so there's no point talking to her. What do you think we should do, Inspector?'

'Keep digging. I do know that Mrs Palmer had a sister,

or perhaps it was a cousin, who helped to care for her when she first became ill. I ought to look into family ties, Lady Gwendolyn. Perhaps a relative may have information that helps.'

'You're right, Inspector. For example, did Laura have a brother? Someone who wants to hurt my great-niece? Or maybe Ralph's family want to punish Lady Diedre, probably in the belief that she ruined Ralph's marriage.'

'I shall work on the matter on my day off next week, m'lady. We'll solve this riddle. Trust me.'

'I do, Inspector. I truly do.'

Once Inspector Howard Pinkerton had left, Lady Gwendolyn went into the small parlour which opened off her bedroom. She immediately picked up the telephone and dialled Vanessa's number, then seated herself at the small writing desk.

After the third ring, the phone was answered, and it was Vanessa herself at the other end of the line.

'It's Aunt Gwendolyn,' she said in her warmest voice. 'I just wondered how you were, my dear, and whether or not your official engagement to Richard was imminent.'

'How nice of you to phone me, Aunt Gwen. Actually, Richard and I are planning to announce it next week. In *The Times*, of course.'

'That's wonderful news. Congratulations, my dear. I would like to give an engagement party for you, Vanessa, unless someone else has already offered to do that.'

'Oh my goodness, Aunt Gwen! That's so kind of you, and I know Richard would like that as much as I do. Thank you.'

'Then it shall be done. I just need to have a date from you, and then we will plan the party together. Now tell me, how is Lavinia? Is she feeling any better?'

'She is, from what I gather. That little romance, which

started at Charles's wedding, is still going strong . . . with Mark Stanton, you know.'

'Oh yes, I do remember. Daphne pointed that out to me. She also said that Diedre and Paul Drummond appeared to be somewhat attracted to each other that same evening.' Gwendolyn forced a chuckle, and asked, 'Did that romance blossom too?'

'I saw Daphne for lunch yesterday, and she told me that Diedre had been out with Paul several times. But she didn't know if it was anything more than a friendship. It would be nice if Diedre had met the right man at long last.'

She spoke for a short while longer with Vanessa before hanging up. She was pleased she had all the information she needed to understand what was happening in the family.

Gwendolyn remained seated at her French *bureau plat*, staring out of the window, thinking about Diedre. She came to the conclusion that she must get Diedre married off, no matter what. That would be Diedre's salvation, and secure her future. But was Paul Drummond the right man?

Her thoughts stayed with her great-niece, whom she had always loved, almost as if she were her own daughter. They were alike in various ways – of similar build and colouring, and, of course, Diedre had the same acerbic wit, was ready to offer her opinions as boldly as Lady Gwendolyn herself usually did.

Although she had managed to conceal her feelings, Gwendolyn had been somewhat startled by Howard Pinkerton's revelations about Diedre and Laura Upton. However, not being judgemental, she was not concerned with Diedre's love affair with Laura. What saddened her was that Diedre had not trusted her enough to confide in her after Laura's untimely death. At the time she must have needed love and support in her sorrow. How isolated and alone she must have felt; and then again after

158

Maxine's sudden death and the strange circumstances surrounding it.

Gwendolyn's thoughts went to Paul Drummond, who handled Hugo's business in New York. She had met him in the past with Hugo and Daphne. He was a fine man, likeable and full of charm. Anyone whom Hugo valued as much as he did Paul had her stamp of approval.

She reached for the phone, having the sudden compulsion to telephone Diedre, but changed her mind. She must let things take their natural course. In the meantime, she would start to make plans for Vanessa's engagement party.

TWENTY-FIVE

They sat together at a table near a window overlooking the Thames. The dining room at the Savoy was busy this particular Friday, and as Miles glanced around he saw that everyone was smartly dressed; the women especially, wearing stylish gowns and jewels. It was quite a glittering evening.

But to him there was not one woman in this room who could compare to Cecily. She was lovelier than ever tonight, her complexion peaches-and-cream perfect, her dark hair burnished with auburn lights. She wore a grey lace frock, with silver threads running through the weave, and crystal drop earrings that sparkled like her lavender-grey eyes. She was incomparable.

'Miles, you're staring at me so hard, as if you'd never seen me before,' she murmured, smiling at him, shaking her head.

'I know . . . it's because I don't think I've ever seen you looking as beautiful. Oh, you've always been beautiful to me, I even thought that when we were little. But you've never been like this, not really. You are radiant.' He reached for her hand and brought it to his lips, kissed it. 'You are the most perfect woman.'

At this moment the waiter stepped over to the table and refilled their champagne flutes. Miles picked up his glass and so did Cecily. 'Here's to you. And me. And us,' he said, clinking the rim of his flute against hers.

She smiled at him and took a sip of champagne.

He held his breath for a moment as he saw the orb of the full moon floating high in the dark sky, just immediately above her head. He couldn't help exclaiming, 'Someone's hung the moon for you tonight, Ceci. It's shining right above you.'

She turned her head to look through the window, saw it for herself. And felt a cold shiver run through her. She recalled what Genevra had said to her once years ago:

Full moon shines on glass.

Shines on water.

Shines on you.

She had asked the gypsy girl many times what she meant but Genevra would never explain.

He gazed at her, reached out and took her hand in his. After a moment, he murmured, 'It's so nice, just sitting here like this, listening to Carroll Gibbons and his romantic music . . . I could sit here forever.'

Cecily leaned back in her chair, studying him, thinking that he looked less tense. Certainly he was more relaxed tonight, even though the meeting had gone badly with Clarissa. Especially since he had believed his wife would agree to a divorce. For some reason, she had believed the opposite. Poor Miles, she thought. Six years of hell, with nothing to show for it. A bleak future ahead without his freedom.

No, it doesn't have to be bleak, she suddenly thought. Aunt Charlotte was right. He was only doing his duty when he married Clarissa, doing what had been planned for him since before he had been born.

Even though Cecily had been friendlier, warmer to him,

161

a bit of a grudge had lingered in her. Now, unexpectedly, it was gone; even the hurt had evaporated. She felt lighter, happier, and she gripped his hand more tightly.

He looked across at her. 'What is it? What're you thinking? You've been so quiet.'

'I was wondering what I could give you as a present, and now I know. I am going to give you the books! The leather-bound books in my flat. They're the kind of history books you love.'

Miles was taken aback. 'You can't give them to me, Cecily. They're worth a fortune.'

'Yes, I can. I can. They're mine. I want you to have them. They're all about Julius Caesar . . . they're meant for you.'

Miles asked Cecily to dance, and she agreed. Now he led her out onto the dance floor, held her tightly, but not too close to him. He was afraid she would be annoyed if he did that. He didn't want to step over the line.

She had been so much more relaxed with him lately, not so cold and aloof. And tonight she had almost been like her old self, obviously attempting to make him feel better. He must maintain the status quo.

'Thank you for being so nice,' he murmured against her hair. 'It's been a lovely evening with you, Ceci.'

'I wanted it to be fun,' she whispered back. 'And you needed a happy evening. So did I.'

The slow foxtrot finished and abruptly the tempo of the music changed. Suddenly everyone was dancing the Charleston, Cecily included.

Miles stared at her. She was laughing, full of gaiety. He felt so heartened that he too took up this latest craze, adroitly moved around Cecily, hopping and swaying as if his life depended on it.

*   *   *

162

Later, when they returned to the table, Cecily leaned forward and said, 'I had some wonderful news from Dorothy today. I've had my biggest year ever in business.'

A huge smile spread across Miles's face and he exclaimed, 'Congratulations! And why didn't you tell me earlier?'

She shrugged and laughed. 'I wanted to just be . . . with you . . . enjoying being together.'

'Well done, my darling Ceci.'

'Thank you. I was startled because Dottie told me we made a lot of money from the accessories, which I've been designing for the last six years, but more as a hobby.'

Looking into her eyes, he murmured, 'You are the most remarkable person I've ever known, Cecily Swann.'

TWENTY-SIX

He sat in front of the fire in the sitting room, holding the book. Earlier he had put a match to the paper and wood chips in the grate, since it had turned cold, and the fire burned brightly now, taking the chill out of the air.

He leaned back against the sofa cushions, and finally looked down at the book, his right hand moving across the beautiful burgundy leather. Then he opened it and turned the pages. It was in perfect condition, a valuable book, and he did not want to take it, especially since it was part of a set. He knew he had no choice. She would be hurt if he refused to accept it.

She had put it in his hand when they had returned to her flat in Chesterfield Street, after their lovely evening at the Savoy. Now she was in the kitchen making tea. She had given him a cognac when they had first got back, because he had told her he felt chilled to the bone. He reached for the balloon, took a swallow of the Napoleon brandy, then put it back on the table next to him.

He realized she had given him the book because she wanted him to have a special memory of tonight. They had often done that as children. And it was a good memory after a bad day. The evening had been unique, had made him feel happy, an emotion long absent in his sad life.

He smoothed his hand over the book again, liking its silkiness. It was about the childhood of Julius Caesar, a childhood he knew by heart. But he would read it again, because he couldn't help himself. History had been his best subject at Eton; it was a hobby these days, one he shared with Harry. Cecily's brother also found comfort, solace and wisdom in the histories of great men, long dead. It was a bond between them.

Hearing her footsteps, he glanced over his shoulder. She had changed her clothes, was wearing the loose casual trousers she had made so popular with women the world over, and a floaty matching top, and he saw why they were such a favourite. Comfort, he thought.

'Here I am,' she exclaimed. 'And I've brought lemon slices and a pot of honey for the tea. You know how prone to colds you are.'

He smiled inwardly at her comment, a line she had learned from Mrs Jackson throughout their childhood. Cook had fussed over him like a mother hen. Seemingly it was Cecily's turn to do the same.

Placing the tray on a circular table near the window, she poured cups of tea, plopped in teaspoonfuls of honey, and brought the cups over to the fireplace.

'It's warmer now, with the fire,' she murmured, and sat back in the chair. Her eyes fell on the book. 'Every time I think you need a gift to cheer you up, I shall give you another book. There are ten in the set.'

'I know that, Ceci, and that's why I didn't want to take this one. They are too valuable, really they are. You must keep them.'

'Oh pooh! They're meant for you. And I didn't pay much for them anyway.'

'Because the woman probably didn't know their true value.'

'But they are mine now, and I can do what I want with them.'

Miles sighed, placed the book on the table and drank some of the tea. After a moment, he asked, 'Why did you buy this flat in Chesterfield Street?'

Looking puzzled, she frowned. 'It was the right size for me, with four bedrooms. I can have Harry and my parents to stay, and I still have the fourth bedroom, which I use as an office. Don't you like it?'

'I do, yes, very much. It's a nice size, you're right, Ceci.' A small smile flickered on his mouth. 'I remember how you often said you wanted to live in Mayfair when you were living with your aunt Dorothy in Kensington.'

She laughed. 'And now I do.'

'I also recall one night, years ago, when I walked up Curzon Street, feeling morose, sombre and ready to run as far away from Mayfair as I could get. And suddenly I was in South Audley Street, and standing outside your little hole in the wall. I think I'd gone there purposely, just to feel your vibrations. It was late at night; I knew you weren't there. But I hoped your spirit was floating about. I just wanted to be near you. There was a sign on the door. It said SHOP FOR RENT. I couldn't believe it. I panicked, couldn't imagine where you'd gone, I was so worried about you. I knew then, without the slightest doubt, that I would worry about you for the rest of my life. And love you for the rest of my life . . .'

Miles cut himself off, leaned back against the sofa, his throat tight with overwhelming emotion. He was unable to say another word as that awful night came rushing back to him in every painful detail.

Cecily, sitting in the chair opposite him, remained quiet, understanding his suffering. Her heart went out to him. Every vestige of her hurt and anger with him had dissipated in the last few weeks. She had only love for him now.

Once she realized he had regained his equilibrium, she asked, 'And what did you do then?'

Slowly, in a gruff voice, he explained, 'At first, I did nothing. I just stood there. Frozen. I truly understood I was stuck in a place from which I could not retreat. There was no way out. And unexpectedly I thought of Caesar when he had stood at the Rubicon, wondering if he should cross the river and march on Rome. He was a Roman, about to make war on the Senate and his own city. He fully understood that he would be committing treason. And for a moment he hesitated . . .'

Miles paused, took several deep swallows of the cognac, and was silent for a moment. Nursing the cognac, focusing on Cecily, he went on, 'Caesar looked behind him and saw his great army. Thousands and thousands of men in armour geared up to do battle for him. He knew he had no choice. "The die is cast," he said to the general by his side. And so he marched on Rome. And there was I, six years ago now, also caught in a trap. And I thought to myself: The die is cast. In other words, the decision has been made and is irrevocable.'

He shook his head and then put the cognac down on the table. 'I knew I had to follow the road I'd been put on. Look where it got me! Unlike Caesar, who won, I did not. I lost you, and in doing so I lost everything of value in my life.' Miles put his head in his hands and began to weep, overcome by his feelings.

Cecily had tears in her eyes and she jumped up, went to sit next to him on the sofa. Reaching out, she gently pulled his hands away from his face, wiped away the tears on his cheeks with her fingertips.

She said quietly, her voice full of love, 'It's all right, Miles, I am here now. I'm going to be with you for the rest of my life. And yours. No matter what happens, I will never leave you. Never. I promise.'

For a split second, Miles thought he had not heard her correctly. Blinking, straightening, he stared at her, puzzlement lurking in his eyes. And at that moment he saw the yearning on her face, and the love and desire for him.

Instantly Miles grabbed hold of her, pulled her into his arms and held her close. Against her hair, he said, 'Oh God, I love you so much, Ceci. I can't live without you. Life means nothing if you're not by my side.'

'And I feel the same . . . we must be together now, whatever happens, Miles. We can't worry about the rest of the world. It's just the two of us now.'

They drew apart, stood up. Still clutching each other, they went down the corridor to Cecily's bedroom. In the dim light they frantically struggled out of their clothes, then they stood apart, gazing at each other in disbelief.

At exactly the same moment, they moved towards each other, their arms outstretched, desire flooding their faces. They clung together in the middle of the bedroom.

The years fell away, and they were at ease with each other, as they had always been. They knew what was going to happen.

They could hardly wait, as thoughts of the pleasure and joy they would share took hold of them. Already their bodies were aflame, just as their thoughts were racing in great anticipation.

Cecily felt she was burning up. The heat started between her legs and was running all the way to her face.

Miles was pressing her closer to him, his hands tight on her buttocks, and she felt his hardness against her stomach. He had an enormous erection; a thrill shot through her. She could hardly wait to hold him in her arms, to love him, make him hers.

Taking a step backwards, she took hold of his hand and led him to the bed.

They lay down together, stretched out side by side. Miles murmured, 'I can't believe we're here together like this, Ceci. It's a miracle.'

'A miracle wrought by Charlotte Swann. And I, for one, am thankful. I can't wait, Miles. I want us to make love. Now. Please touch me. Please. I want you so much.'

Pushing himself up on one elbow, Miles looked down at her, his love spilling out of him. 'I want you, too. I'm aching with desire for you, Ceci. I feel as if I'm about to explode. But I'm also afraid to touch you, to begin . . . because I'll devour you too fast. I want to love you, give you pleasure, and savour you. It's been so long, I want our loving to last for a while, not be over in a few minutes.'

Looking up into those bright blue eyes she had known and loved for as long as she could remember, she said, 'Whatever you wish, Miles. I do know I need you to touch me everywhere, have your hands all over me . . .' Her voice trailed off.

He grew even harder, bent over her, kissed her passionately. His tongue went into her mouth, curled around hers. She responded ardently and he went on kissing her, their tongues entwined. Her arms were around his back, her hands tight on his shoulder blades. She was trembling, her passion for him soaring.

Responding to her fervency, Miles kissed her breasts and nipples. They hardened, exciting her more, and thrilling him. A moan escaped her lips and he knew instantly she was ready for him, wanted to possess him, have his body joined to hers.

He held himself still for a moment, trying to control his own surging desire. And then he gave in to it; he just couldn't help himself. They were both at fever pitch.

Slowly he began to stroke her breasts, running his hand down over her stomach and onto her thighs. He let it linger there for a moment, and then he found her womanhood, touched her. As his strokes became more insistent, he felt the beginning of her spasms. She stiffened, crying out.

Miles stopped abruptly. He moved her legs, rolled on top of her and slid into her expertly. Wanting to share her oncoming pleasure, he went deeper, filling her with himself. His hands slipped under her buttocks and he lifted her closer to him. Then he stopped moving, realizing he was on the very edge.

'Mine,' he mumbled, his voice thick with desire. 'Mine.'

'Forever,' Cecily whispered, and thrust her body against his. Her long legs went high around his back, and she gave herself up to him completely. Her arms were hard against his shoulders, her hands in his hair.

'Is this what you want?' she asked, her voice as hoarse as his.

'Yes, oh yes,' he moaned. His passion flared, grew more intense. He was wallowing in the warm damp heat of her, the velvet softness. She was his woman. There could be no other. And he was her man, the only one who could turn her into this voluptuous lover, the only man who could give her pleasure.

Cecily was whispering his name over and over again. They were both filled with the same urgent passion they had shared time and again, aware it was a melding of their bodies and souls. They belonged to each other. Waves of intense pleasure carried them into a state of ecstasy and, when they reached the pinnacle, they were one being, one soul, and were complete.

Miles lay on top of Cecily, for a moment unable to move. He was weak from pleasure, love and total happiness.

Realizing he was probably too heavy, he slid out of her, curled his body around hers and kissed the back of her neck. 'I'd like to stay the night, Ceci. Can I?'

'I wouldn't have it any other way,' she answered, smiling.

'Is Mrs Granger off until Monday?' he asked.

'She is, yes.'

'Shall we stay in bed for the entire weekend then?' Miles said, grinning.

'I thought you'd never suggest it. Of course. And there's plenty of food, we can have picnics in bed.'

'And make love,' Miles added, and pulled her into his arms. 'Starting right now.'

TWENTY-SEVEN

After she hung up on Miles, Daphne's hand remained resting on the receiver, her expression reflective, her mind on Cecily and Miles. He had spent the night with her. They were back together. They were in for trouble, she was certain of that.

She worried about Miles. What if Cecily decided she did not want to marry him? After all, she had a huge business. Cecily might break his heart in the long run, by rejecting him if he became free.

Daphne sat back in the chair, glancing around the library. She couldn't help thinking, yet again, what an enormous room it was.

In fact, the whole house was enormous. They didn't need a house as big as this in London; the family hardly spent any time there. We could sell it, she thought, her mind always on money these days. If her father agreed. Before going off on his honeymoon, he had confided that he might well spend more time in London, now that he was married to Charlotte.

Sighing under her breath, Daphne rang the bell for Eric Swann, the butler; they called him by his first name because there was so many Swanns around.

172

She walked over to the fireplace and stood with her back to it, liking the warmth of the flames. It was a cool day for September, and there had been a chill in the air for several days.

A moment later there was a knock on the door, and Eric entered. 'Yes, m'lady, do you need me for something?'

'I do, Eric. Please close the door and come in. There are a couple of things I need to speak to you about.'

The butler nodded. Eric Swann had the look of Walter Swann, Cecily's father. They were first cousins, but could easily be mistaken for brothers, so alike were they in appearance. Both of them were striking, tall, and carried themselves well. The London butler was as devoted to the Inghams as Hanson was in Yorkshire, and in particular to Lady Daphne.

Once Eric was standing next to her near the fireplace, Daphne said, sotto voce, 'I have to confide something, Eric. I know it will go no further.'

'I took the oath, Lady Daphne,' Eric reminded her, putting out his clenched hand. 'Loyalty binds me.'

She placed her clenched fist on top of his, and repeated, 'Loyalty binds me.' A moment later, she drew closer, and murmured in the same low voice, 'Can you provide me with someone who can pick a lock?'

If the butler was startled, he did not show it. 'It all depends, my lady. If it's an innocent picking of a lock, I can do that myself, with a small tool I have. Do you have a problem with a lock in the house, Lady Daphne?'

She shook her head. 'No, I don't, and it's not so innocent either, Eric, I'm afraid. That's why I asked for your confidence. Let me explain.'

Eric listened attentively as she told him about the missing jewels, the discovery made in July, on the day of the Earl's marriage; the absence of Felicity on holiday in France, her return to London only recently, and now the necessity of reclaiming the pieces.

'It's been very frustrating for me,' Daphne explained. 'Not being able to do anything for so long. However, now that my mother is back, I must go to her house and get the jewels. They're in a locked cupboard. Wilson is my ally, and she will do anything to help. I just need a plan.'

'Doesn't Wilson have the key to the cupboard, m'lady?'

'No, she doesn't. My mother keeps that key herself. And Wilson has no idea where she hides it.'

Eric gave Daphne a long thoughtful look, before saying, 'If you have to get the jewels yourself, actually steal them, then you obviously believe Mrs Pierce won't give them to you willingly. Is that the case, Lady Daphne?'

'It is. You see, she'll be mortified. So embarrassed that she's been caught out, she'll lie. She'll say she doesn't have them. And there's another reason . . . she wants to keep them.'

'I understand,' Eric replied, and he did. He had never liked the Countess when she was married to the Earl; had considered her a tricky woman with some sort of agenda of her own. He had been suspicious of her for years. After a moment, Eric said, 'With all due respect, m'lady, if there's any lock picking to do, it's going to be me doing it, not you. However, that may not be necessary. If there is any chance that Wilson could get hold of the key for just a few minutes?'

'I honestly don't know. Why?'

'I could get her some soft wax, which she would have to keep on her at all times, and she could press the key into it and get an imprint. I have a good locksmith who could then copy the key.'

'I think that might be a bit complicated for Olive. She's rather nervous as it is.'

'Is there a reason His Lordship can't go and see her

when he's back? And simply demand the jewels. Wouldn't that be the best thing?'

'I know my father would be willing to do that, Eric, but I know she'll deny it. Anyway, I don't want him troubled. You know he hasn't been well. It would be awful if he had another heart attack. She'll be beastly to him. I heard on the grapevine that she's been rather mean about him . . . since his marriage.'

'Yes, m'lady,' Eric responded, knowing full well what she was talking about. He said, 'I have several chaps I know, who know other chaps, who could pick a lock in two seconds. But they would obviously have to do the job when Mr and Mrs Pierce were out for the evening. Or away for the weekend.'

'I understand. I'll have to send Lady DeLacy to see her, because at the moment I'm not very popular. We have to mend our fences, winkle our way in again – that'll give us a chance to know her plans and find the opportunity to do the job.'

'What job?' Dulcie asked as she came into the room. 'Are you talking about the jewels again?'

Daphne nodded.

Dulcie looked across at the butler. 'I think we should just go in and bash the door down, Eric. Or use a stick of dynamite.'

Daphne burst out laughing, and even Eric couldn't manage to stifle the laugh that rose in his throat. 'Too much noise, Lady Dulcie,' he said, swallowing his mirth. 'Picking a lock is quieter.'

'Only too true,' Daphne nodded. 'To move on, I like the idea of a cold supper, served buffet style, Eric. And we shall be nine altogether tomorrow evening.'

'Yes, m'lady. And, in the meantime, I'll try to find a solution regarding the lock.'

* * *

The sisters sat down near the fire, and Dulcie said, 'The house is so quiet. Where is everyone?'

'Poor Charlie has a bad cold, as you know, and I kept him in bed today. He has to go back to prep school next week. Alicia and the twins went to the zoo with Pettigrew, and Nanny took Annabel out for a walk.' Daphne smiled, thinking of her adorable two year old, and amended herself. 'Or rather, Nanny took her out in her pushchair. They'll all be back in time for tea.'

Dulcie laughed. 'That's grand. I do love them all, you know. And where's Hugo?'

'He went to lunch with Paul Drummond. They're both having second thoughts about an investment they made in America, and Hugo wants to thrash it out with him.'

For a moment Dulcie looked thoughtful, and then she asked, 'Do you think Paul is serious about Diedre?'

'I don't know,' Daphne was quick to answer. 'His wife died about eight years ago, and whilst there have been a few women in his life, I know he hasn't been serious about any of them.'

'And what about Diedre? She might not want to give up the War Office. She's always been a career girl.'

Daphne nodded. 'I've thought of that myself. On the other hand, I think Paul's quite a catch.'

'But he's fifteen years older than her, Daphers! Isn't that too big an age difference?'

'He's very athletic, doesn't look his age, and he's a man who's involved in the world and what's going on around him. I invited him to supper tomorrow evening.'

'I shall concentrate on him, weigh him up, and give you my verdict later,' Dulcie announced.

Daphne laughed. 'You're a hoot, Dulcie darling. You really are.'

'You've not told me about your meeting with Wilson. Is she being a cowardy custard?'

Biting back another smile, Daphne nodded. 'She is a bit nervous . . . of overstepping the mark, I suppose.'

'But you told me she was coming to work for you at Cavendon. I think she should just leave Charles Street and be done with it.'

'I want her to do that, Dulcie. But not until I have the jewels safely back at Cavendon. She's my inside ally.'

'You were asking Eric about picking the lock . . . don't you think a cat burglar would be a good idea? He could go in through the window at the dead of night, nick the jewels and be gone.'

'Dulcie, your imagination is priceless. I think Papa is right. You should really consider being a writer.'

'I might do that on the side, but I've decided I want to deal in art and antiques after I finish my art history course. I might even open a shop.'

Daphne gaped at her. 'A shop! Goodness me, what will you think of next? And I can just hear Great-Aunt Gwendolyn exclaiming, "A shop! We're not tradespeople." She'll have a fit.'

Shrugging nonchalantly, Dulcie said, 'It's a new world, Daphers . . . the nineteen twenties not the eighteen hundreds. Time moves on, and everything's different these days.'

'You're certainly right about that.'

'Why are you having this supper party tomorrow?' Dulcie now asked, leaning forward, eyeing her sister with interest. 'You always say Sunday night is your quiet night with Hugo.'

'It is. But I do want to keep the family together, and having informal suppers now and then is a good way to do it. At the family reunion I realized how much I missed being with my siblings and the aunts. I think it's vital that we stay close, share our lives with each other. Family is extremely important to me.'

'That's a beautiful sentiment,' Dulcie responded, getting up, joining Daphne on the sofa. She took hold of her hand, added, 'You're the best sister in the world, and actually the best and noblest person in this family. None of us would know what to do without you. You're our rock. Oh, and is Miles coming to the supper?'

'I believe so. I'm trying to mother him a bit, Dulcie. He's had such a rough few years.'

'So he is back with Cecily?'

'I'm not sure . . .' She left her sentence unfinished.

TWENTY-EIGHT

Diedre was putting the final touches to her hair when the rattling ring of the phone brought her to her feet. She dashed across her bedroom to answer it, breathless as she said, 'Hello?'

'Diedre, it's Aunt Gwendolyn. Do you have a moment, my dear?'

'Of course, I do, Aunt Gwen. Do you have news for me? I hope so.'

'I do indeed. I saw Howard Pinkerton on Friday evening, and he told me that he has spoken to someone at the War Office. He says the rumour about you leaving, or being pushed out, is a whisper rather than a roar. Good news, isn't it?'

'Yes, it is. But I can't help wondering why Alfie Fennell made it sound so . . . huge, as if everyone was gossiping about me.' Diedre sounded baffled.

'I wondered that too, and I came to the conclusion that things tend to grow when they're repeated. The Inspector agreed. Most people exaggerate, he pointed out.'

'Do you know who he spoke to, Aunt?'

'I don't have a name, if that's what you mean. However,

he did say that he spoke to someone at the middle level, not one of the bigwigs.'

'Oh, I see. Why didn't he go to the top?' Diedre asked, sounding disappointed.

'Apparently he thought better of it, and decided that it would be wiser not to draw attention to your name at all. I tend to agree with him there.'

'Oh yes, yes, I think he was right, Aunt Gwen. And I'm grateful to you for helping in this way.'

'Inspector Pinkerton is of the opinion that the rumour has been put out by someone in your private life. Does this bring anybody to mind, Diedre?'

'No, it doesn't. What friend would start that kind of nasty rumour about my work at the War Office?'

'Someone who is not a friend, I believe. Someone who wants to hurt you. Or frighten you, perhaps. Give you a scare, is the best way I can put it.'

Diedre, grasping the receiver harder, was silent for a moment. And then she said, 'I suppose I must have a friend who is really an enemy. But I don't know who that could be.'

'Think about it, my dear – someone may spring to mind. Now I must go. I shall see you later at supper. I thought it better to speak of this matter privately.'

'Thank you, Aunt Gwendolyn. I'll see you at Daphne's.'

Diedre had just returned the receiver to its cradle when the phone began to ring once more. 'Hello?' she said as she picked it up.

'Diedre, it's me,' Paul Drummond said. 'I was wondering what time I should pick you up?'

'In about twenty minutes, half an hour . . .'

'Let's say twenty minutes. I need to speak to you about something.'

'Are you all right? You sound . . . a bit terse, Paul.'

He laughed. 'Never with you. Be there shortly.' He hung up without another word.

That was the way he was: very decisive, businesslike about certain things, precise and practical as well. They were of like minds. She was as efficient as he was.

Returning to her dressing table, Diedre sat down and finished brushing her hair, looking at herself in the mirror. She swept the top wave of her short bob to the left side, then fastened the diamond and tortoiseshell clip in place, above her left ear. She liked this new hairdo, thought it cheeky but chic.

Sitting back, she stared at herself, deciding that the thin line of blue pencil on her lids emphasized the blueness of her eyes even more. And so did the black mascara. She enjoyed using cosmetics, creating a new look for herself.

Ever since they had crept out of the wedding dinner at Cavendon on the occasion of her father's marriage to Charlotte in July, Paul and she had been seeing each other.

Paul had whispered he wanted to be alone with her – somewhere, anywhere – just to talk, to be together in private. She had refused to stay in the house, knowing only too well that staff lurked everywhere when there was a big event.

And so she had taken his hand and led him down to the gazebo in the park. It had been a clear, starry night, with a full moon floating over the lake, and he had liked the idea of being outside, away from the others.

Once in the gazebo, they had seated themselves on two wicker chairs, and within minutes he had his arm around her shoulders and was kissing her. She had kissed him back and they had soon found their passion flaring, their physical attraction to each other obvious.

It was when he reached over to touch her breast that her chair rocked and she went down, grabbing his arm as she did so. His chair also tipped over, and he fell on top of her. They were a mass of tangled arms and legs, and as they looked at each other in shocked surprise, they began to laugh. She recalled now how they had been almost hysterical with laughter, and, of course, the intensely sexual mood was broken.

But not for long. Later the following week, in London, Paul had invited her to have dinner with him. Being the perfect gentleman, he had arrived to pick her up, but they never left the flat. He cancelled the reservation and they ended up making love instead.

He was an ardent lover. Passionate, sensuous and virile. That evening, here in her flat, their affair had begun. His affection, attention, warmth and genuine interest in her had helped soothe her troubled spirit. Her sorrow had begun to dissipate.

Now, suddenly, after Great-Aunt Gwendolyn's call a short while ago, she even felt better about her job at the War Office and the rumours. Reaching for the string of pearls Paul had given her, she put them around her neck, and as she did so she glanced at the photograph of him with his half-brother Timothy. He had given it to her when she had asked him for one. 'This is it, I'm afraid,' he had explained. 'Tim helped to bring me up after our father died. It's the only one I have with me.'

She gazed at Paul's image. He was clean-cut, with a chiselled nose, fine features and a broad brow. He reminded her of the All-American College Boy. Fair hair, clear, light grey eyes, a sincere smile. Even now, at forty-eight, he still had that youthful collegiate look that so appealed to her.

The Drummonds of New York and Connecticut were a banking family, part of the social elite of the city, and traced their ancestry back to England and the *Mayflower*. Paul's mother, Alexandra, was still alive and in her early seventies. Timothy, son of their father's first marriage, ran the family bank, and was married with twin sons and a daughter.

Paul had told her about his family over the two months they had known each other, but had never mentioned his wife. And Diedre, being well bred, had never asked him one question. All she knew was that his wife had died.

She tore her eyes away from Paul's photograph and glanced over at the clock. Immediately she jumped up and went to take her frock off the hanger. He would be arriving any moment, and here she was, daydreaming about him instead of getting dressed. Her dress was by Cecily Swann, and was tailored and elegant, with a full skirt. It showed off her legs, and was flattering. Style was her special thing; she thought she looked more streamlined and chic than her siblings. And why not? She was very much a London girl, and with a career.

As she stepped into her shoes, she thought about Paul Drummond, asking herself where it was going, this affair of theirs? She had no idea, but she was enjoying herself these days. Laughing, she went to select an evening bag. She no longer felt like the spinster aunt who did nothing but work.

TWENTY-NINE

Daphne found Hugo in the library, sitting in a chair near the fireplace, looking preoccupied. 'Can I come in, darling?' she asked from the doorway. 'Or am I intruding?'

A smile flashed across his face when he saw his wife. He jumped up, went to her, took hold of her hand and brought her into the room. 'You've never intruded on me in my life. I fill with joy when I see you, Daphne. You must know that by now.' He laughed. 'If I could, I'd take you to the office with me. And everywhere else I went.'

She laughed with him; linking arms, they walked across the room together. They sat down on the sofa and settled back against the cushions.

'I must admit, I was somewhat preoccupied . . . with thoughts of Paul Drummond, actually.'

Daphne gave him a swift glance and raised a brow. 'Why? Is there something wrong?'

He shook his head. 'No, not between us. Or with his work. He's the best, you know, and a really fine man; he has great integrity, an extraordinary work ethic and is as dependable as they come. His half-brother Timothy has been on his back lately. He's pushing Paul to return to New York. His mother is unwell.'

'Oh dear, I'm sorry to hear that. What's wrong with her?'

'Apparently she's had a heart problem for the last few years. That was my understanding. But she was leading a fairly normal life.'

'And doesn't Paul want to go at this time? Is that it?'

'He knows he must. But we do have some important work to finish before he goes. Also, he seems to be taken with Diedre.'

'You told me that before. But she keeps very quiet. Doesn't confide. She's secretive.'

'I know he likes her. A lot, Daphne. But I don't have a clue what his intentions are.'

'I personally think he's a real catch,' Daphne said.

Hugo looked at her, his eyes twinkling. 'I hope you thought I was, and that I still am.'

'The biggest catch of all time, Hugo, my darling,' Daphne declared emphatically.

'Anyway, Diedre's never seemed interested in marriage. What about her job at the War Office? It's always meant such a lot to her.' Hugo personally believed she buried herself in work because she was lonely. In the way Cecily Swann had been all these years.

'Oh, pooh to that! I don't know why she's stayed there. There's no war on at the moment. When would Paul leave?'

'He said he wanted to finish our work here, consolidate our future plans. His mother's not at death's door. Under the weather, I believe. He wanted my advice yesterday, and I said I thought we could finish up in three or four weeks, something like that.'

Daphne was thoughtful, and after a moment she asked, 'When would he come back to London? Do you know?'

'In about two months. At least, that's what he said to me over lunch. Perhaps he might tell her he's serious. Mind you, that's an assumption on my part.'

Daphne sat back against the sofa, staring into the distance.

185

Then she said, 'I never make assumptions,' and got to her feet.

Hugo stared up at her. 'What an odd thing to say, darling.'

Smiling at him, she bent forward, kissed his cheek. 'I know. Actually, I must leave you for a while. I need to see Eric and Laura.'

Hugo glanced at the carriage clock on the mantelpiece, and exclaimed, 'But it's only seven fifteen! No one will arrive for a while.'

'Oh yes, Great-Aunt Gwendolyn is bound to get here first, at least twenty minutes early, if not sooner. She likes to have a chat with me alone, pumping me for news.'

He laughed as she hurried out, his eyes following her. How lucky he had been in finding her, his beautiful Daphne.

Laura Swann, who was now thirty-nine, had been in service at the Grosvenor Square house of the Inghams since she was fourteen. She had started as a kitchen maid, had worked her way up to head housemaid, and had been appointed housekeeper twelve years ago. Daphne, like her father, considered Laura to be a treasure.

For her part, Laura Swann believed it was a great privilege to work for such a fine family as the Inghams, who were, in her eyes, quite unique.

She stood back, surveyed the buffet table she had just finished arranging. It stood at one end of the dining room, in the bay-window area, and had been brought up from the basement for the supper.

It had been her brother Eric's idea, just as he had suggested that they remove three leaves from the huge dining table. This made space for the buffet table, and also created a more intimate seating plan for the nine people at the supper.

'What a splendid sight,' Daphne said, as she walked

into the dining room and stood next to Laura, adding, 'You've outdone yourself.'

'Thank you, m'lady. I'm glad you're happy.'

'My goodness, what a lovely selection of food. How on earth did you manage it?' She swung around to face Laura, smiling warmly, impressed by the starched white tablecloth, floral arrangement and candelabra, as well as the food.

'As you know, I always keep several chickens in the cold pantry, m'lady, along with other meats. Yesterday, when you informed Eric about supper tonight, I went to Harte's in Knightsbridge. They have a wonderful food department, as you know. I picked up the whole smoked salmon, a veal and ham pie, a game pie, and some of the small pork pies, which I know Mr Hugo enjoys. I roasted one chicken, and the other I used for my chicken-and-vegetable casserole. There's also a ham I made at the other end of the table, Lady Daphne. I thought it was a good idea to have two or three hot dishes, for the guests who don't relish cold food. And Eric suggested I make a vegetable Lancashire hotpot. That's on the other hot plate.'

'And I see a wheel of Stilton cheese, a green salad, and quite an array of steamed vegetables. How on earth you've produced this all by yourself, I'll never know, Laura.'

'It wasn't such a lot of cooking, m'lady, because I did buy the readymade food from Harte's. Just the two chicken dishes, the ham, the hotpot and the vegetables.'

Laura looked across at one of the parlour maids, Bella, who was now entering the dining room pushing a tea cart. 'Bella was a great help, Your Ladyship, and here she is now. With the desserts, which I will place on the sideboard.'

Marvelling to herself, Daphne went over to look at the desserts as Laura put them on the wide Chippendale sideboard standing against the back wall. 'They all look delicious,' she pronounced.

'We always have custards, blancmange and jellies in the cold pantry for the children, m'lady.'

'Yes, I know, and thank you, Laura, and you too, Bella. And the sponge cake looks positively delicious!'

A moment later, Eric arrived in the dining room, wheeling the large wine trolley. 'Here are the selections Mr Hugo made, Lady Daphne,' the butler said, pushing the trolley into a corner of the dining room. 'I will service the table from here, and, of course, the water will already be poured in the glasses when everyone sits down. The two parlour maids will serve the bread . . .' Eric cut himself off, and said, 'That's the doorbell, m'lady, I think it's probably Lady Gwendolyn.'

'I'm certain it is,' Daphne responded dryly.

'Please excuse me, Lady Daphne. I must go and let Her Ladyship in.'

'Are you telling me you let both footmen go?' Lady Gwendolyn said, looking at Daphne closely, frowning. 'Are things that bad?'

'No, they're not bad, as you call it, Great-Aunt Gwendolyn. Not at all. With Hugo, Miles and Harry on the job, things are going extremely well. They've handled everything with great success during Papa's absence.'

'That's truly heartening, I must say. Very good news, my dear.'

'I let the footmen go because it was a waste of money. We're not in London enough any more. Diedre has her own flat, as do you. DeLacy has her flat in Alford Street. In fact, it's only us who stay here when we come to town – and Miles occasionally, of course.'

'I do understand, Daphne. I'm not being critical, I assure you. Just curious.' She smiled knowingly, added, 'I realize you think I'm unusually nosey, but this family is all I have, you know. You're my life.'

'Dearest, darling Great-Aunt Gwen, I don't mind your questions. Not at all. And I welcome your advice. We all love you, you should know that by now.' Daphne spoke warmly and with great sincerity.

Lady Gwendolyn reached out and grasped Daphne's hand, squeezed it. 'It's mutual, my dear. And I must say, Daphne, your eyes look bluer than ever tonight, and you're not even wearing blue.'

Smiling at her great-aunt, Daphne explained, 'Cecily made me the outfit earlier this year, and it's a sort of greyish colour with just the merest hint of a pale, pale blue. Anyway, she predicted it would make my eyes look bluer than ever, and she was right. I think she's as fed up as you with the blue frocks we all own.'

'She's very clever – brilliant, actually – and I must say I love the skirt and jacket you're wearing. So different,' Lady Gwendolyn replied.

'Very Ceci style. Loose and casual, so comfortable. And the skirt is actually a pair of wide trousers which she calls the Divided Skirt,' Daphne said. 'The little top and the long jacket are called the Kimono Set. She has names for everything.'

'Do you think it would suit me?' Lady Gwendolyn asked, and then laughed. 'I don't suppose so, not at my age.'

'Of course it would!' Daphne jumped up, turned around slowly, modelling the outfit, saying as she did, 'As you can see, the wide trousers do actually look like a skirt; the cropped blouse is neat and unobtrusive, and the kimono jacket is loose, flowing, with lovely wide sleeves. You can ask her what she thinks. She's coming to supper with Miles.'

Lady Gwendolyn raised an eyebrow. 'Are those two friendlier? I felt an awful lot of ice at your father's wedding. They were like the Arctic Circle.'

'I think she has thawed tremendously. Cecily has taken pity on him. Poor thing, he's been so sad and very lonely all these years. And she does love him. They love each other.'

'I know that,' Lady Gwendolyn murmured, and thought to herself: Ingham and Swann. They just can't resist each other, that's the God's truth. I should know. I've only got to think of my brother and also Charles to understand the pull.

Seating herself in the chair again, Daphne leaned closer to her aunt and said, sotto voce, 'Miles went to see Clarissa to ask for a divorce. She turned him down. She doesn't want one.'

Lady Gwendolyn sat up straighter and peered at Daphne, then said slowly, in a low voice, 'I can't imagine why Charles ever allowed Miles to marry that ghastly girl. As for her father, Lord Meldrew, I think he's a piece of work. A jumped-up nobody. Can't we buy her off? I'm willing to throw a whole heap of money into the kitty. Whatever it costs, it's worth it.'

At this moment, Dulcie floated into the blue and white sitting room where Daphne and Lady Gwendolyn sat chatting. As usual, she had just caught the end of the conversation, and asked, 'What kind of kitty? One that says "meow"?'

'The kind that's a money pot,' Daphne replied. 'A lot of money to buy off Miss Mildew.'

Dulcie laughed. 'I remember when we all used to call her that. And she is perfectly ghastly, Great-Aunt Gwendolyn. I'll add my paltry savings to that kitty in a shot. Actually, I found a lot of gorgeous paintings in the attic here. We could sell some.'

The two women looked at her aghast, and Daphne said, 'We'll talk about that later. In the meantime, here's Diedre with her lovely fellow, Paul Drummond.'

'Oh, I must see him again,' Lady Gwendolyn announced,

immediately rising, and gliding over to greet the couple as they walked into the room together.

After welcoming Diedre with a kiss on the cheek and a breezy smile, Lady Gwendolyn offered her hand to Paul Drummond.

He took it in his and shook it, his smile as wide as hers. 'It is so nice to meet you again, Lady Gwendolyn,' he said. 'As I recall, you and I had rather an interesting conversation about jewellery when we last met. Most informative for me.'

'You have a good memory, Mr Drummond,' she responded and, turning to Diedre, she added, 'I must say you do look extremely lovely tonight, my dear. I like that colour . . . pale lavender, isn't it? And no doubt it's a Cecily Swann frock. Everyone seems to be wearing them these days. My friends are awed that I can get an appointment to see her so quickly.' Lady Gwendolyn chuckled. 'I don't tell them I've known her since before she was born. I let them think I have some other kind of special pull.'

Diedre and Paul laughed, and Paul said, 'Her talent is amazing, and although they have a similar look, the dresses are quite different.'

'No frock is quite the same,' Diedre pointed out. 'They just have a certain cachet that's kind of like . . . a label. And she uses the most unusual colours, all those pale hues. And then, at the other side of the spectrum, vivid shades that make an impression. I have a purple gown that everyone admires.'

'Her success is phenomenal, and I can only say I am glad she and Miles are together again. It was such a cruel thing, the way they were wrenched apart. But that is the way of our world. Or should I say, that *was* the way. Nowadays, anything goes, I suppose.' Lady Gwendolyn shrugged. 'I just go with the times.'

Dulcie came over to join them, followed by Daphne,

191

and a moment after this DeLacy arrived on the arm of Hugo, who had bumped into her in the hall.

Daphne hurried over to DeLacy and hugged her close. 'I'm so happy you're looking better, darling. I've been worried about you lately. You've seemed too frail, and sad.'

DeLacy smiled at her older sister. 'You were always the little mother, and you never change. But thank you for caring so much. I do feel better than I have in ages, Daphers.'

They stood around, chatting together, until Miles and Cecily arrived. They were the last. After they had mingled for a short while, Daphne found Eric in the dining room and asked him to announce supper.

He did this a few minutes later, and they trooped into the room, all of them exclaiming how welcoming the dining room looked in the firelight, and with the candles flickering on the table. When they saw the buffet table, Dulcie was the first to declare it a veritable feast, which it was.

THIRTY

Daphne was elated that everyone had enjoyed the evening and the food. They had all gone up to the laden buffet table, where they had been served by Eric and Laura. There had been many compliments given about the various dishes on display; later the men, in particular, had eaten the meat pies from Harte's, the Lancashire hotpot and the chicken casserole with obvious relish.

'Lovely men's food,' Miles had whispered to her as they had surveyed the buffet table together. 'I'm going to have a pork pie.'

'I told Laura to be sure to make things which were easy for them to serve. And I think going to Harte's for certain foodstuffs, such as the smoked salmon and the game and meat pies, was a stroke of genius.'

Her brother agreed. 'She's always been quick and inventive,' he reminded Daphne. 'You were right to get rid of the cook here.'

Service at the buffet table was swift and almost everyone had seconds, followed by dessert.

Now it was time for the men to go into the library for cigars and cognac; Daphne would take the women into the blue and white sitting room for coffee, tea and liqueurs if anyone wanted them. She also planned to discuss the missing jewels with her sisters later.

Rising, Daphne cleared her throat and said, 'Shall we adjourn?' Glancing at Hugo at the other end of the table, she went on, 'I will take the ladies to the blue room, so that you, Miles and Paul can have a bit of masculine chitchat in the library.'

Hugo nodded and gave her a loving smile, 'Come along, chaps, let's take the hint and leave the ladies to their own devices. For a short time, at least.' As he spoke he pushed back his chair and made to leave, followed by his brother-in-law and Paul.

Lady Gwendolyn, as fast on her feet as any of them, instantly rose, glided across the dining room, and slid her arm through Diedre's. They headed through the entrance hall together. 'We must speak about Paul,' Lady Gwendolyn murmured in a low tone. 'Let us sit down over there, my dear, I have some thoughts to offer.'

Diedre glanced at her swiftly. 'I hope you like him, Great-Aunt Gwendolyn. I think he's special.'

'So do I,' her aunt responded. 'And, as the matriarch of this family, I would certainly be happy to welcome him into it, let me assure you of that.'

Diedre gave her a huge smile.

The two of them settled down in a corner of the room, near the bay window. Lady Gwendolyn said, 'You never told me he'd been married before. And that he was a widower.'

'We haven't had much chance to speak about him, Great-Aunt Gwendolyn,' Diedre pointed out, giving her aunt a faint smile. 'I'm just getting to know him myself.'

'I know. I'm not taking you to task, my dear, simply making a comment. When did she die? And of what?' Lady Gwendolyn asked in a quiet voice.

'He never explained anything. Paul merely said he was a widower. And before we . . . well, before we became involved, I didn't know anything at all. Because I was hardly ever at Cavendon.'

'More's the pity. I missed you. And Paul wasn't around. He was looking after Hugo's American interests and living in New York. I truly do understand.'

Lady Gwendolyn paused, sat back in the chair, was thoughtful for a moment or two. Finally, bending forward, leaning closer to her great-niece, she said softly, 'Did he ask you any questions? About your previous relationships?'

Diedre stared at her aunt, shook her head. 'He asked me if I had ever been married, and I said no. I did add that I had been in a couple of relationships, and left it at that.'

'He didn't ask you any questions about other men?'

'No,' Diedre murmured, frowning at her aunt.

'Smart man. And you were smart not to volunteer anything, Diedre. At least I'm assuming you didn't. You didn't, did you?'

'To be honest, Aunt Gwendolyn, there wasn't much to tell. And we became involved so unexpectedly, it never occurred to me to question him about his late wife. I didn't want to know about her. And I'm sure he felt the same.'

Lady Gwendolyn sat back, smiling at Diedre, filled with relief. 'Is it serious?'

'I'm not sure. It's too soon to tell,' Diedre said evasively.

There was a small silence.

Diedre glanced around the room and saw that Cecily and DeLacy were sitting together on the sofa. She was glad that these two old friends had made peace with each other. Cecily was a good influence on DeLacy. Diedre loved her younger sister, but she knew she was still upset about her divorce, and needed the support of a loving and genuine friend like Ceci Swann. They were happily chatting, as if they'd never been estranged.

Dulcie hovered in the doorway of the room, and when her eyes caught Diedre's she smiled, waved and moved towards her. She now loved Diedre, and had always thought that Great-Aunt Gwendolyn was very special; she enjoyed their company.

'I rather like the idea of the women getting to spend time together after dinner, don't you?' Dulcie laughed and winked at Great-Aunt Gwendolyn. 'We can talk about things men don't actually understand. They're so dense in certain ways.'

'You've never spoken a truer word, Dulcie. However, they are also rather sweet, and definitely essential, don't you think?' Lady Gwendolyn gave her a knowing look and winked back.

Dulcie burst out laughing. 'You're such a treat, Great-Aunt Gwen. There's nobody like you. Oh, here's Daphne, and she's looking very serious. She told me she had something special to tell us.'

Daphne closed the door firmly behind her and walked over to the fireplace, where she stood staring at the women of the family gathered there. They had been served coffee, tea and water, and some even had liqueurs. They looked comfortable and relaxed, and this pleased her.

Daphne said, 'All of us here are fully aware that some of the Ingham jewels are missing, and understand full well who the culprit is. I promised Papa I would get them back. And I shall.'

Without any further preamble, she filled them in about Felicity's return to London, her Friday teatime chat with Olive Wilson, and her plan to steal the jewellery with Wilson's help. And, perhaps, a burglar, if they were not given to her voluntarily.

Her sisters laughed when she told them about needing the lock of a cupboard to be picked, while Great-Aunt Gwendolyn looked askance when Daphne added that Eric would be looking for an experienced burglar to assist them.

'You must confront your mother before Wilson leaves,'

Cecily exclaimed. 'You need her. She's the best witness you have. She can corroborate what you say.'

Daphne nodded, wondering whether Wilson would remain strong, or lose her nerve.

Lady Gwendolyn said, 'I think Cecily is right. Wilson is the vital element in this matter. I also think you should be armed with a legal letter from our solicitors, a demand for the return of the "borrowed jewels", shall we call them? So that Felicity could save face.'

'Why not start out first in a friendly way?' Cecily suggested, looking around the room, finally fixing her eyes on Daphne. 'You told me you and your mother have been estranged, so perhaps someone else has to make an overture, go to see her, and—'

'I had tea with Mama yesterday,' DeLacy announced, cutting in and taking everyone by surprise, including Cecily.

Dulcie cried, 'Why didn't you tell us you'd seen that monstrous woman?'

'I haven't had a chance,' DeLacy protested. She looked stricken, stared at Daphne. 'I tried to telephone you this morning, and this afternoon. Your phone has been perpetually busy.'

'It's all right, DeLacy, I understand,' Daphne answered gently. 'So, please do tell us how this tea came about. And give us a picture of Mama, and what's happening at Charles Street.'

When DeLacy remained silent, looking around nervously and twisting her hands in her lap, Daphne walked across the room and sat down in a chair nearby. DeLacy had always been sensitive and fragile of nature; since the divorce she had become nervous and easily upset.

Reaching out, holding DeLacy's hand, she said, 'Take your time, darling, nobody's in a hurry or about to leave. Just be relaxed and tell us slowly.'

DeLacy nodded, gave her sister a small smile. She had been close to Daphne since childhood, and was devoted to her, understood how kind and compassionate she was. It was Daphne she trusted wholeheartedly.

Taking a deep breath, DeLacy began, 'It all came about like this. A few weeks ago I was feeling lonely, very sad, and I suddenly thought of Mama. I realized that over the years I had missed her from time to time. I know she behaved badly . . .' DeLacy paused and cleared her throat. 'She ran away because of another man and, well, she abandoned her children. All of us. Still, I did have an unexpected longing to see her, to talk to her.' There was another pause.

Then she began to speak again. 'At first I thought of phoning her. But I sort of, well, I lost my nerve I suppose. So I wrote her a letter instead, telling her that I would like to see her, to catch up over tea. The note was brief and simple, but friendly. I didn't get a reply.'

'Did you go to see her?' Dulcie asked, staring hard at DeLacy, not exactly happy to learn that her sister had weakened in her resolve, had broken the promise they had all made to each other years ago: that they would limit their availability to their mother.

But DeLacy has seemed bewildered and lost since the breakup of her marriage, Dulcie now thought, and she said quickly, 'Please tell us about it, DeLacy. I'm so sorry I interrupted you.'

'Out of the blue, I received a phone call late on Saturday morning,' DeLacy explained. 'It was Lawrence, inviting me to tea that day—'

'Lawrence,' Diedre exclaimed. 'Do you mean her frightful husband? You call him Lawrence?'

DeLacy simply nodded, withdrawing again, noting the angry tone in Diedre's voice. She suddenly wished she hadn't told them.

Daphne was fully aware of this and of DeLacy's growing nervousness, and she said somewhat sternly, 'Please let DeLacy speak without any interruptions. That only makes her more anxious. And it is very important for me to hear what she knows. Come along, darling, do continue.' As she spoke, Daphne reached out again and took DeLacy's hand in hers, giving her an encouraging smile.

'Lawrence Pierce sounded very cordial on the phone, and said if that afternoon wasn't convenient, I could go for tea on Sunday. I chose to go on Saturday because I was coming to this supper tonight. And I did try to get hold of you, Daphne, to tell you.'

'I remember the phone was busy a lot . . . Hugo was using it, and so was I. But no one is being critical of you, darling.'

'I know. So I went to tea. Mama was lovely. She's had bronchitis, and she appeared to be somewhat . . . fragile. That's the best word. She's still beautiful, you know. I told her about my divorce and Simon, and she and Lawrence were so nice, and sympathetic. Later they spoke about their holiday in Monte Carlo. That was it, more or less. Mama did ask about everyone, but I didn't reveal too much. Oh, and she was very nice about your success, Ceci.'

'I bet she didn't ask about me,' Dulcie exclaimed. 'And, do tell us, what's the crazy knife-wielding surgeon really like in the flesh?'

Everyone laughed, DeLacy included, who said, 'He's pleasant, and he does have a certain charm. Very handsome. Nobody's exaggerated about that. But there was something about him that I couldn't quite fathom.'

'What do you mean, DeLacy?' Lady Gwendolyn suddenly looked perturbed. 'He doesn't have a very nice reputation. So I've been given to understand.' She scrutinized DeLacy intently.

'It's nothing like that, nothing strange. Or nasty. I suppose he's distracted, I think that's the best way of describing his demeanour. It's as if he's extremely preoccupied, and that his mind is on other things.'

Diedre remarked, her eyes narrowing: 'In my experience, anyone who displays those traits is highly involved in something, is focused on that and nothing else. The body is there, but the mind is absent. Do you understand what I mean, DeLacy?'

'I do. And you've described him perfectly. He was absent mentally. That's it.'

'How did he treat your mother?' Lady Gwendolyn probed.

'He's nice with her, courteous, Great-Aunt Gwendolyn. But . . .' DeLacy's voice trailed off, and she bit her lip.

Leaning into her, Cecily said, 'There's something else, isn't there, DeLacy? Something you're not saying.'

DeLacy stared at Cecily, then looked across at Daphne, her face suddenly filling with sadness. 'He doesn't seem interested in her as a woman. She is very affectionate with him, loving actually, but he's not like that with her.'

Lady Gwendolyn said, 'I'm sure Felicity is still romantically involved with him, is still in love with him. However, it is quite possible he does not have those same feelings.'

No one spoke for a moment. Finally Daphne broke the silence. 'It sounds as if he's lost interest in her. Sexually. And perhaps that preoccupation you mentioned, DeLacy, is with another woman.'

'How about women, plural? I've heard he's a real chaser of skirts,' Dulcie exclaimed, and laughed. 'You know what they say . . . revenge is a dish best served cold. And if he's got another woman and doesn't love his wife, then this is my moment of revenge. She abandoned me at the age of six, and I've waited a long time for this moment. Revenge served cold can also be very sweet.'

THIRTY-ONE

DeLacy sat at the small desk in her bedroom, writing a letter to her father. She missed him, and would be much happier when he returned to England. He had been away far too long for her liking. He was the rock of her life, as he was for all his children. Somehow she felt safer when he was around. More secure.

She sat back in the chair, suddenly thinking of her mother. Felicity had been so warm and loving at tea, she had been quite startled by her demeanour, but had responded with warmth herself.

She grimaced. Now she was to be the pawn in the plan to get the jewels back, and she dreaded the thought. She would do it, though, because Felicity was in the wrong. And she was on the side of the Ingham Estate; after all, she was an Ingham born and bred, and would protect their interests.

The ringing of the phone brought her up with a start; she reached for it and said, 'Hello?' in a quiet voice.

'May I speak to Lady DeLacy, please?'

It was a masculine voice, and she knew at once that it was Lawrence Pierce. Whatever could he want? 'This is Lady DeLacy,' she said. 'It is you, Lawrence, isn't it?'

'Yes,' he replied, sounding pleased that she had recognized his voice.

'How are you?' DeLacy asked politely, and quickly added, 'Having tea with Mama and you was so nice.'

'Yes she, we, enjoyed it too. Your mother was thrilled that you approached her, DeLacy. The reason I am calling is to do with your mother, actually. I've been trying to think of a present for her, something that would be a genuine surprise. And I've come up with an idea that is wonderful, in my opinion. But it would involve you.'

'Oh,' she answered, sounding surprised. 'What is it?'

'A portrait of you, DeLacy. Which would be painted by Travers Merton. Have you heard of him?'

'He's very famous. A fantastic artist. But why me? Why not one of my sisters?'

'In many ways you are the closest to her, DeLacy. You must be aware of that.'

'No, I'm not.'

'Diedre is somewhat aloof. Daphne is your father's . . . possession, in a certain sense. And always was. And by the time she had Dulcie she had met me . . .' He wisely let his voice peter off, said no more.

'Perhaps you're right, and if you think my mother would want a portrait of me, I would be willing to sit for it.'

'Thank you, DeLacy, I am glad. Obviously, I must now get in touch with Merton and commission him to do the portrait. I am sure he will be thrilled. He enjoys painting beautiful women. Don't forget this is a secret, so your mother mustn't know. Otherwise, it won't be a surprise.'

'I understand. Just one question, Lawrence. If Mr Merton agrees to paint me, will it be immediately? Oh, and where would he do it?'

'If he's available, I will ask him to start as soon as possible, and I imagine you would have to go to his studio to sit. That is the usual procedure.'

'I understand.'

'You are going to be in town for a while, aren't you, DeLacy?'

'Yes, I am.'

'That's good, and I will be in touch by the end of this week.'

Dulcie sat in Cecily's office at the main shop in the Burlington Arcade. 'The reason I want to work here for a while is because I want to open my own shop one day.'

She had taken Cecily by surprise, who exclaimed, 'Your own shop? Selling what?'

'It would be a gallery really, and I would be offering paintings, *objets d'art* and certain pieces of antique furniture.'

'You're just finishing your art history course. So why do you want to go into commerce?' Cecily asked.

'Because I want to work. I don't want to lead a life of indolence and social boredom. And I want to make money, to be self-supporting.' Dulcie said this in such a firm voice, and sounded so determined, she had gained Cecily's entire attention.

'That's very admirable of you, but what will your father say?'

'I don't know. When I told Daphne, she was a little shocked, and warned me that Great-Aunt Gwendolyn would be horrified.' Dulcie laughed and made a face. 'I'm not so sure Daphers is right. I think Great-Aunt Gwendolyn might well approve – she's a good sport.' A little sigh escaped, and Dulcie added, 'Cavendon is a thief, you know. It steals the money Hugo makes on the family investments. So I want to help.'

Cecily digested these remarks, and was silent for a moment. She had long known things were not the same at Cavendon Hall and that money was short. So many different elements had depleted its finances. Finally, she said carefully, 'Are you saying that Cavendon is now really in trouble?'

'No, no, I'm not. But there is a big overhead. That's why Daphne keeps making the cuts. You know, getting rid of the two footmen and the cook at Grosvenor Square. And she's forever telling Hanson we're on a budget. And we're managing. I just want to be useful, help out if I can.'

'I understand. How will you find your product? The paintings and furniture? That might be difficult, and you do need some sort of inventory,' Cecily said.

Dulcie leaned forward and explained, 'The attics here in London – and at Cavendon Hall – are jammed with paintings, other objects and antiques. I'm going to use those for the gallery, and find other things as I go along.'

'Will your father allow that?'

'I intend to persuade him. And I can be very persuasive.'

Cecily turned and looked at the door as it opened; Dorothy stood there. 'You'll never guess who's just arrived?' she said, sounding especially pleased.

'Don't make me guess.'

'It's Lady Diedre, and she has Paul Drummond in tow. They wish to see you. Shall I send them up?'

'Of course.' Cecily rose and walked into the middle of her office. Glancing at Dulcie, she asked, 'Is that relationship serious?'

'Nobody seems to know. Diedre is secretive, and not a bit confiding at all. Perhaps because she doesn't know herself how she feels.'

A moment later, Diedre and Paul came into the office and Cecily greeted them, kissing Diedre on the cheek and shaking Paul's hand.

'How nice to see you,' she said.

Diedre said, 'Paul so admires your dresses. He wants to give me one as a present. Can we look at some?'

'How lovely,' Cecily said. 'Let's go down to the next floor

and we'll show you the Winter Collection. I know there are things you will like, and which will suit you.'

Diedre smiled at her, and then at Paul. 'This is such a treat,' she said to him.

Dulcie took hold of Cecily's arm and whispered, 'Can I please work here for a while? Learn the ropes?'

Cecily put an arm around Dulcie's shoulders, full of affection for her. 'You can start right now,' she answered. 'Come with me.'

Travers Merton stood staring at Lawrence Pierce, who had just arrived at his studio in Chelsea. 'Obviously, you're not slicing into someone's flesh today,' he said, grinning at his closest friend. 'So, what brings you over here? Just a social visit, Pierce? Or what? Knowing you as well as I do, I have the distinct feeling it might be about a woman.'

Lawrence Pierce did not respond. He walked across the studio and leaned against the mantelpiece, his expression neutral. The studio was a spacious room with big windows at one end, filled with perfect light. Just the kind of light a painter required, and couldn't properly work without.

Finally, Pierce said, 'I have a commission for you, Merton. If you're interested.'

'Depends what it is, old boy. I hope it's not another nude of one of your women. I'm a bit sick of those, and where the hell do you keep them? I've often wondered that.'

Travers Merton said this in such an odd voice that Lawrence Pierce couldn't help but be amused. He smiled. 'You've made good money with me. And what I do with the paintings is none of your business.'

'How about a spot of bubbly to seal the deal?' Travers said.

'Why not? I don't have surgery tomorrow. I was thinking of a night out on the town. Are you free? Want to go slumming with me? We might duck into a couple of places we both know well, find a few fancy women to heat up our loins.'

Travers Merton burst out laughing. 'You do have the oddest expressions. In the meantime, let me get a bottle of bubbles to cheer us on our way. You know I'll come with you. I enjoy sharing your escapades.'

There was a small flat attached to the huge studio, and Travers went into the kitchen, opened a bottle of Dom Pérignon and filled two champagne flutes. Only the best for Lawrence Pierce, he thought, be it wine, women or song . . . he chuckled.

A second or two later he was handing a flute of champagne to the famous surgeon, and couldn't help thinking what beautiful hands he had. He'd noticed them before, but they seemed unusually elegant today. Perfect for wielding a scalpel, and also to be painted. He suddenly had the idea of doing that: pale hands clasped, resting on black velvet. He would do it, and give the painting to his friend. Travers knew it would please Pierce, who had quite an ego.

The two men touched their glasses, said cheers, and took a swallow. Lawrence Pierce had a reflective look on his face when he said, 'I want you to do a painting for me, Merton. Of my wife's daughter, Lady DeLacy Ingham.'

Travers looked at him swiftly, 'Not a nude, then?'

Pierce said nothing, swilled some of the champagne. 'No, not a nude,' he answered at last. 'A portrait. For Felicity. A surprise gift for Christmas, if you can have it finished by then.'

The painter nodded, intrigued, and asked, 'What does Lady DeLacy look like? Does she resemble Felicity?'

'No. None of her daughters does. They're all Inghams, through and through. And DeLacy is the most beautiful woman I've ever seen in my life. Glorious. Golden hair, the deepest of blue eyes and a perfect complexion. There's something about her that is quite . . . intoxicating. Wait until you set eyes on her, Merton, you'll be startled. She'll knock your socks off.' Lawrence turned to face the artist and chuckled.

Travers stared at Lawrence. 'Does she do that to you, old chap? Knock your socks off? Is that why you're bringing her here? To me. To soften her up for you? Like I've done so many times in the past? Teach a few tricks? Because I'll be delighted to romp with her. And I'll paint her as well.'

'Nothing like that, Travers, just paint her portrait. You see, this one is forbidden. She's my stepdaughter, for God's sake.'

'Scruples? You? Come off it, my lad. I wouldn't trust you alone with any woman anywhere. You're insatiable.'

'Not this one, Travers. Understood?' He stared the artist down, and then a slow smile spread across his face. 'But you can court Lucy, if you wish. It's all over between us, and I know she's been keen as mustard about you for quite a while.'

'How do you know that?'

'She's told me. Many times.'

'Then why don't we go to see her later?'

Lawrence Pierce shook his head. 'I feel like going out on the town tonight. And if you think about it, you do too.'

'I have to admit you're right,' Travers Merton said, smiling in anticipation.

THIRTY-TWO

Lady Gwendolyn realized, quite unexpectedly, that she was going to be rather busy today. Starting in the late afternoon yesterday, she had received phone calls from two of her great-nieces, and Mark Stanton, all of them asking to see her today. And then this morning, quite early, Inspector Pinkerton had phoned to tell her he had information for her. And that he needed to speak to her in person.

Staring at herself in the mirror on her dressing table, Lady Gwendolyn put on pearl earrings, adjusted the pearl brooch on her navy blue jacket and then nodded to herself. She looked businesslike, yet without being too severe in appearance, and this pleased her.

Rising, she went into the small parlour where she preferred to receive visitors.

Lady Gwendolyn, nobody's fool, fully understood that her great-nieces were running to her for advice of some kind because Charles was still in Zurich. Otherwise they would have sought out their father. Nonetheless, it pleased her that they came to her, the matriarch of the family. She was looking forward to seeing them.

As for Mark Stanton, he no doubt wanted to speak to her about Lavinia. She couldn't help wondering how serious that relationship was. And she was curious, too, about Howard Pinkerton's visit, arranged for later in the afternoon, eager to know what he had found out.

Glancing around the room, she was pleased to see that her housekeeper had a fire blazing in the hearth and had put fresh flowers in the vases. The parlour was her favourite room. It had a handsome Georgian desk, overflowing bookshelves, and comfortable overstuffed sofas and chairs. A mellow room, with its antique pieces set against deep rose walls; this was the dominant colour, repeated in the heavy brocade draperies at the tall windows, and in the fabrics used for the sofas and chairs.

Since it was a gloomy, overcast day, Lady Gwendolyn went around turning on the pale pink silk-shaded lamps, and then sat down to wait for Dulcie, who was usually on time. As the carriage clock on the mantelpiece struck ten, the doorbell was ringing.

A few moments later, Dulcie came rushing into the parlour, a huge smile on her face. 'Good morning, Great-Aunt Gwendolyn!' she cried, kissing her aunt on the cheek.

'Hello, my dear. The parlour is very cosy on this dull morning. In a moment Mrs Fontaine will bring us tea. Or would you prefer coffee?'

'Tea is fine, thank you,' Dulcie answered. She sat down on the opposite sofa, and said, 'I came to test the waters with you, Great-Aunt Gwendolyn. Before I speak to Papa. I don't want to go romping around on a project of mine, and then find out I've blundered into a bog like a blind bull and am sinking fast.'

Lady Gwendolyn shook her head. 'My goodness, Dulcie, your language does get colourful at times. So what is it you wish to discuss?'

Leaning forward, clasping her hands together, Dulcie fastened her eyes on her great-aunt, and said, 'I will be finishing my art history course at the end of November, and I know what I would like to do. But I wanted to pass it by you first, because Daphne said you wouldn't approve. Which means Papa might not either.'

'And what do you wish to do, my dear?'

'I want to open a shop. Oh, dash, I shouldn't call it that, Cecily said. Let me correct myself. I want to open an art gallery. What do you think?'

'Cecily's right, it is certainly better to call it that. A shop resonates of tradespeople, don't you think?'

'I do now.'

Lady Gwendolyn was about to say that she thought Dulcie was a bit young to start a business, then instantly changed her mind. Telling an Ingham they were too young to do something was always a mistake. They were not only headstrong but wilful. Anyway, Dulcie would be nineteen soon. She said, 'Do you have a business partner? Someone who will run this gallery with you?'

'I have a financial partner, and that's Ceci. She's putting up a good deal of money, and will advise me.'

'That's very admirable of her. And she does have a good head on her shoulders. She must believe you can pull this off.'

'I can. But I need your help with Papa. You see, I think he will object to another aspect of my project.'

'What is that?'

'I want to sell a lot of the paintings, antiques and *objets d'art* stored in the attics of Cavendon Hall and the Grosvenor Square house. It would all be my inventory.'

'Good Lord, Dulcie, that's rather a startling proposition! I don't know how to answer you. I can't second-guess Charles.' She paused, shook her head. 'I have a feeling he won't allow you to do that.'

'I believe it's economically impractical to store all those things nobody uses or needs when they could be sold. I would like to support myself, but I also want to help Daphne. She works hard at keeping Cavendon afloat.'

'I know, and I also realize what a great help Hugo is, and Paul Drummond. Also, Miles is learning fast, and he is helping to put the estate on a good footing.'

'Cecily told me Cavendon should be run as a business, and not as a family home only.' Dulcie sat back, waiting for the explosion.

Lady Gwendolyn did look startled, and exclaimed, 'What on earth does she mean? It is a family home. Ours.'

'Yes, and she doesn't mean it shouldn't be that. However, she thinks Cavendon should earn its keep.'

'How? What else did she say?'

'To answer your first question, she thinks my gallery would be a good start, getting rid of all the things stored away. Now, here's another thing. She's heard that some aristocratic families are thinking about opening their stately homes to the public. You know, inviting people to tour the house, and charging an entrance fee . . .' Dulcie stopped abruptly when she saw the shock sweeping across her aunt's face.

After a moment, Lady Gwendolyn said in a somewhat tremulous voice, 'Allow the public to tramp around Cavendon Hall? That's outrageous, Dulcie! And what if they steal something?'

'They can't very well carry out a Hepplewhite table, now can they?' was Dulcie's rapid response.

'There are all sorts of small objects of value around on table tops, like the Fabergé collection of snuff boxes, things like that,' Lady Gwendolyn pointed out, sounding anxious. Her face had paled and her hands were clasped tightly.

'Yes, I know, and we did talk about that. Cecily said certain areas, mostly the rooms where the family actually live, should be closed off. And other more general areas could be roped off, but made easy to view. We have so many treasures; I think other people would enjoy seeing them. Learning about our history, the history of Cavendon.'

'I understand. Still, I'm afraid you'll have to give me time to get used to having strangers roaming around Cavendon Hall and Cavendon Park. It's rather a lot to take in, Dulcie.'

'I know. However, Cecily suggested that the public must be accompanied by a guide, a person to explain the house, talk about the paintings, the family portraits by such famous artists as Gainsborough, Lely, and others. They would be led on a guided tour.'

Dulcie paused for a moment, finally finished, 'I know it's shocked you, Great-Aunt. But I do think we have to look ahead, to the future. In the coming years there will be death duties, and other taxes, as well as the cost of upkeep and repairs to the house.'

Lady Gwendolyn sighed, knowing that Dulcie spoke the truth. She tried to adjust her mind to the thought of allowing the public to come into Cavendon. The rooms where Charles and his family lived were sacrosanct, private. Yet, deep down, she was genuinely convinced that Cecily Swann was the most brilliant woman she had ever known. Her extraordinary talent and successful business proved that.

After a moment, Lady Gwendolyn broke the silence. 'Let me think about this suggestion, Dulcie. Perhaps then I can help you with your father. First, you must win Charlotte over to your side. She has the greatest influence with him, and always has.'

'So you do think it's a good idea?' Dulcie raised a blonde brow questioningly.

'Perhaps. But I must adjust to it. And certainly your father will have to be convinced. By the way, what about strangers wandering in the park?'

'Cecily thought of that, too. She said we would have to use some of the outdoor workers as sort of . . . wardens. That's what she called them. She said they would have to wear a uniform, and a badge that said "Cavendon Hall" on it. She also told me of an idea Harry had. I think that's brilliant too.'

Lady Gwendolyn's ears pricked up when she heard the name of her favourite. 'What is Harry's idea?' she asked, sitting up straighter.

'As you well know, we have a carpentry shop at Cavendon. They make many things, such as tubs for plants and flowers, garden seats, buckets for logs and a variety of smaller things. Harry thought people might want to order some of those items. If there was a shop selling them.' Dulcie smiled. 'Harry is awfully clever, don't you think, Great-Aunt Gwendolyn?'

'He is, and he's a truly talented gardener. I miss him,' Lady Gwendolyn said. 'So it would be an actual shop? On the grounds?'

'I'm not sure. Cecily said orders could be taken and the work fulfilled by Ted Swann, who is head of carpentry and maintenance at Cavendon, as you know. Say something, Great-Aunt, you're looking shell-shocked again.'

'Not so much shocked as impressed. As the saying goes around here, "Whatever would the Inghams do without the Swanns?" Let's face it, they're invaluable.'

Dulcie noticed that this had been said in a more light-hearted way, and she felt certain her aunt would in the end be her ally. She prayed she would. Now she said, 'Oh, and by the way, Cecily has agreed to let me work at the main shop in the Burlington Arcade. Just to learn the ropes, and also to understand what it's like to deal with the public. I hope that doesn't upset you, Great-Aunt Gwen?'

'On the contrary, I think it is quite remarkable – laudable on your part, Dulcie. Your devotion to Cavendon and its future is most impressive.'

Lady Gwendolyn rose, and went to sit next to her great-niece, taking hold of her hand. 'I am very proud of you and your initiative. Ingham women before you, and before me, actually, have always stood tall. As you do in my eyes today. As for Cecily Swann, I shall telephone her myself and thank her personally for her immense loyalty to this family.'

'Thank you for those lovely words,' Dulcie murmured, leaning closer, kissing her aunt's cheek. 'Ceci will be so happy. She loves you too.'

A short while later, Mrs Fontaine brought in the tea tray and departed. Lady Gwendolyn liked to pour the tea herself, and did so now, then said, 'Mark Stanton's coming to see me in a short while, and I've not an inkling why. Have you heard anything about Lavinia? Or them? On our grapevine?'

'No, nothing. But she got cut off by us. You know that. Because of the way she spoke about Charlotte. Everyone was furious with her. She's no longer a member of the inner circle.'

'But she's not cut out of the family,' Lady Gwendolyn asserted.

'That's true. On the other hand, perhaps she's decided she's better off without us.'

THIRTY-THREE

Lady Gwendolyn was full of admiration for Dulcie, impressed with her determination to work and to help Cavendon in doing so. Her great-niece had also given her a lot to consider, and on a very serious level.

She sat in front of the fire, thinking about the attics at Little Skell Manor in Cavendon Park, where she lived. They were full of discarded items, all valuable, that could be sold. She would have them sorted when she was next in Yorkshire. Something told her Dulcie would indeed have her art gallery, and in the not-too-distant future.

Standing up, she went over to the Georgian desk, sat down and took out her notebook, jotted in it a few important things she had to do.

Lady Gwendolyn now knew she must change her will, and to do so she must go and see her solicitor next week. She must also telephone Charlotte in Zurich to ask when she and Charles would be coming home. And she must visit Cecily at her Burlington Arcade shop, not only to thank her personally for giving good advice to Dulcie, but to buy the Kimono Set she had so admired on Daphne. Cecily would tell her the truth . . . whether it suited her or not. Ceci Swann. True blue. She would trust Cecily with her life.

A moment later the doorbell was ringing, which told her that Mark Stanton had arrived. Mrs Fontaine brought him into the parlour just as she was walking across the room to greet him.

'Let's go and sit in here, by the fire,' Lady Gwendolyn suggested, smiling at him. She liked Mark, and always had; he reminded her of Hugo, not only in appearance, but also in his manner. She had watched the cousins growing up together as young boys.

'It's a good day for a fire, Lady Gwendolyn,' Mark said. 'Very gloomy outside, and I'm afraid it's going to rain later.'

The two of them sat down on the sofas facing each other. Mark began to speak immediately, knowing that Lady Gwendolyn liked to get right to the heart of a matter, and at once. He said, 'You must have guessed I've come about Lavinia.'

'Yes,' Lady Gwendolyn answered. 'I haven't seen her since the wedding in July. How is she?'

'Doing quite well, actually. My reason for being here is because I would like your advice. Also, I want you to intervene in a particular situation. So it's twofold.'

'I will do anything I can to help you, Mark; I have been very fond of you for years. And of course, I love Lavinia. Please tell me what's on your mind. I must admit, you do look worried – and a little weary, I might add.'

Mark nodded, settled back against the sofa. He said quietly, 'I want you to know that I have been in love with Lavinia for years. But she was married to Jack, and there was no way I would approach a woman with a husband, however much I cared about her. Not my style.'

'So you loved her in silence, and she never noticed you. Am I right?' Lady Gwendolyn gave him a speculative look.

Surprised by her words, Mark exclaimed, 'How did you know that?'

'I just made a guess. That's often the way it is in life.

Someone can love from afar, hoping and praying the object of their desire might one day notice them and see it all very clearly.'

'It was something like that. And then Jack died. I don't wish anybody ill, and I was sorry he had passed away. He was a nice man, very entertaining. Anyway, as much as I loved her, I believed it would be inappropriate to make any kind of approach. Lavinia was in mourning. So I just got on with work, hoping.'

'I understand,' Lady Gwendolyn murmured. 'Do go on.'

'It was at the wedding in July that I finally decided the time was right. I saw her standing alone, admiring the indoor garden that Harry Swann had made, and I just took my courage in both hands and went over to her. She seemed happy to see me, to talk to me. We spent the evening together. And I knew I was going to pursue her, no matter what. No one, nothing was going to stop me now. And so I did precisely that.'

Lady Gwendolyn studied him for a few seconds. 'That night she understood, and succumbed to you?'

Mark shook his head. 'Not exactly. But she realized how much I loved her, because I told her everything. My yearning for her over the years; the longing I felt whenever I saw her. And how I couldn't stay away from Cavendon, when Hugo invited me, knowing she would be there. I told her that was why I'd never married. I love her with all my heart, you see.'

Lady Gwendolyn believed him, recognized his passion and sincerity. 'Does Lavinia love you, Mark?'

'Yes, she does. The problem is, she won't marry me. And it's destroying me. I want to live with her, take care of her, provide for her. But she won't say yes, won't give in.'

'That's extremely odd, if she cares about you.' Lady Gwendolyn scowled, puzzlement in her eyes. Throwing

Mark a keener look, she asked, 'You want me to advise you. But perhaps you think I can persuade her to marry you? That's what you really mean. Why is that?'

'Because she respects you. She will listen to you.'

Lady Gwendolyn shook her head. 'I simply don't understand what's holding her back. Why won't she agree to become your wife?'

Mark took a deep breath. 'She doesn't want anyone in the family to know this, but she is ill, Lady Gwen, very ill. She says she doesn't want to be a burden to me.'

'I knew it!' Lady Gwendolyn exclaimed, her chest tightening. 'I just knew it, Mark, and at Charles's wedding. She didn't look well. Lavinia seemed so drained and I asked her if she was all right, but she kept saying she was, that she was just tired. I felt instinctively that she was poorly. Oh, why didn't I pay more attention?' Tears glistened in Lady Gwendolyn's eyes.

'It wouldn't have done any good; she's very stubborn and awfully independent.'

'It's serious, isn't it?' Lady Gwendolyn's voice trembled as she spoke.

He nodded. 'She has a tumour in her lung. It's small. The cancer was caught in the early stages. I found her the best specialists, the best doctors in the world. And the finest treatment. I'm hoping she will get better. I pray for her. But what do you think I should do?'

'I don't know. However, do you want me to see her? Is she in hospital? Or at home?'

'Not in hospital now, although she has been. She's at home. And actually she's looking so much better.' He leaned forward, focused on her. 'Even if Lavinia has only a year or two left, I want to be with her . . .'

His voice broke and he cut off his sentence. Sitting up, he blinked and took control of himself. 'I love her so much, you see.'

'And she's very lucky that you do, Mark. I will make a great attempt to get you both to the altar.' Her smile was a little quavery, but she took herself in hand, pushed back her flaring emotions. She said, 'What else did you wish me to do? You said it was twofold?'

'I want you to talk to the family. It's broken her heart that they cut her out of the inner family circle. She did apologize to everyone at the time, and tried hard to make amends. But it didn't work. Please, Lady Gwendolyn, you are the matriarch of this family. Tell them they must allow her to come back. She does not have all that long left on this planet. It would be so cruel to keep her at arm's length as they've been doing.'

'It would, most especially under the circumstances. I will talk to them, I promise. If necessary, I will telephone Charles in Zurich. I will speak to Daphne tomorrow: at the moment she rules the roost, so to speak, with her father away.'

'Thank you so very much, Lady Gwendolyn. I can't tell you how relieved I am that I confided in you.'

'There's just one thing, Mark,' Lady Gwendolyn said, shaking her head, letting out a small sigh. 'I will have to tell them she's ill, you know. Otherwise, they may not agree to forgive her and bring her back.'

There was a long silence. 'So be it,' he said at last.

'Speak to Lavinia; tell her I would love to see her, be friends. I'll take her to lunch, or she can come here, whichever she prefers. Mark, please tell her I am truly on her side. That I will pray for her.'

'Thank you,' Mark responded, feeling as if a great weight had been lifted, now that he had the matriarch of the Inghams on his side.

Lady Gwendolyn ventured, 'I wonder if I can ask you something now?'

'But of course, anything. How can I be of help?'

'I heard a rather strange thing . . . that certain aristocrats who are having financial problems are opening their stately homes to the public, providing guided tours. Have you heard of this?'

'As a matter of fact, I have. Well, a sort of whiff of it. I know John Bailey slightly. He's the chairman of the National Trust, which was founded mostly to protect open spaces. But now the Trust is talking about helping to preserve country houses and gardens. Not a bad thing, in my opinion.'

'I suppose the guided tours do make money?' Lady Gwendolyn threw him a questioning glance.

'I think so. If you wish, I could endeavour to find out more.'

'I would like that, Mark. But please, let's keep this between us. Don't mention it to anyone, not even Lavinia.'

'You have my word.'

After Mark Stanton left, looking more cheerful than when he had arrived, Lady Gwendolyn went back to her Georgian desk. For a long time she stared at her notebook, but did not pick up her pen. Instead her thoughts took over, and she sat staring out of the window, lost in contemplation.

It had started to rain but she barely noticed it. Her mind was on Lavinia. Knowing her niece the way she did, she realized that Lavinia would not want to be a burden to Mark. It was the way she was made – the Ingham way, actually.

The man plainly loved her, very much so. Surely his love, kindness and devotion would help her through this terrible ordeal. Perhaps I can make her see this more clearly, she thought, sighing under her breath, filled with love and compassion for her niece.

Lady Gwendolyn fully understood how hurtful it must

be for Lavinia to have been cut out of the inner circle of the family. She had been in the centre of it all her life. On the other hand, Lavinia had said things about Charlotte which weren't acceptable. Everyone had been shocked and offended by those awful remarks.

A thought struck her. Maybe Lavinia's illness, and the pain she was most likely suffering, had been responsible for the curious nastiness she had displayed. Whatever Lavinia was, she had never been a mean or unkind person. Quite the contrary.

Now she wondered how she would manage to persuade the family to relent. Only by telling them the truth. They would have to know that Lavinia was ill, suffering from cancer.

Slowly it came to her. A plan. She would have to make a point of speaking to every member of the family, but alone. One by one. They would fall in line, she hoped and prayed. She had to be persuasive.

She knew that Lavinia needed a little tender loving care at this time in her life . . . surely the last part of her life.

Tears suddenly flooded Lady Gwendolyn's eyes, and she wept inconsolably for her niece, no longer able to hold them back. Far too young to be struck down like this; far too young to die. Unable to stem the tears, she rose and went into her bedroom, closed the door, and lay down on the bed. And she continued to weep into her pillow as if her heart would break.

Eventually she calmed herself, got off the bed, and went into the bathroom. She wiped her eyes, washed her face, combed her hair and put on fresh lipstick. She always wore lipstick in defiance of her age. And life.

Returning to the parlour, she sat down at the old desk and wrote her notes, answered letters, and made several phone calls.

Life must go on, she reminded herself. Later today she would be having tea with Diedre, and then Inspector Pinkerton was coming to see her. With new information about Diedre's problem. She must be on her toes, on top form to deal with them both.

THIRTY-FOUR

'Dulcie! I didn't expect to see you here,' Diedre exclaimed as she entered Cecily Swann Couture in the Burlington Arcade and closed the door behind her.

'Oh, hello, Diedre. I'm going to be working here for a while. You see, I will soon be opening my own shop – or rather, an art gallery. Ceci's teaching me the ropes, you know: how to handle customers, all that sort of thing.'

Diedre was genuinely surprised. 'Opening an art gallery! Goodness, that's awfully ambitious of you, darling. Do you think Papa will approve?'

'I hope so. But it won't be opening until next year, when I've finished my art history course. In the meantime, I'm making my plans and raising capital.'

'Capital?' Diedre was even more startled, and a brow lifted eloquently.

'Yes. I have to have funds. To run the art gallery. Cecily has already given me quite a lot of money, and even Great-Aunt Gwen hinted that she might put something up. What about you, Diedre? Do you want to throw in a few quid?'

Diedre laughed; Dulcie had that effect on her these days. 'I don't know. How much are we talking about?' There was a pause, then she said, 'I might. What's your idea of a few quid?'

'A thousand. Or even two thousand. Pounds.'

'Good God! You can't be serious.'

'Of course I'm serious. This is a business I'm opening, not a silly game I'm playing. Anyway, that amount would certainly expunge the last vestiges of dislike I've harboured for you all these years. Let's not forget, you made my life hell when I was little. Sometimes you nearly frightened me to death. Two thousand pounds is about right to settle the matter, don't you think?' Dulcie grinned at her cheekily.

Diedre was gaping at her youngest sister, and then she began to chuckle once again, thinking what a nerve Dulcie had. No, it was spunk. And she couldn't help but admire that.

'So, are you going to invest with me? You'll get shares. And I do intend to make money. Pots of it.'

'You're still a little brat, do you know that? But yes, I will invest with you. Not to clear my reputation with you, but because I admire your ambition. And I also love you. How about three thousand pounds? Is that all right?'

Dulcie jumped up and down, laughing, flung her arms around Diedre, and hugged her tightly. 'Thank you, thank you, and your bad reputation has now been expunged from my mind. Forever. I harbour only abiding love for you.'

Swallowing her laughter, Diedre said, 'If it's not a rude question, how much did Cecily invest?'

'Ten thousand pounds,' Dulcie replied truthfully, trying not to look smug. 'She said she would give me more, if and when I need it.'

'Ceci must believe in you, and now so do I.' Diedre opened her bag, took out her chequebook and asked, 'Who shall I make this payable to?'

'Me. Cecily's in the process of forming a company for me. In the meantime, it will go into the escrow account.

224

Next week I shall acknowledge your investment properly, and send a letter.'

'I understand,' Diedre murmured, realizing that Cecily Swann had been diligent when advising her little sister about business.

At this moment Dorothy Pinkerton came out from the back office, and smiled when she spotted Diedre; she came to greet her with cordiality. 'Cecily's waiting for you on the next floor, Lady Diedre, whenever you wish to come upstairs.'

'Thank you, Dorothy. I shall come now.'

Looking at her sister, Dulcie asked, 'Can we have tea together later, Diedre?'

'Oh dear, we can't. I'm sorry, Dulcie. I'm busy today.'

Diedre followed Dorothy up the stairs to the showroom. And she couldn't help thinking that Dulcie could be really incorrigible at times. But no one ever took offence, because she made them laugh.

DeLacy was adding up her chequebook and doing paperwork at her desk, when the phone rang. She answered it at once, to discover Lawrence Pierce on the other end of the line.

'I hope I'm not disturbing you, DeLacy,' he said, sounding extremely friendly.

'Not at all,' DeLacy answered. 'How is Mama?'

'So much better, my dear. And I'm happy to tell you that Travers Merton is currently finishing a painting, and will soon be available to paint you. He took my word for it that you are a very, very beautiful woman and worth painting. I told him that he must put all his great talents to work.'

DeLacy smiled to herself, enjoying this unexpected compliment. She said, 'Oh I'm so glad. I think it was a lovely idea of yours, Lawrence. And Mama will be surprised. I haven't told a soul.'

'Please don't,' he said swiftly. 'I don't want it to get back to her. Now, Merton wants to have a meeting with you, but he's not available this week because he's finishing that other portrait. And neither am I. So sorry about that.'

'That's all right. I know you're in enormous demand, Lawrence, a great surgeon like you. We all understand how brilliant you are.'

'Thank you, my dear. However, I'm going to Paris tomorrow. I have to attend a medical conference, a very important one, where I will be giving the main lecture. I shan't come back until Saturday. So let us make an appointment to meet with Merton next week. When are you available?'

DeLacy flicked through the pages of her engagement book. 'I could be free on Wednesday or Thursday.'

'I'd better make it Thursday, just in case I get delayed in Paris. Let me give you Travers Merton's address in Chelsea. And shall we say six o'clock?'

'Oh, you want me to meet him in the evening, do you?'

Suddenly catching a hint of reserve and anxiety in her voice, Lawrence Pierce explained, 'That is Merton's preference, actually. He is painting during the day, you see, because of the light. He thought it would be nice to have a drink, a toast to the beautiful Lady DeLacy with champagne, was the way he put it. How does that sound?'

'Lovely, thank you, Lawrence.'

'Do you wish me to escort you on Thursday week?'

'Oh no, that's all right. But thank you. I will go there by myself, and meet you there. What is the address?'

He gave it to her, and said, 'Until next week, then.' Lawrence hung up after murmuring goodbye.

DeLacy sat staring at the phone, suddenly feeling nervous about the whole idea of sitting for the painting, although she wasn't really sure why. Travers Merton was famous;

he had an extraordinary reputation. Was it Lawrence? His friendliness?

Pushing these thoughts away, she realized that she had most important news for Daphne. But how to explain to her sister that she knew about Lawrence Pierce and his trip to Paris? She couldn't say Wilson had told her, because Wilson was in close contact with Daphne. Perhaps she should simply telephone her mother and suggest a visit later this week. It was the only thing she could do, unless she confided about the portrait.

Before she lost her nerve, DeLacy dialled her mother's house in Charles Street. It was Ratcliffe, the butler, who answered, and he put her through to her mother immediately.

'Hello, Mama,' DeLacy said. 'How are you?'

'I'm much better, DeLacy, and I'm actually up and about. It was so nice to see you, darling.'

'Mama, I was hoping I could come again this week. I have a present for you, and Daphne is longing to see you, and to bring the baby. Annabel is two now, and gorgeous. Please say we can come. Daphne's missed you and, as you know, I have too.' DeLacy held her breath and crossed her fingers.

There was a moment of silence before Felicity said, 'Why does Daphne want me to meet Annabel? She has refused in the past.'

'The child is two now, and is in London for the first time since she was born, Mama. What a treat for her and for you. Please say yes.'

Felicity, aware that Lawrence would be in Paris doing God knows what – seeing another woman, no doubt – made a sudden decision. 'You always have good ideas, DeLacy. Why not? I'd love to end this estrangement with Daphne, and meet my newest granddaughter. Let us do it. Be friends again.'

'Shall we come around four o'clock on Thursday, Mama?'

'That will be fine.' There was a pause, then Felicity said, 'How lovely of you to buy something for me, DeLacy. What is it?'

'I'm not telling you, Mama,' she answered, laughing. 'I want it to be a surprise.'

Once they had hung up, DeLacy reached for the phone again, anxious to speak to Daphne, tell her about the date she had just made. They would get the jewels back at last. Now it was imperative that they made the plan.

It was early afternoon when Diedre left the Burlington Arcade shop. She cut quite a swath as she crossed the street and went into Fortnum & Mason, the famous old department store on Piccadilly.

Tall, slender and elegant, with a shapely head of shining blonde hair, she drew numerous glances. Being a beautiful young woman, and chicly dressed, women admired her style, whilst men looked after her longingly, wondering who she was. Somebody. No doubt about that.

Once she entered the store, Diedre headed directly to the chocolate counter at the far end of the food department on the ground floor. She bought a large box of her great-aunt's favourite milk chocolates and, once it was packed in a shopping bag, she walked over to the lift and went up to the lingerie floor.

Her intention was to buy beautiful peignoirs, night-gowns and camiknickers, which were Paul's favourite.

Paul. How lucky she was to have found him. He had been right under her nose for ages, and yet they had never spent any time together until her father's wedding.

As Diedre looked at the beautiful chiffon and silk night-gowns, she put a hand on her stomach. She could feel nothing at this stage. Yet she was positive she was carrying Paul's child. The mere idea of this frightened her. She would know later today, after the doctor's appointment. And she would be facing a dilemma if she was with child.

The scandal would infuriate her father. He loathed scandal. She suspected he felt guilty about divorcing her mother, who had created her own scandal after running away with Lawrence Pierce when they were both still married. And now Miles too was separated and seeking a divorce from Clarissa.

Deep down, Diedre knew she would have to tell Paul immediately. She had a strong feeling he was in love with her, and certainly she was deeply involved with him on an emotional level. But would he marry her? She had no answers to that. And what would she do? And then there was her job at the War Office. She loved it and always had. Now there was that rumour about her, another bit of nastiness hanging over her head. And what if someone knew all about her past? Told Paul? She pushed that thought away.

After buying a pale blue silk nightgown and peignoir, she left the store, took a cab to her office in Whitehall. Once inside, she locked the door, sat down in her chair and put her head on her desk. She felt the tears pricking behind her eyes, but blinked them back. What help was crying? It solved nothing.

A baby. The thought terrified her, because she was single, yet the idea of having a child also thrilled her. She had never imagined this would happen. And if she really was pregnant, part of her would be jubilant. In the inner recesses of her mind she had always wanted a child.

THIRTY-FIVE

'Thank you for agreeing to see me earlier than we planned, Lady Gwendolyn,' Inspector Howard Pinkerton said as he walked into the hallway of the Mount Street flat at two o'clock instead of six.

Lady Gwendolyn shook his hand. 'No problem at all, Inspector. My next appointment is not until four. Do come into the parlour.'

'Thank you, m'lady,' he answered, and handed his wet trench coat and hat to the housekeeper.

Once they were seated, facing each other in front of the fire, Lady Gwendolyn asked the Scotland Yard detective if he would like tea or coffee, or maybe something stronger?

'A cup of tea would do the trick, m'lady,' Howard answered. 'It's turned a bit chilly, and thank you.'

Lady Gwendolyn rang the bell on the wall, and a moment later Mrs Fontaine appeared in the doorway. 'Yes, m'lady?'

'Could we have a pot of tea for two and some sweet biscuits, please, Mrs Fontaine?'

'Of course, m'lady.' The housekeeper hurried off.

Inspector Pinkerton started to speak at once. Clearing his throat, he said, 'Life is funny in certain ways, m'lady.

By that I mean things can happen quite unexpectedly, and they often solve a problem just by chance.'

'Correct. And that happened to you, Inspector?'

'It did indeed. On Sunday, Dorothy and I drove down to see my cousin Patsy, who lives in Bath. And, quite out of the blue, she mentioned a name I knew . . . Johanna Ellsworth, the friend of Alfie Fennell, the two people involved in the rumour about Lady Diedre.'

Leaning forward, her eyes riveted on the detective, Lady Gwendolyn asked, 'Why did her name come up in Bath?'

'My cousin likes to paint. She's an amateur, of course. Although she's good, mind you. She belongs to a group of local women, and men, who take painting trips. They go to local places, and sometimes abroad. My cousin happened to mention that next spring she was going to France with the group, and that the trip had been planned by Johanna Ellsworth, who was the founder of the group.'

'You discovered something of importance, didn't you, Inspector?'

'I'll say. I didn't want to make a fuss, alarm Patsy in any way. I just asked a few casual questions. I discovered, in due course, that Johanna Ellsworth had had a half-brother, who had been killed in the Great War. His name was Ralph Palmer. I inquired if he'd been married to Laura Upton Palmer, and my cousin answered in the affirmative. Naturally she wanted to know how I knew Laura. Fortunately I had an explanation at my fingertips. I said I'd been looking at an open case, that of the death of Maxine Lowe, and that Laura Upton Palmer had been a friend of hers. Patsy knows I often dig around in cases that are still open, so my explanation worked. I just let the matter go.'

'Tell me about Ralph Palmer and Johanna Ellsworth, would you please? I'm extremely curious, Inspector.'

'Johanna's mother, Margot, had a first husband. His name was Horace Palmer, and together they had a son,

Ralph. Horace died quite young, when Ralph was only three. Two years later, Margot Palmer married Joseph Ellsworth. A year after that, their daughter Johanna was born, who grew up with Ralph. They were devoted to each other. Apparently she was grief-stricken when he was killed in action. My cousin thinks her half-brother's death devastated her, and damaged her badly.'

Lady Gwendolyn nodded. 'If you love a half-brother that much, perhaps a little abnormally, then you must surely dislike a person who came between him and his wife, Laura Upton.'

'I agree. A grudge, perhaps. The thing is, it all checks out properly. It was my day off yesterday, m'lady, and I went to Somerset House. I checked out births, marriages and deaths, and the certificates are there. They are who we think they are. Everything matches up, and there is no mistake.'

'Do you believe it is Johanna Ellsworth who started the rumour about Diedre and the War Office being unhappy with her work?'

'Yes, I do, Lady Gwendolyn. I honestly felt it was wiser not to press my cousin for any more information, but Miss Ellsworth does sound a bit odd, from what Patsy said. I believe she might be just the sort of person to seek some kind of revenge. Let's face it, whoever it was who started the rumour, they wanted to destroy or badly damage Diedre's career. Diedre was the target.'

'But we can't really prove it, can we?'

'No. Normally, I would have asked for a meeting with Alfie Fennell and Johanna Ellsworth, explaining I was acting as a friend of the family. I would've said I wanted to know if they could provide any more information. It wouldn't have provided anything worthwhile, but meeting with an inspector from the Yard would have alarmed them.'

Howard paused as Mrs Fontaine came in with the tea tray. She put it on the table and departed without any fuss.

As Lady Gwendolyn poured the tea, Howard suddenly said, 'I hope I'm not being impertinent, but is Lady Diedre likely to get married to Mr Drummond?'

Glancing up, Lady Gwendolyn gave him a swift glance, and exclaimed, 'Oh Howard! You are married to a Swann, and the Swanns know everything, often before the Inghams.'

He laughed, and so did she.

Howard said, 'If Lady Diedre did marry Mr Drummond, then the rumour has no relevance, because she will probably live part of the time in New York.'

'Did the rumour have relevance?'

'I don't believe it ever did. As I told you, the person I spoke to at the War Office said it was a mere whisper. But it obviously troubled Lady Diedre. That's why you and I wanted to get to the bottom of it. And quash it.'

'It is quashed. My very great thanks to you, for taking the trouble to find out all that you did.'

'I am always delighted to help you, Lady Gwendolyn.' After sipping the tea, and eating a ginger biscuit, the Inspector said, 'I don't have the time to follow through on the Maxine Lowe case at the moment, but I am going to do so. I don't believe she committed suicide, nor do I think it was a murder. In my opinion, it was an accidental death caused by constantly inhaling two things. The poisonous fumes from lead paint. She was always repainting her homes, apparently; and also the inhalation of arsenic which comes from the ground. There's a lot of it in surface soil. Maxine Lowe was not merely a devoted gardener, but a fervent one. Her gardens at her country house were famous. I'm going to speak to Harry about this when I have a moment this week.'

'Harry is a brilliant young man, and he'll be happy to

help you. There isn't anything he doesn't know about gardens. And what you say is very interesting.'

Howard nodded, and stood up. 'If you will excuse me, m'lady, I've got to be going. I have a meeting at the Yard at five, and I have to unravel my notes and prepare for it.'

'Not a murder, I hope,' Lady Gwendolyn said, as usual filled with curiosity about everything.

'It might be. And it's no secret, it was in most of the newspapers this morning.'

'Oh dear, I haven't looked at them yet.'

'A well-known art dealer, Elliot Converse, was found dead at home a day ago. An apparent heart attack. There are some oddities, shall we say, and Scotland Yard have been called in. His wife went off to Paris a few days before. According to some, she went to meet her lover. Or he was coming to join her. Whatever. But there are suggestions of malice aforethought. Converse was young, in good health, and his death shocked those who knew him. Seemingly the wife's behaviour has been question-able for some time, and there's a lot of money involved. Converse was well off, successful in the art world. She's his only heir.'

'I wish you luck, Howard,' Lady Gwendolyn said, as she walked with him into the hall. 'And thank you again for being such a good friend.'

'It is always my pleasure . . . remember, I am of the same ilk as the devoted Swanns.'

After giving her great-aunt the box of chocolates, and being led into the parlour, Diedre related her tale about her visit to Cecily Swann's shop.

Lady Gwendolyn couldn't stop laughing when Diedre spoke of her encounter with Dulcie. 'What an unusual child she is,' she finally said, when her laughter subsided.

'Not a child! A tough little negotiator, not to mention

one who is also a blackmailer. Selling me back my good reputation, indeed!'

Suppressing her mirth, Lady Gwendolyn exclaimed, 'Look, you've got to admit it, Diedre, she's a clever one. And you were rather mean to her, you know. Very acerbic and unkind. She's obviously never forgotten how you treated her, and now she's found a way to make you pay. That's just like an Ingham.'

'I paid through the nose!' Diedre shot back.

'You didn't have to, though. You chose to, my dear.'

'Yes, I did. Because I rather admire what she's doing. My hat's off to her.' Diedre gave her great-aunt a questioning look when she added, 'She said you would probably invest. Will you?'

'I think so. I did sort of hint I would. I will certainly give her a lot of paintings and antiques stored at Little Skell Manor. For the gallery. Now, that's enough of Dulcie. Come over here and sit next to me.'

Diedre did as she was asked.

Lady Gwendolyn said, 'What is happening with your friend, Paul? Is it serious?'

Diedre took hold of her aunt's hand and held onto it. 'I'm not absolutely sure, but I think he's in the right frame of mind. He's in his forties and I am thirty-three.'

'A good age, take it from me. You've had time to live life a little, before settling down. And you're still young enough to have scads of children. I suppose you want them, and that Paul does also.'

'I don't know. We've not discussed it.' Diedre stared hard at her great-aunt and, taking a deep breath, she went on, 'I'm sure I'm pregnant. I've been noticing certain changes in my body recently.'

If she was surprised at this statement, Lady Gwendolyn was not inclined to show it. She asked swiftly, 'Have you seen a doctor yet? And have you told Paul?'

'I haven't told Paul. I didn't want to until I was really sure. I'll know later today.'

'Quite right.'

Diedre said quietly, 'I believe I'm with child, Great-Aunt, I just know it. Instinctively.'

'Most women do.' Settling back against the sofa, Lady Gwendolyn asked, 'How do you think Paul will feel? About you being pregnant?'

'I've no idea.'

'He made you pregnant, Diedre, and it's his responsibility as well as yours. Personally, I think he'll be thrilled, and he ought to be. He would be getting a superb woman for a wife – and anyway, he is forty-eight. About time he had a son, or daughter, don't you think?'

Diedre merely nodded.

Lady Gwendolyn said, 'You must tell him as soon as possible. We need to know how to proceed.'

'Yes, I know. I want the baby, Aunt Gwen, I really do. I thought it would never happen.'

'If you are pregnant, I think you ought to marry as soon as possible, Diedre.' Lady Gwendolyn stood up. Walking across the parlour, she added, 'Excuse me for a moment.'

Lady Gwendolyn went into her bedroom and took a flat green jewellery box off the dressing table. Returning to the parlour, she handed the box to Diedre, a smile lingering in her eyes. 'I picked this out for you long ago, since you are the eldest of Charles's daughters. It is one of my most treasured possessions, and it's my gift to you, my dear.'

Diedre's eyes were wide with surprise and pleasure. She lifted the lid and gasped. Placed on the black velvet was a brooch in the shape of a long, curling feather made entirely of diamonds. 'It's gorgeous. Thank you so much, Great-Aunt Gwendolyn. How generous of you.'

'It was always intended for you, and I'm so glad you

like it. Now it seems most appropriate, since a man also called Paul gave it to me . . . my late husband.'

'How lovely to know that, and it's exquisite.' Diedre held the brooch, admiring it.

'Paul actually designed it and had it made. You see, he wasn't titled, though his family were landed gentry. He used to say he wasn't good enough for me, which made me laugh. To me, he was the most wonderful man, a true gentleman. I would tease him, and say he was the feather in my cap. And, just before our marriage, he handed me that diamond feather. To wear in my cap, he said.'

'You know I'll treasure it, and pass it on if I have a daughter. Or a daughter-in-law one day.'

'Getting back to your Paul. Tell him as soon as you know if you are pregnant.'

'I will. But what if he doesn't want to marry me?'

'He will. I saw how smitten he was with you at the supper party.'

'I realize I'm in love with him,' Diedre finally admitted.

Her great-aunt said, 'If he proposes, get married here in London. And as soon as possible.'

Diedre nodded her head. 'I will.' She took a long swallow of the tea her great-aunt had poured and ate another cucumber sandwich. She was suddenly starving.

Lady Gwendolyn drank some tea and poured herself another cup. She then said in a low, quiet voice, 'I had a bit of bad news today, Diedre. Mark Stanton came to see me. Apparently Lavinia is quite ill. She has a tumour on her lung. Cancer.'

'Oh no! How terrible. Poor Lavinia.' Diedre scowled. 'You know, I thought she didn't look very well at Papa's wedding. And, to be honest, I've often wondered if she was ill that day, because she was so mean. She isn't normally like that; she's usually so nice and friendly to us all.'

'Mark Stanton wants to marry her, but she won't agree.

She says she doesn't want to be a burden. He's apparently been in love with her for years.'

'Is she having treatment? Can she be cured?'

'I don't know, nor does he. But he thinks she has a few years left, with the right medicines. So I am praying for her.'

'Oh God, so will I. Pray, I mean. Poor Lavinia, and she's not that old.'

Lady Gwendolyn had detected a certain compassion and sympathy in Diedre, and she rushed in: 'I want her back in the inner circle of the family again. It's been a difficult time for her. She cannot be punished any longer, Diedre, not when she is ill, probably even dying. Do you agree with me?'

'I do. How can I help you?'

'By standing by me, if push comes to shove in the family.'

'I am by your side,' Diedre avowed.

'I shall rely on you . . . Now to another matter, Diedre. I had a visitor a short while ago. Inspector Pinkerton, whom you know.'

'I do know him, yes; he was looking into the rumour being spread about me. Which he discovered was a whisper. You told me all that.'

'He found out something else. He was in Bath, visiting his cousin, and by coincidence the name of Johanna Ellsworth came up. She is a member of the same painting group as his cousin. Seemingly, Johanna had a half-brother who died in action in the Great War. His name was Ralph Palmer, and he was married to a friend of yours and of Maxine's. Laura Upton Palmer. Apparently they separated before he joined the army.'

Diedre held herself perfectly still and simply nodded. 'Yes, the three of us were friends, in the same circle. Laura died, and then later Maxine passed away, as you know.'

'According to Inspector Pinkerton, Johanna adored her

brother; they were extremely close. He is certain she is the one who invented the rumour about you being pushed out of the War Office. His theory is that she hated you for various reasons.'

Diedre was unable to say a word. She sat staring at Lady Gwendolyn, trembling all over. Her heart was palpitating rapidly; she was floundering.

'The Inspector reminded me of his earlier conclusions, which were that there was never much of a rumour. I related this to you, Diedre. Earlier this afternoon he confided that this whole matter was a downright lie, created to harm you, or scare you. He says the matter is closed. So we must now push it away from us and get on with our lives.'

When Diedre remained silent, continued to sit immobile, staring at her great-aunt, Lady Gwendolyn added, 'If Paul proposes to you, then you will be handing in your letter of resignation to the War Office imminently, and getting married. *Finis*, as the French say. If you don't get him to the altar, you can still work at the War Office. After a leave of absence.'

Diedre was at a loss; she did not know how to respond. She was staring into the distance, wondering how much her great-aunt knew about her past. And what if Paul found out about her love affair with Laura? This thought troubled her. How would he react?

As if reading her mind, Lady Gwendolyn said, 'I'm not a person who judges anyone, Diedre, and you certainly know that. We are alike in so many ways. Live and let live, that has always been my philosophy of life.'

Lady Gwendolyn sighed and shook her head. 'I just wish you had trusted me enough to share your grief with me, when Laura died, so that I could have comforted you. You see, I do care about you, Diedre, and what happens to you. You are part of my family. I love you.'

239

Diedre was sitting bolt upright, a look of profound shock on her face. She opened her mouth but no words came out. Leaning back against the cushions, she closed her eyes. Very slowly, tears leaked out from under her lids and trickled down her cheeks.

Lady Gwendolyn rose, left her alone and went into her bedroom. She returned a moment later with a handkerchief. Sitting down on the sofa next to Diedre, she pressed the handkerchief into her hands.

'Look at me, Diedre,' she finally said. 'Please look at me.'

Eventually Diedre turned her head, faced Lady Gwendolyn, and answered her. 'I was afraid to tell you about my friendship with Laura. To tell anyone. Not even Maxine really knew. No one did. We were discreet.'

Diedre paused, bit her lip. 'Ralph knew, and now I realize Johanna did. But at the time I had no idea she existed. Laura never mentioned her husband's family. It had been a difficult marriage . . . Ralph abused her, and his family were hostile. That's all I knew about the Palmers.'

'Oh my dear, how terrible. For her and for you. But now it doesn't matter, not any of it. However, I'm still very sad that you had to live with your grief alone, without comfort.'

'I did. And I worked very hard, threw myself into my work. There was never anyone else in my life. Then I was suddenly lucky, this past July, when I got to know Paul better, and became involved with him. Finally my pain went away.' Diedre paused, then added, 'I've begun to realize how important he is to me.'

'I know that. He loves you, too. Take my word for it. I've been around. The old story no longer exists, that's my attitude. It has vanished into thin air.'

'But what about Howard? He knows the full story about Laura, doesn't he?' Diedre sounded concerned.

240

'He's more than likely forgotten it already . . . that silly rumour about the War Office and Laura Upton. He's working on a murder case. I know that's not the answer you want, but you should know that this is how his mind works. He's a brilliant detective. The new case has taken over.'

Diedre nodded and wiped her eyes. 'I understand, Great-Aunt. And I suppose it was all just a piddling thing to him.'

'It was, Diedre.'

'The past is gone,' she murmured softly.

'It has indeed. It's lost in the mists of time. And you must never forget one thing.' Lady Gwendolyn stared into her eyes. 'Howard Pinkerton is married to a Swann. And that's tantamount to being a Swann. He will protect you always, Diedre. You are safe.'

THIRTY-SIX

'It's funny, isn't it, the odd things that make us love people?' Paul Drummond said, taking hold of Diedre's hand resting on top of the table.

She stared back at him, raising a brow. 'What do you mean?'

He did not answer at once, studying her contemplatively, wondering where to begin. The two of them were seated in the restaurant of the Ritz Hotel, at a corner table overlooking Green Park.

Diedre sat waiting patiently, glad he had invited her to lunch. Yesterday she had discovered she was pregnant. He had called her at eight this morning, insisting she meet him. Naturally she had agreed, because she planned to give him her news. She had a mountain of work at the War Office, but she knew she could catch up later. And now, here she was. Her heart was in her mouth, knowing what she must tell him. She hoped he would be pleased.

Finally he spoke. 'You're a beautiful woman, but that's not the only reason I love you. It's also because of your quirkiness, your bluntness, the way you tell it the way it is, and yet without giving offence. I love your mouth, and how you purse it when you're thinking. And I particularly love your brain and the brilliant way it works. It's gratifying to be in love with an intelligent woman and to be loved by her. I want—'

'Oh Paul, what lovely, flattering things to say,' she cut in, startled by his words. 'And I love you too. And also for many reasons. You're right about that.'

He reached into his pocket and took out a small box. 'So will you wear this? Become engaged to me? Be my wife?'

Diedre had not been expecting his proposal at this moment, and she was speechless, gaping at him, truly taken aback. But also filling with happiness. Her baby was safe. Her heart lifted with happiness. Her baby was safe; she filled with relief and a rush of pleasure.

Paul looked at her intently.

She noticed the flicker of worry in his eyes, and exclaimed, 'Yes, I will, I will! Of course, I will!'

A happy smile spread across his face, and he stood up, went around the table, kissed her on the cheek. He then opened the box, took out a diamond ring and slid it onto the third finger of her left hand. A second later he was in his chair again, gazing across the table at her, his eyes brimming with love.

Diedre stared down at her hand, and blinked when she saw the size of the diamond ring. 'Oh Paul, it's beautiful! I love it.' There was laughter in her eyes when she asked, 'Whenever did you find the time to go and select a ring? You're so busy working with Hugo.'

'Actually, I went looking for it the first week we knew each other – in the biblical sense, that is,' he answered. 'I've had it for weeks.'

'You already knew you wanted to spend the rest of your life with me?' Surprise echoed in her voice and was reflected on her face.

'Yes, Diedre, I did. I thought we were meant to be together. Didn't you feel that?'

'I did have strong feelings, but I wasn't sure you felt the same way. Despite our fantastic attraction to each other.'

He began to laugh. Sitting up a little straighter in the chair, he went on, 'So we are engaged. And we will be married, but there are some things I must talk to you about. First, let's order lunch. Get that out of the way,' he finished briskly, his manner changing slightly.

After beckoning for the waiter, he ordered a bottle of Dom Pérignon and asked for the menus. Once the waiter had sped off, Paul said, 'Last night I told you my mother was not up to par, and that I would be going back to New York sooner than I thought. What I didn't mention was that I also have to work out a business problem there. Thankfully, Hugo and I are on the same page, but it may take some time.'

'Are you telling me you won't be coming back to London as soon as you expected?' she asked quietly.

'Yes, and that's why I want you to come with me. Will you?'

'Of course, I will, but . . .' She broke off for a moment and then plunged in. 'I have something to tell you, Paul. I'm having your baby. I'm pregnant.'

'Oh my God! How wonderful, Diedre! Why didn't you tell me before?' A mixture of surprise, joy and gratification mingled together to create sudden euphoria in him.

'I just found out. I think we should get married as soon as possible, don't you?'

'Of course we must. I'm thrilled I'm going to be a father. Actually, that's the understatement of the year. I'm over the moon.'

They toasted each other, clinking glasses, and he saw the happiness on her face. Paul relaxed, glad that he had finally proposed today. 'Let's order lunch, shall we?' he said.

Diedre nodded and picked up the menu, glancing at it briefly. She did not feel hungry, and for this reason she selected the grilled sole.

Paul did the same, and then lifted his glass, savoured the champagne. He knew they would be good together. Diedre would make the perfect wife for him, with her elegance, impeccable manners, and bright mind, not to mention her beauty. And she was loving, kind. And she would make a wonderful mother. What glorious news this was.

He had never known women like the Ingham girls. The four Dees, as they were called by the staff at Cavendon. Nor had he ever been in the middle of a family as eccentric and unique as theirs. They were full of *joie de vivre*, and a certain craziness that captivated him. And Diedre, he had discovered, was as sexually motivated as he was, and he was thrilled by her sensuality and enthusiasm in his bed.

'What is your business problem about?' Diedre asked, breaking into his thoughts. 'Or don't you wish to discuss it?'

'I can talk about it, sure. A few years ago Hugo and I made an investment in a small manufacturing company, because we believed in it. Frankly, we thought it had a lot of potential. Lately, they've been asking for more money, and we're not feeling easy about that. Nor about the head of the company either. Hugo and I dislike the way he's now running it. I need more information before we put in another nickel, and Hugo agrees with me. In fact, we've been wondering if we could sell them our shares and get our money out.'

'What do they manufacture?' Diedre asked, as always filled with curiosity.

'They make airplanes. We invested in the company because of its potential, and because I have long believed that airplanes will become a mode of travel for the entire world. One day. Imagine boarding an airplane and floating up in the sky, crossing the English Channel or the Atlantic Ocean and landing in a foreign land. Marvellous.'

'That it would be,' she agreed, then asked, 'Why are you so unsettled about the company now, all of a sudden?'

'It's not all of a sudden. I've thought it was dicey for a while. Gut instinct, I guess, and I always pay attention to that. It's what my father taught me to do. And I never ask myself how much money am I going to make on this deal? Rather, I ask myself how much could I lose?'

'And you think you'll lose a lot, if you're having qualms about the deal,' Diedre asserted.

'Correct. And we can't afford that. Cavendon can't afford it. The estate is a big burden for your father, but then you know this. Hugo and I hope to sell our shares to the company, and put the proceeds into a new roof on the North Wing of the house.'

'I know the upkeep is costly, as well as repairs,' Diedre murmured, thankful that Hugo and Paul were making sure Cavendon was safe. For the moment.

Paul said, 'Here's our lunch, darling. I don't know about you, but I'm starving.'

She did not respond, took a sip of champagne.

'After lunch, I thought we might walk across the street to Cecily's shop in Burlington Arcade again. So that you can choose some more of her clothes. They would be my engagement present to you, Diedre.'

'How lovely of you, Paul. That's so thoughtful. Thank you.'

'New York can be quite cold in winter,' Paul explained, then continued, 'How shall we celebrate our engagement, Diedre? I would like to invite the family to dinner at the Savoy. Rather a nice place for a celebration, with Carroll Gibbons and his band, the music and the dancing. What do you think?'

'It would be fantastic. You're very spoiling.'

'You ain't seen nothing yet, lady,' he said in a very heavy American accent. 'I'm gonna spoil you to death.'

Diedre laughed, and then felt a little cold shiver run down her spine. Somebody walked over my grave, she thought, remembering the old Yorkshire explanation for such shivers.

She picked up her fork, took a bite of the sole. As she did so she felt a wave of nausea sweep over her, and put the fork down.

Looking across at Paul, she said, 'I think we should get married in London, don't you?'

'I do indeed. And then we'll sail off to New York on the *Aquitania* – that will be our honeymoon.'

THIRTY-SEVEN

The theatre was as quiet as the grave. Not a rustle, not the faintest whisper. The silence was a palpable thing. Dulcie was certain that if she so much as sighed it would sound like a loud cough.

The concentration of the audience was on the man who had just walked back onto the stage. It was so intense, this scrutiny of him; there was electricity in the air, expectation bordering on tension.

The man paid no attention to the actress curled up on a chaise towards the back of the stage. He halted at a low jutting stone wall, half broken, set in the centre of the boards.

He stood there in total silence. Then he moved. Not much, only one step, but Dulcie felt everyone stiffen around her.

He lifted his right leg and put his foot on the low wall. Then he rested his right hand on his right knee, and leaned forward slightly. His face was in profile, and what a profile it was. He was the most handsome man Dulcie had ever seen.

Finally he spoke. His voice was mellifluous, rising and falling with a superb musicality. 'To be . . . or not to be. That is the question.'

He paused for a long moment, and then went on swiftly in a rush of words, 'Whether 'tis nobler in the mind to suffer the slings and arrows of outrageous fortune or to take arms against a sea of troubles and by opposing . . . end them?'

The actor moved once more. He straightened his back and looked off into the distance, his face reflective.

He dropped his voice an octave or two when he spoke again. 'To die . . . to sleep . . . No more.' There was a tiny pause, and then he went on, again in the swift rush, 'And by a sleep to say we end the heartache and the thousand natural shocks that flesh is heir to. 'Tis a consummation devoutly to be wish'd.'

Seating himself on the wall, his elbow on his knee, he cupped his chin in one hand, and looked out at the audience. Lifting his head, he spoke, his voice deeper, richer, now. 'To die . . . to sleep . . . perchance to dream.' His voice became sharper when he continued, 'Ay, there's the rub! For in that sleep of death what dreams may come . . . when we have shuffled off this mortal coil, must give us pause . . . There's the respect that makes calamity of so long life.'

Dulcie was captivated, completely mesmerized by James Brentwood, whom she had never seen in a play before until tonight. He was brilliant. She understood now why they called him one of the greatest actors on the English-speaking stage, if not the greatest. His rendering of Shakespeare's famous soliloquy was more conversational than declarative, and that was why she better understood its meaning. His interpretation of Hamlet was different. New, fresh, bold; she felt he *was* Hamlet, and that he was speaking directly to her. And she supposed the entire audience felt the same.

As the play continued she became more and more wrapped up in the actor and his words; was totally oblivious to everyone else. Her eyes never left the stage and she was unaware of Daphne looking at her, surreptitiously.

249

She had even forgotten her sister and Hugo were in the theatre.

What existed for her was this superb man, an actor of extraordinary talent and power, who had transported her to another level, another place. To be able to act like this . . . what a gift. That was what it was. A gift from God.

His voice washed over her, lilting, warm, cold, hard, gentle and crazed. Every emotion seemed to pour out of him and his mouth. She had always understood it was a play about love, jealousy, revenge, lust and madness, and yet she felt as though she had never seen it before.

She gave herself up to him and his art. He commanded the stage and his presence on it was charismatic.

He had the audience in the palm of his hands . . . the world in his arms, she thought, unable to tear her eyes away from him. She had become his devotee.

The play had come to an end at last. And Daphne was taking hold of her arm and speaking to her, but Dulcie did not hear her. Her mind was on James Brentwood. Gone from her. No longer dominating her. He was off the stage after six curtain calls. Hamlet had gone, for this night at least.

I have to come back tomorrow, she thought, I must. I must see it again . . . and again and again.

'Dulcie, are you paying attention? What's the matter with you?' Daphne was holding her arm tighter, and Hugo was staring at her, puzzled, as they edged their way up the aisle towards the exit signs.

'I'm sorry,' she mumbled, forcing herself to speak. 'I'm just stunned by him, by his acting. What a performance.'

'He's marvellous, that's true. And now we are going to the stage door. We were invited to go to his dressing room by Mr Lambert. I told you. Don't you remember, Dulcie?'

'Oh. We're going to meet him. Actually meet him?' Dulcie sounded startled.

'Why yes, darling, I told you. After I ran into them at Brown's Hotel, and mentioned I was coming to the play, Mr Brentwood invited us to come backstage. And then, a day later, I received a charming note from Mr and Mrs Lambert inviting us to supper. At Rules, the lovely old restaurant in Maiden Lane. And I accepted.'

Dulcie scowled. 'I don't remember . . . I think you must have told me when I was busy going around with my tin cup.'

Hugo laughed. 'I shall have to put something into that tin cup of yours, Dulcie. Now, come along the two of you, don't dawdle. We must go out and around to the stage door. I don't want to keep people waiting.'

'But he has to take his makeup off,' Daphne said, as she hurried after Hugo, holding onto Dulcie's arm.

James Brentwood had two dressing rooms at the Old Vic, both with stars on their doors. The one he actually used was private. It was there that he did his makeup, took it off; dressed, undressed; relaxed or dozed when he needed peace and quiet. Only three people were allowed inside for any length of time: his dresser Sid Miller and Felix Lambert and his wife and business partner, Constance.

The room next door, also his dressing room, was the place where he saw friends and colleagues after the play, mingled, chatted for a while, being congenial. There was a tall, folding Chinese screen standing along a wall on one side of the room, which concealed a door to his real dressing room. And that was how he managed to get out when he wanted to slip away, to bring an end to the evening without being too obvious about his need to escape to his personal life.

Felix was with James in his private dressing room as

he took off his makeup. He confided in a low voice, 'I thought Helen was a bit off tonight, didn't you?'

'I did,' Felix responded. 'But only you and I noticed it.'

'And Constance,' James added, glancing over his shoulder at his manager and best friend.

'That goes without saying – she's never missed a trick in her life. At least to my knowledge. But Helen has been off several times this past week. I think she's fighting a cold. Something ails her.'

'I'll talk to her tomorrow, pay her a few compliments, it always seems to do the trick,' James said. 'With Helen, anyway.'

'I think she's done extremely well, considering. She's young – a novice, really. This is her first leading role, after all, Jamie. And, frankly, Ophelia's a lousy part. Even the most talented and experienced actresses groan aloud about it. It's a thankless role, in fact.'

Before James could respond, there was a knock on the door, and Constance poked her head around it. 'Lady Daphne has arrived. Take your time, Jamie, and you too, Felix. I shall look after them. Oh, and Jamie, I just had a message. Avery Cannon is popping in to say hello shortly.'

Swinging around in his chair, James gave her a loving smile. 'He's always welcome . . . what would we do without him? And it's Lady Daphne, plus her husband? I do know his name, but I can't recall it at the moment.'

'Stanton, Hugo Stanton. And she has her sister with her as well. Dulcie Ingham, Lady Dulcie, actually.'

James nodded. 'I'll be out soon. Why don't you go and join them, Felix, share your considerable charm. It'll be much faster if I'm here alone with Sid. He'll have me dressed in a tick.'

'Good thought,' Felix agreed, and left the private dressing room with his wife.

Sid, who had just taken out a clean white shirt for James, said in a low, confiding voice, 'None of me business, Jamie, but she ain't keepin' good company. Helen, that is. She don't use her loaf, that she don't.' Sid was a Cockney, like James, and came from Bow, where James had grown up.

Wiping off the last of the makeup, James frowned. 'She's not using her head about the company she keeps? Who is he?'

'Some bloody toff. Don't know 'is name, but mebbe she's burnin' a candle at both ends. Get what I mean?'

'I do indeed, Sid. Thanks for the tip.'

Sid merely grinned. He took the shirt, shook it, slipped it on a coat hanger and hung it on the doorknob. 'She's a real looker,' he announced.

'I'm well aware of that, but she was definitely off her mark tonight.'

'Not Helen, Jamie. I'm talkin' abart Lady Muck.'

James laughed. 'I know she is, I've met her before, and she has a very nice husband, by the way. Bring me some real news.'

'Ain't got none.' He disappeared into the small closet and returned holding a suit on a hanger. ''Ere's yer whistle and flute. I picked the dark blue, and it's pressed.'

'Thanks. Pour me a shot, Sid, will you, please?' As he spoke, James went into the bathroom to wash off the last vestiges of the night's makeup with soap and water.

A moment later he came back and Sid handed him the small glass of Scotch. 'Thanks.' James drank it in one swallow, and then put on his white shirt, buttoning the sleeves.

Sid took the trousers off the hanger, and James stepped into them, added a light blue tie around his neck and tied it. With Sid's help he was ready to join his guests within a few minutes. He glanced in the dressing-table mirror and then turned and strode towards the door.

'Into the valley of death rode the six hundred,' Sid declared, sounding his usual warning. He stared at James. 'Watch yerself, matey.'

'And you have a nice evening too, my lad,' James retorted. 'See you tomorrow.'

Constance Lambert was standing in the doorway of the other dressing room, talking to Avery Cannon, the theatre critic, and one of the most astute journalists in London. Cannon was one of his biggest boosters and a good friend.

James kissed Constance on the cheek, and told her she looked as elegant as always. He embraced Cannon, and promised to return in a moment or two.

Entering the second dressing room, he walked over to Lady Daphne and her husband, Hugo. They were talking amiably to Felix.

After greetings and introductions, Daphne said, 'We enjoyed your performance enormously, Mr Brentwood. I've never seen a Hamlet like yours. You were superb.'

'Thank you, Lady Daphne, you're most kind.'

'My sister was transfixed – that's the only word I can think of to describe how she reacted to your performance,' Lady Daphne added.

'I believe she was just as mesmerized as I was, Mr Brentwood,' Hugo said. 'Congratulations. You have an extraordinary talent.'

'Thank you, Mr Stanton. And where is she? Lady Dulcie? Isn't she coming to supper with us?'

'Well, yes, she is.' Daphne glanced around, looked puzzled. 'She was here a moment ago; now I don't see her.'

James peered down the room. He noticed a couple of actor friends who had stopped by and raised his hand in greeting. And then he suddenly spotted a flash of pale blue, the bottom of a skirt, and a matching blue shoe disappearing behind the Chinese screen.

The two actors, moving towards him past a couple of people he hardly knew, now blocked his view of the screen. As they stopped by him, he said in a rush, 'Back in a moment, chaps,' and hurried in the direction of the folding screen.

A young woman in a blue silk dress had opened the door and was going into his private dressing room.

He followed her inside on silent feet.

She had no idea he was right behind her.

'Lady Dulcie,' he said.

He had surprised her. Startled, she swung around swiftly, almost bumping into him. She took a step backwards to avoid a collision.

So did he. And then he pushed the door shut with his foot, not taking his eyes off her.

They stood staring at each other, eyeball to eyeball almost. He was six feet tall, and she was probably five feet nine – not quite as tall as he was. She had been startled by his arrival. He was startled by her appearance.

She was dazzling, the vividness of her colouring unique. Her eyes were so blue they looked unnatural, and yet they were beautiful. And the golden hair was a shining silvery halo around her lovely face; the features were delicate but well defined. She was a girl of the most incomparable beauty . . . and she was just a girl.

'I'm trespassing, aren't I?'

'You are indeed.'

'I'm so sorry.'

'Were you looking for me?'

'No. I saw you coming into the other room. I was escaping.'

'Didn't you want to meet me?'

'Yes. But . . . well, I was angry.'

'Why?'

'Because there were other people present. You see, I felt

you were speaking to me, and only to me, when you were on stage. You were Hamlet, confiding in me.' She shook her head, as if in puzzlement at herself.

Sid, opening the door, cleared his throat.

Looking across at him, James said pointedly, 'Give us a moment, will you?'

His dresser nodded, closed the door quietly, and left them alone.

'Please continue,' James said, fascinated by her.

'It was the suspension of disbelief, I suppose,' Dulcie said at last.

'What do you mean?' James asked, even though he understood exactly what she was referring to. However, he was genuinely surprised this girl had such knowledge at her fingertips. Few people did, unless they were from the theatre.

'What I mean is this. A play is a play, written by a playwright. Actors act the roles. So there is always a bit of disbelief in my mind, because I know it's not real life . . . it's a play, an entertainment. But you made my disbelief disappear. I suspended it. Because you convinced me you were actually Hamlet, talking just to me. And then I was here, and all those other people were arriving in the other room. And it annoyed me.'

He stared at her for the longest moment. She had impressed him. Also, he had the oddest feeling that he knew her, and knew her well at that. 'Have we met before?' he asked.

'No. But I have the strangest feeling that we have, and that I've known you for a long time, James. Oh, I'm sorry, Mr Brentwood.'

'Call me James. May I call you Dulcie?'

'Yes, you must.'

There was a long silence.

James stared hard at her once more. She stared back at him. Their eyes locked. And then they understood that

256

this had been a moment of recognition. They each accepted that they had found their soulmate. A deal had just been struck without a word being spoken. How to proceed? They were both wondering that . . .

There was a knock on the door, and it flew open, as Felix came bursting into the dressing room. 'There you are, Jamie! Everyone's been asking for you. Come on, your friends are waiting. Cannon must leave in a few minutes.'

'I need a word with Sid, and then I'm all yours, Felix.' He looked at Dulcie, and back at Felix. 'Lady Dulcie somehow got lost. Thankfully I managed to find her.' He smiled at her, inclined his head. 'Follow Felix, Lady Dulcie. I'll soon be with you.'

'Thank you for finding me, James. I'm so very glad you did.'

Felix, slightly baffled, took hold of Dulcie's elbow and ushered her out of the room, asking himself what all this was about.

James said, 'Come in, Sid, don't loiter in the corridor.'

Sid did as he was told and shut the door behind him. 'Bleedin' hell, wot was all that abart? Fancy that, comin' in 'ere without so much as a by-your-leave. Blimey, she's got cheek.'

'Actually, she's got it all, as far as I'm concerned. She's extremely intelligent, and a stunning beauty.'

'She looks all of sixteen, if that. Better watch yer step.'

'She's older than that, surely,' James murmured almost to himself, hoping he was right. Then he said, 'I need another drink, Sid. Pour me a shot, please.'

James went into the bathroom and looked at himself in the mirror. He grimaced. He was tired and it showed. He took a face cloth, ran cold water on it and held it against his eyes for a second. Then he combed his hair. He looked his age tonight, and certainly too old for her. But there wasn't much he could do about that. About anything, actually. He shrugged. He would take his chances. He always had.

Sid was waiting with the shot-glass. 'Thanks,' James said, and threw it back, then gave the empty glass to Sid.

'Watch yer step, James. Be careful.'

'No need to warn me. I'm fully aware of the grave danger she poses to me. And I will watch my step, as you call it. And everything else.'

'I'm sorry, Avery,' James said a moment later, as he joined the famous theatre critic, who was now in conversation with Felix. 'I had to sort out a bit of important business.'

The three men stood talking for a short while, and then James moved on to greet his other friends. Felix remained behind with him, whilst Constance left with Lady Daphne, Hugo and Dulcie.

James watched her go through the corner of his eye, and smiled to himself. She floated past him and out of the dressing room without giving him a backward glance. Style, he thought. She's certainly got style. He couldn't wait to leave and join her at Rules.

THIRTY-EIGHT

The moment James walked into Rules with Felix he felt better, less tense. This old place near Covent Garden was first opened in 1798 as an oyster bar, and it was a favourite of his.

He liked the warm and welcoming atmosphere, and its connection to the world he occupied. The walls were covered with sketches, cartoons and oil paintings, mostly referring to the theatre and its history. As for the food, it was the best of traditional English fare, which he preferred.

Constance stood up as they entered the main restaurant, and walked across to greet them. She was their hostess tonight, at her insistence, and had informed Felix earlier that she was in charge.

'I've bagged you for myself, Jamie,' she whispered, taking his arm and leading him to the table, followed by Felix. 'You're sitting between me and Lady Daphne, who's a sweetheart by the way.'

James looked down at her, his brown eyes warm and loving. 'I'm happy about that,' he said. Constance had been like a mother to him since he was fifteen, and he treasured her. So did his adoring sisters. Thankfully. There was no competition there. Ruby, Dolores and Faye

259

were her co-conspirators, looking after his wellbeing and guarding him possessively. Somewhat too possessively at times. But he managed to dodge around them when it was absolutely necessary.

Once he was seated at the table, James realized he was facing Dulcie. Whilst this pleased him in one way, it presented a problem in another. He had to be careful he didn't stare at her too much, or show his intense interest in her.

He reminded himself he was an actor. Which solved the problem, didn't it? Maybe. Maybe not. And that was because he wanted to look at her, to study her, to devour her with his eyes. Her beauty was unique. It took his breath away. Even her lovely older sister paled in comparison.

Constance turned to him almost immediately, and said, 'I ordered champagne for everyone, but perhaps you'd prefer something else?'

'The champagne is fine, and I suppose you've also ordered my usual dinner?' He laughed as he asked this, thinking how lovely she looked. Her short sleek hair was full of auburn lights and her green eyes sparkled. Constance, who was now in her mid-fifties, looked much younger, and she was never anything but chicly dressed. She did Felix proud as his wife and business partner.

'You know I had to do that,' Constance remarked. 'Because of the time element. They close at midnight, remember.' Looking across the table at her husband, she added, 'And I ordered the same for you, my darling. Oysters and grilled sole.'

Felix thanked her and then turned to his dinner partner. 'You probably know about this old restaurant, so I won't bore you with its history, Lady Daphne.'

Daphne nodded. 'Yes, I do – we all do. Papa often brings us here, mostly for lunch. We enjoy Rules, actually.'

Hugo made a comment about the food, and Constance joined in extolling the virtues of certain dishes she preferred.

And James felt the pressure easing off him to be charming and entertaining. He sat back in his chair and looked, for a short while, at Dulcie, fascinated by her. In an odd sort of way he found her presence soothing, even comforting. How strange, he thought, and picked up his glass, sipping the champagne. She seemed to touch him on so many levels.

As the evening progressed, James was struck by the charm and ease of Lady Daphne and her husband, Hugo. They were friendly and companionable, able to talk about anything. Good conversation whirled around the table as they sipped their wine and ate their oysters – which everyone had ordered, he noticed.

Dulcie was quiet, not saying very much at all. She glanced at him occasionally, and carefully, when she thought no one was watching her. He was not talkative himself, pre-occupied as he was with the girl seated opposite. He longed to get her alone, to find out about her, to ask her so many questions about her life. Which he couldn't very well do here.

This thought made him wonder what Dulcie knew about him. He was often written about in the papers, but it was mostly stories about his acting, his career, not his personal life. Perhaps she had questions, too. He could do something about that, and he would.

But before he got a chance to do this, Constance looked at Dulcie and asked, 'How long are you staying in London?'

'I live here,' she answered. 'I have a job. I work with Cecily Swann, the designer. At her main shop in the Burlington Arcade.'

James smiled inwardly. Thank you, clever girl, he thought. Now I know where to find you.

'How wonderful,' Constance exclaimed, obviously impressed. 'I love her clothes; they are simply gorgeous. And how did you get the job? Did you study fashion design?'

'No, I didn't, Mrs Lambert, art history. But Ceci and I grew up together at Cavendon Hall, our family home in Yorkshire. I asked her for a job because I wanted to learn about dealing with the public. You see, one day I'm going to open my own art gallery.'

James sat up straighter in the chair and stared at her. He was pleased by what he was hearing. This was not an indulged and indolent girl, a socialite; this was someone who had a purpose. It made him happy for some reason.

Daphne said, 'The entire Swann family are very much part of our lives, not only Ceci. The Inghams and the Swanns have lived together at Cavendon Hall for many, many years. And, in fact, we even have Swanns working with us here at our Grosvenor Square house.'

'Do you really? How interesting. And I think we are neighbours, Lady Daphne,' James said. 'I live in Brook Street, near Claridge's. As a bachelor, I do like to be close to a hotel. It makes life so much easier. I can always get a meal, or tea on Sunday afternoon.' He stared at Dulcie when he said that.

Felix let out a huge laugh, and exclaimed in an amused voice, 'As if you need a hotel, what with your three sisters and Constance always clucking around you like mother hens. What a life. I wouldn't mind it myself, Jamie.' Felix continued to laugh.

James had the good grace to laugh with him and, turning to Lady Daphne, he said, 'There must be a wonderful story behind that relationship . . . the Swanns and the Inghams. What an extraordinary show of devotion and loyalty on both sides.'

Before Daphne could say anything, Dulcie exclaimed, 'Papa just married a Swann, the first Ingham ever to do so; although there was always a lot of . . . messing around going on . . .' Dulcie stopped speaking when she saw Daphne's scowl and looked at James helplessly. She winked at him surreptitiously.

It took all of his self-control not to burst out laughing. But then Hugo did exactly that, and so Jamie did, too, and so did Dulcie.

Only Daphne and Constance did not join in, remaining poker-faced.

Hugo finally said, 'There are quite a number of record books at Cavendon, James, and history has it that there have been all sorts of relationships between the two families over the generations.' He glanced at his wife. 'I don't think we have to hide that, Daphers, because the whole world knows anyway. And Dulcie was right.'

James, wishing to change the subject, said, 'And when do you plan to open this art gallery of yours, Dulcie?'

'Not until late next year. There's rather a lot to do: finding the art, that sort of thing.'

'I hope I can be your first customer,' James announced. 'I don't own much art actually, and I certainly need some for my flat in Brook Street. The place looks barren.'

She nodded but remained silent; waiting, wanting him to take the lead, he understood that.

After sipping some of the white wine, James said, 'I know you have a job with Cecily Swann, but perhaps some time in the next week or so, when you have an hour to spare, you might help me find a painting or two.'

'I would love to do that. And I'll make the time to suit you.' Dulcie flashed him a smile.

He nodded. Done and dusted, he thought. And I don't give a damn who knows I'm interested in her. And apparently, neither does she.

THIRTY-NINE

'You're going to be painted by Travers Merton! How wonderful. And very flattering,' Cecily exclaimed, smiling at DeLacy.

'Ssssh,' DeLacy said, glancing around. 'It's a big secret. I just explained, you can't tell anyone. Lawrence Pierce arranged it. As a surprise for Mama.'

'I've never broken a confidence of yours, and I never would,' Cecily responded, reaching out, touching DeLacy's arm with affection.

The two women, now fast friends once more, were sitting in the main dining room of the Ritz Hotel in Piccadilly. Cecily used the Ritz often, because it was close to the Burlington Arcade and her shops.

Leaning closer to Cecily, DeLacy said with a mischievous smile, 'I never told anyone that you and Miles used to go up into the attics at Cavendon, to fiddle around with each other, when you were only thirteen.'

Cecily laughed. 'And that's all we ever did, you know. We just fiddled around, touched each other. Nothing too adventurous.'

'Yes, I know. You told me that then, and I believed you, although most wouldn't,' DeLacy countered.

Cecily sighed. 'And thankfully we're back together, and I'm happy, and so is he, and if you can tell me how to kill someone without getting caught, please do so.'

DeLacy made a face. 'Clarissa is just being mean and vengeful to punish him, I think.' She shook her head. 'None of us ever liked her when we were younger. Don't you remember, we used to call her Clarissa Mildew?'

'We weren't nice girls, were we? Very cliquish.'

'No. Oh, there's Miles. He does look well, Ceci. He's put on weight, and he's much better dressed, thanks to you.'

'I have spruced him up a bit, that's true, and he's almost like his old self. And happy, DeLacy, that's the most important thing.'

'You do wonders for him.'

'Good morning, ladies,' Miles said, approaching the table. 'This was a nice surprise, being invited to join two of my favourite women for lunch. Thank you, Ceci.'

After kissing Cecily on the cheek, and then his sister, he sat down. A huge smile spread across his face and he patted his jacket. 'I picked up the letter this morning from the solicitors, and I can't wait for the meeting this afternoon.'

'Let's hope you don't need the letter, that she gives you the jewels without a murmur.' Cecily turned her head, beckoned to the waiter, then asked Miles, 'Would you like something to drink? A glass of champagne?'

He shook his head vehemently. 'No, nothing. I have to be alert and on my toes this afternoon, but thanks.'

DeLacy said, 'Shall we order? Because I have to get home and change, and then go to Mama's first, before everyone else arrives.'

'Why is that?' Cecily asked.

'We made a master plan as you suggested,' Miles answered. 'Lacy goes first, at exactly four o'clock, bearing a gift. At about ten past four, or thereabouts, Daphne will arrive with Annabel and Nanny. They will have tea, it will be cosy, Mama will get to meet her new granddaughter. All lovey-dovey. At around ten to five, which is about the time Annabel will start getting cranky, Nanny will leave with the child, and I shall arrive. And that is when the real business will begin.'

'Will she be expecting you? Or are you surprising her?' Cecily gave Miles a pointed look.

'No surprises, that's not the right way to do it. Lacy will tell her during tea that I want to pop by, that I've something to tell her.'

'And what's that?' Cecily probed, her curiosity getting the better of her.

'I shall explain to her that I want a divorce, and that I'm having trouble with Clarissa, and let her think I'm looking for sympathy. Felicity's always enjoyed being needed. It was her stock in trade, the sympathy-kindness bit. And she likes getting family news; I've long heard on the grapevine that she's felt very cut off from her children over the years.'

'Not our fault,' DeLacy exclaimed, and picked up the menu, glancing at it quickly.

'I understand, Miles, and it's a good plan,' Cecily interjected. 'And so much better to have Annabel and Nanny gone when you ask for the jewels. Oh, and by the way, I have a bit of other news you can give her . . . Diedre's having a baby. She's coming to see me this afternoon to order some things. A wedding gown, a trousseau for the winter in New York, and maternity clothes. The baby is due in the spring . . . late April, I think she said.'

Miles stared at Cecily in surprise. 'Gosh, that is a bit of news. Incidentally, I had a phone call from Great-Aunt Gwendolyn.' He looked at his sister, and added, 'About Lavinia. Did you?'

'I did, I told her she could count on me. I think Lavinia

should be allowed back into the inner circle. She's very ill.'

'That's what I said.' Miles also looked at the menu and put it down immediately. 'They have fish cakes today, and those are for me.'

'I'm having the same,' Lacy murmured.

'Oh so will I.' Cecily looked amused as she said this, and added, 'We usually ate the same thing when we were growing up, so why not now?' Beckoning to the waiter once again, Cecily, Miles and Lacy ordered their food; Cecily and DeLacy both asked for a glass of white wine.

Miles shook his head when the waiter looked at him, and picked up the glass of water. 'I mean to be as sober as a judge,' he muttered to the two women, and then asked Cecily, 'When is Diedre getting married to Paul? Do we know yet?'

'She said in October when we spoke on the phone, but didn't say exactly when. I explained I needed a bit of time to make everything and to do proper fittings. She explained she was going to speak to your father tonight, call him in Zurich. And that she would let me have the date by tomorrow. I believe it depends on when he and Charlotte are coming home.'

After lunch, DeLacy rushed back to her flat, and Cecily and Miles walked over to the main Swann shop in the arcade. Suddenly Cecily stopped dead in her tracks, and cried, 'Oh my God! I can't believe it!'

Miles turned to her quickly. 'What? What's wrong?'

'Nothing's wrong, but isn't that James Brentwood, the actor, looking in my shop window?'

'It is,' Miles replied, and took hold of her arm. 'Come on, let's go and meet him. I'm a tremendous admirer of his. Nobody does Shakespeare like him, and I've read that he's quite the history buff. Perhaps that's the reason he understands Shakespeare as well as he does.'

By the time Cecily and Miles reached the shop at the top of the Burlington Arcade, James Brentwood had gone inside. Opening the door, Cecily was highly amused when she saw Dorothy talking to the actor. She was obviously so flustered by this unexpected encounter, and all of a dither, stumbling over her words.

The moment Dorothy spotted Cecily and Miles coming in together, she exclaimed, 'Ah, Cecily! I'm so glad you're back.' A look of relief flooded her face. 'This is Mr Brentwood.'

James swung around, walked over to join Cecily and Miles. Cecily caught her breath when he came to a stop in front of them. He was incredibly handsome and had enormous presence. It seemed to Cecily that he had sucked all the air out of the room.

'James,' he said, shaking hands with them both.

'It's wonderful to meet you,' Miles said. 'You were spectacular in *Henry V*. I went to see it twice.'

'Thank you,' James answered. 'I always enjoy doing that play. Agincourt, eh? Quite a battle.'

Cecily said, 'How nice of you to come to my shop. How can I help you, Mr Brentwood?'

'James,' he said. 'Please call me James. There are two things, actually. I would like to buy a gift for someone, but mostly I must find Dulcie. Is she here?'

Taken by surprise though she was at this unexpected reference to Dulcie, Cecily managed to conceal this. At that moment she was caught up in his voice; she could listen to it forever, so mesmerizing was it. Pulling herself together, Cecily said, 'She must be here somewhere.'

'She's upstairs in your studio,' Dorothy interjected. 'I'll go and fetch her.'

'I wasn't aware you knew Dulcie. She's my sister,'

Miles said. He was genuinely as puzzled as Cecily about Brentwood and the baby of the family.

'I'd guessed you were related,' James said with a faint smile.

Cecily walked across the room to the Art Deco desk, leaned against it and asked, 'What kind of present are you looking for?'

'I was thinking of a handbag, for my manager's wife. She has a birthday soon, and I'm aware she admires your designs.'

'Do I know her? Does she come here?'

'No, not to my knowledge. Her name is Constance Lambert, and she is very elegant. Your name came up the other evening; she apparently likes your clothes.'

'Most women covet our golden-box evening bag, so I'm sure she would like it. Obviously it's not actually real gold, but gold-coloured metal, and the front looks like the back of a sealed envelope. We also have a pleated silk evening bag with chains—' Cecily broke off, turning her head at the sudden clatter of heels against wood.

Dulcie was rushing down the stairs at breakneck speed. So hurried was her descent that she almost tripped and fell when she reached the last few steps, but she righted herself at once.

James, swiftly stepping forward, took hold of her arm and steadied her. 'Be careful, darling,' he said, and was amazed that he had actually used this term of endearment.

Cecily and Miles exchanged knowing glances, and Cecily raised a brow; Miles half smiled at her, then nodded.

Cecily said, 'Miles and I have some business to attend to. So, if you'll excuse us, James, we'll go upstairs. We can look at the bags later, whenever you wish.'

Once they were alone, Dulcie moved closer to James and touched his arm tentatively. 'Why are you here? We're supposed to meet on Sunday.'

'It suddenly seemed too far off. I wanted to see you now. Today. Isn't it all right, my coming here?'

Her face dimpled with smiles. 'It's very all right.'

James sat down in one of the chairs, stretched out his long legs, crossing them at the ankles, smiling inwardly. There was something so adorable about her; he found her irresistible.

Dulcie lowered herself into the other chair and focused on him. 'And it is a long time until Sunday. Three days and three nights . . . ages away.'

His generous mouth twitched with hidden laughter, but somehow he managed to keep his face straight. He remained silent, gazed back at her, caught up in the amazing vividness of her colouring and extraordinary natural beauty.

Dulcie was studying him intently. She had so many questions on the tip of her tongue, wanted to know everything about him. Yet she would not ask him one thing, sensing that he was a very private person in many ways. She did not wish to intrude on him.

James suddenly said, 'Is there something wrong? You have a strange look on your face. What is it?'

'I was just wishing you were standing up. Then I could hold onto you, very tightly, and know that this was real.'

'That's not a problem.' He instantly rose.

So did Dulcie. She walked across the floor, stood in front of him and leaned her head against his chest. He immediately wrapped his arms around her, drew her into him and held her close. She did the same, and put her hands on his back. And they stood together without moving or saying a thing. Words were not necessary with them, and they both knew it.

From the first moment he had seen her, he had wanted to touch her, to hold her like this. He was breathing in the fragrance of her skin, the lemony tang in her hair.

She was wearing a scent that smelled of tuberoses, and – forever after – roses would always bring the memory of this moment rushing back to him. And for the rest of his life.

It was obvious that there was a sexual attraction between them, but James already accepted he was involved on an emotional level. And he was certain she was. But it was enough for now to stand here together, enjoying this first moment of intimacy.

Dulcie unexpectedly leaned back, looking up at him. 'I want you to kiss me, James. Will you?'

He did so. She kissed him back, and they went on kissing. Finally, he asked, 'So, is it real?'

'Wonderfully real. The most real thing I've ever known.' She leaned into him once more, putting her arms around him, and let out a long sigh. 'I've a confession to make.'

'Do you now? And what is it?'

'I came to the theatre last night. I sat at the back and wallowed in you.'

He smiled against her hair. 'How was I?'

'Wonderful.'

'You should have come backstage to see me.'

'I would never intrude on you; besides, it was Wednesday. You had a matinee. Two performances in one day is a lot.'

He was silent, his mind focused on her. She was amazing, and unusually wise for a young woman.

'How old are you?' he asked, finally getting the words out.

'Eighteen.'

Oh God, no, he thought. She's too young.

When he said nothing, she asked, 'And how old are you?'

'Thirty-three. And far too old for you.'

Stepping away, staring at him, biting her lip, and pushing down the laughter bubbling up, she said, 'No, you're not, you're really not.'

271

'You want to laugh,' he said. 'And I don't understand why my age amuses you. But go on, laugh. I don't mind.'

She did laugh, then calmed herself and said, 'My sister Diedre is thirty-three, and she's about to marry a man who's forty-eight. A man who has just made her pregnant. And Hugo is forty-five, fifteen years older than Daphne. They were married when she was seventeen, in fact. Younger than I am now.'

James was frowning. 'How amazing, Hugo doesn't look forty-five.'

'No, he doesn't. Having a young wife keeps him young.'

'Touché,' James said, and began to laugh. 'You're a little minx, do you know that?'

'No, and I don't like names. Diedre used to call me a little madam. But I suppose you can call me a minx if you want to, because you're special.'

'But am I real?' he asked, laughter in his dark brown eyes. He was enjoying teasing her.

She merely nodded.

He sat down in the chair, and said, 'So, go on, tell me why the Ingham girls are obviously attracted to older men.'

'I have a theory. I think it's because we were brought up by a man. Our father. He took charge of us when we were little, long before his wife ran off with her lover. Papa spent all of his time with us, even when he was hard at it, running the estate. He was a tremendous influence on us, especially us girls. Papa was our moral compass. He taught us the difference between right and wrong, how to be grownups. He said we must stand tall, that we shouldn't weep over anything. He brought us up to be compassionate, kind and well mannered.'

Shaking her head she finished. 'We got used to being with older people. I don't think we'd know what to say to a man of our own age.'

Gazing at him, she said softly, 'Will you hold me again, quickly, before they come downstairs with bucketfuls of bags and other stuff to sell you. Dorothy Swann loves to make a sale.'

'I think you must be an original, Dulcie.' Chuckling, he stood up and pulled her into his arms. He kissed her on the mouth for quite a while.

They clung together. He stroked her hair and, as he did so, he began to realize that the emptiness he frequently felt inside had fled. It was her presence in his life, he was aware of that. He had never felt like this before about any woman. This one's a heartbreaker, he thought. Better hang onto her. Make her mine. I can't let her escape.

Diedre had come into the shop quietly, and was standing staring at a man's broad back. She didn't know who he was, but she certainly knew it was her baby sister in the man's arms.

She cleared her throat.

The two of them drew apart. The man turned around, and smiled when he saw her.

Oh my God, Diedre thought, gaping. It's James Brentwood. Tall, dark and handsome, and larger than life. And what was Dulcie doing in his arms?

Dulcie cried, 'Oh hello, Diedre! This is my boyfriend, James Brentwood.'

'Boyfriend,' Diedre repeated, truly amazed by this incredible scene she had walked in on.

'Yes, boyfriend,' James repeated, understanding that his little minx needed support.

Thrusting out her hand, Diedre said, 'Hello, Mr Brentwood. And welcome to this crazy family called Ingham.' Looking across at Dulcie, she went on in a loving tone, 'Why didn't you tell me you had a boyfriend? And such a glamorous one. You can't hide him under a bushel, you know? And why would you want to?'

Dulcie and James started to laugh, and so did Diedre, and James said, 'What have I unwittingly stumbled into? A lunatic asylum? I've never met anyone like you and your sister, Dulcie.'

'Oh I know, we're unique,' Dulcie replied and, looking at Diedre, she went on, 'Will you get married on a Sunday please?'

'As a matter of fact, we're planning to have the wedding on a Saturday, and a few days later we take the *Aquitania* to New York. But why are you asking me to have it on a Sunday?'

'Because I want James to come. And he won't be able to on a Saturday. He's working. Please make it Sunday. And I promise I will expunge that last bit of bad stuff about you that's still lying dormant in my mind.'

'Ah ha, still my little blackmailer, eh! I paid you three thousand pounds to wipe that slate in your head clean,' Diedre reminded her.

James was staring at Diedre, mystified by this extraordinary conversation.

Diedre noticed his expression, and said, 'Pay no attention to this. We joke around a lot, James, and accuse each other of all sorts of things. We stir the pot.'

'So it seems,' he answered pithily, but nonetheless he was amused.

Diedre went to Dulcie and hugged her. 'I'll change the day to Sunday, so that your boyfriend can attend. To make up for the nasty way I treated you. If he wants to come, that is.'

'I want to,' James answered. 'And thank you in advance, Diedre. You're very kind.'

And you're the most gorgeous thing on two male legs I've seen in years, Diedre thought, walking towards the staircase. Turning, she said, 'I must go up for my fittings.'

'Thank you, Diedre, for being the best big sister in the world.'

274

Diedre smiled at her, her heart full of love for Dulcie, who had undoubtedly hit the jackpot snagging James Brentwood. Fancy that. Her 'little madam' and the greatest actor in England.

FORTY

James Brentwood hailed a cab on Piccadilly and went to the Old Vic, deciding he did not have time to go home. He had been at Cecily Swann's shop with Dulcie for almost two hours. Glancing at his watch, he saw that it was three thirty already. Anyway, he liked going to the theatre early. It gave him time to relax, shed the world, get into his part.

Settling back against the seat, he found himself smiling. Dulcie had that effect on him. Aside from her stunning looks and warm personality, there was something refreshing and unspoilt about her. He enjoyed her colourful expressions, the way she used the language, her forthrightness and intelligence. She was clever. And her sister act with Diedre had been hilarious.

Quite aside from these characteristics, James was relieved that she was not in awe of him, or intimidated by his fame. Some women had been in the past, and it made him feel uncomfortable.

But then Dulcie Ingham knew exactly who she was, where she came from and where she belonged in the world. She was the daughter of an earl, with a title in her own right, an aristocrat born and bred. And yet there was nothing snobbish or stuck up about her, and her determination to work was admirable.

After paying off the taxi, James hurried down the alleyway to the stage door. Once inside the theatre he ran into Sid in the corridor, and greeted him warmly.

His dresser, who was devoted to James, beamed when he saw him, and followed him into the dressing room.

'Blimey, you're really early today, Jamie.'

Taking off his jacket as he moved rapidly across the floor, and hanging it on the back of a chair, James explained, 'I was out on an errand, finished early and decided I might as well come in.'

'Best place to relax,' Sid said. 'Fancy a Rosie Lee?'

'I'd love a sandwich, actually, and I won't say no to the tea, Sid. I haven't had lunch.'

'Comin' right up.' Sid headed for the door, then stopped abruptly. 'The miss was 'ere last night.'

'Why didn't you tell me?'

'I dint know. Just found out.'

James looked at him closely. 'Who told you she was in the theatre?'

'That usherette I know, Doris, who lives down Bow way. She recognized the miss.'

'Why on earth do you call her the miss, Sid? It sounds rather strange.'

'She ain't a missus.'

'That's true. And you probably didn't realize she has a title like her sister. Call her Lady Dulcie when she's here.'

'She's coming back then, is she?' Sid probed, always eager to know everything about James's private life. Always protective of him.

'I bloody well hope so!' James exclaimed, and winked at his dresser.

Laughing, Sid rushed out without another word. Staring after him, James shook his head, bemused, and sat down at the small desk. He rummaged around in the bottom drawer and found his treasured copy of *Henry V*, filled with his notations.

As he flicked through the pages of the play, he wondered if he should suggest it to Felix. Perhaps he ought to have a go at it again. After *Hamlet* closed, and after he'd had a rest. A long rest.

But Felix wouldn't agree, and neither would Constance, he was certain of that. They would want him to do something very different, take a break from Shakespeare. And they were usually right. They had guided his career for eighteen years, and he was thankful he had them.

The phone on the dressing table rang, and he jumped up, went to answer it. 'It's Felix, Jamie.'

'Hello, Felix. Something wrong? You sound angry.'

'I'm not angry, just perturbed. Helen's brother, Andy Malone, called in for her. Apparently she's ill.'

'Oh bugger! What's wrong? Did he tell you?'

'He mumbled something about a female problem, and that she'd only be out a couple of days. Back on Monday. I thought you'd better know you've got the understudy tonight. But Pauline's rather good. Anyway, you always carry the play.'

'I like Pauline, and you're right, she is quite a good Ophelia. I'll manage. Sorry to hear about Helen. She has looked off it lately . . . sort of done in.'

'There's something troubling her, I think, and as soon as she's better I'll have a word with her, attempt to get to the bottom of it.'

'Better make it a gentle word,' James said.

'I will. I've been trying to get hold of you since one thirty, Jamie, and you're in early today. Is everything all right with you?'

'Never felt better. And yes, I went out early. Around the

time you were probably ringing my flat. I went to Cecily Swann's shop. To see Dulcie.'

There was a silence. A moment later, Felix asked, 'Dulcie Ingham?'

'Yes.'

'Why?'

'I've fallen for her, Felix. And rather heavily.'

'I'll be right over,' Felix exclaimed, and hung up without saying another word.

James looked at the receiver, laughed and then put it back in the cradle.

Within a few minutes Sid came rushing into the dressing room, carrying a large mug of tea and a brown paper bag. These he placed on the desk, 'Here's yer mug of Rosie Lee, and I got yer favourite sandwich from the café. Fried egg on bread. Just like yer mum used ter make.'

'Thanks, Sid.'

'It's a good fing I'm 'ere ter look after yer,' Sid told him, opening the top drawer of the desk, taking out a plate and a white napkin.

James leaned back in the chair and said, 'Along with three sisters, plus Constance. Let's not forget that team.'

Sid nodded. 'Do yer fink I do? And they'd never bloody let me.' He put the brown bag on the plate. 'Better eat. It's still warm. I 'spect yer know Helen's not coming in. Poorly, she is.' He always said Helen with great emphasis on the 'aitch', mostly because he usually dropped them.

'Felix told me while you were out getting the sandwich. I can't help thinking there's something really seriously wrong with her.' Standing, James walked over to the desk.

'She looks half dead these days,' Sid announced dourly.

'Please, Sid.'

'Oh, sorry. I fink it's man trouble, if yer get me drift.'

279

'I do.' James opened the brown paper bag and took out the sandwich, realizing how hungry he was when he bit into it.

'It's good, ain't it?' Sid asked, watching James munching on the sandwich.

James nodded.

Sid said, 'I'll let yer eat,' and disappeared through the door.

Mum, James thought, as he ate his sandwich. He only vaguely remembered her now, but he certainly remembered how she had lovingly made him fried egg sandwiches, baked apples, and a dish he still enjoyed, cottage pie. And sometimes, far back in his head, he heard the echo of her singing, and his father telling her she sang like a nightingale. Little things like that came back to him, occasionally. Most of the memories of the woman herself had faded over the years.

She had died when he was seven, in 1900, and he had been taken over by his eldest sister Ruby, who had loved him to death and put him before everybody else in the family, including her husband, Ted Mount, who, nonetheless, had loved him too.

And he, little Jimmy, had loved her to death back, clinging to her for dear life, like a tiny barnacle on a sturdy boat. She was his anchor, his protector, his safe haven. And she was very beautiful. Surely it was she who had given him his taste for beautiful women. Where else had he got it from, except from looking at her? Golden hair, pale blue eyes, skin as white as driven snow. And as smooth as silk. Ruby, who always smelled of everything clean – scented soap, lemons and lavender – and had stroked his hair and wiped away his tears.

She was clever and strove to push them all up the ladder, to better places, better lives. There was something fine about Ruby, and her dignity was always in place. And so was her pride and self-respect.

Their neighbours in Bow Common Lane, where they had lived, spoke well of her, and with something like awe. 'There goes Ruby Mount,' they would say when they saw her walking down the street. 'Tall and proud and beautiful. Elegant, like a queen. She slaves all day and night, cleaning the house till it shines, cooking the meals and ironing the white shirts, sending her men out looking starched from head to toe. And handsome, too, with shining faces and slicked-back hair. And look at their shoes, like glass they are. That's Ruby Mount. And see how she looks after the boy. Little Jimmy Wood. Her youngest brother, ironed from head to toe as well, just like the others. A mother she is to him. That's Ruby Mount, walking down there, proud and elegant in her Sunday best.'

That's what the neighbours in Bow had said about his Ruby. And then there was his middle sister Dolores, who had never stopped tutoring him. Making him read and read until the book fell out of his hands as he fell asleep in the chair. A slave-driver, but loving. And then there was Faye, the youngest of the sisters, who had a voice as clear as a bell, like their mother's had been. It was the musical Faye who had taught him to sing, to recite poetry and the plays of Shakespeare, until he was hoarse. And she had fine-tuned his God-given talent for acting. Those were the three Wood sisters, who had made him who he was by the age of fifteen.

He had two brothers, David and Owen. They had taught him as much as they knew about being a man. How to box, to fight back if he was picked on at St Saviour's in Northumbria Street, the school they had attended. From these two big brothers he had learned how to run fast, climb the tallest wall, ride a bike and catch a fish. They had even bought him a bat and given him lessons in cricket.

It was David who had worked on the docks with their father. West India Docks, close to Bow, one of the greatest docks on the busy River Thames. Strong men, his father and his brothers. Owen had been trained as an engineer. When the Great War came, David had rushed off to join the British Army, gone to fight for King and country. Owen had not passed the medical, and David never came back. Their father had grieved for a second time. For his eldest son.

Now Owen was an engineer, brilliant at what he did, building enormous bridges that spanned the widest rivers around the world, which brought him accolades and wealth and prizes galore.

The Woods. They came from a mixture of English and Welsh stock, and were proud of it. Their father Alfred had married Jenny Jones, from the Rhondda, a lovely girl with a song in her heart and forever on her lips. A black-haired beauty who had fallen in love with the handsome Alfred, a Cockney through and through. And this bright young couple had created their little clan, the Woods of Bow. They had had six children, and all had lived. And they were brought up to fear God, honour the King, have good morals, compassion for others and loyalty to their siblings.

Alfred, the docker from Bow, had died eight years ago. But he had lived long enough to see his youngest son's name shining in bright lights on the marquee of a West End theatre. 'The proudest moment of my life,' he had told James that night. He was somewhat awed that this mesmerizing actor with the thrilling voice, who stood on stage to thunderous applause, belonged to him.

Memories, James thought, thank God we have them. They help us to recall what's long gone, and we can live again in the past with those we once loved. For a moment or two at least.

James glanced at the door as it flew open, and Felix walked in purposefully.

Closing the door behind him, and leaning against it, Felix threw James a long, searching look without saying one word.

Standing up, James stepped forward, gave his manager a warm smile and embraced him.

Felix hugged him back, but still remained silent.

'You got here quickly, Felix. You must have run all the way,' James said, eyeing him curiously, then grinning.

'Actually, I didn't, but I certainly felt like it after hearing your latest news. It brought me up with a start, I've got to admit that.'

'It did me, too,' James answered, walking over to his dressing table, lowering himself into the chair. 'Don't stand there, Felix. Why don't you sit on the couch? It's very comfortable for an interrogation.'

This was said lightheartedly, and Felix had to laugh. 'Is that what I look like, Jamie? An interrogator?'

'From the Spanish Inquisition. Go ahead, start questioning me. I'll be glad to talk, but there's not much to tell, actually. At least not many details to relay.'

Felix sat back on the couch, gazing at him, caught up for a moment in the aura of this man and his extraordinary presence, wondering where it came from. Inside himself, he supposed.

James had adopted his usual position when he sat in a chair, with his long legs stretched out and crossed at the ankles, his body slightly slumped. And yet, however relaxed he was, he retained his elegance. Bred in the bone, Felix decided.

James Brentwood had 'it', Felix thought. Whatever 'it' was. A combination of staggering looks and a charisma that spelled glamour. Even when Felix had first met him

283

all those years ago, at the children's theatre school, he had had the beginning of it. The handsomeness, a certain bearing, a way of holding himself, of walking decisively, striding out, holding his head high. At fifteen he had a patrician air about him, and it was more pronounced now.

Confidence. Belief in himself. The sense he was going places, instilled in him by Ruby. And the other two sisters, but mostly Ruby. Those three young women had never had any doubts about their gorgeous, talented, versatile brother. They knew he would be a star.

They just hadn't realized what the magnitude of the stardom would be, the road he would leap along, taking everything in his stride, without vanity or boasting, almost humble in a certain way. And often surprising himself by his own huge success. And he had become, over the years, a well-balanced man, with integrity, decency and compassion. A good man, in fact, and Felix was full of admiration for him. He was also protective of James Brentwood, as was Constance, who cherished him.

'Why are you staring at me like that?' James asked, interrupting Felix's thoughts. 'You're really giving me the once-over.' He sat up straighter, somewhat abruptly, and shook his head. 'I thought you'd come over to the theatre to ask me about Dulcie.'

'I have, but for a moment I was sidetracked by you, how you look today. Pretty damn good for an actor who's been playing Hamlet for almost a year, and without a break,' Felix improvised, not wanting to reveal his true thoughts. He knew how much James hated it when people gushed over him.

'Gee whiz, Felix! And here was I thinking you were wondering what the Lady Dulcie saw in me,' James quipped, his dark eyes suddenly filled with amusement.

'Walking over here, I reminded myself that I came into this dressing room only two days ago and found you and Dulcie here together. And I couldn't help wondering then what was going on between you.'

'I did also. For the first few seconds. But within a very short time she and I were staring at each other, practically eyeball to eyeball, and we both understood we had recognized each other. We'd never met before, but we knew each other. Hard to explain . . . the shock of recognition is quite astonishing.'

'I understand what you're saying, Jamie, and the clever French call it a *coup de foudre* . . . struck by lightning.'

'That's exactly what it was! I also accepted that we had made a pact, unspoken though it was, and it happened again when we were at Rules . . . that peculiar feeling that we had connected on a very deep level.'

'I remember how you were gazing at each other most of the evening.' Felix cleared his throat. 'And today you were compelled to go to the shop where she works, because you just had to see her again. Am I right?'

'Naturally. Nobody knows me better than you.'

'I came over because I sensed you needed to talk to me.'

'I did. I do, Felix. And when I said there wasn't much to tell, there isn't. And yet something quite momentous happened. My entire life was changed today. And so was hers. Let me explain . . . we held each other tightly and kissed several times. And I confirmed that we were having tea at Claridge's on Sunday.'

'Claridge's,' Felix repeated, a reflective look crossing his face. 'Close to home, Jamie.'

'Yes, it is. But we will not be going up to my flat in Brook Street, if that's what you're thinking. I'm not looking to have an affair.'

Felix nodded his understanding.

James said, 'I have fallen in love for the first time in my life. I am going to marry Dulcie.'

There was no doubt in Felix's mind that James meant every word. He wasn't given to loose talk, and furthermore he sounded serious. 'I must admit you've never mentioned being in love or getting married, ever, even though you've had several romantic relationships. You've always referred to those entanglements as infatuations.'

'And that's what they were. The reason I broke up with Allegra Norman last year was because she wanted me to marry her. That wasn't possible. I couldn't because I knew the marriage wouldn't last very long. With Dulcie it's quite different. I'm in love. And I'm fairly sure she's a virgin, and I aim to keep it that way until we're married.'

Felix exclaimed, 'You'll have to have a will of iron, Jamie, to keep your hands off that girl. She's impossibly beautiful, and undoubtedly completely bowled over by you . . . let's not forget who you are.'

'She feels the same way I do. She's in love, I can tell. I shall ask her to marry me on Sunday.'

'And I'm positive she'll say yes,' Felix assured him.

James was silent for a moment before saying, 'We belong together, she and I. And she's said enough to me already to make me understand her true feelings.'

James shifted in the chair, leaned forward, his expression earnest as he focused on Felix. 'Her father is abroad. But he'll be returning in two weeks, and will be in London. I'm going to see him immediately, ask his permission to marry her. And Dulcie will arrange for us to be married as quickly as possible.'

'How old is Dulcie, James? She looks awfully young and innocent.'

'Eighteen. And you're right, she looks even younger. But she's actually quite wise for her age, and practical. Dulcie is marvellous – very spontaneous, forthright, says what comes into her mind. She's also hilarious, makes me laugh, makes me feel good in general.'

'It's quite an age difference, though . . . you're a thirty-three-year-old man who's been around; you're experienced, sophisticated.'

'That doesn't worry me. Neither does the age difference. Dulcie told me Hugo is forty-five, fifteen years older than Daphne. Her sister, Diedre, is about to marry a man who is forty-eight to her thirty-three.'

'How interesting. It seems that the Ingham women like older men . . . runs in the family, apparently. And I will say this, Jamie, you look happier than I've seen you for a long time.'

'I am. Actually, what I feel is complete.' There was a pause, and then he continued, 'There's something odd I must tell you, something which I found fascinating. Dulcie knows all about the suspension of disbelief, and I'm absolutely certain she figured that out for herself. No one told her.'

Felix gave him a hard stare. 'Few civilians ever understand that. Tell me what she said.'

He did.

Felix was impressed. 'She must be very intelligent, obviously. But she was awfully quiet at Rules, so there was no way to tell. Too absorbed in you, of course. Smitten.'

James laughed. 'As I am with her.' He then confided, 'I want to do everything right. Conduct myself properly. Felix, that is why I wish to see her father. And then we can proceed from there.'

'He's not going to say no, Jamie. And don't even mention to me that you're a docker's son from the East End and she's the daughter of an earl. Those class things don't matter in the world we live in today. It's 1926, for God's sake, and the world has changed.'

'I wasn't going to mention anything about class. And I'm well aware the world can change in a minute.' He pursed his lips. 'After seeing the Earl, I will have to tell Ruby. And Dolores and Faye.'

'Please wipe that worried look off your face. They're not going to make so much as a ripple. They worship the ground you walk on, let me remind you, just in case you've forgotten.'

'I don't suppose anyone will object. I'm a true blue Englishman, a decent man—'

Interrupting him, Felix said, 'No, you're a big star, James, and don't you ever forget it.'

FORTY-ONE

DeLacy was relieved when she heard Daphne's voice in the entrance hall of her mother's Charles Street house. Ever since she had arrived, her mother had been somewhat churlish – or perhaps gloomy was a better word.

Wilson had whispered hurriedly to her that Mr Pierce had been delayed for a week in Paris, and that this had gone down badly with her mother.

Felicity had not been particularly interested in her gift, a distinctive white satin headband edged with diamanté studs, with a white osprey feather attached at one side. It had been expensive and was very stylish, and DeLacy realized she was hurt by her mother's lacklustre reaction.

But now Felicity was smiling. She had also heard Daphne's voice, and here they were, all of a sudden, coming into the blue and white sitting room. Daphne was in the lead, holding Annabel's hand, followed by Nanny. Bending down to look at her daughter, Daphne said, 'This is Grandmama, Annabel. Let us go and say hello to her, shall we?'

Smiling, her pretty face dimpling, the child nodded. Felicity got up from the sofa, her own face full of smiles. Instantly, the two year old broke free of Daphne and tottered across the room on her two plump little legs, heading for her grandmother.

Felicity immediately crouched down and opened her arms to this child she had yearned to see for two years. Almost as if she understood this, Annabel flung herself into Felicity's arms. Mangling the word slightly, she said, 'Amama,' obviously unable to pronounce it properly.

DeLacy smiled, enjoying this moment, seeing the pleasure on Felicity's face. Unexpectedly, much to her surprise, her mother looked younger, and her expression was full of warmth. Obviously this was because of the presence of the two-year-old toddler, who had a mass of curls and looked adorable in a blue dress and matching cardigan.

And yet Annabel was not her first grandchild. Daphne had five children, but only one other was a girl, Alicia. Seemingly, Felicity had never really liked her for some reason. DeLacy had never truly understood her mother's attitude, her coolness towards Alicia, who was lovely, well behaved and pleasant, if a little serious.

After a moment, Felicity straightened. 'Shall we sit on the sofa together, Annabel?'

The child nodded, and Felicity lifted her up in her arms and put her on the sofa, then sat down next to her.

Daphne bent forward and kissed her mother's cheek. She said, 'It's lovely to see you, Mama, and Annabel has fallen in love with you, I think. And given you a new name.' Stepping back a few steps, Daphne said, 'And do you know, she looks a lot like you? Her hair is the same strawberry blonde, and her eyes pale green, just like yours. Not the deep blue of the Inghams.'

These words pleased Felicity, and she said, 'Thank you, and for coming, Daphne, and bringing Annabel to see me . . . I hope we can all be friends again.'

'Of course we can, Mama. Diedre was longing to join

us, but unfortunately she couldn't.' Daphne sat down on the other sofa, next to DeLacy, and Nanny excused herself, saying she would go to the servants' hall downstairs to wait for them.

'How is Diedre?' Felicity asked, curious about her eldest daughter.

'She's very well,' Daphne answered. 'She's getting married soon, to an American who runs Hugo's New York office, Paul Drummond. He's been here for a few months, and – well – they fell in love.'

'How wonderful for Diedre. When is the wedding?'

'They haven't set a date yet, they only just got engaged.' Daphne decided to be vague, since she did not know if Diedre was going to invite their mother to her wedding, planned for next month.

DeLacy said, 'Mama, something very important, Miles is in London. And he hoped he would be finished with his meetings in time to join us for tea. I thought that might please you.'

There was only the merest hesitation on Felicity's part before she exclaimed, 'I would love to see him.'

At this moment, Ratcliffe the butler appeared in the doorway, accompanied by two parlour maids. 'Excuse me, madam, but shall I serve tea?'

'Yes, please do so, Ratcliffe, thank you.'

The butler inclined his head, and motioned for the two maids to wheel in the tea trolleys. He added, 'Nanny suggested I include a small glass of milk for Miss Annabel.'

'Oh, thank you very much, Ratcliffe,' Daphne said, smiling at him.

'You seem so much better, Mama,' DeLacy murmured. 'You've made a good recovery.'

'Yes, I have. I had a heavy cold, not bronchitis apparently. And how do you feel, Lacy darling? A little happier, I hope.'

'I am. But I think it takes quite a while to get over a divorce. I always seem to be on the verge of tears, although I try hard to be strong.'

'You are strong, darling,' Felicity replied in a positive voice. 'I come from good stock, and my father, your grandfather, always told me to be courageous. He had a line he often used, and I think of it often. He would say that life has a way of taking care of itself, and that happens to be true, I've discovered. It helps if one tries not to dwell on problems.'

The two parlour maids passed plates of finger sandwiches around; Ratcliffe poured the tea, and then carried the glass of milk over to the sofa, where he set it down on a small table.

As they ate their sandwiches and drank their tea, Daphne and DeLacy managed to keep up a cordial conversation with their mother. Without knowing it, both young women were thinking how odd it was that Felicity had not mentioned Dulcie, or asked how she was.

Daphne was about to introduce the baby of the family into the conversation, when Felicity said, 'I heard from my friend Rebecca Gosling. She told me that Vanessa got engaged to someone called Richard Bowers. Is that so?'

'That's correct,' DeLacy answered. 'She is engaged. He's a Barnard, I believe, and he has some top job at Scotland Yard. You know, high-level management.'

'Really. How interesting. I also heard that Lavinia has cancer. Have you seen her lately? How is she?'

'She's not too well, Mama.' Daphne's expression became sad. 'Great-Aunt Gwendolyn is in touch with her, but I'm afraid Aunt Lavinia hasn't been able to socialize at all. She has become friendly with Hugo's cousin, Mark Stanton. He's looking after her, and I got the impression that her illness is terminal.'

'How truly awful that is. I remember what my sister

Anne went through all those years ago. It's a monstrous disease.' Felicity shook her head and sat back on the sofa.

At this moment Annabel began to wriggle and, looking at Felicity, she mumbled, 'Amama, down, down,' and endeavoured to slither off the sofa. Daphne immediately leapt up, and caught hold of her before she took a tumble.

'Oh dear, I think she's getting rather restless,' Daphne muttered. 'I'd better go downstairs and fetch Nanny.'

'You don't have to do that, Daphne,' her mother said. 'I can simply ring for Ratcliffe, and he will inform Nanny she's needed.'

'I want to have a word with Nanny anyway,' Daphne explained. 'I won't be a moment. Back in a jiffy, Mama.'

Drawing Annabel towards her, holding onto the child, DeLacy said, 'If you ever want to visit Cecily's shop in the Burlington Arcade, I can arrange it for you. She has lovely things.' DeLacy knew she must distract her mother for a moment or two, because Daphne had actually gone to speak to Olive Wilson. They had to stick to the plan and the timetable.

'I would like to go, if you'll come with me,' Felicity said. 'Everyone raves about the clothes.'

'I would be happy to take you any time you wish.'

Daphne returned to the sitting room and took charge of her daughter. 'Nanny will be here in a moment. She's just having a cup of tea. Then I think she should take Annabel home, Mama. It's about time for her to have a little nap.'

It was with some relief that Miles saw Nanny wheeling the pushchair up Charles Street, heading in the direction of Grosvenor Square. Everything was going to plan. It was exactly fifteen minutes to five, and he was on time. In a moment or two, he would have to confront his mother, and leave her house with the jewellery she had taken from Cavendon Hall years ago. He prayed it would not be too much of a verbal struggle, and that he could handle her. Felicity Pierce was no longer the woman he had known as a child.

From the moment he walked into the blue and white sitting room, Miles Ingham knew two things: he must be in total control of the situation at all times, and he must not antagonize his mother at the outset of this visit.

He therefore smiled warmly, walked over and kissed her on the cheek, and said, 'It's lovely to see you, Mama. And, I must add, you look positively beautiful. You never get any older.' He took a chair facing her, his smile intact.

Felicity, who had been hesitant about seeing him earlier, now wondered why she had been apprehensive. He was his usual pleasant self, and very gallant, which had always been his way. Miles had a lot of charm as well as good looks, and a very astute brain. In certain ways, he had been her favourite of all her children, perhaps because he reminded her a lot of her father, Malcolm Wallace, the famous tycoon.

Felicity said, 'I shall ring for Ratcliffe so that he can bring us a fresh pot of tea. Would you like some of the finger sandwiches, Miles?'

'Thank you, Mama, so kind. But I had rather a late lunch. And you don't have to ring for Ratcliffe. When he let me in, I told him all I wanted was a cup of tea.'

As if on cue, a moment later, Ratcliffe arrived with a tray set with tea things; he placed it on a table, poured a cup of tea for Miles and departed.

Daphne said, 'You look smart, Miles, my compliments on your suit. Savile Row?'

'Yes, but old, I've had it for years. Giles, my tailor, did a few crucial alterations and spruced it up a bit.'

'What on earth is going on in your life, Miles? I know you and Clarissa are separated, but isn't there going to be a divorce?' Felicity held him with her eyes.

'I'm afraid not, simply because she refuses to give me a divorce,' Miles told his mother, grimacing. 'She is as unmovable as a rock. She doesn't need money and she doesn't want a divorce. And that's that.'

Felicity let out a long sigh. 'I never understand women who want to cling onto men who don't want them. It's ridiculous. And what you're saying is that you have nothing to bargain with, because of her father's great wealth. She doesn't need your house or your alimony.'

'Exactly.'

'Would you like me to go and see her, Miles? Intervene for you? Clarissa always liked me – a lot, actually – and I might be able to drill a bit of sense into her.'

'That's so nice of you, Mama, very kind, but it won't work. I know her, and she won't give an inch. But look, you never know, do you? Life can come up and hit you in the face, give you a hard blow. Or it can caress you and make your dreams come true. Yes, that's life. Unpredictable.'

Felicity laughed. 'Certainly my life has been unpredictable.'

'It surely has,' Miles agreed. He leaned forward, and focused his gaze on his mother. 'Whilst I'm here, I need to ask you something, Mama.'

Looking at him swiftly, detecting a change in his voice, she said, 'Yes, of course, what is it?'

'I can't help asking how much of a muddle your jewellery is in?'

'My jewellery? It's not in a muddle! It's all well taken care of, I can assure you of that.' Felicity appeared to be genuinely puzzled by his question, and stared back at him, looking askance.

Miles said, 'I'm glad to hear it. Because you won't have any trouble sorting out the pieces which belong to me, as the heir to the earldom and the Ingham Estate.'

'What? What are you talking about?' Felicity's voice rose an octave as she spoke.

'Look, Mama, I am not accusing you of anything, just explaining that when you left Cavendon years ago, you inadvertently took jewellery you might have thought was yours. But it wasn't. Isn't, I should say. It belongs to the Ingham Estate.'

'All of my jewellery was given to me by my father,' she cried, outraged.

'No, it wasn't. Some of it comes from the vaults at Cavendon. You wore it for many years, and you therefore may believe it's yours. But, as I just said, it isn't.'

Felicity swallowed, knowing that she was in trouble. It had never occurred to her that anyone would notice, come asking for it back. Charles was so careless about possessions. But this was Miles, and he was very different.

Looking directly at him, about to start a string of lies, she stopped herself. His blue eyes were full of ice, and there was such a cold expression on his face, she shrank back on the sofa. His father was soft, weak; Miles was just the opposite of Charles. Tough, ruthless, and he could be as hard as nails. These traits had been inherited from her father, that she knew. And at this moment she understood she could never win with her son.

Before she could say anything more, Miles was handing her a piece of paper. 'This is the list of the items which belong to the Ingham Estate. I think it might refresh your memory. I know how easy it is to get things mixed up.'

Felicity took the paper from him, knowing she had no choice. Her eyes ran down the list. It was correct. She glanced up as Miles began to speak once again.

'I'm sorry, I didn't hear what you said,' Felicity muttered.

'I was explaining that I was at our solicitors' the other day, and they drew up a legal document, requesting the return of all the pieces. Immediately. To be handed to me,'

Miles said in a level voice. 'This is just a simple letter, Mama, but if you do not comply with their request on my behalf, I will have to instruct them to send you a legal writ. And you may have to go into a court of law to defend yourself.' He handed the letter to her.

'My God, Miles, I'm your mother! How can you say things like this? You are accusing me of—'

'Stop right there,' Daphne said. 'Miles hasn't accused you of anything, Mama. He has asked you to sort out the muddle of your jewellery boxes and give back those that are ours. That's all.'

Miles said, 'Perhaps Wilson could help you, Mama. After all, she's been handling all of your jewellery for years. She probably understands what's what better than you.'

DeLacy stood up. This was her cue. 'I'll go down to the servants' hall, Mama. I think Miles has had a good idea. Wilson will certainly know where everything is, won't she?'

Felicity did not answer. She looked from DeLacy to Daphne, and back to Miles. And she understood then, knew suddenly what this had all been about. Bringing Annabel to tea had simply been a ploy to get them into her house. And now they were ganged up on her, the three of them, and about to take away her precious jewels. All that she had left in her life that gave her any pleasure these days. Certainly she didn't get any pleasure from her husband, Lawrence Pierce, the world's greatest fornicator. He was in Paris with his mistress, she knew that. Her jealousy rose up in her throat like bile as she thought of him with another woman, giving her what she was meant to get from him. And when he returned to London he would be giving it to Helen Malone, the actress and his other whore.

Unable to stand being in the room any longer, Felicity jumped up at exactly the same moment Olive Wilson walked in with DeLacy.

Glaring at them, Felicity said in a choked voice, 'Let us all go upstairs and we'll catch them.'

Miles glanced at Wilson swiftly, scowling, a quizzical look in his eyes. Wilson shook her head slightly and stood aside to let Felicity walk past her.

'Go ahead, Daphne, and you too, DeLacy. You can both help Mama.'

They did as he suggested.

Miles put out a hand and held Olive Wilson back. 'What does she mean . . . catch them?'

'It's not important, sir. Mrs Pierce sometimes makes mistakes like that these days. I think what she meant to say was "we'll get them". Meaning get the jewels.'

'I understand. Come with me, Wilson. You are the best person to help us sort it out. She trusts you. I'm perfectly certain she doesn't trust me.'

Felicity sat in a chair in her bedroom saying nothing as Wilson and DeLacy brought out velvet bags of jewellery. They were all in the safe. This was inside a locked cupboard in Felicity's dressing room.

Miles and Daphne opened the bags, checked everything off on the list, and when they were satisfied, Miles said to DeLacy, 'Please go downstairs. When you open the front door you should find Eric there, with Hartley in the Rolls. And Harry, too. They'll come up with suitcases, help us to carry everything down. And Eric and Harry will put them in the vault at the house. They'll be transferred to Cavendon as soon as possible.'

FORTY-TWO

It was DeLacy who knew all of the best nightclubs and restaurants in London. This was because Simon, her ex-husband, was a dashing young man about town, a dandy who fancied himself, and loved to go out every night to show himself off. That's what they had done when they had been married. He had been proud to have DeLacy on his arm, looking beautiful in a very short dress, the style favoured by the flappers, and wearing lots of the jewellery he had given her.

Her ex-husband's favourite nightspot was the Gargoyle Club on Meard Street, a regular haunt for artists and aristocrats. It had been founded in 1925 by Simon's friend, another aristocrat called David Tennant. It was sumptuously decorated, and some of the glamorous interiors had been done by the French painter, Henri Matisse. The Gargoyle boasted a four-piece orchestra, and, as in all nightclubs, food had to be served with the liquor because of the law. A lot of it went uneaten because most people arrived late, after dinner.

DeLacy's favourite club was the Kit Cat. She loved to dance, and the club had a black jazz band from America which she thought was the best in town. She could do the

Charleston, the Black Bottom, but mostly favoured the foxtrot and the tango. The other reason she liked this club was because Simon hardly ever went there.

After a happy celebration supper at the Grosvenor Square house, Miles suggested they should go to a night-club to celebrate the return of the jewels. These were now safely locked up in the vault down in the basement.

Several of the women demurred, and Miles exclaimed, 'Oh come on, let's go out and have a bit of fun for once. All we do these days is work and worry about keeping Cavendon safe. I could use a bit of a bash and I bet every-one else could.'

'Yes, it would be lovely, come on, don't be spoilsports,' Cecily cajoled. 'It'll do us good.'

Diedre declined. She explained she felt queasy and wanted Paul to take her home.

Dulcie was adamant about not going, murmuring something about drawing up plans for the interiors of her art gallery. But, in truth, she preferred to go up to her room and think about James. He had asked her to meet him after the play ended tomorrow evening. He wished to take her to dinner at the Savoy. 'And at least I can hold you in my arms on the dance floor,' he had said. And she had agreed to go to the stage door to pick him up.

Hugo, noticing that Miles now had a glum expression on his face, decided they should humour him. Hugo had been unable to accompany them to Charles Street earlier today, because of a business meeting. But Miles had assured him that Lawrence Pierce really was abroad, and that Daphne would be perfectly safe with their mother, they all would. Felicity would have no one there to intervene or throw them out.

'Yes, let's go!' Hugo exclaimed. 'Daphne and I will join you.' He smiled at his wife as he said this, and added, 'I would love a whirl with you, darling. And it has been ages since we've had a night out. Miles is right about that.'

Daphne agreed at once, looked at her sister and said, 'Come on, DeLacy, you're the expert. Where shall we go?'

'The Kit Cat. I love it and they know me well there. But we'd better leave soon. They get awfully busy after eleven.' DeLacy stood up and walked across the dining room. 'Hurry up,' she called, going out into the foyer.

They were welcomed with open arms and a lot of bowing and scraping by the staff of the Kit Cat. And, naturally, because it was Lady DeLacy, they were given the best table in the nightclub. The decorations were glamorous, and there was a great buzz. But it was smoky, the light a bit murky. On the other hand, the black jazz band were playing their hearts out, and the atmosphere was exciting – thrilling, really. They had arrived just in time. Within half an hour the club was packed with flappers, beautiful girls in short frocks accompanied by handsome young men, smoking cigarettes and holding glasses of champagne in their hands.

Automatically, several waiters brought champagne, a bowl of caviar, and a plate of toast fingers along with lemon wedges to their table.

'God, caviar,' Miles said, glancing at DeLacy. 'I love it! But I'm not sure I can eat it right now.'

DeLacy smiled at him. 'You might later, we all might. And they will bring other small things, like smoked salmon on toast, small steak sandwiches. They have to serve food because of the liquor laws. Anyway, you might be hungry in an hour or two.'

'I understand.' Miles lifted his champagne flute and said, 'Cheers everyone. And thank you, ladies, for being on my team. We got the jewellery. Part of our safety net is back in our hands.'

'Cheers,' they all said, echoing him.

Hugo said, 'Thank goodness it went off without a hitch. But then she was outnumbered and outmatched. I recently heard that Felicity was not quite as bright mentally as she used to be.'

'Oh, I don't know about that,' Miles asserted. 'I thought she was very alert. Didn't you, Daphne? DeLacy?'

DeLacy said, 'Very much so. And she was the other day, when I had tea with her and Pierce. But I do think she gets a bit flustered when he is away. Wilson sort of indicated she was possessive of him.'

'I agree with that,' Daphne interjected. 'And I'm just thankful we managed to accomplish our . . . mission, shall we call it, without there being any kind of scandal. You know Papa wouldn't like that at all. And, incidentally, they'll be back in London in about two weeks. He has to give Diedre away, you know.'

Miles asked Cecily to dance, and together, hand-in-hand, they went onto the dance floor, smiling at each other, happy to be together. At one moment, against his cheek, she said, 'I'm so happy you managed to retrieve the jewels, Miles. However, you must always remember that when you have something to sell, you must have a buyer. If you don't, you have nothing of value.'

Miles kept on dancing, but he was startled by these words, and leaned back slightly, staring down at her. 'What do you mean?'

'Exactly what I said. There must be someone who wants the commodity, whatever it is, otherwise it's a worthless commodity.'

'That's a depressing thought. You've just thrown cold water on my jubilant mood,' he said in a low voice, trying not to show he was annoyed.

'No, I haven't,' she answered, drawing close to him again. 'I'm just pointing out the reality of things . . . because when your father comes back I want you to advise him to sell certain pieces of jewellery. And I think he ought to allow Dulcie to open her gallery and sell the items in storage in the attics. What good are they doing there?'

'Why this desire to sell things all of a sudden?' Miles asked, trying not to sound worried.

'Because the world is in a buying mood, on a roll right now. There's a lot of money around. People are in a good mood because business is roaring along non-stop. Everyone has telephones and cars. Women are buying . . . and especially my clothes. In other words, it's boom time.'

'I see what you're getting at, and I suppose you're right. There's an awful lot of jewellery at Cavendon, even without these pieces we just got back. I will talk to him. And you must talk to Charlotte. You know she has the most influence over him.'

'I certainly will. And Charlotte has a lot of common sense. But let's forget it now, and enjoy ourselves.' She kissed his cheek and whispered, 'I love you, Miles Ingham. I love you with all my heart.'

'And I love you, my smart, clever, adorable Cecily Swann.'

A few moments later, Miles and Cecily both noticed that Hugo and Daphne were now dancing. And they edged closer to them, moving through other couples on the floor.

Miles glanced at Daphne, and asked, 'Did you leave DeLacy alone? I think Ceci and I should go back to the table. She might be a bit forlorn. You know how she gets.'

'Oh she's not forlorn, not one bit. Some extremely handsome man came over to the table and introduced himself to us. It was the well-known painter, Travers Merton. He asked if he could speak with her privately, so Hugo and I got up and came onto the dance floor.'

'Travers Merton,' Miles repeated. 'My goodness.'

Cecily murmured, 'DeLacy can handle herself, Miles. She'll be fine. Let's enjoy this dance.'

When Travers Merton arrived at the table, asking if she was Lady DeLacy Ingham, DeLacy had nodded, wondering who this man was.

Now the two of them were chatting earnestly and drinking champagne together. When Hugo and Daphne had done their disappearing act, she had asked the artist to sit down. He had done so at once.

'What a stroke of luck,' Travers said now, gazing at DeLacy. 'Pierce said you were beautiful, but he underplayed it. You are staggeringly beautiful, Lady DeLacy. The most beautiful woman I have ever seen. It is my honour to paint your portrait. And I wish to thank you in advance for agreeing to sit for me. I just hope I can do you justice.'

DeLacy was beaming at him, flattered by his words. He was not only charming, but a darkly handsome man with a certain bearing, and it was obvious he was from a good background. She thought he was about thirty-five or thereabouts, certainly younger than she had expected him to be. She felt drawn to him; he had a certain magnetism.

Finding her voice, she said, 'I am the one who is honoured. Thank you for agreeing to paint me, Mr Merton.'

Leaning across the table, he said in a soft voice, 'I wish we could start the portrait tomorrow. You're not by any chance free, are you?'

'I am, yes. In the afternoon.'

'Oh that's marvellous. Could you come to my studio at about four o'clock? The light will still be good. I could do the preliminary sketches.'

'It's a perfect time for me,' DeLacy replied, feeling suddenly hot all over. She hoped she wasn't blushing.

Travers Merton was filled with pleasure, and he lifted his champagne flute. 'To our collaboration. I think it is going to be rather exciting, don't you?'

DeLacy clinked her glass to his, and merely smiled.

Travers smiled back, and knew at that moment he was going to make her his. He wouldn't be able to resist her. She was delectable, sexually arousing to him. No wonder Lawrence Pierce wanted her for himself. He had never said that exactly, but Travers Merton realized she would be Pierce's ultimate prize. Lawrence Pierce had taken everything from Felicity. Her love. Her sexuality. A great deal of her money. And lately her peace of mind. To Travers it was obvious Pierce would want her gorgeous daughter. That was the way the man was made. And Travers was positive the surgeon suffered from Don Juan syndrome. Certainly he couldn't resist women. He was a serial womanizer of the worst kind.

'You're rather quiet,' DeLacy said, looking across the table at Travers Merton, wondering what he was thinking.

'Oh, I'm so sorry. I'm afraid I was caught up in my thoughts about your portrait. I was wondering what you planned to wear. Perhaps we could discuss it?'

DeLacy nodded. She felt relaxed with the artist, found him attractive, and he gave her a certain confidence. 'It will be head and shoulders, will it?' she asked.

'I think so. Yes, yes,' he answered swiftly, studying her in the dim light of the nightclub. 'You do have the loveliest neck, swan like, and I can see part of your shoulders. They are perfect, smooth as white marble.' He paused, sipped his champagne. 'If you have a gown that is off the shoulders, or a blouse with the same neckline, either would be ideal. I would like it to be white . . . very virginal. Ideal for such a beauty as you.'

'I have a number of suitable things,' DeLacy said, enjoying his flattery, his lovely manner with her.

'Are you free over the weekend? We could really make progress if you can sit for me then. Perhaps I could start on the canvas.'

305

At this precise moment, DeLacy saw Clarissa walking into the club on the arm of a good-looking young man. Miles had told her that Clarissa had put on weight, and looked blowsy and unkempt. But not tonight. She was plumpish but elegant, her brown hair cut in a sleek bob, and she was wearing makeup and looked quite beautiful in a yellow chiffon gown. A bit of a transformation had obviously taken place. DeLacy couldn't wait to tell Miles.

Travers cleared his throat.

'Yes, I am available on Saturday and on Sunday also,' DeLacy announced. 'I know Lawrence wants to give the portrait to my mother for Christmas, and that's not so far off.'

'I will give him the portrait of you in time,' Travers Merton answered. But I won't give you to him, he thought. You are going to be mine. I shall save you from him. There was no way Travers could know that night that DeLacy would be his greatest love. Or that she would cost him his life.

FORTY-THREE

Paul Drummond sat at his desk in Hugo's London office, going over a few notes he had made about the dinner in New York, which he had recently planned. It was to be a celebration of his marriage to Diedre, in fact, for family and old friends. It would be small but elegant.

He leaned forward and looked at the calendar. It was Thursday 30 September today. In exactly ten days, on Sunday 10 October, they would become husband and wife.

Diedre was thrilled that her father would be giving her away, relieved that Charles and Charlotte would be returning to London next week. The marriage would be in London and the reception at the Grosvenor Square house.

He, too, was thrilled that his half-brother Timothy was already in London. He had arrived several days ago, and was ensconced at the Ritz Hotel in Piccadilly with his wife Elizabeth, their fifteen-year-old daughter Gwynneth, and twin sons, Lance and Cole, who were twelve. Tim was going to be his best man.

Dulcie, DeLacy and his niece Gwynneth were going to be Diedre's bridesmaids, in frocks designed and made by Cecily, who had also created the wedding gown for the bride.

They had both wanted a small wedding, but Diedre had insisted on certain things, including four ushers. When he had asked who they were, just out of curiosity, she had said, with a twinkle in her bright blue eyes, 'James Brentwood, Miles, Hugo and Harry Swann. How do you like them apples?'

He laughed to himself now, remembering how she had picked up that phrase from him, as well as many others. He had told her he liked 'them apples' a lot.

After the wedding, they would spend a few days in London, then sail to New York on the *Aquitania*.

Once they arrived in Manhattan, they would be living at his triplex apartment on Park Avenue. Two years ago his mother had moved out and given it to him. It was too big for her and the stairs were troublesome. Since then, she had occupied his small bachelor apartment on Fifth, which Elizabeth had revamped for her. It was much more comfortable for his mother, and it was on one floor.

He could not help thinking what a great idea that switch had been. He had a lovely home to take Diedre to, plus the family mansion in Connecticut, left to him by his father in his will.

The ringing phone brought Paul up with a start, and he reached for it. 'Drummond here.'

'Hello, Paul,' his brother said.

'This is a nice surprise.' Glancing at the clock, seeing that it was just twelve noon, he asked, 'Do you happen to be free for lunch, Tim?'

'Yes. But I'd like to come over to your office first. Ask Hugo to join us, will you?'

'I will, but he might not be free.'

'He'll have to make himself free. I have something important to tell you. It's urgent. I'm leaving the hotel now, so I should be there in about fifteen minutes. See you.' Tim hung up.

Pushing himself to his feet, suddenly hit by a rush of anxiety, Paul left his office, wondering what had happened. Something was wrong. And it had to be about business, not his mother's health.

He knocked on Hugo's door and walked in uninvited, so anxious was he.

Hugo was on the phone; he stared across at Paul. 'Can you give me a minute or two?'

'Sorry, no. Something has happened, has to be business. Tim wants to see us. Right now. He's on his way over here.'

'I'll have to go, Daphne,' Hugo said. 'I'll ring you later, darling.' He put the receiver down and said, 'Didn't he tell you what it was?'

'No. But I know him intimately. He was tense, terse, and I've a horrible feeling it's to do with us.'

'I got a call late yesterday afternoon from Allan Carlton. As you know, Paul, he's my vice-president at the bank,' Tim said, and looked over at Hugo. 'Brilliant guy, well connected, has his ear close to the ground, knows a lot no one else knows in the banking world and Wall Street.'

Hugo nodded. 'In other words, he's a reliable source.'

'More than reliable. He doesn't pass anything to me unless he's absolutely certain it's true.'

'How does he manage that?' Hugo asked, sounding doubtful.

Timothy said, 'I don't know, I don't ask, but he's never been wrong.'

'What did he tell you yesterday?' Paul gave his brother a searching look, his worry escalating, his impatience starting to show.

'He said that from information he has just received, he believes Transatlantic Air is in dire straits, desperately trying to raise money. He predicts they could go belly-up, and real soon.'

'Oh my God!' Hugo exclaimed, reeling with shock. His face was ashen.

Paul had also lost his colour; his face was pale. His voice was shaky, when he said, 'When will this happen? Did Allan say?'

'No, he could only hazard a guess. He thinks it will be some time soon, within this month. Al Birkin, the guy who runs the company, has a few tricks up his sleeve. And a possible buyer for Transatlantic – some German tycoon. But can he pull it off? That we don't know.'

'They won't buy us out now, will they?' Hugo muttered.

Timothy exclaimed, 'They don't have anything to buy you out with! No cash.'

'We had twenty million invested,' Paul managed to say. 'Which we're about to lose if the company does go belly-up.'

'*When* it goes belly-up, Paul, because it will. And they'll declare bankruptcy. So, yes, the investment is gone, kaput, out the window,' his brother said in a firm voice, shaking his head.

Hugo gaped at them both and slumped back in his chair, looking as if he was about to pass out.

Timothy went on, 'You've both lost five million bucks each. You can eat that loss, Paul. It won't ruin you by any means. But what about you, Hugo? Can you afford to lose five million dollars?'

'I think so, and I do have some other investments I can cash in to fill the gap, keep us financially secure. My family, that is. But Cavendon had ten million invested in Transatlantic. That's a loss they can't afford. The money we invested was for the future: death duties, taxes, and future generations . . .' Hugo did not finish his sentence.

The silence in the room lasted a long time. The atmosphere was filled with gloom, a palpable sense of worry and despair. Each man was hunched in his chair, struggling with this horrendous news.

Paul suddenly said, 'I can't let Cavendon take this loss. It's my fault. I was the one who brought Transatlantic Air into the picture. I am going to sell some real estate. I must return the money to them. Wipe the slate clean.'

'What real estate are you referring to?' Timothy asked.

'My flat in London. When we come back we will live at Diedre's. There's the house in Connecticut. About eight hundred acres in Litchfield County, plus the mansion itself. That's large, as you know, and has all the amenities. Pool and tennis court, gardens. And I have some buildings in the meatpacking district – lofts and factories. They should bring something worthwhile.'

'Yes, I think they will,' Timothy agreed. 'But real estate can take time to sell.'

Paul said, 'I want Drummond-Manhattan Bank to lend me that ten million dollars, Tim, for that reason. The real estate will be my collateral. Once it's all sold, the bank gets their money back.'

'All right, I'll do it,' Timothy agreed at once, without any pondering. 'I do have a board to answer to, Paul, obviously. But I doubt they'll create a problem.'

Standing up, he walked over to Paul and stretched out his hand. 'Signed, sealed and delivered,' he said. 'You've got a deal.'

Paul nodded. 'Thank you, Tim. I'm immensely grateful. I want to do this as quickly as we can. Because no doubt the news about Transatlantic going bankrupt will be in all the papers. And perhaps sooner than we think. I don't want Charles to be worried. Or Diedre. Let's not forget, I've got a wedding in ten days.'

'We'll clear it up before then,' Timothy said, 'I promise.'

Hugo, almost at his wits' end with worry, managed to say, 'Thank you, Paul. I'm very grateful, and Charles will be too.'

'Do we tell them anything about Transatlantic's problems this weekend?' Paul asked, glancing at Hugo.

'Perhaps we'd better not,' he said swiftly. 'Why spoil all the excitement and happiness about your upcoming marriage?'

'I agree,' Paul replied. 'Knowing Tim, he'll move quickly. Won't you?' He looked at his brother expectantly.

Timothy nodded. 'I sure will. I'll call Allan later. He'll get things moving, and talk to our real-estate people.'

Much later in the day, when he was finally alone in his own office, Hugo Stanton sat pondering. Paul had turned out to be as true blue as he had always thought he was. Hugo was thankful Timothy Drummond was in London and willing to help them.

On the other hand, Hugo knew what bank boards were like. Difficult. All boards were difficult. And that was what worried him. The board of directors of the Drummond-Manhattan Private Bank could turn the loan down. Then what would happen?

If the Ingham Trust didn't get their ten million dollars back, eventually Cavendon would go down. Not now. Not next year, because they still had funds. But not enough. The estate wouldn't survive very long, and the Inghams would eventually fall.

Hugo's heart was heavy as he went home, wondering how to keep this from Daphne. He had to. He would pray to God to save them.

PART THREE

Women Warriors
January–June 1927

Every lover is a warrior, and Cupid has his camp.
                                                    Ovid

Sweet is revenge – especially to women.
                                              Lord Byron

FORTY-FOUR

Charles Ingham, 6th Earl of Mowbray, sat at his Georgian desk in the library at Cavendon Hall. There was a broad smile on his face as he looked at the papers spread out in front of him. In particular, he was thrilled by the news in the telegram he had just received, and he was smiling because – for the first time in the last six years – their finances were relatively stable. His relief was enormous. And it was all due to Hugo and Paul who had pulled a prize rabbit out of a hat.

The ten million dollars, which had been retrieved from their disastrous Wall Street venture, thanks to these two men, had gone back into the Ingham Trust. It would not remain there for very long. Some of it had to be carefully invested in a number of safe English companies, chosen by him and Hugo – because money had to be made to work, to earn more money. But they wanted to lower the risk; they were taking no chances. Part of it had to be put aside for government taxes, as well as the weekly running of the house and the estate.

But at least they weren't on the brink of disaster. For the moment. Unfortunately, there were a lot of repairs to be done, mostly in the North Wing. That entire wing needed a new roof, and numerous windows had to be replaced, as did several floors in the main downstairs rooms; the dining room and the library needed the most work.

There was a knock on the door and, before he could say anything, Hanson's face appeared around it.

'A word, my lord?' Hanson said. 'Or am I interrupting?'

'Not at all, Hanson. Don't loiter there. Come in.' Yet again he couldn't help thinking how well the butler looked. When he and Charlotte had returned from Zurich in October they had both been surprised at Hanson's ruddy health. And pleased that he was in such good shape.

As he glanced at the butler, Charles detected a hint of worry, and asked swiftly, 'What's wrong, Hanson? I can tell by your expression we have a problem.'

'Unfortunately. There's a bad leak in the West Wing—'

'Damnation! Most of our guests are staying in that wing. Where's the leak? In a bedroom or one of the suites?'

'The Wedgwood Suite, my lord.'

'Good God! I hope it's not the ceiling and the walls. That room is a masterpiece, and full of valuable antiques.'

'It's a plumbing problem, Lord Mowbray. Luckily, Mrs Thwaites spotted it this morning when she was up there with one of the maids. The pipes in the bathroom have burst. I have Ted Swann in there already, fixing the leak. But it seems to be a job that will take a few days. We can't use that suite for a week at least, Your Lordship.'

'There're plenty of other bedrooms in that wing. Any suggestions, Hanson?'

'I've done a quick tour with Mrs Thwaites, and we selected two bedrooms and one suite. The bedrooms are the Gold Room and the Apricot Room, and there's the Venetian Suite, so beloved by your grandmother, Countess Florence, m'lord.'

'It's got rather a lot of rare Venetian glass in it, Hanson. That's why it's not often used. I'll think about it. In the meantime, what about the Chinoiserie Suite in the South Wing?'

'Do you think Lady Daphne will mind having guests in her wing, Lord Mowbray?'

'I don't suppose so, Hanson. But we can ask her. We'll work it out – after all, this old pile is full of bedrooms.'

'That it is, m'lord. When the festivities are over, I think we should have Ted Swann and his staff look at every bathroom and every bedroom. In each wing. The weather has been so bad for the last two months. Such a lot of snow and ice. It's imperative that we pay attention to all of the pipes in particular.'

'You're right, Hanson, as usual. Better do a good overall check with Mrs Thwaites and Lady Charlotte. I'll make her aware of the problem later.'

Hanson nodded and was gone.

A short while later, Charlotte came into the library; as she walked towards him, he thought: My wife. Charlotte is my wife. Mine to have and to hold for as long as I live. How lucky I am.

He rose as she came to his desk. Putting his arms around her, he kissed her cheek.

'You have a cold nose,' he said, leaning away from her, laughing.

'Just like a puppy.'

'A beautiful puppy,' he answered, still laughing.

His happiness with her was something sublime. He had never been so happy in his adult life. Charlotte truly was his better half.

Putting his arm around her shoulder, he walked her over to the fireplace, where they stood in front of the roaring flames. She said, 'That feels good . . . the warmth. It's rather cold out today, Charles. If you go for a walk, you must be properly dressed.'

'Where were you, darling? I was looking for you earlier.'

'I popped down to see Lady Gwendolyn. She wanted to discuss what to wear for the various events this weekend,' Charlotte told him.

Charles said, 'I don't suppose she mentioned what she did the other day, did she?'

'No. What happened?'

'She wrote me a cheque for five thousand pounds and wouldn't take no for an answer. When I refused, she forced it on me, and I just didn't have the heart to push it back at her. She would've been hurt.'

'Why was she giving you five thousand pounds?'

'She said she wanted to contribute to the cost of Dulcie's wedding, and that since I was her heir, she thought I might as well have some of the money now instead of later. When she was dead.'

Charlotte saw the mirth in Charles's eyes, and she was amused too. 'There's really nobody like her. Oh, and by the way, she insists I now call her Aunt Gwendolyn.'

'And so you should. She's right about that.'

'Anyway, that was a lovely gesture on her part, and the money will come in useful. I've had to hire fifteen women from the village, Charles, and they do expect to be paid.'

'Fifteen women! Whatever for?' He looked aghast.

'To look after the guests. We will have approximately twelve additional people staying in the house. It's bad weather, snowing. There are various events, both during the day and in the evening. And we have outside guests coming, too, Charles. I asked Mrs Thwaites to prepare a couple of rooms, the parlour and the mud room for Wellington boots, raincoats, topcoats and umbrellas. And I suggested Ted should put in racks. We need an extra cloakroom or two, you see.'

'I do see. And you've done the right thing.'

'Cook also needs extra help,' Charlotte pointed out.

'The guests who are staying here have to be fed . . . breakfasts and lunches. That's why I've hired a caterer to help Cook with the dinners on Saturday and Sunday. That is my contribution to this wedding, by the way.'

'Charlotte, no! I won't have it. I can well afford to pay—'

'Too late, Charlie,' she interrupted. 'I have already paid the caterer in advance. It's done and dusted.'

Charles let out a long sigh. 'Whatever am I going to do with you?' he asked, shaking his head.

'You can always kiss me, Charlie – whenever you want, and wherever you want, these days,' she replied, laughing. 'We're married now. No more sneaking around.'

He grinned at her, loving her so much. She could do no wrong in his eyes. The only time he'd ever been cross with her was when she had bossed him around when he was a boy.

Charlotte said, 'I heard about the leaks in the West Wing. Mrs Thwaites just told me. I'll get to it with her and Hanson next week, I promise.'

There was a knock on the door and Daphne came in. She walked across to the fireplace, saying as she did, 'I'm so glad you're both here. Hugo's had a call from Mark, a short while ago.' Tears welled in her eyes, and her voice was shaky. 'Aunt Lavinia can't come tomorrow. She's apparently taken a turn for the worse.'

Daphne sat down on the sofa. Charlotte joined her, putting an arm around her comfortingly. 'I'm so sorry,' she murmured.

Charles was momentarily stunned. His sister had been in remission. He felt an overwhelming sense of helplessness, followed by a sudden premonition that Lavinia would not survive. Cancer was a killer. He sat down in a chair, consumed with worry and apprehension. And much regret.

A moment later, Hugo came in and joined them at the fireplace. He said to Charles, 'Mark apologizes for not speaking to you. He just felt he couldn't talk coherently, he's so upset. That's why he spoke to me instead, Charles. Lavinia is quite ill. He feels it's wiser that she stays in London.'

'I understand,' Charles answered. 'I shall speak to him later, and perhaps Lavinia will be able to come to the phone as well.'

Daphne exclaimed, 'I think we were so unkind to her. Now I regret it terribly. I was hoping to make her feel better this weekend. About us. I wanted her to understand we love her.'

'I'm sorry you felt you had to shut her out of the inner circle because of the things she said about me,' Charlotte interjected. 'I really didn't care, you know, and I knew she would accept me. After all, we've been friends since childhood.'

'You knew!' Daphne exclaimed, and then let out a long sigh. 'Of course you knew, you're a Swann.'

'Vanessa is coming, isn't she?' Charles asked, looking across at Charlotte.

'Yes, darling, she's arriving tomorrow with Richard.'

'Personally I'm glad Great-Aunt Gwendolyn cancelled that engagement party for Vanessa and Richard,' Daphne remarked. 'Lavinia was ill, and Vanessa did the right thing, asking our aunt to postpone. Also, the date was very close to Diedre's wedding.' There was a pause, and then she added, 'I'm sorry Diedre won't be here this weekend. What a disappointment. But I suppose she has to follow doctor's orders.'

'Yes, she does, Daphne. Nobody ever wanted to be here at Cavendon more than she did,' Charles said. 'Paul explained in his letter to me that the doctor didn't want her to travel. They're afraid Diedre might lose the baby. That's why it's bedrest for the time being.'

Charlotte said, 'I'm absolutely positive that Diedre will be fine, Charles. Do try not to worry.'

Wanting to change the subject, Daphne said, 'Oh, by the way, Papa, Wilson was touched that you thanked her for helping us to get the jewels back.'

'I was very grateful to her, as well as to your little team.'

'Miles calls it *his* team.'

'Let's just call it the winning team,' Charles murmured. 'And is Wilson now working here permanently, Daphne?'

'She is, Papa, and she's wonderful. A very efficient lady's maid. And she makes herself useful in other ways. She's also a nice person.' Daphne smiled inwardly, thinking how Olive Wilson had changed her life for the better, had made it so much easier.

Daphne looked at her father and said, 'Miles says those jewels are contaminated. He thinks we ought to auction them off, Papa.'

Charles was surprised by this comment, and exclaimed, 'We're not selling anything. We're managing very nicely, at the moment. There's no reason to make any reckless moves.'

FORTY-FIVE

The grand entrance hall at Cavendon was empty when Travers Merton walked downstairs on this cold Friday morning in January. He glanced around, once again admiring the extraordinary paintings on the walls. All of them were by some of the greatest English portraitists of the eighteenth century. And it was quite an array of ancestors, going up along the staircase wall and around the entrance hall as well.

After slipping into his overcoat and wrapping the wool scarf around his neck, Travers strode towards the front door. And then, out of the corner of his eye, he caught sight of Hanson. Now he hurried in the direction of the dining room where the butler was heading.

'Mr Hanson!' he called. 'Oh, Mr Hanson. Could I have a word with you, please?'

Hanson swung around at once, smiled when he saw Travers. 'Yes, of course you can, Mr Merton. How can I be of help?'

'I was wondering if it would be all right for me to go into the church? I don't want to disturb anyone working there.'

'You are talking about the little church here on the estate, aren't you, Mr Merton?'

'Yes, the one up the hill, behind the stable block.'

'There is no one in there, sir. You see, the wedding is to be held in the village church. It's much larger and quite a crowd is expected. Friends of the groom, as well as his family.'

'Oh I see. I hadn't realized it was at a different location. I love old churches, Hanson. I enjoy prowling around them, studying the architecture.'

The butler nodded. 'I knew your grandfather, Mr Merton. I haven't had a chance to mention that before. Lord Noyers was such a lovely gentleman; he came here for the grouse. He was one of the Guns.'

Travers nodded. 'Yes, I know. He was a close friend of Lord Mowbray's father, the Fifth Earl, and he enjoyed his trips to Yorkshire. So did my grandmother. They're long gone now, I'm afraid. They died within a few weeks of each other, seven years ago now.'

'I did know that, Mr Merton. It must have been a big loss for you.'

'It was. They brought me up. I was an only child. Anyway, thank you, Hanson. I shall wander up to the church. Oh, and by the way, is Lady DeLacy anywhere around? I looked for her after breakfast, but no luck.'

'I'm not sure where she is at the moment. I do know that she is meeting with her sisters and Miss Cecily later. A ladies' get-together of some sort, sir.'

'She did mention that. Well, perhaps she's gone for a walk. I might run into her outside. Thank you again, Hanson.'

'My pleasure, Mr Merton. It's icy. I'm glad to see you're wearing a topcoat. Enjoy your visit to the church, sir.'

'Thank you,' Travers said, and hurried on towards the front door.

It was a white landscape outside. The fields and moorland were totally covered in snow, which glistened brightly in the sunlight.

Not even a bare black branch, Travers thought, as he walked up the hill. Even they are weighted down by snow. I couldn't even do a black-and-white etching in grisaille.

He was surprised when he pushed open the old oak door and stepped into the church. It was warm; then he noticed the paraffin stoves standing against some of the walls. Somebody knows their job, he thought, moving forward, his attention caught by the extraordinary stained-glass windows, their vivid colours brilliant from the sunshine pouring into the church.

He sat down in a pew and looked around, noticing flowers on the altar. The church was well taken care of: that was patently obvious. But then so was this great stately home. The Inghams knew what they were doing, preserving it so well. Hats off to them, he thought, and with admiration.

He had grown up in a lovely manor house, not a great stately home like Cavendon, but that, too, had been looked after scrupulously by his grandparents. Compton Noyers was a Tudor house, not far from Cirencester in Gloucestershire, and he tried to go down at weekends. It was his. Both of his parents had died in an accident when he was a child. He had promised his grandfather he would not sell the house, and would one day bring up a family there. He kept a housekeeper and a caretaker, and the house was always ready to receive him.

A small smile flickered around his mouth. He might well be able to keep that promise now. And all because of a girl he had lusted after, thinking only of sexual conquest and his own pleasure. But with whom he had fallen deeply in love.

His beautiful, tender, loving DeLacy, the girl of his dreams; the kind of girl he had never thought he would meet. Golden hair, blue eyes like a summer sky, and a complexion like a summer rose. Her features were delicate, finely sculpted. What a beauty.

But he had met her and had known within the first week that this was no lady to be lusted after and left. This was a special and unique young woman. A woman he wanted to love and protect, and keep close to him forever. And, much to his own amazement, she had eventually reciprocated his feelings.

Looking back, he remembered how difficult things had been at first, when, after weeks of painting her portrait, he had managed to woo her into his bed. Now he recalled his shock when he realized how terrified she was of physical contact with a man, and genuinely afraid of sex. Only after a great deal of gentle coaxing, touching and endless foreplay had he managed to make her feel relaxed enough to finally make love. His gentleness, tenderness and genuine feelings for her had won her over at last. But it had been quite a task to quell that awful fear she harboured.

It was only after they became sexually bonded and truly close that she told him about her marriage, and the way Simon Powers had treated her. It was virtual rape on their wedding night. Later, he was so demanding, so rough and uncouth with her, she had frozen. He had called her names – rather vulgar names at that; said that she was frigid, a bitch, and on and on. Their quarrels had been violent at times, and yet she had wanted to make the marriage work.

When he had finally asked her why that was, she had simply said it was the way she had been brought up. Her father had always frowned on divorce, even though he had been divorced himself. But that was all her mother's fault, she had explained.

It's a good thing Simon Powers had gone to live in South Africa, Travers thought now, his mind still on DeLacy's marriage. If I ever meet that bastard, I'll beat him to a pulp. Powers was an Etonian, as he was, and came from a good family. But he had behaved like a lout.

DeLacy Ingham. She was the great love of his life. He

wanted to marry her, and he fully believed she would accept him. He hoped her father would not object, throw a spanner in the works.

After all, he had a bit of a reputation, had been a womanizer in the past, carousing with the likes of Lawrence Pierce. He didn't see him any more. Travers had grown to detest him, in fact, because he knew that deep down Pierce lusted after DeLacy and wanted her for his mistress. Travers had never said a word about this to DeLacy, having no wish to frighten her in any way whatsoever.

Nor had Pierce said anything, but Travers knew him well. He had gone carousing with him – slumming, as Pierce called it. They had picked up fancy women in bars together, but Travers had never been to one of Pierce's famous orgies. And sometimes he wondered if they had really happened. No one else he knew had been either, and Travers believed they were probably an invention on the surgeon's part.

He had fallen out with Pierce because of his callousness and ungentlemanly behaviour towards the actress he had been seeing. Also, Travers had discovered Pierce was a liar, and a cheat at cards.

He thought of the painting he had been going to do, of Pierce's beautiful hands. He had never managed to get around to doing it, and now he was glad he hadn't, and also that Pierce was no longer part of his life. They had almost come to blows at one point, when Pierce had made derogatory remarks about Lacy.

Fortunately the portrait of DeLacy had been wondrous – no one could deny that. It had been painted with the deepest of love. Pierce was impressed. And so was Felicity.

Pierce had been happy to pay for it immediately; he had told Travers that because of the portrait he was back in Felicity's good graces and that she was also pleased because he had stopped going to Paris. Most importantly, he was occupying Felicity's bed once more, giving her what she wanted. And her money was flowing to him again. But he did confess to Travers that he was still having an affair with Helen Malone, the actress, because she helped with his stress, he had added. Good riddance to bad rubbish, Travers thought.

The sound of footsteps echoed, and Travers turned his head. Immediately he jumped up. DeLacy was coming into the church. He rushed to her, taking her into his arms at once, filled with sudden happiness.

'Hanson told me you were up here,' she said, kissing his cheek.

'I've enjoyed sitting here, musing quietly to myself, admiring the stained-glass windows, and thinking about you.'

'What were you thinking about me?'

'Lovely things.' He took hold of her hands, slipped off her gloves and put them in his pocket. Hand-in-hand, they walked together towards the altar. One day he would marry her here.

They stood together in front of the altar, their arms around each other. They kissed for a long time, happy to be together.

And they made promises to be faithful to each other, never to be apart, and to stay together for the rest of their lives.

Charlotte had taken refuge in her upstairs parlour, a room that had been used by nannies in the past. It had been redecorated whilst she and Charles were in Zurich last year. Because she liked the blue and white bedroom in the West Wing, she had asked Daphne to use that colour scheme here.

Now, as she sat in front of the fire, she was happy to have a little time to herself. Fortunately none of the guests had yet arrived; they would come tomorrow. Except for Travers Merton, of course, who had driven up to Yorkshire with DeLacy earlier in the week.

She was pleased DeLacy had taken to him the way she

had. He appeared to make her happy, and obviously Travers was bowled over by her, truly in love.

Charlotte had met his grandfather, Lord Noyers, many times in the past, when he had come to shoot in August. He and David had been very close friends indeed. Sometimes, when they wanted to go away together, she and David had been Lord Noyers's guests at Compton Noyers. He had been in on their secret, and glad to help them.

Lunch had been easy, with just the family present, and Travers. Charles and Travers had now gone for a walk, along the paths which had been cleared of snow by the outside workers.

She was wearing the swan brooch on the jacket of her suit, and now she unpinned it, held it in her hands. What a lovely piece of delicate workmanship it was, a beautiful pin that was so significant to her.

There was a knock on the door, and as she said, 'Come in,' Dulcie did so.

'They've sent me to see you, Aunt Charlotte,' Dulcie said. This was the way they had been told to address her by their father.

'Who are they?'

'Daphne, DeLacy and Cecily. We had a little drink this morning in the love nest in the attic. Where Cecily and Miles used to have their daily rendezvous. And they decided you should be the one to tell me about sex, and what I had to do on my wedding night.'

'Why me?'

'Because you brought me up. With Nanny helping. They say you're married to Papa now, and so it's your responsibility.'

'They're playing a joke on you, aren't they, Dulcie?'

'I don't know . . . perhaps it's a joke on both of us.'

'Do you know anything about sex?' Charlotte asked, giving her a keen look.

'Of course I do, I'm nineteen. I may not know about . . . well, some intricate things, but I do know about having intercourse.'

Charlotte frowned, wondering what this was all about. Suddenly she said, 'You haven't had an affair with James, slept with him, have you?'

'No. And that's not because I didn't want to. Actually, I've really tried to seduce him. But he wouldn't succumb to my charms.'

'I understand. James has been a true gentleman because he knows you're a virgin. You are, aren't you?'

'Unfortunately yes. And he said he would not touch me until I was his wife.'

'Very admirable, but it must have been hard for him. After all, you are very beautiful, Dulcie.'

'It was hard for me too! I mean, let's face it, he's gorgeous. It's hard not to scramble all over him and eat him up.' Dulcie laughed. 'I think DeLacy must have told them we hadn't had sex, and they sort of . . . set me up. It is probably a joke, Charlotte, because everybody sleeps with everybody these days. Before they're even engaged.'

Charlotte nodded. 'We're living in modern times indeed.' There was a pause and she laughed and said in a teasing manner, 'However, since he's arriving tonight, you still have time to get him into bed. You're not getting married until Sunday. You have tonight and tomorrow night, in fact.' The amused smile remained on Charlotte's face, her eyes twinkling.

'I'm not going to even try,' Dulcie answered, laughing. 'He told me he had a will of iron. He does. And stop teasing me, please.' Dulcie went over and hugged Charlotte. 'Thank you for being who you are, Charlotte. And he is very gorgeous, my James, isn't he?'

'Heart-stoppingly gorgeous,' Charlotte agreed.

FORTY-SIX

It was a winter wedding at the church in Little Skell village, nestled amongst the snow-covered moors. Fortunately, it had stopped snowing on Friday evening, and on this Sunday afternoon the sky was a brilliant blue without a cloud, and the sun was shining.

Over the course of Saturday, the village had been cleared of snow, and so had the land surrounding the church. The Earl knew only too well that everyone from the three villages would gather at the church. It was an ancient tradition; their people always came to see an Ingham wed. And this particular Ingham girl was especially popular with everyone.

There would be a lot of guests arriving at Cavendon, and Charles had realized that the villagers would have no option but to wait outside. The church would be full. But, once the bride had arrived, they would go next door to the church hall where Hanson had arranged for hot drinks and sandwiches to be served. Later, once they heard the church bells ringing, they would know it was time to rush back to the church to see the bride and groom leaving as man and wife.

The villagers had never seen anything like this wedding.

Nor had anyone else. The bridegroom was one of England's greatest classical actors, and the handsomest man they had ever seen. Tall, dark-haired, with sparkling brown eyes, he was elegant in his morning suit, with a white rosebud in his lapel and a wide smile on his face.

He arrived at the church first, with his brother Owen, who had flown all the way from Australia, where he was building a bridge, to be his brother's best man.

After them came Miles Ingham and his little band of ushers: Hugo, Harry Swann and Felix Lambert, James's manager. They were also smart-looking in their morning suits with the traditional white rose of Yorkshire in their buttonholes. None of them wore their top hats, because Dulcie had forbidden it in no uncertain terms, much to their relief.

James Brentwood and his brother had gone into the church, but the ushers waited on the steps for the two bridesmaids, Daphne's daughter Alicia and DeLacy. And, following them, Daphne's twin sons, Thomas and Andrew, six years old, were the pageboys. With them was their older brother, Charlie, who had no role, but had been allowed to come home from prep school for the weekend to attend the wedding.

Because it was winter, Dulcie had agreed with Cecily that the wedding gown and bridesmaids' dresses should be warm, and that elegant coats designed to match would be a wonderful addition.

Cecily had dressed the bridesmaids in lavender-coloured gowns made of heavy satin. They were ankle length, with long sleeves, and worn with high-heeled boots made of lavender leather. The long wool coats were the same lavender shade, and were in a tailored military style. They wore small Juliet caps made of lavender satin that matched their gowns.

The twins looked adorable, and the crowds outside the

church cheered and clapped as they marched proudly up the church steps after their sister and aunt, escorted by their elder brother. Cecily had put them in white riding breeches, knee-high polished black boots, and red, military-style jackets with brass buttons. They looked like miniature copies of the guards at Buckingham Palace.

Thomas and Andrew grinned and waved to everyone before they went into the church, loving the applause and attention. Charlie made sure the three of them stood with the ushers; they all felt very grown-up today.

Miles led the bridesmaids to a quiet corner at the back of the church, as the many guests began to arrive. He noticed that the pews were filling up swiftly now. The bride's family and friends were on the left, the bridegroom's on the right. Miles hadn't realized how many people were coming, and he recognized a number of famous show-business faces, obviously friends of James's. It was going to be quite a fancy affair – no doubt the wedding of the year.

James was standing at the front of the church, a few steps away from the altar, just off to one side. Owen was with him. 'Do you have the rings?' he asked, his voice low but urgent.

'No. Miles has them in his pocket.'

'You should have them!' James hissed.

'No. Miles needs them. They have to be placed on the cushions . . . pageboys carry the rings. On the cushions,' Owen responded.

'Oh, sorry. I forgot . . .' James let his sentence fade away. He was shaking inside. He knew he was having an attack of nerves. It was something like stage fright, he thought. That was something he had rarely had in his life. But then he had never been about to be married before.

He stared out into the centre of the church. The audience, he thought. I must think of them as the audience, and I'll be all right. I won't make a mistake.

The pews were filling up rapidly. A sea of faces. Some he knew, others he didn't. He took a deep breath and looked towards the front pew.

Finally he smiled, felt the anxiety easing. Ruby, his dearest Ruby, had her eyes focused on him; they were full of love. She offered him her most encouraging smile and, quite suddenly, he knew everything was fine.

There they were, his adoring sisters . . . Ruby, Dolores, and Faye, sitting with their husbands and grown children. His niece Amanda, his nephews, Julian and Frank. And Sid. He had been so upset when James had told him he wouldn't be needing a dresser for his wedding, that it wasn't like a play. 'But I could be yer valet, Jamie. That's wot toffs 'ave: valets.' And Sid's feelings were so very hurt, James had not had the heart to refuse him. Sid had been helpful, as it turned out. Especially today, helping him to get into the morning suit. And he was full of glee, mixing with the staff, boasting about his job in the theatre.

Next to Ruby was Owen's wife, Elaine, and in the row behind them was Constance Lambert, in her beautiful new purple outfit from Cecily Swann Couture. His sisters were wearing Cecily Swann as well, and all of them looked as proud as punch. He chuckled quietly to himself. The Woods never wanted to be outdone by anybody, and they were full of pride. He loved them even more for that, plus their integrity and dignity.

His sisters had been awed by Dulcie at first, mainly because of her title, he suspected. But with her hilarious use of the language, her forthrightness, and her humour, she had put them at ease. They had fallen in love with her. And who wouldn't? he wondered. He was so smitten he could hardly see straight.

Glancing around, James couldn't help thinking how truly beautiful this ancient church was today, filled to overflowing with flowers. He could smell the fragrance of roses, instantly reminding him of her, as if he needed any reminders. There were hundreds of candles throughout the church, many of them tapers, and they created a magical feeling.

What pleased James was the effort that had been made to keep the church pleasantly warm. Her father had told him that he was going to make sure that the paraffin stoves were placed everywhere in the church, and along the walls near the pews. Obviously this had been done. The Inghams thought of everything. He had liked Charles and Charlotte immediately. And Charles especially, the night they had had dinner in London, after the Earl had said he could marry Dulcie. He had been accepted immediately as a member of the family, and he felt at ease with them.

Pulling himself away from his thoughts, glancing around again, James realized that the church was now full to overflowing. He looked at his watch. It was ten past three. The bride was late. Where was she? Where was his little minx? His indefatigable temptress?

How hard she had tried to seduce him, lure him into her bed. I'll have to find a way to get my own back for that endless torture, he thought, his mouth suddenly twitching with suppressed laughter. Yes, pure torture it had been. Felix had been right. It had been a struggle to keep his hands off her. But he had, despite her.

Owen touched his arm. 'She's arrived,' he whispered.

James straightened, and strained to see her, staring down the centre aisle. He spotted Miles, then Felix, and the two little boys stood out in their red jackets. Alicia came to the forefront, and then suddenly there was DeLacy, blocking his view. They were in some kind of

334

huddle at the back of the church and he hoped nothing had gone wrong.

Swallowing hard, he chastised himself for being so anxious. He reminded himself to stay calm. She was here. In this church. That was a relief.

There was a sense of anticipation in the air all of a sudden. People had become aware that Dulcie was about to walk down the aisle, and they were looking around, trying to see her.

The organ music started. It was Wagner's famous 'Bridal Chorus'; James recognized the melody of 'Here Comes the Bride'. The organist was going all out, filling the church to the rafters with his music.

Unexpectedly, there she was, standing at the top of the nave, her arm through her father's, holding onto him tightly. And, very slowly, they began their walk to the altar.

Taking a deep breath, James steadied himself. His legs felt so weak, he thought they might give way; he was so nervous. His eyes remained on her, taking in her amazing beauty, thinking it was hardly possible that any woman could be this beautiful. But she was. And she was going to be his wife. His.

She looked like some being from a fairy tale, he decided, and so glamorous it was almost unbearable. She wore a floor-length cape of white brocade, trimmed with white fox. This went around the neckline and down and around the entire hem. It sat on her shoulders, revealed a wedding gown of pure white satin, the skirt covered in tiny crystal beads which gleamed in the candlelight.

His heart missed a beat when he saw the wide diamond choker he had given her for a wedding present, and the matching diamond earrings. They were the chandelier style, and dripped down from her ears. The jewellery appeared to illuminate her face, and he thought she shone like a bright star. My little minx, he thought. And when she finally arrived, and he stepped forward to take her hand from her father, his eyes filled with tears.

James blinked, gave her a half smile, saw that she was crying too.

He wanted to take her in his arms and hold onto her forever. To kiss her again and again. Later, that was later, he reminded himself.

The ceremony started but all he heard was her voice saying, 'I do.' And his own, uttering those same words. Thomas and Andrew were coming forward with their cushions, and gold rings went onto their fingers.

They stared at each other. Their eyes were still moist.

They were married.

FORTY-SEVEN

Church bells pealing. Villagers cheering. Cameras clicking. Confetti falling. That was the scene outside when James left Little Skell church with Dulcie clinging to his arm, looking up at him adoringly.

The cheering stopped when the bridal couple stopped in the middle of the path. Everyone fell silent, momentarily struck dumb. They were the most beautiful couple any of them had ever seen.

Dulcie thanked them all for braving the cold weather to see her married. James thanked them for their best wishes, then ordered them back to the warm church hall where they should enjoy their own party, his mellifluous voice ringing out in the cold air, stunning them. It was a thrilling voice, like none they had ever heard before. But then he was one of England's greatest actors, wasn't he, they said to one another, nodding their heads.

James and Dulcie walked down the path, their happiness shining in their eyes. When they got to the Rolls-Royce, DeLacy and Alicia were already there, and they helped Dulcie into the back seat, lifting up her gown and the long cape, arranging them carefully.

Once the car was driving towards Cavendon Park, James

turned to Dulcie and touched her face lightly with his fingertips. 'You're my wife,' he said in a low voice. 'Imagine that, my little torturer is now my wife.'

Dulcie's eyes opened wide. She stared back at him. 'Torturer,' she repeated. 'I would never torture my husband.'

'No, you won't,' he replied more emphatically, and grinned at her. 'But you certainly made a good job of it when I was your fiancé.'

She squeezed his hand, leaned against him, and whispered, 'I know I was a temptress, and I'll never stop being that, you know.'

'I certainly hope not.'

They fell silent after that, and several minutes later the car was pulling up outside Cavendon Hall. Miles and Cecily, who had been put in charge of the wedding weekend, were standing on the front steps waiting for them.

After Hartley had helped Dulcie out of the car, Cecily took the small bouquet of white orchids from her, so that Dulcie could lift the cape and gown as she went up the steps.

Once they were inside the entrance hall, Miles and Cecily hugged them both and congratulated them. Then Miles said, 'I want us to get the usual formalities over as quickly as possible.' Glancing at his sister, he turned to James, winked and said, 'Dulcie wants things to move fast, so she can have you all to herself, I suspect.' He threw her a suggestive look, his eyes full of mischief.

'Miles!' Dulcie exclaimed, and found herself actually blushing.

James, amused by her reaction, said, 'Well, Miles, I've discovered my wife usually has very good ideas indeed. So come, let's start moving it along. What are we doing first?'

'Here's the drill,' Miles answered. 'There are newspaper and magazine photographers waiting for you both in the yellow drawing room. Felix is looking after them for me, since he's used to dealing with the press. They're being served hot tea and coffee, and finger sandwiches. So in about fifteen minutes that room will be your first stop.'

Cecily interjected, 'The press already adore you, James, from what Felix says, and I'm sure they'll feel the same way about your wife.'

'How could they not?' James murmured, and blew a kiss to Dulcie, who laughed, her happiness spilling out of her.

Miles took over, and said, 'This is the right time to do it, if either of you want to freshen up. Then we'll take you to meet the photographers, have your pictures taken. Half an hour, maximum. After that you'll join our families for the traditional family portrait. In the West Wing ball-room.'

Dulcie, looking at Cecily, said, 'Do I need to do anything?'

'I don't think so, you look wonderful to me.' As she spoke, Cecily went over to Dulcie and studied her face for a moment. She shook her head. 'Perfection, even the lip rouge hasn't smudged. And the little Juliet cap has held your hair in place very nicely.'

'Thank you, Ceci. And thank you for everything you've done for me, and for my beautiful gown and cape.' She leaned forward and kissed Ceci's cheek, and whispered against her hair, 'It'll be your turn to get married next, you'll see.'

Cecily smiled, but this suddenly faltered and she turned her head as her eyes filled.

Only Dulcie noticed the unexpected tears.

James was efficient and disciplined, and Dulcie was used to traditional family weddings. And with Miles and Cecily in charge, guiding them, things moved along without a hitch, and at great speed. The Inghams and the Woods were patient, and willingly allowed themselves to be moved around and rearranged, and rearranged again by Miles

339

and Cecily. After a gruelling hour, the photographer sighed with relief that the session was over.

James and Dulcie were the last to leave the ballroom in the West Wing. It was mandatory that they had photographs of themselves alone together, and they had stayed behind to do the shots.

Now they walked to the South Wing, where the wedding reception and dinner were being held. The reception was in full swing when they arrived in the pale green sitting room, where they were welcomed by members of their families and guests.

They both took glasses of champagne and moved around together, greeting as many as they could. They then turned to their right, into the pink dining room. Earlier in the week this had been revamped by Hanson and Mrs Thwaites, who had turned it into another sitting room, as they had done in the past.

The first person to greet them was Great-Aunt Gwendolyn, who had taken a fancy to James. 'Like every other woman,' Dulcie had muttered when her aunt first met him. Great-Aunt Gwendolyn looked quite extraordinary in one of her royal purple gowns and masses of diamonds. Charlotte came over next, and DeLacy with Travers, and then the bridal couple moved on once again, not wanting to miss anyone.

Dulcie, who had bonded with Ruby weeks ago, gravitated to her when James got caught up with Ralph Shore, an actor friend of long standing. A moment later James was surrounded by some of his other male cronies, and trapped for the moment.

'We make quite a fantastic clan, don't we, Ruby?' Dulcie said, and raised her glass to her sister-in-law. 'Twenty-four of us in that photograph and we all looked marvellous.'

Ruby raised her glass and clinked it against Dulcie's.

'The Inghams and the Woods, and not a bad match at that.' Ruby gave her a loving smile. No flibbertigibbet, this one, she thought. Dulcie was the real thing.

There was a moment's pause, and Ruby drew closer. 'I'm so happy James found you, Dulcie. You're good together. He's always needed a woman like you.' Ruby meant every word. She had faith in Dulcie; she knew that she was steady, practical and had her feet on the ground. And there was a smart brain behind that gorgeous face.

'I adore him, Ruby. You must never worry about him. I promise you I'll take great care of your James. And mine.'

Before Ruby could respond, Constance Lambert came to join them, her face full of smiles. She too was wearing purple, but her outfit was a Cecily Swann. It was chic: a long, straight taffeta gown, enhanced by a shower of amethyst beads.

'What a wonderful wedding, Dulcie. And so many flowers! Wherever did they come from in this harsh winter? The church and the house look unbelievable.'

'We have several greenhouses at Cavendon, and our head gardener grows orchids. So some of them came from here. The rest are from Harte's in London. They import flowers from the Scilly Isles all the year round. They were driven up from London in a Harte's van yesterday.'

'How amazing,' Constance replied, and went on, 'And so are you, Dulcie. You look breathtaking. Cecily has done you proud; your wedding dress is out of this world. And so is the cape.'

'That's also very warm,' Dulcie said with a laugh. 'I was glad to take the cape off during the photography. And leave it off. Thank you, Constance, I love the dress too. But I asked Ceci to keep the bodice plain, that's why there are only crystals on the satin skirt. I didn't want anything competing with my diamonds from James.'

'What has James done now?' James asked, coming up

next to Dulcie. 'What are my three favourite women saying about me?'

'Only that we love you to death,' Dulcie answered.

James took hold of her hand and brought her closer to him, somewhat possessively. He said, 'Hanson is about to announce dinner, and Daphne thinks we ought to slip out to the hall, disappear so that he can get everyone else to sit down. We'll be the last to go into the blue ballroom, Dulcie. Hanson will come and get us.' He smiled at Constance and his sister. 'We're going to slip out now. See you in a few minutes.'

James led Dulcie through the two rooms and into the entrance foyer of the South Wing. 'We can wait here,' he murmured, kissing her on the cheek.

She looked at him coquettishly, raised a brow and said, 'If we hurry, maybe we can have a quickie. Upstairs in your suite. What about it?'

'Dulcie Ingham, you're incorrigible!' he exclaimed, laughing.

'I'm Dulcie Brentwood now. Your missus, and don't you forget it.'

When they entered the blue ballroom a short while later, even Dulcie gasped, along with James. It was really a large sitting room but, like the other rooms, it had been transformed. Furniture and carpets had disappeared. Eight tables of ten, to seat eighty people, had been arranged around the room; the centre had become a dance floor. The room itself was decorated with flowering plants, banks of orchids, roses and other species. There were white tapering candles everywhere and little votive lights twinkled on window ledges, the mantelshelf and the dinner tables.

A five-piece band was situated in one corner; as James and Dulcie walked in holding hands, they struck up, 'Here

Comes the Bride' again. And everyone clapped at the sight of them.

The food was delicious, the wines superb, and the room buzzed. People were chatting and laughing. It was not only a lavish wedding but a joyous one.

There were, over a period of time, many toasts and speeches. The latter were kept short, following Miles's stern instructions. Some were very funny, others touching.

At one moment, James and Dulcie went onto the dance floor. It was their first dance of the evening. Once they had been around twice, other couples followed, and it seemed to Dulcie that there had not been such gaiety and happiness at Cavendon for years. Not even at her father's marriage to Charlotte last year. It pleased her that people were having a good time.

After dessert had been served, Miles came to speak to James. 'You should do your speech now, before the wedding cake is wheeled in. That's quite a performance, cutting it, and all that. A bit of a fuss, actually.'

James agreed with him. 'Yes, it's best to do it now,' he replied, at the same time wondering if he and Dulcie could escape after that.

A few minutes later, Miles and Cecily tapped their crystal goblets with their spoons and the room fell silent.

Squeezing her hand, James stood. Everyone was staring at him, including his wife. But he was used to that after all these years on the stage, and he never minded an audience after hours. It was part of his life, a given.

'I will never forget my beautiful wedding in the snow,' he began. 'Marrying my incredible Dulcie is the happiest day of my life. I could sing her praises to you, and tell you how unique she is, but I would prefer to say something to my wife instead.' He looked around the room, and added, 'If you will permit me?'

'Yes, yes, go ahead!' Ralph Shore cried, and all of his

male friends started to clap. 'Go ahead, say it to her, Jamie!' Ralph exclaimed. 'We'd love to hear it, too.'

'Since I'm an actor and not a writer, I'm used to speaking other people's words. I would like to do that now, in order to express my feelings about my wife.'

He looked down at Dulcie, sitting on his right, her bright blue eyes huge in her face.

He stood there without speaking for a moment. And yet he was charismatic and compelling in his silence and stillness. The moment he began to speak again, in that memorable voice, the entire room went quiet. There was not another sound, his voice ringing out across the ballroom.

'How do I love thee? Let me count the ways. I love thee to the depth and breadth and height my soul can reach, when feeling out of sight for the ends of being and ideal grace.'

He paused for a moment, his voice becoming slightly softer as he continued, 'I love thee to the level of every day's most quiet need . . . by sun and candlelight. I love thee freely as men strive for right. I love thee purely as they turn from praise. I love thee with the passion put to use in my old griefs and with my childhood's faith . . .' There was another pause, and his cadence changed again. 'I love thee with a love I seemed to lose with my lost saints. I love thee with the breath, smiles, tears of all my life . . .' He inclined his head. He had finished saying the words written so long ago by Elizabeth Barrett Browning.

James leaned down to Dulcie, took hold of her hands and brought her to her feet. Looking into her face, he said, 'Oh, how I love you, my darling wife. So very, very much.'

Tears glittered in Dulcie's eyes and in his. And everyone else's. There wasn't a dry eye in the room.

The two of them remained standing, gazing at each

other, and then she put her arms around him and kissed him, holding onto him tightly, as he now held her.

Everyone began to clap, and Dulcie walked him out to the dance floor. The band began to play a waltz and they danced around the floor, still gazing at each other. The guests were mesmerized and remained seated.

A few moments later, two footmen and Hanson came into the ballroom. Gordon Lane and Ian Melrose were pushing a rumbling trolley on which stood an enormous three-tiered wedding cake, a masterpiece of icing sugar and fantastical decorations.

They positioned the trolley in the middle of the floor. Hanson beckoned to James and Dulcie. They joined him next to the cake, and Hanson handed Dulcie a large silver knife.

'Put your hand on top of hers, sir,' Hanson said to James. 'You must cut the cake together.'

They did so. There was more applause from the guests, and laughter from the bride and groom.

Hanson beamed at them, and motioned for the two footmen to wheel the cake to the other end of the room, where it would be cut into slices and served.

The band began to play on cue from Miles. James took Dulcie into his arms and beckoned to their guests and family members. 'Come and join us!' he called. 'Dance with us! Celebrate with us!'

Cecily and Miles came onto the floor first, followed by Daphne and Hugo, Ruby and Ted. Owen and Elaine followed. And so did Charles and Charlotte, with DeLacy and Travers hard on their heels. The floor was soon filled with couples enjoying every moment of this quite extraordinary wedding.

'Let's go,' Dulcie whispered after a few seconds.

James nodded; holding her firmly in his arms, he danced her across the floor and out of the door of the ballroom.

They ran down the corridor and into the hall, and up the main staircase to the East Wing. This was where the Inghams lived, and Dulcie had insisted James have a suite near her room.

Dulcie stopped when she came to her bedroom. It was just three doors away from the Marmaduke Suite where James was installed.

He stared at her, asked worriedly, 'Do you think I can get you out of this complicated dress?'

'I doubt it,' Dulcie answered, and looked over her shoulder. 'Cecily agreed to follow us when we left the ballroom. She'll get me undressed. Go on, go to your suite. Oh look, here she comes. I won't be a minute.'

'After waiting four months, I think I can manage a minute,' he said, giving her a theatrical leer. 'Hurry up, though.'

FORTY-EIGHT

The light was dim in the bedroom of the Marmaduke Suite. James had turned out most of the lights, had left only one on. But there was firelight in the grate, and moonlight streaming in, so she could see him quite clearly.

He was standing in front of the window, looking out at the long stretch of park towards the lake. He had not heard her come in, and she remained there in the doorway, studying him intently, wanting him so much, but wanting to savour every moment of her wedding night.

James was so still he seemed like a statue. She was aware this stillness was part of him, an internal calmness that was natural. Perhaps it was even part of his success. He had hardly moved on stage when she had seen him in *Hamlet*, taken just a few steps. But he had been riveting. That stillness was a powerful tool. And it added to his natural elegance, refinement and grace. She also understood that his voice was his greatest gift of all.

He happened to turn around as she walked further into the room, and was startled when he saw her, exclaiming, 'I didn't hear you come in. How long have you been standing there?'

'Only a minute.'

A smile flickered around his mouth. 'It took more than a minute for you to get out of that wedding dress.'

'I know, but I'm here now.'

He came towards her. She saw that he was wearing a dark blue silk robe, tightly belted, and he was in his bare feet, as she was. She did not move, suddenly awed by him and his great fame, and an unexpected shyness came over her. She was frozen to the spot.

James noticed her sudden hesitation; he also noticed how ethereal she looked in a filmy white peignoir that floated around her. But it was short, fell just below her knees and showed her shapely legs provocatively. He hurried to her.

James grabbed hold of her and pulled her into his arms, then stood there breathing in the smell of her hair, the scent of roses on her skin. She was his. They were married. What a blessed relief.

He tilted her face to his and looked down at her. Her eyes were a deeper blue in this light, and he saw in them a yearning for him. It was a yearning he shared. How he had ached to be with her like this, able to make love to her properly, without any rushing or anxiety or, later, regret.

His heart turned over. But oh God, how young she was. Only nineteen. So innocent, untouched, inexperienced. For a split second he was almost afraid to make love to her. She was so vulnerable, defenceless.

As if reading his mind, she said, 'I took two minutes instead of one, because I asked Cecily what I should do to you in bed.'

This startled him. 'You didn't!'

'I did. And she said I shouldn't try to do anything. Because you were thirty-three and obviously you were an experienced man; you would know what to do to make me happy and you would look after me.'

'I do. And I will,' he said. He bent down and brought his mouth to hers. She moved into him, her shyness evaporating. He was already aroused. He held her away and exclaimed, 'Don't move.'

'Where are you going?' she asked as he rushed out of the bedroom.

'To lock the door of the suite,' he answered, and a moment later he was standing in front of her again.

She stepped forward and laid her head on his chest, putting her arms around him. 'Do you remember when I did this in Ceci's shop? I told you I wanted to make sure you were real.'

'Well am I?'

'Oh yes, very real.' She stood back, looking up at him. 'I know I've been a temptress, that I've driven you mad, but I couldn't help it. I wanted to make love to you so much – whenever I saw you, actually, and whatever time it was.'

'Do you think I didn't?' he asked softly, his dark eyes fixed on her, his brilliant gaze quizzical.

'No, I knew you wanted me as much as I wanted you.'

He couldn't wait any longer. He was fully aroused, his heart clattering in his chest. Grabbing her by the shoulders, he pulled her to him, took off her peignoir and the filmy nightgown, slipped out of his robe.

Their eyes met and locked. They moved at the same time, stepped into each other's arms. He held her very tightly; she pressed her body against his, moved slightly and felt his hardness. Her heart quickened as heat rushed through, her desire for him flaring.

'I love you, James.'

'I love you, too.' Against her hair he said, 'That bed we've needed since the day we met is over there. Let's not waste any more time.'

They lay down next to each other and the world

exploded around them. Their hands were all over each other; their sexual desire, their need to be together a driving force between them. They couldn't wait to possess and be possessed. Their passion soared. He kissed her deeply, their tongues entwining, their hearts clattering in unison. He stroked her breasts, her hands roamed over him greedily, not an inch of him was left untouched by her.

He was experienced and deft. She was his eager pupil, giving herself up to him willingly, asking him to touch her, to arouse her any way he wished. He did. When his fingers found the golden silk between her legs, she gasped. He felt her relax eventually, and he knew he was giving her pleasure. And this aroused him even more.

Suddenly there was no time left for him. He slid his body on top of hers, took her to him swiftly and with some force, knowing this was the best way to ease any pain for her. She stiffened almost instantly, and gasped, but he paid no attention, went deeper. And when he heard her sighs of pleasure against his cheek he knew she was all right.

Her hands were on the nape of his neck, in his hair, sliding down his back. A moment later, she was gripping his shoulders, wrapping her long legs around him. Instantly they found their own rhythm.

He discovered she was as sensual as he was, and her eagerness to please him, to make love without any inhibitions, only served to inflame him more.

When she began to quiver, found his mouth with hers, and tightened her grip on his shoulders, he moved against her swiftly. She met his need, cried out with pleasure, said his name over and over again.

James thought he was falling through space . . . faster, faster, moving with her, giving himself to her without restraint. Her hands pressed the small of his back and, as

350

she cried out yet again, he was burning up, then dissolving into her, and cried out himself, whispering her name.

James was still trembling as he lay on top of Dulcie, his face resting against hers. He knew he had not made love like this ever before, not with any other woman. It had not only been overwhelming physical pleasure, but he had loved Dulcie with his heart and soul and mind. He belonged to her, and she to him, and they were well matched. A sense of contentment he had never experienced flowed through him, and he knew it was because of her.

He moved, slipped off her.

She touched his face, almost tentatively. He noticed she looked anxious.

He frowned, 'What is it? What's wrong?'

'I was just wondering if I was worth waiting for. Was I all right . . . in bed?'

He couldn't help it, he started to laugh. He took hold of her, brought her close. 'Oh, my little temptress, my very sweet seductress, of course you weren't all right. Wrong word altogether. You were wonderful.'

She smiled, leaned closer, and kissed him lightly on the mouth. 'When can we do it again?'

'Not just yet,' he answered, stifling his laughter. He brought her into his arms, cradling her against him. 'I didn't hurt you, did I, darling?'

'No. You made it fast, and I was fine.'

He pushed himself up on one elbow. Looking down into those glorious blue eyes, he said, 'You are my first wife and my last. I just want you to know that. I told you once that I was playing for keeps, and I was. I am. I'm afraid you're stuck with me.'

'Just try to escape!'

Nestling against him, she said, 'I'm glad we're having our honeymoon on the *Aquitania*. Because on a ship there's nowhere to go. Except back to the cabin.'

'Yes, I'd already thought of that,' he murmured, although he hadn't. What a wondrous girl she was, his Dulcie. Full of surprises . . . and certainly in bed. Inexperienced though she was, she had been ardent, passionate and responsive. He had found the love of his life, as she had hers.

It was quiet in the bedroom; the only sound the crackling of the logs that James had thrown onto the fire a short while ago. He had pulled the bedclothes over them, turned out the lamp at his side, and brought her close to him. Dulcie had fallen asleep with one arm thrown over his stomach.

Feeling drained, he had dozed on and off, but now he was wide awake, his mind turning endlessly. But there was a deeper contentment in him. He was relaxed, at ease, at peace.

There had been moments in his life when James had had flashes of insight into himself. He had known instinctively that he did not want to spend his life with any of the women he dated, or even those with whom he'd had longer relationships. It wasn't that they weren't beautiful or nice or loving – they just weren't right for him.

He hadn't been able to pinpoint what 'right' was. Until he had met Dulcie, standing in his dressing room looking lost. They had exchanged long and knowing looks, and had understood everything. They had recognized each other as being . . . right. It was a *coup de foudre*, and it had never happened to him before.

He felt differently about her than he had about anyone else. He was protective of her, wanted to shield her, take care of her, and her instincts were perfect when it came to him. She understood him, knew him without the benefit of time. For all of her cheekiness, bold comments and forthrightness, she was highly intelligent, serious minded, and entirely reliable. He wanted to be with her all the time. She satisfied a deep need in him, entirely fulfilled him emotionally.

She stirred next to him, whispered, 'James, are you awake?'

'Yes.'

There was a silence. He said softly, after a moment, 'I belong to you, Dulcie. You've put your imprint on me . . . for life.'

He felt her smile against his shoulder. She slid on top of him and lowered her head, finding his mouth with hers. And so it began again, their passionate lovemaking, and that was the way it would always be with them.

FORTY-NINE

'We just made it under the wire last year,' Charlotte said. 'Much to everyone's relief, and most especially mine. Charles was truly anxious for weeks.'

'I realize that,' Lady Gwendolyn said. 'I was ready to turn my few investments into cash, so that I could give it to him.' A wide smile spread across her face when she finished, 'But it wasn't necessary, thank God! The Ingham luck held. We are fortunate in so many ways.'

'We are indeed. Charles believes he has the best sons-in-law in the world. It was awfully generous of Hugo to sell some of his investments in Wall Street and give the money to Charles. Helping to wipe the slate clean, Hugo calls it. And it did take a bit of a burden off Paul.'

Leaning forward, Lady Gwendolyn said, 'I never quite understood why the Drummond family bank were only willing to go so far, to lend him just half of the money he asked for. Nobody ever really explained that to me, except to say it had to go before the board.'

'It would have been an enormous amount of money to lend one man, even if he is a Drummond and a share-holder in the bank. Paul's not stupid, so he took the offer immediately, without quibbling, and then Hugo jumped in and supplied the rest from his own money.'

Charlotte hesitated for a moment, then murmured, 'Daphne gave me the impression Hugo felt just as responsible as Paul, because it was their decision to put the money from the Ingham Trust into Transatlantic Air.'

'I understand, and thank you for filling me in, Charlotte. Very frankly, I'm so glad you're back at Cavendon. I've missed you and Charles. We all have, and I'm relieved you've taken over from Daphne. She needs a rest.' Eyeing Charlotte, her head on one side, Lady Gwendolyn said with a smile, 'And of course you've settled in as chatelaine of this great pile of ours with the greatest of ease.'

'I've still a lot to learn.'

'Not too much, my dear. Let's not forget, you've lived at Cavendon all of your life.'

'But I was not running it. Thankfully Hanson is by my side whenever I need him.'

Lady Gwendolyn said, 'I must change the subject, Charlotte. The real reason I wanted to see you today was to tell you a story.'

'A story about what?' Charlotte asked, giving her husband's aunt a searching look.

'About the Inghams and the Swanns. A story from long ago.' Lady Gwendolyn sat back in the chair and forced herself to relax. She had been longing to confide in Charlotte ever since giving her the swan brooch, had subsequently regretted not having told her at that time. Now, unexpectedly, she felt nervous.

'First I would like to ask you a question, Charlotte. Where do you keep the famous Swann record books?'

'They're in the safe at my house across the park. I didn't take them with me to Cavendon Hall, because there are so many. And it's best to leave them there, because when I die Cecily will be in charge of them.'

'Don't talk about dying, for heaven's sake: you're a young woman.'

'Why did you ask me where they were?'

'Just curiosity, that's all,' Lady Gwendolyn replied, leaning against the cushions. 'The reason I really invited you to come to Little Skell Manor this morning is to show you something. But first, the story. However, I must begin with a question.'

'Ask me anything you want, Lady Gwendolyn.'

'Aunt Gwendolyn from now on. You're family. Well, in a way you always have been, but it's official since your marriage to Charles. So, to continue, this is my question. Am I mentioned in any of the record books?'

'No, you're not. Some names from a hundred years ago appear, but that's all. Why do you ask?' Charlotte frowned, thinking this conversation somewhat strange.

'Long ago I was in love with a Swann,' Lady Gwendolyn announced, her eyes fixed on Charlotte. 'And he with me.'

Flabbergasted though she was, Charlotte just nodded. Wanting to know more, she sat forward in her chair eagerly.

'Eventually, he and I came together, and became lovers. It was a grand love affair. He was a widower, and I had been widowed six years earlier; my husband died when I was thirty. My Swann was very proper and had loved me from afar, but had never approached me. He was always a gentleman in his behaviour. But one day I couldn't stand it any longer, I wanted him so badly. And I became bold, Charlotte. I manipulated things so that I could be near him as much as possible, and one evening, in a moment of sheer madness, I just stepped up to him and kissed him. We were alone, of course. Instantly he understood that I shared his feelings. And so it began.'

'I never guessed it was you!' Charlotte exclaimed, still stunned by this admission.

'What do you mean?' Lady Gwendolyn gaped at her, genuinely taken aback. Who had known about them?

'There's something in one of the record books, a notation, but no mention of your name. Was your lover Mark Swann?'

'Yes . . . Mark and I were together for some years.'

'I'm going to run over to my house. I want you to see the record book. I won't be a moment, Aunt Gwendolyn.'

Once she was alone, Lady Gwendolyn got up and went over to the black lacquered Chinese chest of drawers, and opened a drawer, lifted out a letter case, took it back to the chair where she had been sitting.

True to her word, Charlotte was back very quickly, coming into the parlour holding a record book in her hand. She opened it to the correct page and handed it to Lady Gwendolyn, who stared down at the page and began to read.

In mine own hand. July 1876.
I loveth my ladie. Beyond all.
The swann fits the ingham glove tight.
I have lain with her. She is mine.
She gives me all. I got her with child.
Oh our joy. The child dead in her belly.
Destroyed us. She left me.
She came back to me.
My nights are hers again.
Til the day I die. M. Swann.

Lady Gwendolyn blinked, sudden tears filling her eyes, and held the book next to her body for a moment, clutching it to her. She closed her eyes and sat very still for a while. Then she handed the book back to Charlotte without saying a word.

It was obvious she was very moved.

Charlotte said, 'I can see you loved him.'

'With all my heart . . . until the day he died.'

'It must have been heartbreaking, losing his child.'

'I was devastated. And so was he.'

Clearing her throat, hesitating, Charlotte finally asked, 'What would you have done with the child, Aunt Gwendolyn? Surely that situation would have been horribly difficult to handle. Especially in those days, fifty years ago.'

'We did think about it a lot, and never came up with a proper solution. And then it didn't matter, because the baby was stillborn.'

'Thank you for telling me.' Charlotte sighed. 'Dulcie's forever announcing that a lot of messing around must have gone on between the Inghams and the Swanns over the years. That's her rather blunt way of putting it, but I believe she's right . . . there must have been many involvements over these many, many years.'

'I agree. How could there not have been? The two families were living side by side in the country, practically under one roof most of the time. They were thrown together constantly, and they were all so compatible, and good looking, and more than likely highly motivated sexually.'

'And now we have Cecily Swann and Miles Ingham,' Charlotte said. 'Joined at the hip forever. And no divorce in sight. A different situation. They won't give each other up, you know. Not again.'

'It will come right in the end, believe me it will, Charlotte,' Lady Gwendolyn reassured her. 'We must all be patient. As you so often say, what is meant to be is meant to be. And things only happen when the time is right, in my experience.'

'That's true.'

Lady Gwendolyn picked up the leather case, opened it and took out some old photographs. 'This is Mark Swann. And this is a picture of me with him.'

'How good you look together. Mark resembles Walter,' Charlotte exclaimed. 'He's very handsome.'

'Aren't they all?' Lady Gwendolyn murmured with a wry smile. She handed Charlotte another old photograph, also well preserved. 'And this is Margaret . . .' She cut off the end of her sentence, fell silent.

Charlotte was staring at a picture of a beautiful baby in an expensive-looking christening gown and a small lace cap. She glanced up and gaped at Lady Gwendolyn, her eyes full of questions.

'Our child. Mark's and mine. You see, we had another baby and she lived. We had been very careful, and I was in my forties by then. I didn't believe I could get pregnant. No one was more terrified and shocked than I was. After all, I was almost forty-eight.'

So startled was she, Charlotte couldn't speak for a moment, and then she said in a low but vehement voice, 'Oh my God! What did you do?'

'The only thing possible at that time, at least for us. We had to give her up for adoption. I told my brother, David, the truth; anyway, he had always guessed about Mark and me,' Lady Gwendolyn explained. 'As you well know, David and I were very close. He was genuinely sympathetic, but adamant that we could not keep the child. Had I been married, we could have explained it away, I suppose, like so many married women did, and claimed it was the child of my husband. But I was a widow.'

'I do understand.' Charlotte's voice was full of sadness. 'It must have been so hard for you. Who adopted your baby?'

'Mark and I were never told. That was the way it was in those days. Adoption was very private – secretive, in a certain sense. David had a solicitor in Harrogate, whom he used for some estate matters. It was this solicitor who handled the matter. David assured me that the baby was

359

going to a good middle-class family, a couple who were desperate for a child. I went out and bought lovely clothes for her, and a certain amount of money was given to the family for her care. And that was the end of it . . .' Again Lady Gwendolyn stopped mid-sentence and sat back in the chair, a sorrowful feeling sweeping over her. She was full of tears, wanted to sob her heart out.

Charlotte, observing her intently, saw that she was extremely upset, and remained silent, fully understanding her pain as she relived those memories of long ago.

Gwendolyn must have been beautiful, Charlotte thought. With a look of Diedre in her late thirties, early forties. The white-haired woman sitting opposite her was still lovely, with the clearest of blue eyes and a fresh complexion.

Suddenly, Lady Gwendolyn sat up straighter in the chair, pulled herself together. 'I said that was the end of it, but of course it wasn't. I have thought about that child, my daughter, every day of my life; wondered about her, worried about her. The good thing was that Mark and I stayed together. We were so in love with each other, we couldn't part. But we did become very careful in every way. Ingham women seem to get pregnant very easily.'

'I'm glad you continued your love affair, Aunt Gwendolyn. You needed each other.'

'We did, and he was always loving and consoling. Somehow we did manage to cope. And we believed we had done the right thing . . . for the child. And we were both certain that David had handled it well.'

'So somewhere out there, in this world we live in today, there is an Ingham-Swann woman called Margaret.'

'I'm sure she is alive and well. I hope so. However, I am not certain that her adoptive parents kept the name Margaret. They probably had her christened something else.'

'Did they know where she came from?' Charlotte asked.

'No. The solicitor assured them she was from a good family, gave them a few scraps about the circumstances, and that was that. However, I have to believe that they brought her up well, for my own peace of mind.'

'Thank you for confiding in me, I appreciate your trust.'

'Charlotte, I would trust you with my life.'

'And I am always here for you, whatever you need, whenever you need it, Aunt Gwendolyn.'

'Thank you. Charlotte, I want you to know something else . . . I fibbed when I told you that the golden swan brooch had been passed down by my mother. That wasn't true. Mark had it made for me. He said if things had been different, we would have been married, and I would have been a Swann. Since you are now both Swann and Ingham, I thought it should be yours. You enjoy wearing it, don't you?'

Charlotte smiled. 'I do. I've been wearing it a lot. In fact, when I told Charles you had given it to me, that it was an Ingham heirloom, he was surprised. He said he'd never seen it before.'

'Don't enlighten him, Charlotte, please. I want my little secret to remain a secret.'

'It will, I promise.'

FIFTY

'So how much did the wedding cost, in the end?' Hugo asked, looking across his desk at Miles.

'A lot. But actually Papa didn't have to pay anything, as it turned out. In fact, I think he might have made some money on it.'

'How?' Hugo asked, sounding surprised by this comment.

The two men were sitting in Hugo's London office, working together on a project, an idea of Harry Swann's. And, as usual, Hugo was worried about money.

Miles took a piece of paper out of his pocket and looked at it, refreshing his memory. 'Now, let's see. Great-Aunt Gwendolyn gave Papa a cheque for five thousand pounds, as you know. It was a gift, because he's her heir, apparently. However, not all of that money was spent, for the following reasons.' He glanced at his list, and continued, 'Dulcie said she didn't want any gifts from the family, but if they did want to give her and James something, she suggested they contribute to the cost of the wedding.'

'That was a nice thought, and practical, as she usually is.'

'I paid for the band; that was my gift,' Miles went on. 'Charlotte paid for the two caterers from Harrogate, who did the Saturday dinner, the wedding reception and the wedding dinner, alongside Cook. And Charlotte's bill did include the food for those occasions.'

'That must have been a big saving for Charles,' Hugo murmured, feeling better already.

'Cecily gave Dulcie her wedding gown and cape. They were her wedding presents. She also paid for the extra orchids and all the other white flowers which came from Harte's department store. She's become quite friendly with Emma Harte, you know, and, in fact, Ceci's opening a shop within the store. It's going to be called the Cecily Swann Boutique, and will sell all of the accessories she designs.'

'What wonderful news that is, Miles. I must congratulate Ceci. She's turned out to be a fabulously successful business-woman.'

'She has. So let me tell you the rest. Daphne paid for the two bridesmaids' dresses from her trust, she told me, and the little soldier outfits for the twins. And Papa used some of the money from Great-Aunt Gwendolyn to pay the women from the village, who came up to help. Oh, and the photographer. But Papa told me the other day he hadn't spent it all.'

'That's good news. We can always use a little extra cash.'

'Hugo, is there something I should know? Something wrong?' Miles now asked.

'No, no, nothing. I guess I've just become a terrible worrier these days. And there are now those leaks in the West Wing bathrooms.'

'Bathrooms! I thought it was only one.'

'Seemingly another one has sprung a leak. They're working now to get them fixed.'

'Oh God.' Miles pursed his lips, leaned forward, and said, 'Not to change the subject, but I do want to discuss something else.'

'What? Now *you* sound concerned,' Hugo exclaimed.

'I'm not. But I've never quite understood everything

about the Transatlantic Air situation. I don't mean about them going belly-up, I mean about exactly how much money we, meaning the Ingham Trust, got back.'

'The full amount. I gave half the sum from my own money, and Paul the same amount. In other words, the Trust got back its entire investment. We'd invested the money on behalf of the Trust, which is why we felt responsible.'

'That I know, and it was very generous of you both. What no one has explained is how much ten million dollars is in English pounds.'

'It's two million pounds, give or take a few pennies,' Hugo answered at once.

'Good to know. What's the rate of exchange, Hugo?'

'At this moment it costs four dollars and eighty-seven cents, give or take a cent, to buy one English pound.'

'Good God! Why so much?' Miles was surprised.

'The pound has a high value, not necessarily a good thing by the way. And the dollar has been devalued. It's all to do with the gold standard, as far as the pound is concerned, and too complicated for me to explain in a few minutes.'

'You don't have to, Hugo. And thanks, I now have a better picture. Papa did tell me you and he had been careful about investing some of the money that came back into the Trust; that you had chosen very conservative and solid English companies.'

'We did, Miles. Don't worry, the money is safe. We kept back cash, of course, in order to pay those bloody awful income-tax bills the government is dishing out these days. And for the maintenance of the estate.'

'So we're basically all right?'

'We are. But, let me add, there are the costs of the new roof on the North Wing, and also the plumbing repairs now going on in the bathrooms.'

Miles nodded. 'Let's get back to Harry's idea. I want us to go with it, Hugo. I think it might work, bring in some much-needed income eventually.'

'I agree. But what we must consider is that if we rent out those empty farms, we will have to train the men who take them on. That takes time.'

'I know. Listen, let's go over it with my father this weekend, get his views and go from there.'

'We're going to manage all right, Miles,' Hugo said, sounding more confident in general. Miles always cheered him up because he was positive, had a good attitude.

Rising, Hugo said, 'Come on, let's go and grab a bite of lunch. Then I'm driving up to Cavendon tonight. When are you coming up, Miles?'

'I'm not sure. Tonight Cecily and I have a dinner. With Felix and Constance Lambert. I'm looking forward to it. They're good company.'

'What news of the newlyweds? How're they doing?'

Miles smiled, had a twinkle in his eye. 'They're head over heels in love, having a great time in New York. Diedre and Paul are thrilled that Dulcie and James are in Manhattan. And Diedre's feeling better, by the way. The bedrest was good for her, and the baby is safe. Due in April, I hear.'

'Thank God for that. I wonder if Daphne knows?' Hugo murmured. 'She's been so worried about Diedre.'

'I only got the news from Ceci this morning. She's had a letter from Dulcie about something, and gave Ceci all this news in it.'

Walking down to Shepherd Market to have lunch at a small Italian restaurant they liked, Hugo suddenly looked at Miles and said, 'Where does Charlotte get her money from? She's very generous to the family.'

Miles smiled, rather proudly in fact. He said, 'Over the

years when she worked for my grandfather, David, the Fifth Earl, he bought her quite a lot of jewellery, and he also created a small trust for her. Also, she's been very frugal over the years. Cecily told me Charlotte gave her a whole lot of brooches and bracelets to sell for her, which Ceci did. And I understand she paid for the caterers with her savings. After all, she is now the Countess, and certainly my father will always see she is taken care of. But she's a good woman. Good to all of us.'

Hugo exclaimed, 'I'll say! And frankly I'm glad she has taken over the running of the house. She's so efficient, and now I see Daphne more than ever. And that's so much joy for me.'

FIFTY-ONE

Constance Lambert stood in the dressing room of their spacious flat in Eaton Square, regarding herself in the long mirror. She was wearing her latest Cecily Swann, and liking what she saw.

The suit was made of white wool, trimmed with black rickrack, and had black buttons on the short flared jacket. The skirt was shorter than she normally wore, just below the knee. But Cecily had convinced her she should show off her legs, and had added that – these days – shorter was sexier.

Her shoes were also by Cecily; she had bought a number of pairs in different colours. They were called the Swann Quick Step. They were a simple court shoe but had a rather high heel, which was flattering to the leg. Tonight she was wearing a black pair which had white high heels. She decided she would carry the Golden Box bag by Cecily, which James had given her for her birthday last year; since it was still February, she would also wear her white cape which matched the suit.

She stood back, her head on one side, thinking she looked elegant and yet up to the minute, as far as style was concerned. That was the beauty of Cecily Swann's clothes. They made women look younger and much more modern. No wonder she had become the most important fashion designer in England. All of the fashion editors in Fleet Street loved her; wrote about her constantly, and most flatteringly. Her publicity was fantastic.

At the sound of the front door closing, Constance went out into the corridor and headed for the hall. Felix was taking off his overcoat and putting it in the closet, along with his scarf.

He smiled when he saw her, and took hold of her arm, walked with her to his study, explaining, 'I need to talk to you before we go to dinner. You do have a few minutes, don't you? You are ready, aren't you? Well, you are, I can see that, looking as beautiful as always.'

'Thank you,' she said. 'Of course we can talk.' Although she had kept her voice even, Constance was alarmed, wondering what had happened. Felix was never brusque with her, nor did he ever sound strained, as he did now. 'Rattled' was perhaps a better word. She had been married to him for so long she knew every facial expression, every mannerism, every quirk; could read him well. 'You're upset, darling, what's bothering you?'

Felix put his briefcase on a chair, and sat down on the sofa. Looking across at Constance, who was still standing, he said, 'Come and sit, Con. I've something to tell you. But first I have to warn you about tonight. You must be careful what you say in front of Miles and Cecily. And you can't repeat anything.'

'I never would, anyway. But please explain what this is all about. You're frightening me.' She lowered herself into a chair, but sat on the edge. 'This doesn't have anything to do with James, does it?'

Realizing she did sound afraid, he said quietly, 'No, no, it doesn't, I promise you. Let me start at the beginning.'

She nodded. 'But James and Dulcie are truly all right, aren't they?'

'They are fine, wonderful – having a ball, as they say in New York. This has to do with Helen Malone and her death last week.'

'Oh. I see. I'm listening, Felix.' She sat back in her chair, relieved. James was like the son she had never had, and she adored him; she was forever worrying about him. And now there was Dulcie to worry about, too. How lucky he had been. That girl was a treasure.

'Long before she died, Helen had not been herself – as you well know since we managed her,' Felix said. 'The rumour circulating in theatrical circles was that she was having an affair, that he was posh, or "a toff", as Sid kept saying. But that's about all any of us knew. However, seemingly he was a married man. And that was the root of Helen's problem. He had a wife. She was the mistress. There was no possibility of a divorce. I've been told it was breaking her heart. Also, it seems the man was not a particularly nice type, a bit of a brute.'

'So this is to do with that man? Helen's lover? Is that it?' Constance threw her husband a questioning look.

'Partially. Since the gossip was rather accurate, I had to believe that the man was indeed from the upper class,' Felix explained. 'However, I had no idea who he was. Nor did I care. Helen was old enough to do what she wanted. Anyway, to get back to the present. Sid came to see me today at the office. He had a suitcase belonging to James, asked me to keep it for him. It was full of scripts, books, notebooks. Because Sid is in the middle of a move to a new flat, he was afraid the suitcase might get lost. It had been in James's dressing room at the Old Vic, and James had given it to Sid to look after.'

Pausing for a moment, Felix took out a gold Cartier case, lit up a du Maurier cigarette and took a few puffs. Then he continued his story.

'In the course of our chat,' he said, 'Sid told me that

369

Helen had actually died of septicaemia. Caused by a botched abortion. She had also lost much of her blood by the time she arrived at the hospital.'

'Oh no, Felix!' Constance exclaimed, her face turning pale. 'How terrible for her. If only she had confided in us, we might have been able to help her avert such a tragedy.'

'That's true. I was most upset when Sid told me. Devastated actually, Con; she was so talented. And so young.'

'How does Sid know all this?'

Felix shook his head. 'The grapevine, I suppose. You know how fast gossip and bad news travels in our world – any world, for that matter. Once Sid had relayed this horrific news, he confided that the man she was seeing was a famous surgeon. His name is Lawrence Pierce. Who is married to Felicity.'

'Miles's mother! Oh my God, don't tell me he performed the botched abortion.'

'I don't think it would have been botched if he had done it. It would have been perfect. Most likely she went to a woman in a back street, who had a knitting needle.'

Constance shuddered at the imagery, and closed her eyes for a moment, pushing back her tears as she thought of Helen Malone, only twenty-seven and far too young to die in such a terrible way.

'This is the thing, Constance. Sid told me that the name of Helen's lover was never actually known by any of her friends, which I find unlikely, but he says it's true. According to Sid, he's been "outed", as Sid calls it. His name's out on the street. Sid believes there's going to be trouble. I believe he was actually trying to warn me.'

Constance sat up straight in her chair, looking aghast. 'Do you mean we could be involved, because we managed her?'

'No, no, I'm putting it badly, darling. I think Sid was

alerting me, making me aware there could be some sort of trouble. He just wanted us to know.'

'Could there be a police investigation?' Constance asked, giving Felix a questioning look.

'I doubt it. Pierce is an eminent surgeon, and a brilliant one. He's an important man, married to an heiress. The police won't touch this with a bargepole. Sid's thinking of Helen's family. They may be out for blood.' Felix paused, stubbed out his cigarette. 'Have you forgotten how Helen became our client?'

Constance stared at him, nodded. 'No, I haven't. It was James who discovered her, in that amateur theatrical company. He brought her to us. Helen's brothers knew the Woods; they were friends of James's father. They are dockers in the East End.'

'That's right.'

'You don't think her brothers would blame James, do you? For bringing her into the professional theatre?'

'No, never. James Brentwood is so ethical, has such integrity and decency, no one would harm a hair on his head. He's an icon, Connie, you know that. Much beloved by thousands – as well as you, Ruby, Dulcie and me.' He took another cigarette from the Cartier case, lit it and smoked for a moment, his face reflective. 'This is another thing not to be repeated. I've been told, and by a very good source, that James will be knighted before he's forty.'

For a moment Constance looked stunned, and then she gave her husband a warm smile. 'I knew it would happen one day. He has to be honoured in that way by the King.'

'Sid is certain there's going to be some sort of bad trouble, that Helen's brothers might go on the warpath. Retribution.'

'I hope not, and I'm awfully glad James is on his honeymoon. I know he would be very upset by all this.'

'I agree. However, he has Dulcie. He found her at last,

371

the woman he had been seeking for years. She'll look after him. She's another Ruby for him. In fact, Dulcie's protective of him already, has been since the day she met him. Or hadn't you noticed?'

'Cecily, you look stunning!' Felix said, standing to greet her and Miles as they arrived at the table in Rules on Maiden Lane. 'And you don't look half bad yourself, Miles,' he added, shaking Miles's hand.

They both thanked him, and Cecily went over to Constance and kissed her cheek, then sat down in the chair the waiter was pulling out for her. Miles did the same; he kissed Constance and then took a seat himself. Within minutes they were sipping pink champagne and toasting Cecily.

Miles, wondering what this was about, looked at her. A brow lifted and then he gave her one of his puzzled frowns.

Cecily laughed and said to him, 'I'm being toasted because something lovely has happened—'

'Oh dear, doesn't Miles know?' Constance cut in peremptorily, looking at Cecily. 'Haven't you told him yet?'

'I haven't had a chance, Connie.'

'So I shall tell him,' Felix announced. Turning to Miles he explained, 'We represent a famous theatrical producer, Michael Alexander, who is putting on a new musical in the West End. He wants Cecily to design the clothes for the show. And, guess what, we got her for him. The contracts will be drawn up within the next few weeks. So we thought it would be nice to have you both to dinner to celebrate.'

Miles beamed at Felix and then at Connie, pushed back his chair and went to kiss Cecily on her cheek. 'You're a naughty girl, keeping me in the dark,' he said, but he was thrilled for her, and almost bursting with pride. 'It *is* lovely news, darling, you're right about that. Gosh, you're going into a whole new world, Ceci . . . into show business.'

Squeezing her shoulder, he returned to his seat, and lifting his glass he toasted her. 'To my talented and very dearest Ceci!' After swallowing some of the champagne, Miles added, 'It looks as if February is your lucky month. Have you told Connie and Felix about your new boutique?'

'I have, and you're right, Miles. I've been most fortunate. I'm a lucky girl.' As she said this, she couldn't help thinking it was marriage to Miles she wanted, not a contract for a musical.

'You deserve it, darling,' Constance said. 'I've never seen anyone work like you do, except for James. He's a glutton for punishment, I always tell him. And he just laughs, like you do.'

'I had a letter from Dulcie this morning,' Cecily said. 'The newlyweds are enjoying New York. And, by the way, Diedre's health has improved and the baby is all right. So it's been good news all around lately.'

Felix said, 'I heard from James last week, and it looks as though he and Dulcie will probably take a trip out to the Wild West, as he calls it. To California, a place called Hollywood, where they've been making those moving pictures for a few years now. It looks like sound is the coming thing. Voices are going to be very important, and who has a voice like James's?'

'No one,' Miles answered. 'I can listen to him forever.'

'So when will they be coming back?' Cecily asked. She missed Dulcie and Diedre, and now that DeLacy was courting, she was spending more time with Travers Merton. Their little band of Cavendon women was scattered. For the moment, at least.

'I don't think James will want to stay longer than a week in Hollywood,' Felix answered. 'I sent a telegram to him a few days ago. I've had an offer for him to do a limited engagement of *Henry V*, here in London. He cabled back he wants to do it. So he'll have to return by the end of this month or early March to go into rehearsals.'

'Oh, how wonderful,' Cecily said. 'He's such a thrilling actor.'

'And a lovely man,' Miles remarked, looked across the table at Cecily and grinning. 'Our little madam has been very lucky, hasn't she?'

Cecily grinned and, noticing the strange look on Felix's face, she felt she had to explain. 'Dulcie was very much like she is today, when she was a child,' Cecily explained. 'Very outspoken, mischievous and a bit cheeky. Diedre used to call her a little madam, and she wasn't very nice to her either. Dulcie was a bit afraid of her. Hence the successful blackmailing of last year.'

'Blackmailing? What was that all about?' Felix asked.

Miles said, 'Well, that's what Diedre called it, but I think Dulcie was being rather clever myself. She asked Diedre to put up some money for her art gallery. Her ploy was to tell Diedre that – if she did – the bad memories of her, which Dulcie still harboured in her head, would disappear.'

Constance and Felix looked at each other and burst out laughing. 'I can just hear her saying it,' Constance said through her laughter. 'How very clever she is.'

'And very beautiful,' Felix added, hoping and praying that no one would want her to be in moving pictures out there in the Wild West. James would never allow it. He wanted a wife, not an actress. He had enough of those hanging on his arm over the years. Besides which, Dulcie was his new Ruby . . . the woman he'd been looking for all of his adult life.

Focusing on Miles, Felix now asked, 'Do you still invest in stocks on Wall Street?'

Miles shook his head vehemently. 'Not on your life, Felix. We had rather a bad experience. It's righted itself, thankfully, through some good help from Hugo and Paul.

But we're out of the American stock market. Paul thinks bad times are coming. He's already starting to unload some of his own investments, and selling real estate. Hugo is thinking about doing the same thing. He has rather a lot of investments from the years he lived there.'

'I'm glad I brought it up,' Felix said. 'I will avoid Wall Street.' The two men sat chatting for a while, about the money markets, investing money, the good and the bad of it all.

Constance and Cecily spoke about clothes and her new boutique at Harte's. They all drank more champagne; finally, they stopped their chatter and ordered dinner.

Once they had selected their food, and Felix had chosen the wines, the talk went back to the theatre, and the new shows being planned for the summer season.

At one moment, Felix and Constance froze in their chairs when Miles mentioned the death of Helen Malone. 'Yes,' he said. 'I was awfully sad to read of her death in the newspapers. I thought she was a most marvellous Ophelia, and James and she played well together,' Miles remarked. 'I know she was a client of yours; it must have been quite a blow.'

'Yes, it was,' Constance said immediately, her expression neutral, her voice even. 'We will miss her. She was talented, and a truly nice person.'

'What did she die of? I didn't quite understand that,' Miles said, probing a little. 'From the stories in the papers.'

Before Constance could say another thing, Felix jumped in swiftly. 'It was some sort of blood poisoning, that's all we were told. She has a family, you know, and they have been dealing with everything, as families usually do.'

Constance, noticing the waiter coming across the room, exclaimed, 'How lovely! The oysters are on their way.' She had managed to change the subject, and continued to do so, suddenly started talking about pearls to the three of them, especially Cecily. 'They're my favourite jewellery. Pearls of any kind, and I love those you're wearing, Cecily. You should market them, don't you think?'

'I've just designed various pearl necklaces, and long ropes of pearls, Connie. I'll send you a long string tomorrow as a gift.'

'Why thank you, darling, how sweet of you.'

It was only when they arrived back at Cecily's flat that she pounced on Miles. 'I couldn't believe it when you mentioned Helen Malone. I almost fainted to distract them. I thought you were going to give them all the gossip on the family grapevine, about Helen Malone and Lawrence Pierce. And I didn't know how to change the subject.'

'But Connie did. I noticed how she suddenly mentioned the oysters and then pearls. She thought she was distracting me. And I let her do it, because I think they know about Pierce and Helen. And I didn't want them to feel obliged to tell me that my mother's husband had been messing around with their client.'

'I noticed something, Miles. They became awfully silent when you asked how she died.'

'How did she? Do you know? I've been puzzled about that.'

'I'm not sure,' Cecily said as she went into the bedroom, taking off her jacket, stepping out of her shoes.

Miles, following her, was removing his tie. 'Come on, you're a Swann: the Swanns know everything. What else did Eric tell you?'

'He doesn't know as much as you think. It's only gossip from his show-business mates. But the suggestion is that she did have some sort of blood poisoning. The other story trickling out onto the street is that she had an abortion, that it went wrong. Also, Eric did mention that Lawrence Pierce's name is out there.'

Miles sat down in a chair to take off his shoes. Looking across at her, frowning, he said, 'Could my mother possibly know about Helen Malone?'

'I just don't know. How could she?'

'Oh well, I don't care really whether she knows or not. He's her problem, not mine or yours. Come on, Ceci, hurry up. Let's go to bed and cuddle up together. I haven't seen you all week.'

When she remained silent, Miles got up and walked over to her, took hold of her and brought her into his arms. 'I love you, Ceci, and so very much. I know you cried at Dulcie's wedding, and I understand why. I noticed, even if you think I didn't. I will work it out, I promise. You will be my wife.'

Cecily had loved him since childhood, and she knew he meant every word. But she also knew the situation was not in his control. Clarissa, his estranged wife, held those strings. And very tightly.

Taking a deep breath, Cecily looked into his eyes. 'I have you, Miles. You're my whole life; all that matters to me. I don't need a piece of paper to tell me that you love me, I know you do. Come on, let's go to bed and make love.' And they did.

FIFTY-TWO

DeLacy and Travers were so drunk they barely made it back to his studio in Chelsea. They had been guests at a big society wedding, extremely lavish, where wine and champagne had flowed like rivers, and the food had been perfection. What else to expect at the Ritz Hotel?

Many of their friends had been present, and Travers had enjoyed himself immensely, mixing with old school pals from Eton, as well as celebrities and socialites he had painted and others he hoped to paint. DeLacy had also enjoyed herself, because Travers kept her close to him, included her at all times, never left her standing alone.

The doorman at the Ritz had helped them into a taxicab later and now they were staggering into the bedroom of his studio, supporting each other as best they could. Somehow they managed to get undressed, fell onto the bed in a stupor and immediately passed out.

It was midnight when the man arrived at the front door of the studio and tried the knob. Instantly it opened, and he stepped inside, smiling to himself. Merton had been so drunk he had forgotten to lock the door. But he had a copy of the key anyway, so what did it matter?

With great stealth, the man crept across the studio and

into the kitchen, where he put on a small light. He took a bottle and a syringe out of his jacket pocket; after filling the syringe, he put the bottle back in one pocket, the syringe in the other.

He did not have to go into the bedroom to see that they had passed out. The lights were still on, and they lay sprawled across the sheets, lost to the world. She was breathing heavily; he was snoring loudly, which told the man his sleep potions from the Chinese herbalist, Fu Yung-Yen in Chinatown, had worked. He had dropped a pellet in each of their drinks at the wedding when neither of them was looking.

Gliding into the bedroom, bending over Travers, the man took out the syringe and lifted Travers's arm, injected the potassium chloride into the fleshy part covered in hair underneath; he pulled the syringe out when it was empty and slipped it into his pocket.

The man glanced at DeLacy. A sneer crossed his face. He didn't want her any more. She was Merton's leavings, anyway. A whore, a bitch, a drunk. Worthless. Damaged goods.

He crept away on silent feet, turned out the light in the kitchen and left the studio. He walked through the streets, breathing in the fresh air, not minding the cold wind. It was refreshing.

By the time he had made it to the King's Road, he felt much better. He had accomplished what he had decided to do months ago. Merton deserved it. That bastard had taken DeLacy for himself, before he had made her his own. That had spoiled his well-made plans: get rid of the mother, install the daughter, live happily ever after on Mama's money. After all, she had made him her heir. Now he was stuck with the mother.

A sudden thought struck him. Maybe in a few months he could start an affair with DeLacy. She would be over

Merton by then. He could clean her up, get her into shape, dress her up just to undress her, and take her into his bed. And give her what she really wanted. Him. The very thought of this aroused him, gave him an erection.

Stepping to the edge of the pavement he hailed a cab, told the cabbie to take him to Charles Street, and let himself in.

Felicity was in luck tonight, he decided. The aroused state he was in ensured that she could romp with him to her heart's delight, the way she liked, and with a little bit of the rough stuff thrown in.

DeLacy was so nauseous it awakened her. She pushed herself out of bed, half stumbled to the bathroom, fell onto her knees and vomited in the toilet. She lay on the cold tiled floor for a long time, eventually began to feel a bit better.

Scrambling to her feet, she managed to get to the kitchen, filled a glass with cold water, drank it down greedily, parched. Then she hobbled into the studio, sat down in a chair, taking deep breaths. She was less woozy, and the feeling of nausea was receding, but she had a raging headache.

The chair was facing the bedroom; all of a sudden DeLacy sat up with a start. She could just see Travers, and realized he was slumped over to one side, half hanging out of the bed. He looked strange.

Pushing herself to her feet, she stumbled towards the doorway, drew closer, peering at him. Then she took a step back. A scream rose in her throat, and she started to shake. Fear was edging into her mind.

His eyes were wide open. And blank. She didn't know what was wrong with him. And then it came to her. He was drunk, wasn't he? Or was he dead? But how could that be? Rushing out of the room, shock beginning to set in, she went to the phone on his desk in the studio and dialled Cecily. She couldn't stop shaking.

It rang and rang, and she was about to hang up, when she heard Cecily saying, 'Hello?' in a muffled tone.

'Ceci, it's me,' DeLacy said in a halting voice that quavered. 'Something's wrong . . . with Travers. Please come. Come and help me.'

'Where are you?' Cecily asked in an urgent voice, now wide awake.

'His studio.'

'Are you dressed?'

'No.'

'Get dressed. Make sure you've got all of your things, jewellery, bag. I'll be there shortly. With Eric.'

'Why? Why Eric?'

'I feel better having him with us. Eric's a man. We might need a man. Get dressed, sit down and wait for us. All right?'

'Yes,' DeLacy said, and hung up. Then she began to sob, shock completely taking over.

By the time Cecily arrived with her cousin, Eric Swann, DeLacy had managed to put on her clothes and find all her things. Her shoes, stockings, handbag, and the pieces of expensive jewellery she had been wearing for the formal wedding.

The light tapping on the front door made DeLacy hurry over to open it. The moment Cecily walked in, she took DeLacy in her arms and held her close, soothing her.

DeLacy was weeping quietly, but after a few moments she pulled herself together and stood away.

'Hello, Eric,' she murmured, then looked at Cecily, her eyes still wide with shock. She said, 'Please look at Travers? I don't know what's wrong with him.'

'Yes, we will,' Eric answered. 'Where is he?'

'In the bedroom. It's over there.'

Together Eric and Cecily crossed the large studio and went into the bedroom. But it was Eric who stepped over to the bed, took hold of Travers's hand and felt for his pulse. There wasn't one. Looking into Travers's face, he shook his head, gently closing Travers's eyelids.

Turning to look at Cecily, and then at DeLacy, standing in the doorway, Eric said, 'I'm so sorry, Lady DeLacy. I'm afraid he's dead. Of what, I've no idea. I would think a heart attack, perhaps.'

'But he's young,' Cecily exclaimed, shaking her head. 'How can that be?'

DeLacy didn't say a word. She just stood there staring into space, tears trickling down her face. Then she walked into the bedroom, bent over Travers and kissed his face. It was cold, and she pulled back. Swallowing, battling to control her emotions, she lifted the sheet with shaking hands and covered him up.

Cecily took hold of her arm and said, 'I think we must leave. Do you have everything?'

'I do, yes.'

Looking at the expensive jewellery, Cecily said, 'Are you sure you do have all of that?'

'Yes, I do.'

Ushering DeLacy into the studio, Eric said, 'Let's sit down for a moment so you can tell us what happened this evening. I'd like to know.'

She nodded and they all sat. DeLacy said, 'Travers and I went to the Coddington wedding at the Ritz. Travers had been at school with Peter Coddington. It was a very lavish affair. Travers and I had quite a lot to drink – more than usual. And especially for me. When we left we were really drunk, but managed to get ourselves here in a cab. We fell into bed and passed out. I woke up around one thirty, feeling nauseous. I vomited a lot. Then I drank some water, and went to sit in here. I saw Travers; he looked so strange, falling out of bed, his eyes blank. I was afraid. I didn't know what was wrong.' Looking across at Cecily she said, 'That was when I called you, Ceci.'

'It was almost two when you telephoned. I know because I looked at the clock on my bedside table.'

'Nobody else was here with you?' Eric asked.

DeLacy shook her head. 'No, we were alone.'

'You say you vomited,' Cecily said, frowning. 'Could you have eaten something that poisoned you? And also Travers?'

'I told you, the reception and dinner were at the Ritz Hotel. The food is the best.'

Eric, who had been looking thoughtful, said slowly, 'It's not the first time I've heard of a young man dying of a heart attack. And, who knows, Mr Merton might have had heart problems. Do you know if he did, Lady DeLacy?'

'He never mentioned it.'

'Could all the alcohol have caused something to happen?' Cecily looked at Eric, raising a brow.

'It could, but I'm not a doctor, you know.'

'I don't think we should just go and leave Travers here like this, after all,' Cecily now said, changing her mind about leaving. 'I think we ought to call Uncle Howard, tell him what's happened.'

'But he's Scotland Yard,' DeLacy whispered, frowning. 'Why do you want to involve Scotland Yard?'

'He's also family, Lady DeLacy. But the normal thing to do when somebody dies is to call that person's doctor. Did Mr Merton have a doctor?'

'No, not that I know of. He was very healthy.'

'Shall we call an ambulance? And have Mr Merton's body taken to a hospital? When somebody dies suddenly like this, there has to be an examination, perhaps even an autopsy,' Eric explained.

'I'm going to telephone Uncle Howard, ask his advice. I'd like to have this matter in the hands of a Swann.'

'He's not a Swann,' DeLacy muttered.

'He's married to one, and that means he is,' Cecily answered.

Howard Pinkerton arrived at Travers Merton's studio in less than half an hour, having told Cecily that he would come over to check everything out himself.

He spoke to DeLacy at length, and she took him through the progression of events of earlier. When she had finished, he said, 'I would like to see Mr Merton's body please, Lady DeLacy. If I may?'

DeLacy took him over to the bedroom, showed him inside, then retreated.

The Inspector pulled back the sheet and scrutinized Travers Merton's body intently. He made a mental note that there were no marks on the body – no bruises, no signs of violence. He covered the body with the sheet and went back into the studio.

He said, 'I'm going to call for an ambulance, have Mr Merton's body taken to hospital for a thorough examination. I will take my pathologist over there myself.'

Sitting down on a chair, he continued, 'Quite frankly, it looks to me like a natural death. More than likely a heart attack. How old was Mr Merton, Lady DeLacy?'

'Thirty-seven,' she answered. 'And he was in good health.' Tears filled her eyes, and she endeavoured to control her emotions, turning her head away, blinking.

Inspector Pinkerton volunteered, 'People can walk around with conditions they are not aware of, and perhaps this was so with Mr Merton. You told me he didn't have a doctor.'

'That's right. I know because I once asked him, and he said he didn't need a doctor, he was as fit as a fiddle. Those were his words.'

Howard Pinkerton nodded. 'I prefer not to speculate. Let us wait for a professional opinion.'

He stood up, went over to the phone, made a telephone call. He then looked across the room at the others and said, 'There's no need for you to wait for the ambulance. I will handle this. By the way, who is the next of kin, do you know, Lady DeLacy?'

'Travers was orphaned, and his grandparents are dead. He does have one relative, on his mother's side. A cousin, and they were quite friendly. Otherwise, there's no one.'

Eric hailed a cab, and Cecily and Eric took DeLacy to her flat in Alford Street. Cecily had invited her to stay with her, not wanting her to be alone at this difficult time. DeLacy refused, explaining that she needed to be in her own home.

'There are a lot of his things in my flat, and I have to be surrounded by them. I'll be all right, Ceci. Thank you for coming to help me.'

'You know I'd do anything for you, Lacy.'

'So what happens next?' DeLacy now asked.

'Uncle Howard will stay in touch,' Cecily replied.

Eric interjected, 'I think we'll know quickly how he died once he is examined by a doctor.'

'Do you know Travers's cousin, Lacy?' Cecily asked. 'I think you will have to be in touch, and there is the matter of the funeral.'

'I've met his cousin, he's pleasant. His name is Vivian Carmichael and he's from the Noyers side of the family. But I'm not sure how to reach him.'

'Don't worry about that. Uncle Howard can handle it, or Miles.'

Eric and Cecily walked through Mayfair, back to her flat in Chesterfield Street. At one moment, he took hold of Cecily's arm, and drew her to a halt.

She looked at him. 'What is it, Eric?'

'I just wanted to say that you acted like a true Swann, the way you wanted to hurry DeLacy away from the studio.'

'I know it must have seemed heartless. But that's the way we're built – protect the Inghams, take the bullet if you have to. And, frankly, I'd no idea what had happened. I felt I had to get her away from the studio and back at home.'

'You did the right thing, phoning Howard. He's the best copper I know. But I think it was a natural death, don't you?'

'Yes, I suppose so. Yet something nags at the back of my mind, something I can't quite put my finger on.'

Eric frowned. 'You surprise me. Do you think they were poisoned? If so, by whom? Who would want to hurt them?'

'I don't know. But why was she vomiting?'

'DeLacy is not used to imbibing a lot of booze, is she? Maybe the tippling made her feel nauseous, caused the vomiting.'

Cecily simply frowned, and they walked on.

Eric said, 'She's still a bit wobbly, you know, and her eyes look glazed. And she'll have one hell of a hangover.'

'She's a fragile person, Eric. I must look after her.'

FIFTY-THREE

There is no place more beautiful than Cavendon Park, especially when the sun is shining, Cecily thought, as she walked up to the house from the village.

It was the middle of April; after weeks of rain and, before that, melting snow, the weather had suddenly changed for the better. She glanced up.

The sky was pale blue this afternoon, with white scudding clouds, and the sun was bright, if not exactly warm. Buds were opening on the shrubs and trees, and daffodils were pushing their way up. Everything was green and growing. Renewal was in the air.

After Travers Merton's tragic death, things were looking up. DeLacy was recovering slowly from her soul-destroying anguish and emotional devastation. He had died of a heart attack, according to the doctors at the hospital, and the pathologist brought in by Howard Pinkerton. It was declared to be a natural death.

Travers's cousin, Vivian Carmichael, had asked DeLacy to help with his funeral, and she had done so willingly. All the Inghams had attended, to give her support, along with many of his old friends.

Cecily had quickly come to realize that this extraordinary

turn-out and display of loyalty and love had been part of DeLacy's healing process. It had comforted her that his friends cared so much for Travers.

DeLacy was living at Cavendon most of the time. She felt at ease within the middle of her family, welcomed their love and affection.

DeLacy was also on the mend, and in no small part because of Cecily's brother, Harry. They had been childhood friends, and in his spare time Harry went riding with her, and sometimes they all went to the theatre in Harrogate. Harry was offering DeLacy some companionship, and this pleased Cecily. There was nothing worse than being alone when you were sorrowful. She knew that only too well.

Cecily was feeling rather chuffed today. Only two hours ago, Michael Alexander, the producer of the musical, had telephoned her to say he loved the first sketches of the clothes. She was enjoying this new venture; she had discovered she liked designing for the theatre.

Her other project, the boutique in Harte's department store, would be opening in the late summer. She was currently designing a new line of accessories exclusively for Harte's. She could sell them in her own shops, but not to any other retailers.

Dulcie had come up with a few good ideas for her, and they were already in production. She smiled to herself at the thought of Dulcie, who had already found a building in Mayfair for her art gallery.

The two of them had giggled together the other day, at the Burlington Arcade shop. Dulcie had confided that she was about to raid all the family attics in order to have an inventory for the gallery. They had both envisaged the furore this would create.

The other bit of good news was that Diedre had given birth to the baby in New York. It was a boy, and mother and child were doing well.

Cecily glanced at her watch. It was just after three thirty. She had been invited to tea by Aunt Charlotte, who had asked her to bring some of the sketches of the clothes for the musical. She had them in her satchel.

As she hurried past the rose garden, Cecily noticed the oak door was wide open. She went to close it, and was surprised to see her aunt sitting on a garden seat. She had her elbows on her knees and her head in her hands. Something was wrong. Very wrong.

Cecily went into the rose garden, closing the heavy door behind her and running down the steps.

She flew along the gravel path; her aunt looked up and saw her, stared at her blindly, as if not seeing her at all. Charlotte's face was stark, and the colour of bleached bone.

'Aunt Charlotte, what is it? What's wrong?' Cecily cried, sitting down on the seat next to her, letting her satchel fall onto the ground.

Charlotte did not answer. She sat there, motionless, as unmoving as a statue. Cecily noticed a vein throbbing in her aunt's temple and there was a look of anguish in her eyes.

Unexpectedly, Cecily, who was afraid of nothing, was very frightened. She knew that whatever had happened, it was big. Enormous, in fact. Was the Earl ill? No, she would not be on this seat if he were. She would be with him. And yet instinctively Cecily was positive that her aunt was in some kind of shock. What was scaring her and creating this state of mind?

Without warning, Charlotte suddenly put her arms around Cecily and began to sob, clutching her tightly, clinging to her like a drowning woman to a raft. Holding her closely, trying to calm her, Cecily wondered where Miles was. She needed Miles. And no one else. It was apparent that Charlotte had a problem that she could not share with the Earl.

After a while, the sobbing lessened, and finally Charlotte sat up, looking deeply into Cecily's face. Taking a few deep breaths, she said in a trembling voice, 'I think I needed that, it helped. And I'm sorry, Ceci, to do that to you.'

Grabbing hold of her aunt's hands, Cecily said softly, 'I love you. I am always here for you. Please tell me what's wrong? Explain why you are so dreadfully disturbed. Perhaps I can help you. I know the Earl must be all right, otherwise you would be with him. Are you ill, Aunt Charlotte?'

'No, I'm not,' she answered, her voice shaking, tears behind her words. 'It's Cavendon that's ill. It's dying, Cecily, it's going to disappear before our very eyes. We have lost. And without Cavendon Hall we have nothing. When Charles finds out it will kill him, I know it will. Cavendon is his life. That's why I'm hiding down here, wondering what to do. I cannot give him this news. I dare not. I'm afraid it will cause him to have another heart attack—'

Interrupting her, Cecily cried, 'But what has happened? You must tell me, and we'll work out how to handle it.'

'It was Ted,' Charlotte said. 'He discovered some major problems in the house—'

'You mean when Ted was having the plumbing in the bathroom repaired during the wedding?'

'Yes. First it was one bathroom, and then two, and now it's ten.' Charlotte broke down again, the tears flowing. 'And that's not all of it,' she said, brushing away her tears with her hands. 'The entire house is in danger. Bad floors, more leaking roofs; the structure is in a weakened state. When Ted came with the first bit of bad news in January, and then February, I told Charles that we had to attend to the bathrooms, bring in extra plumbers. At the time, it was two. Then it grew – the repair work, I mean. To cut a long story short, Ted suggested we call in some reputable surveyors, and so we did. I asked Charles's permission to do this, explaining it was a precaution; that it was nothing too dramatic.'

'But it is, isn't it?' Cecily asserted, grasping the problem now.

Charlotte could only nod. She took out a handkerchief and wiped her eyes. 'The melting snow, the terrible rain lately, have wreaked havoc, and so have many, many years of neglect. Today I received the written reports from the surveyors. They're horrendous, terrifying. I dread to show them to Charles. They are devastating, those reports.'

'The surveyors think the entire house needs a major overhaul, is that it?' Cecily suggested.

'Yes, it is, Ceci.'

'And it's going to be costly. I'm right, aren't I?'

Charlotte nodded. 'Vast. And it's money we don't have.'

Cecily sat back on the seat, thinking hard. She looked at her watch. 'It's almost four. Do you think you can get through tea without displaying any emotions or being upset, Aunt Charlotte?'

'I think so. But why?' Charlotte's voice was a bit steadier.

'I want to formulate a thought I have, turn it into a plan,' Cecily told her. 'A plan that might help a bit.'

Charlotte stared at her. Doubtful though she was that anyone could save them, she nevertheless listened to her niece. 'What is the plan?' she asked.

'I can't tell you that until later. Who's coming to tea?'

'DeLacy, Great-Aunt Gwendolyn, you and Miles, and Charles and myself. I don't know whether you know, but Hugo took Daphne to Paris for a week. She's been longing to go for ages, and she worked so hard all these years . . .' Charlotte's voice broke.

She looked at Cecily and saw the determination on her face, the steely glint in her lavender-grey eyes. There was a toughness in her niece that Charlotte had always recognized, had even admired. And great brilliance as a business-woman.

'Can't you tell me something, Cecily? Just to give me hope.'

'No, I can't. Because it might be false hope. Where are the surveyors' reports?'

'Upstairs in my underwear drawer,' Charlotte replied.

'This is what I think you should do. Go home, go to your dressing room, make yourself look beautiful. Tidy your hair and face and put on a great frock of mine. Then go downstairs to tea, and be the Countess of Mowbray. Tell Miles I'll be a few minutes late. And be prepared to make an announcement when tea is over. Tell them – us – that you have to have a family meeting.'

'When would the meeting be?'

'Right there and then. Once Hanson has cleared the tea things. That is when you will have the meeting.'

'And is that when you want me to give them the bad news? Is that it?'

'It is. But by then I think my plan to give you some help might have been formulated in my head.'

After Charlotte had left, Cecily remained seated in the rose garden. Taking a small notebook out of her satchel, she made several lists, closed the pad and put it away. And then followed on the heels of her aunt.

Walking rapidly, she went up the path to the house, with many different thoughts and ideas whirling around in her head. After sorting them out, Cecily focused on Miles. She decided it was better not to discuss anything with him at all.

He had to be as surprised by Charlotte's devastating news as everyone else. That was an imperative. The Earl must not think Miles was in cahoots with her. Miles had to be an innocent bystander like everyone else. And so did Aunt Charlotte. That was the last thing Cecily had said to her. 'Whatever I say, look startled.'

Once she arrived at Cavendon Hall, Cecily went in through the kitchen door, waved to Susie Jackson, the cook, and made her way up the back stairs to the conservatory. This was Daphne's private bit of space, and no one ever came in here.

Seating herself at Daphne's desk, she picked up the phone. Within a few seconds, she was asking for Mrs Emma Harte, and was put through to her immediately.

They talked for twenty minutes. Cecily asked her three questions. Emma answered yes to each one of them. At the end of their conversation, Emma said, 'You remind me of myself when I was your age, Cecily. You have brilliant ideas, a flair for design and the right take on retailing. But most of all you have tremendous courage. I'm going to enjoy our partnership. Because that is what it has just become. We'll draw up the contracts next week.'

Tea was in full swing when Cecily arrived in the yellow drawing room. No one appeared to mind that she was late, and they greeted her cordially.

Miles and the Earl stood; after shaking hands with Charles, she went over and kissed Miles. She was about to sit down next to him, when Lady Gwendolyn said, 'Come and join me, Cecily, please. I need to discuss something with you.'

She looked at Miles through the corner of her eye, and he muttered, 'Oh go on then, go and sit with her. I've got you for the rest of the day.' He winked at her and whispered, 'And night.'

Cecily kept a straight face, and crossed the room, sat down on a sofa, placed her satchel next to her.

Lady Gwendolyn said, 'I'm so thrilled that Dulcie has

found a gallery. I want to give a party for her, for the opening. What do you think of the idea?'

'It's absolutely marvellous, Lady Gwendolyn, and she'll be thrilled. I believe she has now raised all the money she needs.'

Lady Gwendolyn laughed. 'As long as I give her the spoils from my attic, and Lord Mowbray does the same thing, she'll be in business.'

'I know you won't refuse her,' Cecily murmured, and took the cup of tea Hanson was offering her with a happy smile on his face.

They talked about other things. DeLacy came and sat in a chair next to Lady Gwendolyn and Cecily. And the whole ritual of afternoon tea at Cavendon proceeded as normal.

Cecily was proud of Aunt Charlotte. She had done her hair beautifully, put on powder and lip rouge, and wore a beautiful lavender lace and silk tea gown. Cecily had made it for her last year. It still looked wonderful, Cecily thought, and decided to do a new version of it in black and white for the summer.

The most important thing was that Charlotte Swann Ingham was now in total control of herself. She was the Countess of Mowbray. Elegant, dignified and full of charm, the perfect hostess. Bravo, Cecily said to herself. She's recouped. She's a Cavendon woman again.

It was just before the two footmen began to clear the tea things that Charlotte looked at Charles. 'I would like everyone to stay on for a while, Charles, once everything has been cleared away.'

'Oh. Why is that, Charlotte?' He looked at her, his admiration apparent in his blue eyes. 'Do you have something special to announce? It sounds like it to me.'

'Well, I'm not sure I would call it special. Interesting, perhaps.'

'Whatever you want to do, my darling, is all right by me.' He lowered his voice. 'Has it ever been otherwise since I was twelve years old?'

She looked at him, laughing with him, but her heart turned over. If the Ingham family fell it would destroy him. Her smile remained intact, nonetheless.

Once the family was alone, Charlotte cleared her throat, said in a steady voice, 'I just told Charles that I wanted you all to stay on for a while. I have something to tell you. I hope that's all right? I hope you can stay.'

'Of course, Charlotte,' Lady Gwendolyn said. 'I love this yellow drawing room, and I love being with the family.' She settled back, made herself comfortable.

Taking a deep breath, Charlotte said, 'As you all know, we've been having some repairs done over the last few months. Ted Swann, who does such a beautiful job taking care of the interiors at Cavendon, suggested that we ought to get surveyors to come in. He thought they should do a general check-up of the house. After all, it was built in 1761, such a long time ago. And what a grand and stately home it is. So well worth protecting. I asked Charles if we should do this, and naturally he agreed.'

'And we have now had their reports, is that it, darling?' Charles asked.

'Yes. We have. I just want to point out a detail that perhaps we all forgot. Or maybe never even knew. Cavendon has one hundred and eighty-three rooms in total. Naturally this includes the servants' quarters, kitchens, storage rooms, sitting rooms, bathrooms, bedrooms, plus the private suites we occupy in the different wings. And then there are the reception rooms, dining rooms and so on.'

'Good God!' Miles exclaimed. 'I never knew that!' His genuine surprise echoed in his voice.

'I think I did know once,' Charles murmured, and frowned. He had caught something in Charlotte's voice a moment ago that bothered him. He had known her since they were children, and there had been just a tiny hint of . . . fear? He focused his eyes on her, anticipating trouble.

She continued: 'The good news is that the repairs needed for Cavendon can be done, and done well. In a two- or three-year period. The bad news is that the cost is rather high.'

'How much?' Charles asked, knowing now why she had been fearful. It had to be a large amount, quite a few thousand pounds, he decided.

'To repair and strengthen Cavendon Hall will cost quite a few thousand pounds . . . about a hundred thousand, actually,' Charlotte said, endeavouring to keep her voice steady, clutching her hands together as she spoke. 'Probably even more.'

Charles was shocked. All the colour left his face. He kept himself upright in the chair, but his heart was thundering in his chest. They were ruined. The Inghams would fall. It was the end for them and their dynasty.

Miles was speechless. But he too was the colour of bone. Neither man spoke.

A clear and confident woman's voice rang out. 'I can give you some of the money, Lord Mowbray, so that you can at least begin the restorations,' Cecily said.

Charles was flabbergasted. He simply stared at her.

So did Miles.

It was Charlotte who said, 'But why would you do that, Ceci?' Her voice had risen slightly.

'It isn't a gift, Aunt Charlotte. It's a business deal. In return I would like the Ingham Trust to give me the "contaminated" jewellery, as Miles calls it. The pieces borrowed by the former countess.'

'I'm not sure what they're worth,' Charles exclaimed, looking across the room at Cecily, still stunned at her offer.

He was thunderstruck really. Obviously she had been more successful over the years than he had ever realized.

'I said I will give you the money you need to start the work,' Cecily repeated. Reaching for her satchel, she took out her chequebook and her pen. 'Who shall I make the cheque payable to?'

FIFTY-FOUR

It was Lady Gwendolyn who spoke first. Looking across the yellow drawing room at her nephew, she said, 'I can't help wondering why you haven't accepted Cecily's offer, Charles? The house is crumbling, about to fall down, and you're hesitating. With all due respect, you should sell Cecily the jewels. Nobody here is going to wear them again.'

Charles answered her at once. 'I'm trying to absorb all of this, and the only reason I have hesitated is that I'm not sure it's a fair deal.'

Miles interjected, 'You don't know the exact value of the jewellery, do you, Papa?'

'That's right, Miles. I'm quite certain they might be worth much less than we've always believed. I don't want to cheat Cecily.'

'You won't be cheating me, Lord Mowbray. You see, there is a condition attached to my offer to buy the jewels. May I explain it to you? Because we will have to sign a contract.'

Charles nodded, and glanced at Charlotte, raising a brow. She knew what he was thinking, and said quietly, 'Whenever has there been a written contract between the Inghams and the Swanns, Ceci? Never, to my knowledge.'

'I know that, Aunt Charlotte. There has always been total fidelity between the two families, and I respect that. I also took the oath. However, in this particular instance, my offer involves a third party who insists on a contract with me. I therefore need one from His Lordship.'

Before anyone else could say a thing, Miles asked swiftly, 'Can you tell us who that is, Ceci?'

'Of course I can, Miles. It's Emma Harte, of Harte department stores.'

'Is the money you're offering me her money?' Charles asked, more out of curiosity than anything else.

'No, it isn't, Lord Mowbray. It is my money, which I earned. Let me explain. If you sell me the jewellery, I shall make copies of the pieces. I am going to create a line of jewels in crystal, coloured glass and semi-precious stones. I want to call it The Cavendon Jewellery Collection by Cecily Swann. So I need permission to use the name "Cavendon" from you. And Mrs Harte insists on having it in writing. She will be selling the collection in all of her stores, and I will be selling it in my shops.'

'What a brilliant idea,' DeLacy exclaimed, clapping her hands. 'You're a genius, Ceci. Come on, Papa, say yes.'

'I might have a few fine pieces I would be willing to sell,' Lady Gwendolyn ventured, smiling at Cecily. 'If you're interested, of course.'

'I very well may be, Lady Gwendolyn. We can look at them later if you wish.'

Focusing on Charles and Charlotte, who were sitting on the sofa together, Cecily went on, 'To explain it further, Mrs Harte and I have become business partners in this venture, so obviously she's looking to be protected. It's only natural.'

'Yes, it is,' Charles agreed, and asked, 'Out of curiosity, when did you have the idea for this jewellery collection, Cecily?'

'When Miles showed me the pieces at the Grosvenor Square house, the day he, Daphne and DeLacy got them back. I thought they were beautiful. It struck me then that I might be able to create a line of fake jewellery based on them. Then I got sidetracked, first with the boutique in Harte's, and then the clothes for the musical. But last week the idea surfaced again in my mind. Why do you ask?'

'I was thinking what a lucky break this is for us. I will sell you the jewels and sign the contract regarding the use of the name Cavendon. You've saved the Inghams, saved Cavendon, Cecily, and for that I will be eternally grateful. I thank you.'

'Thank you, Lord Mowbray. Now, who shall I make the cheque payable to?'

It was Miles who answered. 'The Cavendon Restoration Fund, please, Ceci. That's the new company Hugo suggested we start. It is mainly to keep track of the money we are spending to do the repairs to the North Wing roof and the bathrooms.'

'Good thinking, Miles,' Charles said.

Cecily signed the cheque, stood up and walked across to the Earl. She handed it to him. 'You don't have to give it to me now, Cecily. Next week will be fine, when I sign the contract.'

She said, 'I trust you, Lord Mowbray. Your word is good enough for me. You are an Ingham and I am a Swann, and when I was twelve I took the oath to protect the Inghams.' She thrust out her arm, her hand clenched. 'Loyalty binds me,' she said.

The 6th Earl of Mowbray placed his clenched fist on hers. 'Loyalty binds me,' he answered, and put the cheque in his pocket. 'Thank you,' he said.

'This wonderful news and Ceci's great generosity calls for a celebration, Papa,' Miles announced. 'I think we should pop a bottle of champagne and toast our most brilliant girl.'

The atmosphere in the yellow drawing room had changed. The mood of shock and despair had evaporated completely, and there was a sense of relief and hope for the future in the air. Charles and Miles looked more like themselves. Their colour had returned to normal and they were relaxed. But both of them were still slightly stunned by Cecily Swann and what she had done.

And so was Charlotte, and she said so to Cecily as they sat down on a sofa together. Then she asked, 'When did you really think of the fake jewellery line?' She gave her great-niece a piercing look.

'When I said I did, which was when I first saw the pieces. I really did forget about them. So much was happening to me, and in the family. Then this afternoon, the idea popped into my head.'

Charlotte gave her a knowing smile. 'And when did you make the deal with Emma Harte?'

Cecily began to laugh. 'About fifteen minutes after you'd left the rose garden. I sat there thinking what to do. I hit on the idea of telling Emma about the fake jewellery line, and two other projects I have in the works. She was tremendously excited, said she wanted to do all three projects. And become my partner. That's when I knew I could risk the money I'd personally earned and saved over the years.'

Charlotte was silent for a moment, and then she said softly, 'Thank you, Ceci, thank you so very much. You've not only saved Cavendon, you've saved Charles's life. I know the disastrous news would have felled him, had we not been able to offer a solution immediately. I honestly think you prevented him having another heart attack.'

'I'm glad. I really wanted to help you, help the family,' Cecily replied. 'And I enjoy working with Emma Harte. She's an inspiration to me.'

'She's a role model for all women, there's no doubt about that.' Charlotte took a sip of champagne and asked, 'Can you tell me about the other two projects? Or are they a secret?'

'I can tell you, but keep them to yourself for the moment.'

'I will. You know I never discuss things, especially your business.'

'I'm planning on a whole new line of clothing. Bridal gowns and trousseaus, right down to fancy camiknickers, nightgowns and other sexy underwear. Emma said yes to the idea without thinking twice. In fact, she wants me to consider having a third boutique in the store called Cecily Swann Brides. Or something like that.'

Charlotte had an excited look on her face, and exclaimed, 'That's so clever. Brides usually need a trousseau and can never find exactly the right clothes for their honeymoon. But nightgowns and underwear should be separated. Isn't that yet another boutique?'

'Maybe you're right, Aunt Charlotte. I'll give it some thought.' Lifting her glass, she clinked it against her aunt's.

'And what is the third new project?' Charlotte asked.

'One I've been working on for a year . . . with two chemists. A beauty line of creams and lotions, and hopefully cosmetics. Emma was very keen indeed about this line.'

'I'm not surprised. And you really are a genius, Ceci. I've always told you that. And now you've turned yourself into a brand, which is just marvellous.'

Cecily smiled and sat back against the sofa. 'I'm glad I'm here for the weekend. And I want to thank you for giving me your house in the park. It's nice to have some privacy with Miles.'

'It's my pleasure,' Charlotte answered, and then asked quietly, 'Why did you really do it?'

Cecily stared at her, frowning. 'Do what? Give the Earl the money? Is that what you mean?'

'Yes. You didn't have to, and frankly you surprised everyone, including me.'

'I did it for Miles. I did it to keep Cavendon safe for him. I know how much he loves it, needs to live here and run the estate. It's his life. And he's my life. That's why I did it. For Miles.'

It was early evening and still lovely as Cecily walked through the park to Charlotte's house. She liked the house. It was neat, compact, with a big kitchen, a spacious living room looking out onto the garden, a bedroom and bathroom upstairs, with a small study next to the bedroom. She used this as her office, and it was a good place to do her designs. She and Harry would inherit the house one day, but he had his own cottage across the street near their parents' house, and preferred that.

Hearing her name being called, she glanced around and saw her father's brother, Percy Swann, the head gamekeeper, waving at her. She waved back, and went into the house.

A number of Swanns lived in Little Skell village, others in Mowbray and High Clough, the two other villages belonging to the Inghams.

She sat down at the kitchen table and took her notebook out of her satchel, looked at the figures. She nodded to herself. She had been able to buy the Cavendon jewels without taking too much of a risk. And she knew the collection of fake pieces would be popular, make money.

But it was the White Rose perfume and cologne that actually topped everything; these were her biggest sellers.

It had been her mother's idea to create a perfume, and to that end she and Alice had gone to Grasse, the famous perfume town in the south of France. She and Alice had been intrigued and fascinated when they arrived, and overwhelmed by the number of perfumiers who could create scents to please anyone and everyone, and the number of companies who made scents for retailers all over the world.

They had spent days sniffing essence of flowers, oils, musk, and all manner of liquids that went to make the best scents. Her aim had been to have a strong rose smell, and in the end her chosen perfumier had created one she loved which smelled of tuberoses. It happened to be Dulcie's favourite too. The perfume made a huge profit, and was hard to keep in stock.

I've been lucky, she thought, and then heard her mother's voice echoing in her head. 'Hard work, Ceci, and talent. And just a bit of luck.' Hard work indeed. Six years, seven days a week. But work had been her saviour and she loved her profession.

A gentle knocking on the door brought Cecily to her feet; when she opened it she was taken aback to see Genevra standing there.

''Scuse me, Miss Cecily,' the Romany girl said, a smile flickering in her dark eyes. 'I come ter say thank yer. For them frocks yer gave me. They fit.' She did a small curtsy, holding out the sides of the frock, which was an old one of Cecily's, and had been given to her by Mrs Alice.

'I'm glad you like them,' Cecily said. 'I've still got my piece of bone, you know, and so does Miles. We treasure them. Our lucky charms.'

'Aye, that they be,' the gypsy said. 'You be well, liddle Cecily. And thank yer again.'

Before she could answer her, the Romany had hurried away as she usually did.

FIFTY-FIVE

Lawrence Pierce left the Ritz Hotel looking extremely pleased with himself as he set out to walk to White's, his club in nearby St James's Street. He had just spent a glorious afternoon and early evening with his new woman, one he had made his mistress after knowing her for only a few days.

She was an American with the rather common name of Mattie Lou Brown, but then her money was not at all common. It was all-powerful. She was a few years older than him, but good looking and voluptuous.

Widowed and childless, she had inherited a vast railway fortune from her third husband. Her one aim in coming to London, she had told him at their first meeting, was to party, mix with the right social crowd and have plenty of hectic sex, as she called it.

After their first session in bed, in her suite at the Ritz, she had told him she had never experienced such wonderful sex as she had with him. Seemingly he was the only man who had ever satisfied her. And so their long sexual afternoons and evenings had begun.

She constantly flattered him, praised his looks, his prowess in her bed, gave him expensive gifts, and kissed

405

his 'golden hands' as she called them. And then yesterday afternoon she told him she had decided to marry him. She wanted him. 'Forever, honey,' was how she put it. Having said that, she gave him a piece of paper and told him to read it.

He did so, and was staggered. She was mind-bogglingly rich, was planning to give him a large chunk of her fortune as a wedding gift and a life of ease and comfort. She had a yacht, a house in California, and a triplex apartment on Fifth Avenue. 'All yours to share, honey bunny,' she had added. 'And I want an answer tomorrow.'

He knew Felicity would never agree to a divorce. But he had to have Mattie. She was sexually voracious, which pleased him, and she was so bloody rich he could live in splendour, never wield a scalpel again as long as he lived.

This afternoon, after one of their marathons, he had accepted her proposal of marriage. She had been thrilled.

Thinking of this and her anxiousness to board her yacht in Nice, Lawrence had gone to the hospital this morning and picked up a few things. He patted his pocket now as he walked along, smiling to himself. He had the tools he needed to make himself a free man. He would marry Mattie and they would sail from France to Italy and his life would begin again.

Sex usually made him hungry, and tonight was no exception. Lawrence had a hearty dinner with two of his old cronies, and they laughed a lot, imbibed some great wines, and talked about their sexual escapades with fancy women. None of them talked about their mistresses. Or their wives. That was *verboten*.

They drank cognacs and coffee for several hours and puffed on their cigars, but finally his two friends left. Lawrence sat alone in the gentleman's club where he had been a member for years. It had been founded in 1693 and was a club for men only. It was always a relief to be away from women for a while. On the other hand, he couldn't do without them.

Eventually Lawrence knew he must leave, go back to Charles Street and do what he must do. He had sobered up after all those cups of black coffee, and he decided to walk home to Mayfair.

They got him on the corner of Berkeley Square, at the bottom of Hay Hill. A black van pulled up just as he turned to go across the square. The window rolled down as the van stopped, and a face appeared. 'Which way ter Bond Street, guv'nor?' the man asked.

Lawrence said, 'Go around—' A blow to the back of his head felled him before he finished his sentence. 'He's down and out,' a man's voice said.

Two other men jumped out of the van, pressed a chloroform-soaked cloth against his mouth. Picking him up, they threw him into the back of the van.

'Not a bleedin' copper in sight, thank God,' the driver of the van said. He headed toward the docklands and the empty warehouse which was waiting for them. They were going to teach this bugger a lesson he'd never forget.

It was the fifth of June, a lovely Sunday afternoon, and Dulcie had chosen this day for the opening of her gallery so that James could be there. He was starring in *Henry V* at the Old Vic, and this was his day off.

James stood next to her, greeting their guests, smiling and chatting and being his usual charming self. As for Dulcie, she was in high spirits, looking more beautiful than ever, if that was possible.

She was proud of the gallery, had called it the Dulcie Ingham-Brentwood Gallery, and it was on Bruton Street in Mayfair, where most of the family lived. She and James were still in his flat near Claridge's, but were looking for somewhere else a bit larger in this part of London, which they all liked.

Lady Gwendolyn was hosting the party for the opening of the gallery, and now she floated up to them, a huge smile on her face.

'Everyone is here,' she said, beaming at James. 'And that really pleases me. So do the placements of my paintings, Dulcie. What a wonderful eye you have, and you've hung them particularly well.'

'I want to thank you for the paintings and the jade pieces, Great-Aunt Gwendolyn,' Dulcie replied. 'I know they will sell, and you will get your share very quickly.'

'I think Cecily's idea of giving my profits to the Cavendon Restoration Fund was a wonderful idea. I believe Charles is doing the same thing.'

'Yes, he is,' James said, winking at Dulcie and then at Lady Gwendolyn. 'My hat's off to my beautiful bride. I'm glad I was with her when she raided all of your attics. She was like Attila the Hun, the way she ploughed her way through.'

'I agree,' Miles said, coming to join them with DeLacy and Cecily. 'Papa and Charlotte will be a few minutes late. But they're on their way. And they wish the three of you to come to supper.'

The gallery was soon overflowing with people, many of James's acting friends, Ruby and his other two sisters, Felix and Constance Lambert, Michael Alexander, the theatrical producer, and most of the Inghams.

'The whole world is here,' DeLacy said as she strolled around with Miles.

One of the last to arrive was Dorothy Swann, along with her husband, Inspector Howard Pinkerton. The two of them walked around the gallery, admiring the paintings and sculptures. Dorothy was proud of Dulcie and her determination to have a gallery.

When Cecily spotted them, she hurried over to greet the couple. Once the pleasantries were over, Howard said, 'Let's walk over to that quiet corner, Cecily, shall we? I have something to tell you.'

Cecily threw him a quick glance. He had sounded very serious. 'Is something wrong?'

'I wouldn't call it that,' Howard said, steering the two women across the room. 'I was on duty earlier and a case landed on my desk. A bit of a mystery in some ways, actually. However, it concerns Lawrence Pierce.'

'Pierce,' Cecily repeated in a low voice. 'What has he done now? Something probably awful.'

'He's probably done a lot of awful things in his life, but he won't do any more. He's dead.'

Cecily stared at him. 'My God! How? When?'

'As to when, I would say Friday night. He was found on the steps of his hospital on Saturday evening. He was still alive, just barely, but died later of his head wounds. He had been beaten up badly, his face was almost pulp. The worst wounds were to his hands. I went over to the hospital to view the body, and one of the doctors told me they looked as if they had been stamped on by hobnail boots. If he had lived, he would never have operated again.'

Cecily was pale when she asked, 'Does his wife know?'

'She does, yes. Anyway, here's the thing. When he was found he was fully clothed, and in his jacket pocket there was a full bottle of potassium chloride. Do you know what potassium chloride can do, Cecily?'

She shook her head, 'No, I don't.'

'An overdose by injection stops the heart. In other words, it mimics a heart attack. Within minutes the heart simply stops. It's impossible to trace, because the heart muscle tissue releases large amounts of potassium into the bloodstream when it's damaged. So a doctor would say it was a heart attack.'

Cecily gaped at him. 'You're thinking of Travers Merton, aren't you, Uncle Howard?'

'Yes, I am. Because they were friends. I know that from Lady DeLacy. And then they fell out. Badly, I believe.'

'Can you investigate further, Howard?' Dorothy asked. 'Regarding Mr Merton, I mean?'

'No, it's all too late, I'm afraid. But somebody who had a reason got to Pierce. I would call it retribution.'

PART FOUR

Angels in Disguise
December 1928–
September 1929

There shall be no evil befall thee, neither shall any
  plague come nigh thy dwelling.
For he shall give his angels charge over thee, to keep
  thee in thy ways.
They shall bear thee up in their hands, lest thou dash
thy foot against a stone.

Psalm 91

The angels keep their ancient places;
Turn but a stone, and start a wing:
Tis ye, 'tis your estrangèd faces
That miss the many splendoured thing.

Francis Thompson

FIFTY-SIX

'What an odd year 1928 has been,' Dorothy Swann said, shaking her head as she sat opposite Cecily in the office upstairs at the main shop in the Burlington Arcade. 'So much has happened. Bad things, too.'

'Mostly for other people,' Cecily replied. 'Not for me, not for us, actually. Still, the Inghams have had their bellyful, haven't they?'

'They have indeed. They all were sorrowful about Lady Lavinia's death last spring, most especially Mark Stanton and Lady Gwendolyn. And her sister, of course, Lady Vanessa.'

'I know,' Cecily murmured. 'Because they really loved her. The others were regretful and sad, too, but also feeling a bit guilty because of that rift. Miles admitted this to me. He wasn't overly enamoured of his Aunt Lavinia, mostly because she hadn't treated Uncle Jack in a very nice way.'

'So Dulcie said.' Dorothy looked at the clock. 'I'd better go downstairs and see how she's doing. She insisted I come up here to look at her sketches, told me she could easily try on coats by herself.'

Chuckling, Cecily said, 'Well, she can. Anyone can. I'll

413

go downstairs with you in a minute.' Reaching for a folder on her desk, she opened it, took out a drawing and handed it to her aunt.

'This is just fantastic. Dulcie came up with the idea of brooches to be worn on hats, then said they could also work for lapels if someone wanted. But they are large. She's calling the three she's designed Duet Pins. She's even come up with a line for the advertising: Let the man who adores you buy you the Duet Pin.'

After studying the sketch for a moment, Dorothy said, 'It's beautiful . . . a curling diamond feather. Where did this idea spring from? Did she tell you?'

'Oh yes. And she says it has to be called Paul's Feather, because Lady Gwendolyn's late husband, Paul Baildon, designed that brooch, had it made for her as a wedding gift, telling her it was a feather for her cap. She gave it to Diedre.'

'How lovely.' Dorothy smiled at the sentiment behind the brooch, and handed the drawing to Cecily. 'It's an elegant pin, and I like the way it sort of curls at one end.'

'So do I. The original sketch Dulcie did was an exact copy, but then she gave it her own touches. This has more of a flourish.' Passing Dorothy another drawing, she went on, 'This is a gold swan, as you can see, and Dulcie is calling it Swan Song.'

Dorothy exclaimed, 'This is beautiful. Very beautiful. What a talent for drawing Dulcie has.'

'She actually does. However, the swan was also minutely copied from an existing brooch. It's another one from Aunt Gwendolyn, which she gave to Aunt Charlotte. As an engagement present.'

'I'd love to see the actual pieces, Ceci.'

'I don't have them, Dottie. We don't own them. We have the right to copy. They're not part of the Cavendon

Collection of Jewellery, but will be under the name of Swann. Charlotte and Diedre don't want money . . . this was their way of saying thank you for what I did last year. Profits are all ours.'

Dorothy nodded her understanding and gave the sketch back to Cecily. 'And what is the third pin?'

'Here it is.'

'Oh my goodness, this is unique. Was this also another borrowed from Charlotte?'

'No, Dulcie designed it herself. As you can see, it's an oddly shaped golden heart, slightly crooked.'

'It looks as if it's been wrapped in a bit of red lace.'

'I know, that was the intention. It's lace made of small rubies. And she's calling it the James Brentwood Heart.'

'And he's agreed?'

'Absolutely. You know he adores her. In fact, he helped her design it.'

There was a knock on the door, and Dulcie looked into the room. 'You have a client downstairs, Cora Ward. And she's very upset, sobbing. I tried to calm her. But you'd both better come.'

The three women went downstairs to the next floor, where the two dressing rooms were located, one at each end of the room. The middle of the floor was furnished simply, with a few chairs and, in the centre, a platform where clients stood for fittings.

Cecily was alarmed at the sobbing which emanated from the dressing room at the far end. She hurried to it and tapped on the door. 'Mrs Ward, it's Cecily Swann. May I come in?'

'Yes,' Cora Ward answered, between sobs.

Opening the door, Cecily stood there looking at her. 'You're awfully upset. I would like to help you if I can. Do you have a problem? Or are you ill?'

The young woman lifted her head, gazed at Cecily, and shook her head.

Cecily had always thought her rather beautiful, with a mass of glorious auburn hair, dark brown eyes, almost black, and a pure white skin. Black Irish, Cecily thought yet again, as she had in the past. Descended from one of those Spanish sailors whose ships had sunk in the Irish Sea in Elizabethan times, during the Spanish Armada invasion.

'Come and sit with us out here, Mrs Ward. Dorothy will make us some tea. And then perhaps you can tell me what's wrong, if I can help you in some way.'

Nodding her head, Cora stood up, and followed Cecily to the grouping of chairs. Turning to Dorothy, she said, 'I didn't try the clothes on, Miss Dorothy. I didn't want to get them soiled. You see, I can't have them.'

'Don't worry about that,' Dorothy answered. 'Just sit down and talk to Miss Swann and Lady Dulcie. They're very good listeners. Do you like milk and sugar in your tea?'

'Please,' the young woman said, and sat down in a chair. For a moment she was silent, biting her lip.

Dulcie took the chair next to her. 'Do you have a problem with your husband about the clothes, Mrs Ward? Sometimes men do get a bit tired of paying large sums . . .' She purposely let her sentence trail away, and looked at Cecily, raised a brow.

Cecily took over, and said in a kind voice, 'If that is the case, please don't worry. The clothes were made for you, but your size is fairly standard. Someone else will buy them. I certainly won't force you to take them.'

'Thank you, Miss Swann,' Cora said. She stood up, hurried over to the dressing room, came back with her handbag. Lowering herself into the chair, she opened her bag, took out a handkerchief and patted her eyes and her face.

'I'm so sorry I've upset everyone, made a scene here,'

she said. 'But things just suddenly overcame me. I just . . .'
She struggled not to start crying again, swallowed hard
and pulled a sheaf of papers out, clutching them to her.

'These are the last bills from you. He won't pay
them . . . I can't. You see, he took the jewellery he'd given
me.'

Her black eyes pooled with tears and she jammed the
handkerchief against them, pushing back the sobs rising
in her throat.

'From what you're saying, Mrs Ward, I have the feeling
that perhaps your husband must be having financial
difficulties. I do understand your problem. Let's not worry
about the last bills for the moment. I'm sure things will
straighten out for you, and when they do you can pay
them at that time.'

'Thank you,' Cora said and put the bills back in her
bag. 'You're being extremely nice, Miss Swann.'

A moment later, Dorothy came in carrying a tray of
tea. Placing it on a table she filled four cups, added milk
and sugar, handed them around.

After sipping her tea and calming herself, Cora said in
a less agitated voice. 'I will get a job, Miss Swann, and
pay what is owed. Over time. Because he won't. He can't.
You see he's lost all his money; things have gone wrong
for him.' There was a pause, and she cried angrily, 'He's
thrown me away, like he has other women in the past . . .'
Feeling the tears rising inside her, Cora paused and drank
the tea. She was shaking inside, and hurt. He'd abandoned
her without a second thought.

Cecily looked first at Dorothy and then at Dulcie,
frowning. She said, 'I don't quite understand, Mrs Ward.
Are you getting a divorce?'

'No, I'm not Mrs Ward. I'm not a missus. And my
name's not Ward. It's O'Brian. I was born in England, but
my parents are Irish. And I'm not a married woman, I'm

417

single. I have never been married. I had a gentleman friend . . . for four years. But now it's finished. I have a week to find somewhere to live.'

'Can't he help you at all?' Dulcie asked in a sympathetic voice, feeling sorry for her.

'No, he can't. And I know it's all true, because I was quite friendly with his chauffeur, Bert Robinson, and he gave Bert the sack a week ago,' Cora exclaimed, and rushed on. 'Bert came around to see me, told me to get ready for the shove. He said my gentleman friend wasn't a gentleman, that he was a bad man, that he was a crook, had lost everyone's money for them, not only his own. He said terrible things about my friend. And I know some things are not true. You see, Lord Meldrew's just not like that. Whatever he is, he's not a crook. He's not going to jail for fraud, like Bert said. I know he's not.'

There was a total silence in the room after Cora's unbroken rush of breathless remarks, uttered clearly but nonstop. It was obvious she was telling the truth.

Cecily and Dorothy exchanged startled glances, and Dulcie gaped at them, shock registering on her face. She started to say something but caught herself in time. She stopped before the words came out, her eyes riveted on Cecily.

Taking a deep breath, Cecily said, 'Perhaps I can be of help in some way, Miss O'Brian . . .'

'Please call me Cora, Miss Swann.'

Cecily inclined her head. 'I'm sorry your friend has trouble. And I see now you need help. What kind of job are you looking for, Cora? What qualifications do you have?'

'I've worked in a shoe shop, and at a milliner's. I've been a junior nanny, looked after a little girl for a year. I can do a lot of things. But I like shops the best.'

'I shall think about this for a couple of days, and come

up with some suggestions regarding a job. In the meantime, do you have friends who can give you a bed? Just for a week or so, until you get on your feet?'

'Yes, I have a friend, Marie,' Cora responded, now more controlled. 'She was recently widowed. She has a small house in Chelsea. It's tiny but she'll let me sleep on the sofa. She's lonely, she'll like the company.'

'Good. You must try and find somewhere to live within the next week or so. Today is Tuesday, the eleventh. If you telephone Miss Dorothy on Friday of this week, she'll perhaps have news for you about a job.'

'Thank you, Miss Swann, ever so much. You're being so kind. And I will pay these bills. I promise.'

Cecily smiled at her. 'Don't worry about those at this moment. Now, if you'll excuse me, Lady Dulcie and I have work to do in the studio.' Addressing Dorothy, Cecily added, 'Perhaps you can help Cora to collect her things, please.'

'Of course,' Dorothy said, her face a total blank.

Cecily and Dulcie went upstairs, walking slowly and with great decorum. But they were both ready to explode.

Once inside Cecily's office, Dulcie cried in a vehement but low whisper, 'She's Clarissa's father's mistress! My God! What a whole heap of information she has just dropped in your lap, Ceci. What a bargaining tool Miles has now.'

Pushing back her hair, Cecily nodded. 'Yes, indeed he does. Clarissa is soon about to lose the source of her wealth. She's going to need money. She'll come to Miles. And she certainly needs the roof over her head that she has at the moment. Because Daddy can't fork out for anything.'

'Do you believe Lord Meldrew's going to be prosecuted for fraud; that he'll go to jail?'

'I think it's true more than likely. Chauffeurs hear an

419

awful lot, know a lot. He's probably bitter about being sacked, but truthful.'

Dorothy came into the office a few minutes later. 'She left, looking happier. I locked the front door of the shop. I think we've things to discuss, don't you?'

Dulcie stared hard at Dorothy. 'Do you realize what a newspaper would do with all this information? I can just see the headlines . . . Financial tycoon and peer of the realm Lord Meldrew indicted for fraud. Keeps young mistress in lap of luxury. That's just what comes to mind.'

There was laughter, which came as something of a relief after the last hour. Sobering, Cecily said, 'It's true what Dulcie's saying, Dorothy. Any paper in Fleet Street would love to get their hands on this. It's real muckraking, I know, but the public lap it up.'

'We could leak it, Ceci,' Dulcie said. 'James knows a lot of press people, and so does Felix. And just think how embarrassed Clarissa would be. All of her friends would shun her. She'd come crawling on her hands and knees to Miles, wanting money and whatever. She'd agree to a divorce just to keep it out of the papers. He could go and see her, threaten to tell the newspapers about Cora.'

'That sounds like blackmail to me,' Cecily said, and then laughed again. 'But you're right, Dulcie, what you say is absolutely true. Clarissa no longer has control of this situation. And suddenly Miles has acquired a big stick.'

Dorothy said, 'I thought of taking you out of the room earlier to talk for a minute, Ceci, because I considered offering her a job. But then I decided against it.'

'I thought the same thing,' Cecily murmured. 'But I changed my mind. I don't want her anywhere near us. I do want to use her for information, if we can. But I do not want any association with her. She can't be linked to us. Because it could backfire. I will help her, because I think she's a nice girl who's been treated in a rotten way by a bad man. I've never liked him, and I know Hanson, who sees through everyone, can't bear him. That's beside the point, of course. I'm certain I can get her a job at Harte's. Although even that's a bit too close.'

'Let me think about it,' Dorothy said. 'I might get inspired.'

'Are you going to say anything to Howard? Tell him about Cora's comments?'

'No, I'm not. Anyway, if there is a case pending against Lord Meldrew, it wouldn't be under Howard's aegis . . . more like the fraud police. But I'll stay quiet for a while, unless you want him to give us a helping hand in some way?'

'No, not yet. But thanks, Dottie,' Cecily said gratefully.

'I've got to pop over to see Diedre,' Dulcie now said. 'And you should come with me, Ceci. Oh, and by the way, I love my two coats. Do you want to see them on me, Dorothy?'

'I certainly do, Lady Dulcie. Come along, let's go downstairs. Give Cecily a few minutes to clear her desk.'

FIFTY-SEVEN

Diedre stood in the middle of the drawing room of her mother's house in Charles Street, glancing around yet again. She had been coming to the house for the last two weeks, endeavouring to sort out all the possessions housed here.

Felicity had lived for only a year after Lawrence Pierce's murder; had had a stroke in July of 1928, and never recovered. To Diedre's surprise she was the only one of her mother's children to be left anything in the will: this house and everything in it. The only thing she wanted was the fabulous portrait of DeLacy, painted by Travers Merton, hanging over the fireplace.

Embarrassed to be the only child to inherit from their mother, Diedre had recently sold the house and planned to divide the money among the five of them. Miles said he would give his portion to the Cavendon Restoration Fund, and in the end they had all decided to do that, herself included.

None of them had been surprised by the contents of the will. Felicity's vast fortune, inherited from her father Malcolm Wallace, and all of her jewellery from him, had been left to Grace, her sister Anne's daughter, Felicity's niece.

Diedre let out a long sigh. She was tired of coming over here to sort through her mother's things. Daphne had helped a little, bringing Olive Wilson with her, and so had Cecily. DeLacy was living at Cavendon and never came to London; Dulcie had such disdain for 'that woman', as she called her mother, that she had not volunteered to help.

But Dulcie was coming this afternoon, bringing Cecily with her to choose paintings for Dulcie's gallery, along with other objects. Then the furniture and everything else would go to auction next week. Glancing at her watch, she saw that they would be arriving shortly.

Leaning back in a chair, Diedre thought of the events of the last year. She and Paul had finally returned to London permanently in the spring of 1928. His mother had died six months before. Hugo had cleverly taken his investments out of Wall Street and so had Paul. They had both moved everything to London; there was no need for a New York office any more.

Paul had managed to sell the large mansion and land in Connecticut, and his mother's apartment on Fifth Avenue. And once they were settled in her flat in Kensington, his brother Tim had helped him to sell the triplex on Park Avenue.

Paul had been as happy as she was to move to England; he missed her family as much as she did, had understood how homesick she was. He also liked the idea of bringing up Robin in London, surrounded by Inghams. They would soon be moving into their new flat in Eaton Square; her father had given them a suite of rooms at Cavendon where they spent many weekends. Their little son was flourishing, and Diedre was the happiest she had been in a long time.

A moment later Ratcliffe, whom she had kept on to look after the house, was showing Dulcie and Cecily into the drawing room. He asked Diedre if they wished to have tea but they all declined.

Once they were alone, and having greeted each other, Dulcie looked at Cecily and cried, 'Tell Diedre! Get her opinion, Ceci!'

'Tell me what?' Diedre asked, noting the excitement on Dulcie's face, the sparkle in her eyes.

Cecily told her about Cora O'Brian and what had happened at the shop in the arcade; about the young woman's connection to Meldrew, and his financial woes.

Diedre listened attentively, surprise flashing across her face. She was as startled as they had been earlier. 'Without knowing it, this young woman has handed you a bucketful of vital information about Meldrew. It would be fatal if it does leak to the press. Financial ruin is bad enough, but public humiliation is also a killer.'

'We could leak it!' Dulcie exclaimed, sitting down on a sofa.

'We could, but I don't think we will,' Diedre replied. 'Papa would be appalled at us.'

'But Clarissa would be highly embarrassed. Also, she's going to need money, since Lord Meldrew, her horrible father, is out of cash.'

'Seemingly so, according to Cora O'Brian. But perhaps he isn't. Men like Meldrew usually have money hidden, often in foreign countries, and especially in Switzerland. Money that would be hard to find,' Diedre explained. 'Men who specialize in financial finagling usually anticipate possible consequences and provide for the future, their future. Anyway, when is this situation going to become public?'

Cecily said, 'I don't think Cora knows – at least she made no mention of it.'

'Let's not forget she was quoting the chauffeur, Bert Robinson,' Dulcie reminded Cecily, and added, 'Maybe the authorities aren't onto him yet.'

'That's quite possible,' Diedre agreed. 'What we know

is only what the chauffeur told her, plus the fact that Meldrew has left her, and refuses to keep her in style any longer, or pay her bills. He might just want to get rid of her.'

'Well, yes, that's true. However, I think Meldrew is the kind of man who could easily be a financial whiz, as Miles would say.'

'Have you told Miles yet?' Diedre asked Cecily.

'I can't tell him. He's on the train to London at this moment. He'll be arriving in a couple of hours.'

'Good. Having this information does give him the means to bargain with Clarissa Meldrew, if he decides to tell her it might get into the newspapers.' Diedre laughed dryly. 'That sounds like blackmail, in a way, but why not? I'm only worried about Inghams, not Meldrews. Miles has been treated very badly by them. And Clarissa's attitude is unconscionable.'

'I think Miles should do that,' Dulcie announced, and then exclaimed. 'Oh my goodness, what a wonderful portrait of DeLacy over the fireplace. It's the one by Travers Merton, isn't it?'

Diedre nodded. 'I thought I would give it to DeLacy; she should have it. And incidentally, how have you been doing with the paintings Travers left her in his will? Have you sold any yet?'

'Several. Although she was so reluctant to let go of them at first, but she changed her mind when I said Cavendon needed the money for the restoration work. That convinced her. She said Travers would have approved because his grandfather had loved Cavendon.'

'You can have anything you want from here, Dulcie,' Diedre said, needing to move things along, get home to Robin. 'There are some very good paintings by well-known artists, and there are more upstairs. And you can have all of the art objects as well, if you wish.'

'Normally, I wouldn't touch her stuff with a bargepole,' Dulcie answered. 'But when they're sold, the money will go to Cavendon. Shall we wander around together and pick out the best?'

'Let's do it,' Cecily said, looking at her watch. 'I want to be at the flat when Miles arrives.'

'Well, well, well,' Miles said, when Cecily told him about the encounter with Cora O'Brian, and gave her a huge smile. 'It doesn't actually solve my problem, but it does give me a certain amount of leverage, don't you think? With Clarissa.'

'I do,' Cecily replied, moving closer to him on the sofa. The two of them were sitting in front of the fire in the living room of her flat, drinking tea. Miles had asked for tea ten minutes ago when he had arrived from King's Cross railway station. He told her he felt cold, and needed something hot. He had turned down soup, explaining he would have that at dinner.

'You will go and see her, won't you? And as soon as possible, Miles?'

He nodded, and looked at his watch. 'Too late to get in touch with her now. I shall give her a ring tomorrow morning, and try to set a date for a meeting.'

'Won't she want to know why you suddenly want to see her?'

'I expect so,' he replied, looking suddenly reflective, staring into the flames roaring up the chimney. 'I shall be honest, and say I need to discuss something very private, which I can't talk about on the phone. Leave it to me, I know she likes intrigue.'

'I will, but I don't mind going to see her, you know.'

He chuckled. 'I can't let that happen, my love. You'll make mincemeat out of her. Or antagonize her. I have to think of something to hook her . . . perhaps I'll say I

426

heard a rumour about her father having certain problems, and is there something I can do to help him . . .' His sentence floated away as he put his arm around her and drew her even closer. 'I'm suddenly quite optimistic. You'll see, 1929 is going to be our year, Ceci. Our good luck is just around the corner, darling.'

FIFTY-EIGHT

'That was a very special piece of roast beef, love,' Howard Pinkerton said. 'I think I enjoy Sunday lunch better than any other meal of the week. Except for your duck on Christmas Day. And your Yorkshire pudding is the best in the world.'

'Well, it better be, Howard, I come from there,' Dorothy laughed, and picked up his plate. 'And I have your favourite dessert. Apple crumble.'

'Spoiling me, that you are, Dottie. And with warm custard, I've no doubt.'

'That's right. I'll only be a moment.'

Howard sat back in his chair, staring at the window. It was a cold December, and snowing outside, the flakes sticking to the glass panes, making little patterns. Intricate, like fancy lace. Life was intricate. And complex. And sometimes he couldn't help shuddering when he thought of the duplicity and evil in this world, and the bad men, wicked men, who committed all kinds of sins and crimes. On the other hand, there were good men too. Brilliant men. Like that wonder boy who'd flown the Atlantic in a wispy little airplane last year. Charles Lindbergh, his name was, and he had become quite the hero, not only in America, and France, where he'd landed, but here in England and around the world. And Mr Henry Ford, one of his favourites. Howard enjoyed his Ford cars. And one of their own, James Brentwood, the country's greatest classical actor, a man of decency and integrity.

Then there were men like Lawrence Pierce. He stuck in Howard's mind. He thought of him often, convinced that he had murdered Travers Merton. And that he might have been intent on murdering his wife, Felicity Pierce. The night he was on his way home from his club, and obviously got nabbed by somebody who was an enemy, there had been a bottle of potassium chloride in his jacket pocket. An overdose of that was lethal. And who was it intended for that night, if not for his unsuspecting wife? But he had never made it home and a life had been saved.

And then there were men like John Meldrew. Unscrupulous, duplicitous, clever swindlers who took money from ordinary people, lined their own pockets with it. Those were the worst buggers . . . stealing from the poor to make themselves rich.

'Here we are, Howard, apple crumble and custard,' Dorothy said, putting a plate in front of him.

Before he could thank her she had disappeared again, had gone to the kitchen. A few seconds later she was back with her own plate and sat down at the dining table with him.

The apple crumble was delicious, and he didn't speak as he ate it slowly, savouring it. But he was going to talk to her shortly. She was troubled, had something on her mind, he knew that. After all, they'd been married for a long time. He knew his Dottie inside and out, and upside down.

It was over coffee in the sitting room that Howard finally spoke out. After a few sips of his coffee, he put the cup down in the saucer, and said, 'You've been very preoccupied all weekend, love. You have something on your mind, I just know it. Perhaps talking to me might help?'

Dorothy let out a really long sigh, but remained silent. She sipped her coffee, puzzling out what to do. To confide in Howard or not? She made the decision. She was going to ask him if he knew about Lord Meldrew, and when he was going to be arrested. Cecily and she needed to know what was going on. Ceci wanted to be in control of her own destiny.

Looking at him, giving him a slight smile, she said, 'One of our clients came to the shop earlier this week, Howard, and she was very upset. Her name is Cora Ward, and she—'

'She was in Cecily's shop, was she? Well then, you no doubt know that she's been dropped by Lord Meldrew.'

Dorothy nodded, leaning forward eagerly. 'Is it your case, Howard?'

'No, it's not. It's being handled by the fraud people, the police who deal with financial crime. But Matt Praeger, the head of that division, is an old friend. I know his chaps have been gathering information on Meldrew for some time. He'll eventually go to trial, and to jail – no doubt in my mind about that.'

'Is it imminent? His arrest, I mean?'

'Not sure. I think they're still gathering evidence, as I just said. They need a watertight case. I understand your interest, Dottie. His daughter is the estranged wife of Miles Ingham. She's the one who's keeping Ceci and Miles apart. Why was the young woman in the shop?'

'She couldn't pay her bills, and couldn't take the new dresses. She broke down, sobbed out her tale of woe. She's nice enough, trapped in a bad situation. He's cut her off financially, taken back the jewellery, told her to leave the flat he was renting for her. We all felt sorry for her. I got her a job at Madame Arlette Millinery. That was the best I could do – and Ceci doesn't want us to get too involved with her.'

'Don't!' he exclaimed, a little sharply for him.

Dorothy stared at him. 'Have I done the wrong thing, Howard?'

'No, you haven't, everything's all right. I doubt it, but she could get called, become a witness in court. A witness for the prosecution. We don't need her mentioning any names we know, now do we?'

'No, we don't. That's right. Would Richard Bowers know anything more? When the case is coming up?'

'No, he wouldn't. It's not his department. And even though he's now married to Vanessa, I can't go to him. He wouldn't like it, Dottie, he really wouldn't.'

'I just wanted to help Ceci. I want her to get married to Miles.' There was a moment's hesitation, and she was about to confide something else. But she changed her mind, kept her thoughts to herself. After all, she wasn't sure of her facts. Not yet.

Howard said, 'As soon as I hear something important, I'll let you know, Dottie. And I will say this, I think Miles has a better chance of negotiating his divorce now, because Meldrew's daughter is soon going to be penniless.'

On Sunday afternoon, Miles dialled the house he owned in Kensington for the sixth time. There had been no answer for days, and he had gone to the house three times. It was locked up, the draperies drawn. The last time he had been there he had seen the milkman on his rounds, and asked him if the family was away. The milkman had nodded. 'Gone on holiday, I think, sir.'

He was about to hang up again when the phone was answered. 'Ingham residence,' a young voice informed him.

'Could I speak to Mrs Clarissa Ingham, please?' he

431

asked, realizing he was speaking to the young parlour maid, Molly.

'I'm afraid Mrs Ingham is away, sir.'

'I assume you mean out of London?'

'I do, sir.'

'Oh, I see. Do you have a telephone number for her?'

'No, sir, she went to Switzerland for the Christmas holidays.'

'Ah yes, of course. And when is she returning?'

'In early January, sir.'

'Do you have an address for her?'

'No, I don't, Mr Ingham.'

'Thank you, Molly,' he said, and hung up. Turning around he said to Cecily, 'She's in Switzerland for Christmas.' He then explained, 'That was the parlour maid, Molly. She recognized my voice. Once more we are at Clarissa's mercy.'

Cecily shook her head. 'No, we're not. We are going to be back at Cavendon for Christmas, and we're going to enjoy it. We've waited this long, what's a few more weeks, Miles? I know now that you will get a divorce. Eventually.'

He jumped up, went and sat on the arm of her chair, smoothed his hand over her hair. 'There's no one like you, Ceci, and I'm so glad you are mine. And yes, you will be my wife one day. I promise you.'

432

FIFTY-NINE

'I've come for the inspection,' Daphne said, standing in the doorway of Hugo's dressing room, just off their bedroom.

He swung around at the sound of her voice, and his breath caught in his throat. She looked so stunning. She wore a long sheath of greenish-blue silk, simple but stylish, the cut superb, like all of Cecily's clothes. Unlike many other modern women, Daphne had never favoured the sleek hair bob, and tonight her blonde curls were piled up on top of her head.

'You look gorgeous,' he said, walking towards her. 'And the sapphire earrings I gave you, when we were married, match your eyes. Gosh, wasn't I clever to think of that,' he finished, chuckling.

Daphne laughed with him, and said, 'Well, do I pass muster?'

'I'll say you do, darling. Everyone else will be left standing in the shade tonight.'

'I doubt it. I think my sisters are aiming to be quite glamorous.'

'I suppose they always are, like you. And that nanny you had must have been quite a tartar, calling for an inspection whenever you all went out.'

'She was in a way, but she was also quite wonderful.'

'Do you want to go down? I am ready, I just have to slip on my jacket.'

'In a moment. I want to ask you something – well, several things, actually, Hugo.' Her face changed slightly, became more serious as she continued, 'When we were married, you gave me this?' She opened the evening bag she was holding and took out a small envelope, showed it to him.

He nodded. 'Yes, that's right, I did. And I told you to put it in the safe in our bedroom.'

'That's exactly what I did. It's been there ever since. And, I must admit, I haven't wanted to acknowledge its existence because of the words written on the front—'

'Not to be opened until after my death,' he said, cutting across her, repeating the words he had written years ago. 'I understand, darling. Why are you suddenly mentioning it now?'

'Because I want to know what's inside this envelope, Hugo. Please tell me.'

'It's the number of an account at the bank in Zurich, which was opened by my mentor, Mr Benjamin Silver of New York. He gave the envelope to his daughter, my first wife Loretta, and she passed it on to me later, just before she died. All anyone needs to take money out of a numbered account – as it's called – is the number.'

'And there is money in that account?' Daphne raised a brow.

'Yes. He put quite a lot there, many years ago, and no one has ever touched it.'

'I see. And my other question is: what happened to Loretta's inheritance? Is it in this account in Zurich?'

'Partially, yes. But her inheritance from her father was not only money and investments, but also a great deal of real estate, many buildings, which bring in annual rents.

434

As you know, that company – which I've owned since Loretta's death – is run by Neil Coulton, who has moved up through the ranks over the years. There has always been someone in charge, running it on my behalf, ever since I came back to live in England.' He paused, his eyes searching her face. 'Why all these questions, darling?'

'Curiosity really, Hugo. I just happened to notice the envelope when I took out the sapphires, which I've not worn for a long time.'

'The money in the numbered account is my safety net for my family, Daphne. You and the children. It cannot be used for Cavendon, you know.'

'Oh Hugo, I wasn't thinking of anything like that! I know what you've done for Papa. And giving him all that money was tremendously generous of you. I was just being nosey, that's all. Truly, Hugo.'

'All right, darling, don't get upset. I just want you to understand that I need to have you all protected, just in case anything should happen to me.'

'It won't. You're a young man. And thank you, Hugo, for explaining it, and for making sure our little family is safe and secure.'

'I'm glad your father agreed to let Dulcie auction off the collection of eighteenth-century silver finally. It wasn't doing him any good stored in the vaults. You'll see, she'll do a wonderful job. After all, every piece is by a master silversmith, like Paul Storr.' Walking across the room to the clothes closet, Hugo took out his dinner jacket and slipped it on.

Daphne turned, moved towards the door. Hugo caught hold of her hand and pulled her back to him. Looking into her face, his own gaze very serious and intent, he said, 'Promise me you will keep that Swiss numbered account intact if I am dead. You must keep it for a rainy day, or a genuine emergency.'

'I promise I will keep it for our children, Hugo.'

He smiled, kissed her cheek, and led her out of their bedroom.

Bad times were coming, he knew that. So did Paul Drummond. Paul's brother Tim had warned him already that it was the era of boom and bust; 1927 and 1928 had been the boom years. He did not like to think of what was coming next. Nor did he wish to discuss it with anyone. Why spoil Christmas?

Christmas Eve dinner had been a ritual at Cavendon Hall for over eighty years. Charles, being a traditional man, had continued the custom, hosted one for his family every year. It was the most special of the Christmas events and everyone looked forward to it with anticipation.

Now, as he sat at the head of the table in the dining room, he couldn't help feeling a rush of pride and pleasure when he glanced around.

How beautiful the four Dees looked, dressed in lovely gowns and wearing their best jewellery. Four daughters he cherished, as he cherished Miles, his only son and his heir. And there was Cecily, his future daughter-in-law, a shining star.

And what about the three men his daughters had chosen? He believed they had all been made for each other – rather a lucky break, since he considered marriage a game of chance.

For a moment his eyes rested on his first cousin, Hugo Stanton, who had proved to be an adoring spouse and extraordinary father.

Charles moved on, glancing at Paul Drummond, who was cut from the same cloth as Hugo, a genuine man of honour. He had been the first man to make Diedre truly happy after her years of sadness and her lonely life as a spinster, working at the War Office.

And finally, James Brentwood. For all his handsomeness, talent, great fame and stardom, he was a man without vanity, as far as Charles was concerned. Long walks with James had shown him that the actor was a good man, decent, full of integrity and honesty. It was obvious to the entire world, not only to the family, that he adored Dulcie. As for his youngest daughter, she worshipped the ground James walked on.

His heart ached for Miles and Cecily, a young woman he had known since her birth, and who he had grown to love like another daughter. What a ghastly situation they were stuck with. After Christmas, he would go to London with Miles, take advice from their solicitors. The fact that John Meldrew was seemingly a crook did not entirely surprise him. Although he had not realized how extensive his chicanery had been.

Miles had told him everything he knew, and Charles had spoken to Charlotte at length about it. She agreed with him that some strong measures must be taken with the Meldrews to achieve what Miles sought. A divorce. Then marriage to Cecily. And, hopefully, the arrival of an heir, one day in the not-too-distant future.

His sister Vanessa was smiling at him, and he smiled back. She, too, was happy. Her marriage to Richard Bowers had come late in her life, in a certain sense. But Bowers was a gentleman, a fine man, and they were obviously in love.

Perhaps he would speak with Bowers over the holidays and ask his advice. He had to be careful how he handled this, though; he didn't want Bowers to think he was asking for help from Scotland Yard.

Charlotte caught his eye and he stared down the table, admiring her, loving her, his dearest wife. She put him first before anyone else; the family also. He knew she would defend the Inghams and Cavendon Hall with her last breath.

Finally, his eyes rested on the grand dame of the family . . . Aunt Gwendolyn, the matriarch. She looked splendid tonight. Beautiful, vigorous and truly on form. This coming year of 1929 she would be eighty-nine. 'And, don't worry – I shall make it to a hundred, Charles,' she had announced to him tonight. He didn't doubt her. Furthermore, she had good health and a will of iron.

There they were, surrounding him: his clan, his tribe, his ilk, call it what you wanted, they were his. To love and honour and protect. That had always been his aim since he had become the 6th Earl, and it still was. That was his duty.

He glanced at the door as Hanson and Eric Swann came in along with the two footmen, ready to serve the main course. Eric and Laura Swann had come to work at Cavendon for the Christmas and New Year period. Charles had finally sold the Grosvenor Square house two weeks ago.

It had been bought by an Indian Maharajah of great wealth. Eric, not one to waste time, had found a much smaller but charming townhouse in Queen Street, not far from Grosvenor Square. Charles had bought it immediately; was happy they would remain in Mayfair.

After the holidays, Eric and Laura would return to London to prepare the new house for occupancy. Trust a Swann to do his duty, Charles thought. They will have it ready in no time at all, and they would be the only staff except for a general maid.

Hanson and Eric poured the red wine, and Gordon Lane and Ian Melrose served the roast duck, steamed vegetables, gravy and orange sauce, one of Cook's specialities.

Charles noted that Hanson was, as usual, in his element, looking after the entire family, serving them with style. What a devoted and loyal retainer he had been over all these years.

The dinner was full of laughter, chatter, and bonhomie,

as everyone ate the delicious food, drank the best of wines, talking about politics, the government, assessing Stanley Baldwin and his policies.

It was after this course was finished that Charles stood up. 'I'm not going to make a long speech,' he said. 'I just want to say a few words. Firstly, Charlotte and I thank you all for coming to Cavendon to share Christmas with us. We welcome you with much pleasure and love. Now I would like to toast Cecily and my four daughters, who have done so much in the last two years to help keep Cavendon safe. You all know how hard they have worked, raising the necessary money for the restoration, so I don't have to repeat their feats of generosity and dedication. I think of them sometimes as women warriors, at other times as angels in disguise. But tonight let us toast the five of them as Cavendon women of the finest order!'

He raised his glass and so did the others, including the five young women, who toasted each other with smiles on their faces.

Several days after Christmas, Miles was truly worried as he walked down to Charlotte's house on the edge of the park, where Cecily lived part of the time when she was at Cavendon. Quite often she shared the suite of rooms he now occupied in the South Wing. His father and Charlotte never said a word; each turned a blind eye. And now he was on his way to persuade Ceci to come back to the main house with him. Immediately.

Percy Swann, the head gamekeeper, had warned him a short while ago that a snowstorm was coming. Miles did not wish to have Cecily isolated alone in the house on the edge of the park. She would argue, he knew that, because her parents Alice and Walter lived opposite, across the village street. Nonetheless, he would not take no for an answer.

When he went into the house, Cecily was actually putting on her coat, and he noticed she had her satchel on a chair.

'Hello, darling, I see you were expecting me,' he said, smiling at her. 'It must be mental telepathy.'

'Yes,' she replied, with a light laugh. 'My mother came over to see me. She said Percy was warning the villagers about the weather, and she thought I should be with you, under the circumstances . . .' She instantly broke off, realizing she was about to say the wrong thing.

Miles frowned. 'What circumstances?'

'The snowstorm, silly,' she improvised and went on, 'My mother told Percy he ought to perhaps do something about Genevra and her parents and brothers, up there on the ridge in their caravans. They could be trapped, you know – at risk.'

'Percy usually has the right ideas, so he'll do what your mother said. I noticed they don't go away in the winters these days . . . the Romany family, I mean. Just to be sure, I'll see Percy attends to it. They can be housed in one of the empty farms nearby. Much safer for them. If there is a storm, that is.'

The storm did not come that day.

For several days the weather cleared up. But on Friday 28 December, Miles looked out of the window of the bedroom and gasped. The entire landscape was covered in snow that glistened in the wintry sunlight. It seemed to have a coating of shimmering ice. There must be a wind, he thought, still gazing out. There were huge snowdrifts, and the bare black trees had disappeared under blankets of white that weighted the branches.

Looking up at the white sky, he knew, with a sudden rush of anxiety, that more snow would fall soon. He could not help thinking about the North Wing. The roof had now been repaired, but so many rooms had horrendous problems, and they had years of work ahead. It was the wing that caught the most damage, exposed as it was to the moors and the cold blasts from the North Sea.

He glanced at Cecily, who was still asleep, and slipped out into the bathroom. It was only six o'clock in the morning but he knew he had to be dressed and downstairs as soon as possible. He would be needed, of that he was certain.

He found his father in the dining room having breakfast with Hugo and Paul. They all looked as worried as he felt, and they were soon discussing the measures that needed to be taken.

Hanson came in and served him his usual hot pot of coffee, and then Miles asked for sausages and mushrooms for breakfast. The butler did his duty with his usual efficiency and grace.

'What do you think, Hanson?' Miles asked as the butler put the plate in front of him.

'Batten down the hatches,' Hanson said. 'I think we might be trapped here for the next few days. Of course the outside workers will start clearing the snow from around the house. But it will be a hard week ahead, Mr Miles.'

Everyone's predictions had come true. More snow came. Then it rained. And, because of the fierce winds blowing over the moors from the sea, the banks of snow froze, became glassy surfaces. Many paths were dangerous to walk on, and the outside workers scattered ashes and cinders from the fireplaces, as well as sand mixed with rock salt.

The family settled in to wait. James and Dulcie had left Cavendon on the 27th, the day after Boxing Day. They had promised to spend New Year's Eve in London with his sisters Ruby, Dolores and Faye, and their husbands, along with Felix and Constance Lambert. But Diedre, Paul and Robin, their little boy, had remained, as had Vanessa and Richard Bowers.

At one moment, Charles invited Richard to come to the library for a chat, and had told him the tale of Clarissa Meldrew, and also what they had learned about her now disreputable father.

Richard had proved to be amenable and willing to speak about the matter; had confirmed that what Charles knew was more or less the truth. Meldrew had not yet been arrested, but there was no doubt in Richard's mind that he would be, and relatively soon. It was just a question of assessing the evidence and finding witnesses to testify against him.

Charles was happy he had spoken to his sister's husband. Whilst Meldrew's arrest would not get his son a divorce, her father's financial ruin would put Clarissa at their mercy. She would need money and a roof over her head. Miles did have a big stick, Charles believed.

During the snowstorm, and their captivity inside the house, Cecily spent time going over her papers. Dorothy's reports were neatly written, detailed and explicit, and she could tell almost at a glance what was happening at the shops and the boutiques at Harte's.

The partnership with Emma Harte had turned out to be highly successful. The two women got on well, saw things in the same way, and they had the added bond of being hard-working, committed Yorkshire women, filled with drive, ambition and discipline.

Much to her initial surprise, the Brides boutique had proved to be wildly successful. So much so, Cecily had hit on the idea of producing tiaras to go with the veils and the gowns. To this end, she had purchased four valuable diamond tiaras from the Ingham Collection stored in their big square boxes in the basement. She had had them reproduced in crystal and glass, and they sold out quickly. Seemingly every young bride wanted to be a princess or a queen in a sparkling tiara.

The Cecily Swann Cavendon Collection of Jewellery was also a big hit, although she was not surprised by this. The manufacturer was one of the best in England, and his product was superior. She was also contemplating another manufacturer in Paris, whose pieces looked so perfect that women thought they were made of real gems.

It was Dulcie who had come to her one day, and pointed out that it was her accessories, such as the evening bags, day bags, hat brooches and shoes that were other huge sellers. When Cecily had wondered out loud why this was, Dulcie had explained, 'Because young women, with less money than your socialite clients, can afford those things. And they can boast they have a bit of Cecily Swann in their wardrobe. That's why you should do a new collection of the silk white rose pin, and maybe use some other colours.'

Cecily had taken her advice; Dulcie gave her ideas, helped her with many things to do with the merchandise, as well as supervising her art gallery.

Because of her need to be with James during the days he did not have a matinee, or if he was between jobs in the theatre, she had hired an experienced art dealer, Melanie Oakshot, who had been in the business of art for over twenty years. Melanie had brought along her young assistant, Bethany Armitage, and together they did a good job on Dulcie's behalf, running the Dulcie Ingham-Brentwood Gallery for her.

Cecily looked up when there was a knock on the door, and Charlotte came in to the small parlour where she worked when she was at Cavendon.

Charlotte smiled, 'I thought I might give you a little treat this afternoon. If you want one, that is?'

'I always like a treat, Aunt Charlotte. What is it?'

'A tour of the vaults in the lower basement. I've persuaded Charles to sell some more of the Ingham jewellery, and I wondered if you would be interested in creating a second collection.'

'I would. How wonderful! Of course I'd love to come down to the vaults.'

'I thought so. Perhaps I can walk with you to the dining room for lunch.'

Everyone was seated, and greeted Charlotte and Cecily when they arrived in the dining room. Miles had a smile on his face and Cecily smiled back.

He said, 'Good news, my sweet. The snow has started to melt, the weather is warmer, and I think the big thaw is coming.'

Diedre said, 'I hate to tell you this, Miles, but I saw some little trickling leaks in my bathroom ceiling this morning. I did mention it to Hanson, but you should know that there ought to be another check made of the house.'

'Damn and blast!' he exclaimed, and then said, 'Oh, sorry about that, Papa.'

'Ted and his workers will get to everything, Miles,' Charles reassured him. 'Try not to worry so much. The men check areas every day. Let's be thankful it's the North Wing where there is the most damage. At least it's all in the same location.'

The footmen came in and served mulligatawny soup and warm rolls. Miles exclaimed, 'Oh good! My favourite soup, Hanson.'

'Cook made it specially for you,' Hanson whispered as he bent closer, pouring white wine into Miles's goblet. 'Don't tell anyone, though. You're Cook's favourite.'

After the soup, roast chicken and vegetables were served;

dessert was baked apples with clotted cream, a favourite of the Earl's, which everyone else enjoyed too.

At one moment, Miles said, 'Are you all right, Ceci? You do look rather pale. I noticed you haven't eaten much either.'

'I'm afraid I'm not feeling very well, Miles,' she responded and, looking at Charlotte she said, 'May I be excused, Aunt Charlotte? I think I have to go to my room.'

'Of course, Ceci. Shall I come with you?' Charlotte volunteered.

'No, thank you. I'm fine.'

Miles pushed back his chair, and exclaimed, 'I'll escort Ceci upstairs. Papa, Charlotte, if you'll both excuse me.'

Charles said, 'Do help Cecily. If you need Dr Laird, let me know. I think he'll be able to make it onto the estate. The paths and inside roads have been cleared of snow.'

'Thank you.'

Taking hold of Cecily's arm, Miles walked her out of the dining room, across the hall and into the South Wing. 'You haven't been quite yourself since New Year's Eve, darling. Do you think you have a tummy upset?'

'Not really,' Cecily answered, and held onto his arm as they climbed the staircase. Once they went into the sitting room, Cecily walked over to the window and opened it, breathed in fresh air. 'There, that's better,' she said, turning to look at him.

'Miles, there is something I must tell you,' she announced.

He threw her a curious look. There had been the strangest tone in her voice. 'What is it, sweetheart?'

He came to the windowed area and peered at her. 'You do look a bit peaked, actually.'

'I might have eaten too many rich things over the holidays,' Cecily said. 'But actually, there's nothing wrong with me that is remotely connected with food.' She took a deep breath and said, 'I'm pregnant, Miles. I'm ten weeks pregnant with your baby.'

Miles was flabbergasted and stood staring at her. He was speechless, totally taken by surprise. Then his blue eyes lit up, and a huge smile crossed his face. Reaching out, he took her in his arms and held her tightly. Then he drew away, kissed her cheeks, her forehead, her nose. Hugged her again. 'Whoopee! We're having a baby!' he cried.

Cecily couldn't help laughing with him, and then she said quietly, 'I'm afraid your son will be illegitimate if you don't get a divorce before the summer.'

'I will! Don't you worry! I've more incentive than ever to drive this matter through. And Papa will back me to the hilt, have no fear.'

'So you're not upset? I mean, because we're not married?'

'I'm as mad as hell. But not upset. This is our first baby.' He reached out for her, hesitated, then said, 'Can I touch your tummy, please, Ceci?'

She smiled. 'There's not much to feel. But yes, you can touch my tummy.'

He smoothed his hand over her stomach several times, and then asked, 'What do you feel? I mean inside? Do you feel him growing?'

'I feel different, and my body has changed, my breasts are a bit swollen, and I feel nauseated by food sometimes, as I was just now at lunch.'

'Have you seen a doctor?'

'Yes, of course. The day before we came up to Yorkshire for Christmas. He confirmed what I'd guessed.'

'Should I telephone for Dr Laird? Perhaps he ought to come and examine you.'

'I'm really all right now. I just have to be careful about rich food, and also cut down a little. Anyway, if Dr Laird comes to examine me, the whole world will know I'm pregnant with your child.'

Miles bit his lip, trying to stop the laughter bubbling up in his throat. Swallowing hard, he said, 'Well, Cecily, nobody thinks we're playing tiddlywinks up here. I believe most people we know are fully aware we are in a serious relationship.'

She smiled to herself, sat down. 'When will you call Clarissa? It's already the fourth of January. Surely she must be back?'

'I haven't told you this, but I've been calling the house every day, twice a day. There's just no answer. But Papa has agreed we should see our solicitors next week, proceed with a few legalities. Perhaps we can somehow force her hand.'

'She might agree willingly if her father goes into the clink,' Cecily murmured.

'That will undoubtedly happen eventually, and she'll need money, and she will look to me. Don't worry, it will all work out.'

'I hope so, Miles. I don't want our first child to be illegitimate. I want your son to be your legal heir.'

'Trust me, trust in my love, Cecily Swann, soon to be Cecily Swann Ingham.'

Hugo had a hobby that made everyone in the family smile. It was innocent enough, but somehow it amused them. He loved to read newspapers, and especially those which were full of lurid stories.

And so every Sunday morning he retired to his study in the South Wing, closed the door and 'dug in', as he called it, until lunchtime.

Daphne had taught his children to respect their father's special few hours. She knew how much it relaxed him, took his mind off his usual worries about money, investments, Cavendon and the future.

And so it was on that Sunday morning early in January,

Hugo settled down in an armchair in front of the fire and started to read. After only a moment or two of scanning the front page of the *Sunday Times*, the serious paper he always read first, he sat bolt upright. He read it through again, put the paper down and jumped up.

Leaving his study, he raced upstairs, and tapped lightly on the door of Miles's bedroom. It was opened at once, and he saw that Miles was putting his finger to his lips, saying, 'Ssssssh.'

Stepping outside, Miles said, 'I want Cecily to sleep. She's very tired. That's why she didn't come down to breakfast.'

Hugo nodded, got hold of Miles's arm and said, 'Come with me. I have something to show you.'

SIXTY

Hugo led Miles into his study, and picked up the *Sunday Times*. Staring at him intently, he said, 'Look at this, Miles. I think you'd better read it.'

Wondering what this was all about, Miles took the newspaper from his brother-in-law, and stared at the front page. The headline hit him right between the eyes.

PEER INJURED IN HORRIFIC AVALANCHE: DAUGHTER DEAD WITH FORTY-ONE OTHERS

Chamonix, France.   6 January 1929

An avalanche of horrific proportions swept across Mont Blanc yesterday, killing forty-two people and injuring thirty others. Amongst those dead are Mrs Clarissa Ingham, daughter of the tycoon and peer of the realm Lord John Meldrew, and her fiancé, Mr Philippe Meurice, a French financier. Mrs Ingham's father was seriously injured but is expected to live. Lord Meldrew and his party were not on the slopes but were sitting in a ski lift cabin which was

449

descending from the top of Mont Blanc. The ski lift was hit with massive slabs of snow that hurtled at such speed, had such weight, they snapped the cables holding the ski lift. Police say it is a miracle Lord Meldrew lived.

Several eyewitnesses reported they were walking through the town when they heard rumbling sounds – loud, thunderous noises. Great fractures boomed across the slopes of Mont Blanc; half the mountain was tumbling down in a huge swathe which looked to be hundreds and hundreds of feet wide. Giant slabs of snow hurtling forward gained momentum as they tumbled, sweeping everything aside. Many skiers on the slopes are believed to be buried under the mass of snow.

The ski lift cabin was hit by several gargantuan slabs of frozen snow, which broke it away from the cables and sent it hurtling into the air. Everyone was killed except for the British tycoon. Other English people who died on the slopes were Mrs Jessie Green, Mr Peter Pullen . . .

Miles stopped reading, since he did not recognize any of the other names. He gaped at Hugo, shaking his head in disbelief and said, 'She was not in Switzerland, but in France, and with a fiancé, no less. I didn't even know she had a fiancé. Hard to do when there's a husband around, even if he's long gone.' Miles pressed his hands to his eyes. 'What a terrible way to die.'

'Shocking death,' Hugo said. 'And although you and your father are not mentioned in this story, it being the very proper *Times*, I bet some of the other newspapers go to town. So be prepared, there might be some muckraking. Probably be a good idea to keep Cecily up here, rather than in London. Until everything settles down. But I think you and Charles should be in London. You own that house. Being in London protects Ceci.'

'I understand, Hugo. Thanks for the tip, and thank you for coming to get me. It's a hateful thing to read, a bad way for anyone to die, but . . .' he sighed. What was there to say?

'It is, Miles, I agree. I don't need to utter another word, I know.' He stepped forward and gave Miles a big bear hug, murmured against his ear, 'You're a free man, though. Bad as this is, it releases you from bondage.'

'I'd better go to Cecily, and then I'll find Papa to tell him.'

'If you like, I can show him *The Times*,' Hugo said.

'Would you, please? I think I'd better go to Cecily.'

Miles went into his suite of rooms through the sitting room, and sat down on the sofa for a moment. He was slightly numb with shock.

Clarissa was dead.

That was something he had not expected in his wildest dreams, and would never wish it on anyone, however bitter he felt. What an irony that her duplicitous crook of a father had lived. How strange destiny was. But no doubt Meldrew would spend a good many years of his life in jail. Where he belonged.

He heard a noise and looked at the bedroom door and saw Cecily standing there in her dressing gown, staring at him.

'You let me sleep through breakfast,' she said.

'I know, but you seemed exhausted last night.' Walking over to her, he put his arms around her shoulders, and led her over to the sofa. 'Come and sit with me. I've something to tell you, darling.'

Cecily pulled back, stared at him. 'Something's happened. You sound very serious, even dour. What is it, Miles?'

He told her, repeating everything he had read in the newspaper. 'Hugo has loads of other papers downstairs,

Ceci. I'm going to speak to Papa, and then read them. Hugo thinks Papa and I will be mentioned, that we should go to London. And that you should stay up here in Cavendon until this sort of . . . well, blows over. There might be reporters wanting to speak to me and Papa.'

Cecily nodded. 'To be honest, Miles, I think I need to stay here in the country for a couple of weeks. I have some work to do, and I need to be . . . at peace, which I always am here . . .' Her voice fell away, and then she said slowly, 'What a horrifying way to die.'

Naturally the newspapers had a field day with the story. Thousands of words were written about Clarissa Meldrew, her tycoon father, her estranged husband, Miles Ingham, his father, the 6th Earl of Mowbray, and his lover, Cecily Swann. They dug into the dirt, and they wrote their stories, and the Inghams didn't mind at all. And neither did a young woman called Swann. A piece of her beloved Miles was growing inside her.

'What is that wonderful phrase someone once said? "Publish and be damned." I don't give a hoot what they say. I know who I am and what I am,' Charles said to Miles one day. 'My son's bad marriage doesn't define me. Who I am as a man defines me.'

'I agree, and quite frankly, Papa, I don't think the newspapers have been that bad at all. In fact, I think Meldrew has fared much worse than us. And why not? They know he's a criminal.'

Charles nodded. 'I'm glad you got our solicitors together with theirs, and took over the Kensington house. I presume you don't want to live there, do you?'

'God no, not on your life! It should go on the market, don't you think?'

'I do indeed. The money will help with all these new

blasted leaks and broken pipes, and God knows what else. Cavendon's a thief, my father used to say, and he was right.'

'Thanks for ringing me, Uncle Howard,' Cecily said. 'Keeping me posted. Miles likes to know everything.'

'I promised I would stay in touch. And from what I hear, Meldrew will be jailed as soon as his injuries have healed. He actually has police guards round the clock at the hospital. He won't be able to just walk out of there, you know. The fraud police have loads on him. He'll go down for years.'

'He deserves it,' Cecily said.

'We're looking forward to coming to the wedding, Ceci. And here's Aunt Dorothy, who's itching to speak to you.'

'Hello, Dottie,' Cecily said. 'I'm sorry I'm still up here in Yorkshire, but Dr Laird wanted me to rest for a bit longer.'

'Take all the time you need, my little love. I'm holding the fort. Dulcie's in and out, and Diedre offered to come over if I need any help. The Warrior Women are ready, willing and able. Anyway, I just wanted to let you know your dress is ready. Lady DeLacy said she's happy to bring it up to Cavendon tomorrow. Shall I send it with her?'

'That's a good idea, Dorothy. I can't wait to see it.'

'And I can't wait to see you wearing it, standing in front of that altar at Cavendon, marrying the love of your life.'

Cecily laughed. 'I never thought I'd hear those words ... marrying the love of your life at Cavendon.'

'You know what Charlotte says, "What is meant to be is meant to be." And she knows what she's talking about.'

Cecily said goodbye and hung up, and turned around when she heard the parlour door open.

'Can I come in?' Lady Gwendolyn asked. 'And stroke the tummy?'

'You can,' Cecily answered, laughter echoing in her voice.

'I'm really only joking, my dear. But Miles has confessed to me that he loves to stroke your tummy at night. And I do understand how he feels. There's something wonderful about a new life growing.'

Walking into the parlour, Lady Gwendolyn said, 'I have a wedding present for you, Ceci. And I hope you like it.' She handed a small gift-wrapped package to Cecily, and then lowered herself into a chair.

'How lovely of you, Lady Gwendolyn. Thank you.'

'Aunt Gwendolyn, after tomorrow, Ceci. You'll be family then.'

Cecily smiled at her again and untied the white ribbon, took the lid off a red leather box. Inside it was a small strawberry made entirely of rubies, with leaves and a stem studded with diamonds. 'How unusual, it's just beautiful,' Cecily exclaimed, taking it out and looking at it.

'It was one of the gifts my late husband gave me, because I enjoyed eating strawberries and cream. I still do. He was very sweet, had such fanciful ideas. And I don't mind if you want to copy it for your jewellery collection at Harte's.'

Cecily burst out laughing, stood up, and went over to kiss the matriarch of the Inghams whom she had always loved.

It was a small wedding, family only invited, and it took place at the small church on the estate at Cavendon. Cecily wore the dress she had designed to hide her condition, based on one she had made for Daphne years before.

It was in the French Empire style, with long sleeves, a high bust line, with the pleated fabric dropping away into fullness at the front. Made of lavender silk, it had a matching coat. Both were calf length and she wore a matching Juliet cap, a style she had made famous.

The four Dees insisted on being her matrons-of-honour and, much to her amusement, they all wore blue frocks to match their eyes.

Her mother, Alice, insisted she was married from their home, and Cecily agreed that this was absolutely right, very correct.

It was a March wedding, because Miles refused to wait any longer, and Cecily agreed with him. She wanted to wear his wedding ring after all these years. 'And after three proposals,' she had added, winking at him.

Her brother Harry, Hugo, Paul Drummond and James Brentwood were the ushers, as usual wearing the Yorkshire white rose, from the Ingham crest, in the lapels of their morning suits. Miles asked his father to be his best man, and the 6th Earl was happy to agree.

Once again, the church was warm from the paraffin stoves, and filled with beautiful flowers when Cecily walked down the aisle on the arm of her father, Walter Swann. She felt as if she were dreaming when she finally reached the altar surrounded by the glorious stained-glass windows. It was a sunny day and coloured light filtered through like a streaming rainbow.

When she had to say the words, 'I do,' Cecily's voice shook slightly, because in her heart of hearts she never believed she would be married to Miles. There were too many things against their union.

When his voice rang out, clear and strong in the church, her eyes filled with tears. And then he was kissing her, and holding her to him. She could hear his heart clattering against hers, which was also clattering in unison.

'We're married, Ceci,' he whispered, and led her proudly down the aisle to the strains of 'Here Comes the Bride'.

The villagers were outside, waving and cheering and throwing rose petals and confetti, which blew around in the wind.

455

And the first person Cecily's eyes lighted on was Genevra, the Romany girl, all dressed up in one of Cecily's frocks, with a red ribbon in her hair.

'We must stop,' Cecily said to Miles, and he nodded his agreement when he saw the gypsy girl.

Genevra smiled at them, her black eyes shining, and handed Cecily a piece of paper. 'A gift fer yer,' she said. 'Look. Look at it.'

Cecily did. And what she saw was a square box drawn on it, with a bird sitting on top of the box. In strange wobbly writing the words said: *Swann rules.* And instantly Cecily understood. She remembered that drawing Genevra had made in the dirt with a stick so many years ago. Staring at Genevra, she said the words, 'Swann rules?' and it came out sounding like a question. Genevra inclined her head, put her hand on her own stomach. 'Baby Swann rules Ingham,' she said, and blew them kisses, running off towards the fields. And Cecily understood that the box represented Cavendon Hall and the bird a swan.

They went on down the path to the sound of the villagers clapping and cheering again. Cecily said, 'It's a boy. I'm carrying your heir, Miles.'

'Is that what she meant?' he asked.

'It is. And I believe her.'

Later that year, on a lovely sunny day in July of 1929, Cecily went into labour at Cavendon Hall. It was mandatory that an Ingham was born at the house; midwives came from the village for the birthing of the baby.

Although she was in labour for almost ten hours, Cecily didn't care. It was her child, the child Miles had given her, such a great and wonderful gift from him, like his enduring love. When the baby finally arrived, it was a boy. They called him David Charles Walter Swann Ingham, named for his great-grandfather David, the 5th

Earl, his grandfather Charles, and his grandfather Walter, Cecily's father.

'Oh he's so beautiful,' Miles said to her, as they stood at the font in the church on the estate, on the day of his christening a few weeks later.

'Just like his father,' Cecily said. 'Like father, like son.'

Miles bent closer and kissed her cheek. 'Thank you, Ceci. And thank God everything came out right,' he whispered. And she agreed.

Cecily and Miles spent a lot of time in Yorkshire for the rest of the summer. He needed to be on the estate working with his father and Harry, whose plan to rent out the farms had been highly successful. They were also supervising the repairs and the restoration of the house, which never ceased.

As for Cecily, she could work from anywhere, and was able to design a new line of jewellery, as well as accessories, shoes and wedding gowns. Emma Harte had renewed their contract and they were still in partnership.

Cecily doted on the baby, and on Miles, and she was so happy it seemed to her that her life was perfect.

Hugo and Paul sat with Paul's brother Tim in Hugo's study at Cavendon. Tim had been in Paris on business, and he had brought them disturbing news when he had arrived in Yorkshire last night.

'Boom and bust. The usual story. Big speculation, irresponsible investing, putting trust in devious businessmen, stockbrokers and the like. Big business is best, they told us. It rules the world. That's what's been happening, and there have never been any regulations on Wall Street, as you well know.' Tim sighed, 'I see it coming. A Wall Street crash. And soon.'

'This is worrying, and very disturbing,' Hugo replied.

'It's the nineteenth of September today. When do you expect this crash?'

'I don't know. There's so much speculation, buying stocks, reckless dealing, selling and buying, God knows what's going to happen. But you two are all right, aren't you?' Tim glanced at his brother Paul and then at Hugo. 'You got out of Wall Street.'

Paul said, 'I did.'

Hugo nodded. 'I sold a lot of investments and moved my money to the London Stock Exchange. I did keep some of the Ben Silver money in investments in Wall Street, but not much. Why?'

'Many other bankers agree with me that Wall Street will crash. And it will reverberate around the world. It could actually lead to a depression . . . a world depression.'

'Let's hope not,' Hugo said.

It was Friday afternoon, 20 September. Everyone was enjoying the weekend. The weather was lovely. It was like an Indian summer. Cecily and Miles were sitting on the terrace when Charles came out. He looked so shocked, Cecily knew at once that something had happened. Something terrible. Charlotte followed him, and she too was chalk white, appeared nervous.

Miles rose at once, also suspecting trouble. 'Has something bad happened, Papa?' he asked, then glanced at Charlotte, who had a strained expression. And fear in her eyes.

'Not bad news, Miles, catastrophic. Hugo just told me that the London Stock Exchange just crashed officially.'

'My God, why? What happened?' Miles cried, surprise echoing in his voice.

'It's all to do with a man called Clarence Hatry, who had been jailed for forgery and fraud. He's caused all this. Apparently the market has been unstable, severely so for days. Periods of selling, buying, everything going crazy.'

'What does it mean to us?' Cecily asked, looking first at Miles and then at Charles.

'We have lost a great deal of money,' Charles answered.

'Are we wiped out?' Miles asked sharply, fearing the worst.

'Not exactly. But, well, a big portion of our investments has gone.'

'What does that mean to us?' Cecily asked again. 'Are we ruined? Is the House of Ingham about to fall?'

'I sincerely hope not,' Charles answered in a strained tone. 'But things are going to be very difficult. We will have to stop the restorations at once. And make sure we can pay our taxes, maintain the estate, pay the staff.'

'But what about the money I gave you for the jewels?'

'That has been used up. New roofing, acres and acres of it. New floors. The work on the foundation. You know what's been happening. Plus income taxes.'

'Are we broke, Papa?' Miles asked.

'Not quite. Because Cecily has been buying the Ingham jewellery. And Dulcie has been selling off our paintings at the gallery. But we will have to tighten our belts. And trim, and trim and trim. And sell more possessions.'

Charles sounded so depressed, Cecily was wondering if he was telling them the truth. Suddenly, a feeling of enormous indignation came over her, and then immediately dissipated. In its place came a sense of determination, of being in control of her own destiny. She jumped up, took the baby out of its little cradle, ran down the steps and out onto the lawn. She stood in front of the house, staring up at it.

Miles had raced after her. 'What are you doing?' he cried looking perplexed, worried about her strange behaviour.

She did not answer Miles. She turned the baby around to face the house, showing it to him.

459

'This will be yours one day,' she cried. 'You will reign here. The first Swann to sit on top of the house of Ingham. It is going to be yours, I promise you that. Whatever it takes. Cavendon will be yours to rule. It is meant to be. Your heritage. It is a prediction. And it is not just this great stately home, it is so much more.'

Cecily paused, looking around the park, then turning the baby to face her. She went on in her strong, purposeful tone. 'It is thousands of acres of land, a famous grouse moor, three villages with villagers whom you must care for and protect, who depend on you. It is a title dating back for almost two hundred years. You will be one of the premier earls of England. The Eighth Earl of Mowbray, following on after your father. It is a dynasty you must protect with your life.'

Miles, who had listened to her words, was stunned, yet impressed. He saw she was white, noticed her implacability, the determination in her strange lavender-grey eyes, the hint of ruthlessness in her, fleeting though it was. He was awed by her strength, her sense of duty.

Settling the baby comfortably in her arms, cradling him, Cecily turned to Miles. 'I meant everything I said, Miles. We are going to fight and work. And keep Cavendon safe. We must. For you and for this boy . . . the heir whom you've longed for.'

Cecily paused, moved closer to him. 'You are my husband at long last. I've given you this boy, your heir. Will you stand beside me and fight for all this?'

Miles put his arms around his wife and his child, and held them tightly against him, filled with love and gratitude. They were his family.

'I will,' he said.

And he did.

ACKNOWLEDGEMENTS

My husband, a film producer, believes that the public should never know anything about the nitty-gritty that goes on behind the scenes in the making of a movie. He thinks it spoils the magic. And I suspect he feels the same way about all the nitty-gritty behind the writing of the book. I agree. However, I would like to thank the people who have been involved in my creation of this new novel.

Once the writing is finished, the book goes into editing and design, and then production. This is the time other people become involved, and the teamwork begins. I want to thank my team at HarperCollins, London.

I owe very special thanks to my editor, Lynne Drew, Publishing Director. She is a wonderful sounding board and has an innate grasp of character, drama and story-telling. Her insight into people and their motivations is unique, and I appreciate her suggestions and ideas. I must thank Kate Elton, Executive Publishing Director, for her enthusiasm and support; editor Martha Ashby for taking care of innumerable details, and editorial assistant Charlotte Brabbin for keeping track of it all. My thanks go to my editor, Susan Opie, and my copy editor Penelope Isaac, who both do a great job and are dedicated to my novels.

Elizabeth Dawson, PR Director of HarperFiction, deserves a big thank you from me for her promotion and publicity endeavours once the book is published, and for keeping me laughing when we go on the promotion tour. Roger Cazalet, Publishing Strategy Director, and Oliver Wright, UK Sales Director, do a marvellous job of presenting the book to the public and I thank them. Finally, thanks also to the entire team at HarperCollins in London who are involved in all aspects of publishing my novel.

Wendy Jeffrey, my editor at Doubleday many years ago, left publishing and started a new career. We have remained friends for thirty-five years and she still continues to read my manuscripts for her own pleasure, but also at my request. Her comments are invaluable to me, and I thank her for her continuing support. Thanks to Lonnie Ostrow of Bradford Enterprises, a whiz at the computer who helps with the preparation of the manuscript, and areas of research. Thanks also to Linda Sullivan of WordSmart for her work on the manuscript, which is always perfect.

I can never thank my husband enough for his loving and enduring support in every way, and his understanding of my continuing need to write my novels. Not only that, he is my best critic. He always reads my manuscripts in an objective way and says what he thinks. Along with my editors, Bob is one of the first readers, and his quick response is invaluable before I start the editing. A true partner in every sense, it is Bob who guides my career and manages it with the skill of a businessman and the creative mind of a film producer. He also makes the movies of my novels and with wonderful actors in the leading roles. Aside from all this, he manages to make me laugh every day of the year.

The Cavendon Luck

Barbara Taylor Bradford

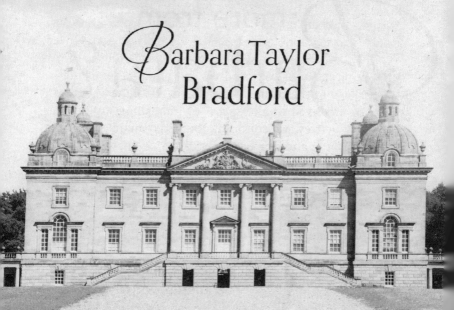

As the clouds of war gather
over Cavendon, it is the
younger generation who
must step forward...

Coming in 2016

Want to hear more from *Barbara?*

barbarataylorbradford.co.uk

You can visit her website for the latest news, reviews and Barbara's own blog.

f /BarbaraTaylorBradford

Follow her on Facebook for updates on all of her books, including exclusive competitions and photos.